THE BLOODLESS BOY

THE
BLOODLESS BOY

ROBERT J. LLOYD

MELVILLE HOUSE PRESS

NEW YORK & LONDON

Melville House Publishing
46 John Street
Brooklyn, NY 11201
and
Melville House UK
Suite 2000
16/18 Woodford Road
London E7 0HA

mhpbooks.com
@melvillehouse

ISBN: 978-1-61219939-9

ISBN: 978-1-61219940-5 (eBook)

Library of Congress Control Number 2021942888

Designed by Richard Oriolo

Printed in the United States of America
1 3 5 7 9 10 8 6 4 2

A catalog record for this book is available from the Library of Congress

TO MY DAUGHTER,
ALSO NAMED GRACE

' . . . these Creatures do not wound the Skin, and suck the Blood out of Enmity and Revenge; but for through meer Necessity, and to satisfy their Hunger. By what means this Creature is able to Suck, we shall shew in another Place.'

Micrographia, Or some Physiological Descriptions of Minute Bodies Made by Magnifying Glasses with Observations and Inquiries thereupon
Robert Hooke (1665)

CHARACTERS

MR. HARRY HUNT, Observator of the Royal Society of London for the
    Improving of Natural Knowledge.

MR. ROBERT HOOKE, Curator of Experiments of the Royal Society of
    London for the Improving of Natural Knowledge, Gresham's Professor
    of Geometry, and Surveyor for the City of London.

MASTER TOM GYLES, Robert Hooke's Apprentice.

MISS GRACE HOOKE, Robert Hooke's Niece.

MRS. MARY ROBINSON, Robert Hooke's Housekeeper.

MRS. ELIZABETH HANNAM, Harry Hunt's Landlady.

SIR EDMUND BURY GODFREY, Justice of Peace for Westminster.

MR. GABRIEL KNAPP, a Constable.

ANTHONY ASHLEY COOPER, the Earl of Shaftesbury.

DR. JOHN LOCKE, the Earl of Shaftesbury's Secretary.

MR. URIEL AIRES, the Earl of Shaftesbury's Man.

M. PIERRE LEFÈVRE, an Assassin.

THE MECHANICAL SCRIBE, an Automaton.

MR. HENRY OLDENBURG, Secretary of the Royal Society of London for the Improving of Natural Knowledge

MRS. DORA KATHERINA OLDENBURG, Henry's Wife

MR. TITUS OATES, a Clergyman, and Perjurer.

MR. ISRAEL TONGE, a Fanatic.

COLONEL MICHAEL FIELDS, a Soldier for Parliament.

MR. MOSES CREED, a Solicitor.

HIS MAJESTY CHARLES II, the King.

FRANCES TERESA STEWART, Duchess Of Richmond And Lennox.

ANNE LENNARD, Countess Of Sussex, Daughter of the King.

HORTENSE MANCINI, Duchesse de Mazarin, the most Beautiful Lady in the Kingdom.

SIR JONAS MOORE, Surveyor-General of the Board of Ordnance.

MR. ENOCH WOLFE, an Eel fisher.

DR. THEODORE DIODATI, a Physician.

MR. GIDLEY, a Chirurgeon.

MR. TOBIAS TURNER, Proprietor of the Angel Coffeehouse.

MR. INVINCIBLE and MRS. FELICITY TARRIPAN, Quakers.

MR. JONATHAN LATHAM, a Carpenter.

MR. NOBLE FISHER, a Builder.

MR. KILL-SIN ABBOTT, a Waterman.

MR. THOMAS BLAGROVE, Proprietor of the Crown Tavern.

MR. THOMAS GARRAWAY, Proprietor of Garraway's Coffeehouse.

MR. DANIEL WHITCOMBE, a Virtuoso Natural Philosopher.

A CAPTAIN, of the King's Foot.

A SERGEANT, of the King's Foot.

A TROOPER, of the King's Foot.

A MAN with a Child on his Back.

A MAN with a Painted Eye.

THE BLOODLESS BOY

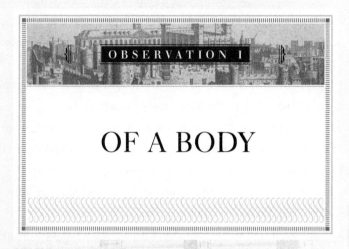

OBSERVATION I

OF A BODY

THE WATER BEGAN TO STICK, SPLASHES fattening on the glass.

Harry Hunt, Observator of the Royal Society of London for the Improving of Natural Knowledge, stopped to look more closely at the change in form, as rain turned to snow. Fingers stiffened by the chill, he wiped at his spectacles, and watched the first flakes settle on the brown leather of his coat.

He committed the observation to his memory and moved on. His purposeful stride took him past the new Bethlehem Hospital sprawling across Moorfields, smudges of light escaping its windows.

He had a slight frame and pale London skin.

South down Broad Street. The narrow buildings shouldered one another, pressing together for warmth. Untouched by the fury of the Great Conflagration, they followed the old scheme.

Harry made his way towards Gresham's College, the mansion used by the Royal Society, to see the Curator of Experiments and Professor of Geometry there, Mr. Robert Hooke.

Falling thickly, the snow had already settled despite the wet ground. The early morning sky was violet, the colour of a bruise.

Harry's steps echoed through the archway leading to the College quadrangle. In the stables, the horses snorted, and he heard the grate of their shoes. He turned for the south-east corner and stopped at a door.

Above him, a window clattered open and the head of a boy appeared.

'Mr. Hunt! Mr. Hooke's already gone!'

Harry put his finger to his lips. Tom Gyles, with a pantomime grimace, acted out his understanding. Ah, discretion was required. No less loudly, he called down again.

'I'll come to you! Mr. Hooke would desire no stranger hear the business.'

Harry let himself in with his key and shook off the snow from his coat onto the lobby's neat flagstones.

Perhaps a philosophical business engaged the Curator. The Royal Society kept him busy with his trials and demonstrations for the Fellows. Hooke also worked as Surveyor to the City of London, with Sir Christopher Wren. A far more lucrative employment, rebuilding the new London. Maybe he went to perform a view.

The rest of the boy belonging to the head arrived, zig-zagging down the stairs. A rope of hair stuck up from his crown, giving him the look of a shaggy sundial.

Harry looked past him, on the chance he might glimpse Hooke's niece, Grace. At this hour, though, she would still be in her bed. A little wistfully, he returned his thoughts to Tom.

'Mr. Hooke is gone to his new bridge at Holborn, to meet with Sir Edmund Bury Godfrey!' Tom was hopping from foot to foot. 'The messenger's knocking woke us all.' So, Grace was awake . . .

Hooke had wanted help with his improved design for a lamp, its self-fuelling mechanism misbehaving.

'I shall return later, then, when his business is done.'

'He asks that you join them there.' Tom looked slyly up at Harry, watching his eyes widen, pleased with the result of his information, happy he had held it back for most effect.

Harry felt a pulse of anxiety. Sir Edmund was renowned throughout London as a pervasive, threatening presence.

'I shall go there. Oh, I forgot—a happy New Year's Day to you, Tom.'

'And to you, Mr. Hunt. A happy 1678 for us all.'

Harry left the boy behind him and walked back across the quadrangle.

Grace watched him leave from her upstairs window, observing the trail of his boots as they dragged through the snow.

THE SMELL OF fish, flesh, and fruit from the Stocks. Breakfast.

By the statue overlooking the market—Charles II and his mount trampling Oliver Cromwell's head—Harry bought a pastry and Dutch biscuits from a man half-asleep by his stall.

The pastry was too hot to eat, and too hot to hold. He swapped it from hand to hand as he walked. Up the gradual climb of Cheapside. Past where the Cross had stood until its destruction by Puritan enthusiasm. This had happened ten years before Harry was born, yet people still referred to it as a landmark—the more pious offered their thoughts on the Whore of Babylon as they did.

Friday Street, Gutter Lane, Foster Lane, and Old Change.

Here, all had burned in the Conflagration. In between these townhouses, warehouses, and shops—brick and stone, to the post-Fire regulations and standards—some spaces still remained. Sad patches of land, never reclaimed, their charred ruins dispersed over time, replaced by litter, nettles, and dirt.

Lines of stones reached up from the wharfs. The largest took days to be dragged from the quayside. The Cathedral awaited them, its ribs and stomach open to the sky. Surrounding it lay more stones, bricks, earth, and timbers. Like organs cut from it, more than materials to build it up.

From where the arch of Newgate used to be, before fire, too, destroyed it, Harry walked down the winding lane of Snow Hill, sliding, almost falling, and then to Holborn Hill.

Wiping the last pieces of pastry from his fingers, he transferred his attention to a biscuit.

He was at Holborn Bridge, spanning the Fleet River.

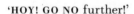

'HOY! GO NO further!'

An old man in a coachman's coat stepped out from the doorway of the Three Tuns, halting Harry with an unsteady palm. His face was a cracked glaze of lines under a worn-out montero. The wool of the hat was wet through, sagging over his shoulders. Despite his age, he was a hard-looking man, and far broader than Harry.

'What happens here?' Harry asked, in as business-like a tone as he could muster, wiping biscuit crumbs from his chin.

'A finding—no mind of yours!'

'If Sir Edmund Bury Godfrey's done the finding, then I'm to meet him. Mr. Robert Hooke accompanies the Justice, does he not?'

The man, a constable of the watch, scowled at him.

'I am Mr. Harry Hunt, Observator of the Royal Society, and assistant to Mr. Hooke,' Harry added grandly.

With a cursory thumb, the constable sent him down to the river.

ROBERT HOOKE HAD shaped this place, overseeing the Fleet's straightening, deepening, and widening. It had taken four years of difficulty and disaster: the riverbed re-dredged after floods, the weight of the banks breaking the new timber wharfs, piles, and footings, the groundwater sweeping away the sluices and drains. The dumping of refuse from the abattoirs and households had continued, and rain washed in the wreckage left over from the Conflagration.

At last, it was finished. Vastly more expensive than the City had envisaged, the Fleet Canal was the biggest project of rebuilding the new London. All the way to the Thames was now smart with paved quaysides, and the watermen in their wherries could reach as far as the new Holborn Bridge.

Before, its main users had been floating dead dogs—their corpses bumping, sniffing one another in death as they had in life. Upstream, the Fleet continued as it always had: a silty, muddy-banked ditch. It disappeared into the hillside through an arch, a huge iron grating holding back the filth from Turnmill Brook.

Hooke sheltered beneath the span of the bridge. Harry easily recognised his hunched form, the twist in Hooke's back diminishing what would have been a tall stature. Without the cover of a wig, his hair hung over his large forehead and stuck to his sharp chin, and his long nose, its nostrils red-rimmed, had a dewdrop hanging from its tip. He wore his favourite overcoat, a natural grey colour.

His protuberant silver eyes acknowledged the younger man's arrival, but he said nothing to him.

Next to him, contrastingly upright, stood a tall, impressive man in a long black camlet coat, black leather gloves, and a large black hat. A sword, sheathed in a black scabbard, poked out behind him. His peruke, also black, swept around his large head and down over his shoulders. A single touch of ostentation: a band of gold fabric encircling the hat lessened his Puritan severity.

Sir Edmund resembled, Harry thought, a large inquisitive raven.

Harry jumped down from the quayside's low wall, slipping on the bank. The Fleet slid viscously over the mud, eroding the snow to a clean, frosty edge.

Hooke merely pointed, directing Harry under the bridge. Northwards, away from the new wharfs of the Canal. Along the old, untouched muddy bank.

Harry walked past the two men, through the shadow of the arch, and back into the brightness of the falling snow.

⌇

HIS REACTION WAS not worthy of a new philosopher of the Royal Society. Harry urged himself to become cooler, more dispassionate, as Mr. Hooke would want him to be.

A dead boy, naked, possibly as young as two years, at most as old as three, lay in the mud on his side. Back curved, head bowed to his chin, arms and legs folded to his body.

The falling snow softened his outline, making it look as if he had come up from the ground. Digested, then expelled.

'A happy New Year's Day to you, Harry,' Hooke said ironically, now striding after him, the mud under the snow sucking at his shoes. Suffering from a cold, his thin, nasal voice struggled through the phlegm at the back of his throat.

Sir Edmund followed them out from under the bridge. His face was the colour of raw meat, long with a solid jaw, and his mouth had lips so thin it looked like an incision. His complexion, with its furrows and broken veins, betrayed a life in the open air.

'Mr. Hooke described you.' Sir Edmund did not wait for Hooke to make the proper introduction. 'Already I am impressed.'

His voice resonated from his diaphragm. Harry thought he felt and heard it in equal parts. Seldom to receive flattery from men of such rank. He wondered how Hooke had termed his description.

'Harry was my apprentice, but is his own man now,' Hooke said. 'To business, Sir Edmund?'

Hooke stooped nearer the body. 'An angler made the find,' he explained to Harry. 'Looking for grig eels, says he. He must be a night-bird for suchlike.'

'Eels tend not to stir by day,' Harry affirmed, swallowing. He tried to control the trembling that had started in his right thigh, hoping the older men would ascribe it to the cold. The vapour in the air signalled his short, shallow breaths.

'There are marks of unusual dispatch,' Hooke said, not noticing, intent on the boy.

'The eel fisher,' Sir Edmund added, removing his gloves, 'ran to tell and cannot bring himself back. He cowers in the Three Tuns.'

The Justice produced a black notebook from his pocket, leather-bound, and a portable pen and ink set. 'A blasphemous crime.' He rubbed at his mouth.

Harry noticed Sir Edmund had a twitch in his *orbicularis oris*, a strand of muscle pulling at his bottom lip.

Still trembling himself, but mindful of the dictates of the Royal Society—and of Robert Hooke, who used to be his master—Harry bent to brush snow from the body.

The boy's skin, pale as the snow he lay in, was untouched by signs of decay.

His eyes, still wide open, had irises an unusual blue. Towards indigo.

An eye withheld the image it last perceived, Harry had heard. Looking into them, he saw only his own reflection.

'The eyes are not filled with a pestilent air,' Sir Edmund observed. 'He is recently dead.'

'Not recently,' Hooke corrected him. He saw the Justice's perplexed look but offered no further explanation. Instead, he placed the end of his finger over his right nostril and ejected snot from the left, directing it into the river.

'What's this rectangle on him?' Harry asked, looking at a thinner dusting of snow on the uppermost part of his ribs.

'A letter was left,' Hooke answered.

'I have it,' Sir Edmund said, producing it from inside his coat. It was small, with a broken black wax seal. 'I shall study it later, in the warm.' He slid the letter back out of their sight.

Hooke held Harry's arm, stopping his question for the Justice.

Instead, Harry brushed more snow from the boy, rolled him onto his back, and moved the limbs to see. 'The manner of death's easy enough to read.'

'Immediately explicable,' Hooke agreed.

'Well, then? How did he die?' Sir Edmund asked them.

'You have seen these puncture marks on the body?' Hooke indicated the insides of the tops of the legs. 'Each with writing by it, in ink.'

'I have. The neatness of lettering next to each hole is remarkable.'

'Going into the skin,' Hooke continued, 'and on, deeper, into the iliac arteries, these holes show the insertion of hollow tubes. They have a similar diameter to the shaft of a goose feather. There are four such apertures, used to drain him of his blood.'

Sir Edmund winced, then made a note in his book.

Hooke inspected the writing by each hole. 'A living body, when pierced, seeks to stem the blood's flow. The blood sticks at the wound, growing thick from coagulation. Losing too much blood brings death by its heat being lost, and elemental or humourical imbalance.'

He loudly cleared his other nostril. It seemed to aid his thinking. 'When the action of the heart has ceased, the flow of blood goes still. The texture of this boy's skin is papery to the touch. The feel of the flesh beneath, with the presence of these piercings, reveals all of his blood was taken.'

'His heart weakened, then stopped, before it could further expel his blood through these holes.' Sir Edmund demonstrated his understanding. 'How, then, was the remainder of his blood taken?'

Harry thought for a moment. 'By making a Torricellian space, the vacuum encouraging the blood to flow.'

Hooke looked at him, pleased.

'Why a need for all this boy's blood?' Sir Edmund asked them.

Hooke shrugged, his hunched back rocking with the gesture. 'These holes show the signs of repeated insertion. This writing on the body shows when.'

They stared at the four holes, each having a cluster of dates by it.

'The oldest is from nearly a year ago,' Harry said, reading *15th Febry. 1676/77*. 'Whoever marked these days clings to the old style of calendar.'

Hooke made a circle with the point of his finger around one of them. 'They show no signs of healing.'

'He was preserved for perhaps a year,' Harry said.

'No signs of freezing, or embalming.'

'Again, a Torricellian space, Mr. Hooke. A vacuum preventing decay.'

'Why, though, this need for blood?' Sir Edmund asked them, writing rapidly in his book. 'It is papistry, mark my words.'

Hooke looked at him mildly. 'You steer us where we do not necessarily wish to go. Nothing here shows Catholicism.'

Sir Edmund's expression darkened, and he snapped his gloves together.

'Infusion?' Harry suggested, a little to cheer the Justice.

'Into another, Harry? Our own trials at the Society have been too often unsuccessful.'

'Mr. Coga received very well the blood of a lamb.'

'He had only small amounts infused. Indeed, he wanted to undergo the procedure again, thinking he benefitted from some symbolic power, the lamb's blood being the blood of Christ, as Christ is the Lamb of God.' Hooke gave a wry smile. 'His religious zeal may have protected him. Other infusions ended in agony and tragedy. Into many others then, Harry? In modest amounts?'

Hooke, ignoring the Justice's irritable look, spoke to Harry with a professorial air, that of a teacher with his favoured student.

Sir Edmund's irritation was a mask for his disgust. The way of this boy's death revolted him, and he had never met two people who discussed such phenomena as *affectionately* as these. Even the lowliest chirurgeons of his acquaintance at least pretended delicacy and deference.

But, he did not doubt, they would be useful to him.

'Pope Innocent VIII,' he offered, 'when given blood from boys to rejuvenate him, received Catholic blood. There was no countenancing any other.'

'The project failed,' Hooke said dismissively. 'He died soon after.'

Sir Edmund growled, and one hand clenched into a fist. 'Elizabeth Báthory bathed in the blood of her victims, to keep her youth.'

'She was a Calvinist,' Hooke replied.

Harry concentrated on the body, avoiding their debate. He wiped off the falling snow with the edge of his hand. On the boy's chest were fine splashes, white, almost transparent. He picked at one, and it folded flakily under his fingernail.

'Candle wax,' he announced. 'Beneath, the skin's unaffected. The wax dripped after he died.'

'Worked on at night?' Hooke wondered, squatting next to him. 'Or in a darkened place. A candle lodged upon his ribs to provide a light to work by.' Hooke looked closely at the wax. 'This is bleached beeswax. An extravagance in most households.'

'Liturgical candles!' Sir Edmund looked triumphantly at them. 'Catholic practices!'

'Such candles are not only employed at Mass,' Hooke said.

Sir Edmund showed them his annoyance by his laboured concealment of it. He gestured at the snow on the ground. 'You see the curious lack of prints.'

'Only our own, and those of the eel fisher,' Harry agreed. 'His steps are clear. He stopped well short of the body.'

'He could not take himself closer when he realised his discovery,' Sir Edmund said. 'How did the boy arrive here? Surely, by water.'

'There are no marks in the mud, leading from the Fleet,' Hooke replied.

The Justice looked around them. 'The fall of snow covers the mud about the body. Any impressions have disappeared.'

'You play the Devil's Advocate.' Hooke indicated the smears on their legs. 'We make deep impressions. Such holes could not have filled.'

'We are close enough to the Thames for the ebb and flow of its tide to reach here. The rising water has removed any footprints . . . ?' The question in Sir Edmund's voice suggested his lack of conviction.

'The tide ebbs, but gently, and we are close to the neap tide, in the first quarter of the moon, when the water does not rise so greatly,' Hooke told him.

Sir Edmund stared through the murky surface of the Fleet. 'There are no rubs from a wherry's keel. The boy was not dropped from up on the quay, he being too far from the wall. Nor was he dropped from the bridge.' He shifted uneasily. 'Everything must have its cause, and leave evidence of its passing. A murderer may conceal the reason for his crime, yet, given the body, his methods at least—of killing and disposal—are always apparent.'

A little further along the bank was the eel fisher's large box of bait. It had ropes attached for transporting on his back. Going to it, Harry saw it was full of lampreys. Their sucking mouths pouted stupidly up at him. A film of slime covered their lengths.

'He wants a large haul, with this much bait.'

They walked back along under the bridge and climbed to the quayside.

'Here in this place openly . . . it is not a thing hotly wrought.' Sir Edmund looked back down at the bank. 'This boy suffered an elaborate killing.'

THE JUSTICE SENT the old constable into the Three Tuns to bring out the eel fisher.

Resembling the fish he preyed on, with an overlarge mouth and expressionless eyes, the man had thick stubble up to his cheekbones. His boots and hands were filthy with the mud of the bank.

He told them his name was Enoch Wolfe.

'Do you remember anything further than you told Sir Edmund?' Hooke asked him. 'Was anything here then that is not here now? No skiff? No wherry?'

Wolfe shook his head. 'Only night and rain,' he replied. 'Traded for day and snow.'

He glanced at Sir Edmund for reassurance he should answer questions from this odd-looking, twisted man with his youthful colleague. The Justice he knew well—who did not?—but who were these two with him?

Sir Edmund, with a snarl, confirmed he should.

'No person on the bridge, by the water, nor upon the quayside?' Hooke enquired.

'Just me, my lampreys, and the eels I was after,' Wolfe declared.

Satisfied he had no more to tell, Sir Edmund committed the eel fisher to silence about the discovery.

'Where can we find you again, Mr. Wolfe, should we have need?' Harry enquired.

The man gestured vaguely westwards. 'Over the bridge. Go into Alsatia. Anybody there knows me.'

'I recognised you, from Alsatia,' Sir Edmund said.

'*God spared not the angels that sinned, but cast them down to Hell.*' Wolfe let a mischievous grin touch his lips, no sooner seen than gone.

'We are, all of us, lower than angels,' Sir Edmund chastised him.

As Wolfe walked away, he became faint in the falling snow.

'We have no hope of his remaining quiet,' Sir Edmund said, wiping at his thin lips. 'I need time to brief my intelligencers, to hear what is said about the town. If the boy is from loving kin, I feel sorry for them.'

They sheltered together in the tavern's doorway. The constable stood morosely in the snow, his rank keeping him in the elements. Although he sensed some guilt at displacing him, Harry made no offer to swap places.

'I need a more close examination of this boy,' Sir Edmund said. 'At the Fleet Prison? It would be convenient there.'

'I have my tools at Gresham's College,' Hooke replied. 'But I cannot promise the participation of the Royal Society. I am merely its Curator. You will need the President's permission.'

'You have the skills to anatomise the body?'

'I studied under Dr. Thomas Willis, and assisted him with his chirurgical and chymical work,' Hooke said, nettled by the Justice's question. 'I can perform an autopsy well enough.'

'Well enough is well enough. It would be more private at Gresham's. I shall not yet make known the finding. The taking of blood from so young a child is irreligious. To my mind, it points to papistry. If word escapes, the mob will add its own shine to the affair.'

'It would influence only the credulous,' Hooke said.

'It may be designed to influence precisely those!' Sir Edmund answered, his temper rising again at Hooke's unsubtle dig.

'We will not divulge a thing of it,' Hooke promised for them both.

Sir Edmund gripped him by the elbow. 'Have you the means, at the College, to renew his preservation? You must do it soon, before he decays.'

The question surprised Hooke, and he sounded suspicious. 'I can preserve the boy. The air-pump is Mr. Boyle's property, rather than the Society's. Engaged in the writing out of his chymico-physical doubts and paradoxes, he has no need of it presently. Any dissection I will not do without the permission of our President, Viscount Brouncker.' He shrugged off Sir Edmund's hand.

'I believe you both together will explain away this killing,' Sir Edmund asserted, his deep voice emphasising his faith. 'Your knowledge of blood and vacua will greatly assist in the finding of this child's murderer.'

He left them abruptly to commandeer a tumbrel. Its owner, at first belligerent, quickly turned agreeable.

'Sir Edmund is persuasive,' Hooke observed.

'You were more willingly coerced.'

'True enough, though I find the Justice to be difficult, like rubbing up against a smoothing paper. Why does he press to keep the boy preserved?'

'In truth, I cannot say, Mr. Hooke.'

Hooke looked anxiously at the scene by the water, the Fleet flowing past them, and past the body of the boy, all being steadily covered by the snowfall.

'Sir Edmund wants a Catholic cause for this murder. The finding of this boy may lead us into unfathomable seas. We must take a care to keep our eyes steadily fixed upon the facts of nature, and so receive their images simply, as they are.' He wiped at his nose with the sleeve of his coat.

Harry nodded, looking pensive. 'You must return to the warmth, Mr. Hooke. Otherwise, we will have a second death. Sir Francis Bacon died from his trial to preserve the chicken with snow.'

'You are entirely right, Harry.' Hooke's stuffed head made his words sound as if he expressed them through treacle. 'Let us return to the College.'

'I'll follow you. I must attend to something first.'

Watching Hooke's twisted spine, and hearing his wheezing breaths and sniffs fading as he went off along the quayside, Harry wondered how far he would want to help. Hooke lived for his natural philosophy and for his building. He had enough demands on his time.

Waiting until Hooke was far enough away, Harry at last allowed his body to react to the finding of the murdered boy. He heaved up his breakfast, then scooped up a handful of snow to take the bitter taste from his mouth. He kicked some over the undigested pastry and biscuits.

'Get yourself to Gresham's College, Mr. Hunt!' Sir Edmund called. 'My man will deliver the boy. I shall meet you there later, to see his preservation.'

OBSERVATION II

OF RELEASE

ONCE THE HOME OF MONARCHS, THE Tower of London was now a prison.

The Earl of Shaftesbury looked back at the room which had been his gaol. A window in a line of many.

Down the timber steps, through the Jewel House, by the decayed ruin of the Hall.

Shaftesbury rested his hand on the wall as he surveyed the falling snow. Its flakes blew about at the mercy of the wind. He threw back his head and opened his mouth, relishing the taste, the delicate fizz, as each snowflake melted on the warmth of his tongue.

An expressionless yeoman urged him on, past the stores keeping munitions, ropes, masts, and tackle.

Shaftesbury had been Chancellor of the Exchequer. Then, Lord Chancellor. Then, First Lord of Trade. How quickly he had fallen from the King's favour.

After authoring a pamphlet declaring the royal prerogative should be restricted, he was charged with contempt of Parliament—even though the King had kept Parliament prorogued for over a year.

Through the gate of the inner wall, then the Wakefield Tower, and to the Watergate. Through St. Thomas's Tower.

His pamphlet also argued Parliament should decide the inheritance.

The King's brother, the Duke of York, was heir to the throne. York was openly Catholic, bringing confusion to those loyal to Crown and tradition, but who feared having his religion pushed upon them.

Another yeoman raised the last portcullis.

Shaftesbury had resisted Danby's Test Oath, which required all in office to declare resistance to the King a crime.

He could not accept that the liberty and property of the people were subject to the pleasure of the Crown. It was against *Magna Carta Libertatum*. It made the King's authority absolute. It swept away the limitations placed on him at his restoration eighteen years earlier, and all of Parliament's gains after the Wars.

Shaftesbury's arguments were gaining popularity, in the Lords and in the Commons. The King had recognised the threat.

It took a year in the Tower before Shaftesbury expressed contrition. Stubbornness kept him in so long, but he had not broken.

The time was right: there were things he needed to do which could not be done inside a prison cell.

He stood outside on the Wharf.

A black coach-and-four waited for him. Its driver wore an oiled goatskin coat to protect him from the weather. The wood of the coach, lacquered and polished, reflected Shaftesbury's image. A long face tapering past fleshy lips to a small chin, jowls grown more apparent during his imprisonment. A bottle-green coat, which brushed the snow as he walked.

Shaftesbury had not wasted his year. He had reflected. He had disputed with himself. At first to order his thoughts, as much as to while the time away. Later, as reason and method and purpose conjoined into a plan convincing even to himself, it became his impetus. His inspiration.

Leaning back and bringing up his fist, he punched his own reflection. The noise made one of the horses start, its hooves scrabbling in the snow.

Now his last doubts were gone.

A crack in the lacquer and a dent in the wood.

The driver soothed the horse, making low sounds to calm it. He did not try to dissuade his employer from further violence to the coach. It was not his place. It was not his coach.

Shaftesbury raised his hand, stinging from the blow, in apology to his driver. He smiled, as much at himself as at his man.

The door swung open. An arm extended from the interior to help him step up.

He settled himself on the cushioned seat, revelling in the smell of his own coach.

The window was a sheet of pierced tin. As the coach lurched forwards, he put a hand to its coldness to steady his view. Through these points of brightness, he observed the Lion's Tower shrink. He listened for sounds from the Royal Menagerie but heard only the thudding of hooves as his horses struggled for grip.

The animals remain while I leave, he thought, feeling pity for them.

Turning from the tin window, he looked towards his companion.

A lady in a long, intricately patterned dark blue coat. She looked about thirty years of age, her beauty not yet faded, although perhaps difficult to tell with her powder and rouge.

She flinched from Shaftesbury's look, pressing back into the cushioning to keep distance between them. He had the kind of stare that looked through you as much as at you.

'This day of freedom marks the start of my revenge,' he said.

Her eyes became glossy as tears formed in them.

He slapped her.

The trace of his hand was clear.

A red print on her cheek.

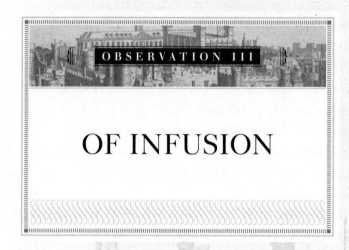

OBSERVATION III

OF INFUSION

THE BRIGHT YELLOW WALLS OF ROBERT Hooke's drawing room made a startling contrast with the view through the window, of the wet slate sky over Bishopsgate and the anaemia of the falling snow.

More strong colours fought for domination. A crimson rug leaked between the legs of blue chairs. Their orange seat covers, imported grogram, clashed with the cerise of the table. At the windows hung purple velvet curtains, reaching to the floor. Sturdy linings reinforced their fabric for the nights when Hooke required complete darkness. A vase of Christmas roses, placed at the table's centre by Mary Robinson, the housekeeper, added bright whites and pinks.

Never afraid to make himself the subject of his own *experimentum crucis*, Hooke had chosen the colours for medicinal effect, to nourish his weak frame. When working with Harry to build a half-scale model of a flying machine, he had suggested such retinal stimulation might hinder the choking of his nerves and discourage black bile.

Surely enough, Hooke soon put Tom Gyles to pulling up the old rush matting and painting the table and wainscoting. He dispatched Mary to Bloomsbury for the rug. Hooke himself chose the wallpaper, bought from an upholsterer at Whitehall.

Everything about Hooke's appearance, on the other hand, was drab. He sat near the fire, trying to warm after his return from the Fleet to his rooms at Gresham's College. His skin was pallid and lustreless. His greying hair, prone to breaking off, was now tied back with a charcoal-coloured ribbon. His silver eyes, which never settled, flickered about the objects in his drawing room.

The room also served as Hooke's elaboratory. Plans and constructions for his demonstrations at the weekly meetings of the Royal Society covered the table behind him. His diary, detailing his busy life, weather observations, the always precarious state of his health and medications used to improve it, his finances and experimental ruminations, lay open across them, next to his microscope and his calculating machine. When Gottfried Leibniz had shown his own calculating machine to the Fellows of the Royal Society, Hooke commented he could make one with a tenth of the number of components, and at a twentieth of the size. He promptly did so.

A glass-fronted cabinet displayed his collection of fossils, the traces of creatures long since disappeared from Earth. Many came from the cliffs near his childhood home on the Isle of Wight, some from excavations for buildings in London, given by the workmen who knew of his interests.

Clocks stood about everywhere, most of them disembowelled, their innards spilt as if Hooke anatomised the grand complication of time itself.

Stalagmitic piles of books grew from the floor, inserted into them hundreds of loose sheets, Hooke's notes written across them in his tiny scrawl. More books filled the shelves lining the whole of one wall.

All his tools—saws of various sizes, vices, clamps, tongs, (one with an extending double joint of Hooke's own invention), turn-screws, perforators, wrenches, and pliers—were organised on a large board. Each with its own place, either hanging from a nail or on a small shelf.

This neatness was not their natural state of rest. Harry had designed the system when he was Hooke's apprentice. Their temporary discipline was due to the previous morning's hunting and sorting by his replacement, Tom Gyles.

A door led to Hooke's observational turret, housing a pair of his larger telescopes and his selenoscope. Harry used to sit up there with Hooke, both of them wrapped in blankets, sipping hot chocolate.

Now it was Tom who learned the mysteries of the constellations, the names of stars and planets, and the mysterious attractions between them. The boy, just ten years old and already apprenticed, sat in among Hooke's things, mixing plaster for a model of the surface of the moon. He dreamed of exploring the oceans, and never tired of discussing with his master the mathematics of navigation, the problem of longitude, magnetic declination, and a clock to keep time at sea.

'I shall blow air through the plaster from beneath the model, before it has set,' Tom explained to Harry, smearing plaster over his forehead, 'to emulate its craters.'

Harry experienced an unsettling nostalgia for times spent at the table or crouched on the same bit of floor Tom now occupied. Shaping, carving, brazing, gluing. Now, he came by invitation, and the tools he knew so well altered subtly to his perception.

Harry had his own workshop, his own tools, his own methods of taxonomy and keeping to hand.

Visible through a doorway, Grace stood in the kitchen. She watched as Mary enticed a hare to leave its skin with a pull of her forearm. Its pelt slid from the animal, a sheath of pink-lined fur. A satisfying ripping sound accompanied her movement.

They spoke quietly, laughing often, but Harry could make out little of their conversation. Grace had the habit of talking behind her hand, so it was impossible to guess at the topic.

'How go the springs, Mr. Hooke?' Harry enquired, surreptitiously looking at Grace.

Hooke's niece was too grand for him. Sir Thomas Bloodworth, Lord Mayor of London at the time of the Conflagration, had wanted her for his son, until she turned him down. Admiral Sir Robert Holmes, Governor of the Isle of Wight and scourge of the Dutch fleet, also harboured an affection.

'Will you be ready with your paper?' Harry added.

An expensive education paid for by her uncle, and the manners of a lady. No thoughts for a lowly Observator.

Hooke grunted at him. 'I hope to have it in *Philosophical Transactions* soon enough.'

On the table was a wooden stand. A copper spring twisted into a claw at its lower end was suspended from it. A pile of weights sat by.

'I consider the spring-like behaviour of the air.' Hooke said. 'A man might fly on the end of a sound-spring. I am too bogged in fantasy. I am like a cripple climbing stairs, my progress slow and painful to observe.'

'And the world intrudes as ever. Sir Edmund's man will be here presently, with the boy.'

'Yes, yes,' Hooke said. 'Come closer to the fire, Harry. Mary has prepared me an infusion of catmint, to fend off the rheum. Somewhere, I have some steel wine. It is no wonder my understanding of this world proceeds slowly. Do my headaches and voidings of jelly signal the slipping of my faculties?'

Taking a place by the fire, next to where his soaking socks already hung, Harry skilfully kept Hooke away from expounding further on his ailments by offering to write an account of the boy at the Fleet. 'We'll be asked pertinent questions should there ever be a trial.'

Hooke sent Tom over to the window, instructing him to watch for Sir Edmund's man. Vigilantly, Tom carried the board with his section of lunar surface, and some tube to blow through. The plaster started to stiffen.

Hooke poured the pan of steaming green liquid into a bowl. The bowl had a chip on its rim, which he avoided. It would not have occurred to him to replace it. He took a chest-full of the steam before swallowing the catmint.

'The tincture resembles that which it seeks to drain out, Harry. A happy coincidence of signatures auguring well!'

Harry, his clothes still damp, would have appreciated the offer of at least a sip of it.

⬱

HOOKE SAT WITH his catmint and stared up at the ceiling. He did not view beams and plaster, but pictured instead mud, snow, and the body of the boy.

'What do we know about blood?'

'To take the blood so completely is a difficult undertaking,' Harry answered. 'To infuse it into another, more difficult still.'

'It demands knowledge of blood, and the course it takes about the body. Its flow, its pulsation, of the fabric of its conduits, of its sticky coagulation, and methods to prevent it stick. Of quills, capillary tubes, and funnels.'

'Arthur Coga, he of the lamb's blood, survived.'

'Professor Denis, physician to the King's cousin, placed the blood of a calf into a man who had suffered from a frenzy. The man pissed out black urine, then died.'

'He's the reason the Society forbade the continuance of infusion.'

Hooke took a tentative slurp of his drink. 'Viscount Brouncker, our President, put a stop to it.'

Harry watched him swallow. 'Witches are drained of their blood, to take away their power.'

'It is not Christian to persecute superstitious people.'

'There's a broken line dividing religion, magic, and philosophy. I test all things according to my own yardstick. You've taught me to do that, Mr. Hooke, over our years together.'

'There was a witch in Umbria, I recall, who used baby's blood stirred with vulture's fat. Another used toads, fed upon consecrated bread and wine. The toads were crushed into a powder and mixed with children's blood.'

Harry felt the need to compete. 'Another witch used the blood of a red-haired Catholic man, who she poisoned by the venomous stings of bees. She suspended him upside down, let his blood into a bowl and mixed it with the corpses of the bees that caused his death.'

'An efficient use of ingredients,' Hooke commented.

'This imparted the power of flight to the witch, who rubbed it on herself.'

'That, I would definitely be interested in,' Hooke said. 'I have long sought assistances to flying.'

He produced a pipe and some tobacco. Harry looked over at Tom, who looked happy enough, despite their conversation. He was busy blowing down a thick length of tube, forcing the almost-set plaster into strikingly crater-like forms.

'Every Scythian soldier drank the blood of the first man he overthrew in battle,' Hooke said.

'The Lydians made wounds in their arms, from which each covenanter sucked.'

'The way of the Arabians, when two men swear their friendship, is that a third makes a cut on the inside of the hand of each, and they all declaim to Bacchus and Urania of their oath.'

Harry tried to think of another one. 'Statues of Mary have been seen to weep tears of blood.'

'St. Catherine of Sienna. She attended executions, resting her head on the block to receive the blood of the sinner, so it would be accepted by Christ.'

'What of Sir Edmund's view, that the boy suffered a papist murder? The Catholics believe in transubstantiation, the changing of wine into the blood of Jesus, in their observance of the Eucharist.'

'It is not my blood that makes me an Anglican, Harry. It is my childhood, my history, and that of my parents.' Hooke stuck a taper in the fire and lit his pipe. 'It is not a thing innate. The Royal Society dictates modesty of aim and expression. We depend neither on Revelation, nor Epiphany. We have learned through this century how such dogmatisers hold a grip on our imaginations, urging men to unpardonable acts.'

Hooke exhaled. The tobacco smoke circled around him, catching the light, a halo missing its saint.

'Yet belief can alter the flesh,' Harry persevered. 'To be brought up a Catholic is to be brought up to believe. Belief in a cure may lead to recovery. Sailors tell of voodoo spells of the Western Indies, where to say a man is dead is enough to kill him, then to show him he can live again is enough to revivify him.'

'Perhaps we should not so easily dismiss Sir Edmund's fears.' Hooke tapped the end of his pipe on his front teeth. 'We are left with the questions: Why was this boy murdered? Why was his blood taken? How was it used? If for infusion, into whom was it infused?'

'Who killed him?' Harry added simply.

'The Justice took the letter left on the body. I am sure that will tell us all.'

'Not if he keeps it from us. Did you see the letter left on the boy? It was just numbers.'

'I will not speculate, Harry, with such little information. I have only *imagination*.'

Hooke used the word as if it were something despicable.

Harry fell silent, seeing the boy on the riverbank again, but moving, pushing himself up through the snow.

His mouth began to water, his own imagination making his nausea return.

Tom Gyles dropped his model onto one of the piles of books, making it rock perilously, before eventually settling.

'A dray arrives, Mr. Hooke,' he announced.

OF SALTPETRE, SULPHUR, & CHARCOAL

THE BOX WAITED ON HIS DESK, a candle on its lid. Wax dripped where the flame's heat breached the rim. He had always enjoyed the smell from beeswax candles burning.

Henry Oldenburg, Secretary of the Royal Society of London for the Improving of Natural Knowledge, put down his pen and stared into the swaying light, thinking of the fretful time when he first sailed from Bremen. It was then he had met John Milton, Secretary of Foreign Tongues for Cromwell's Council of State.

Milton, as his sight diminished, had depended on an amanuensis to assist him in his work, and do his writing for him.

Observing the flame, Oldenburg imagined blindness, wondering at the loss his friend must have borne.

Milton was three years dead. An even more unfathomable state.

The sounds of his wife moving about the house cut into his thoughts.

His Dora Katherina. Her love for him was undemanding. She understood him, understood his passions flowed first towards the New Philosophy.

Everyone who knew of the Royal Society knew of him. He was its Secretary, its Intelligencer, and the producer of its *Philosophical Transactions*, publishing contributions from *virtuosi* throughout the world.

His correspondences drew together hundreds of natural philosophers, mechanics and experimentalists. Famous in elaboratories and workshops across Europe and the New World, he had advanced the design of the Royal Society: to take to task the entire Universe, unfettered by partisan zeal, devoted only to truth and human welfare.

He picked up a coin, a milled copper farthing, from the arm of his chair. The candlelight flickered on its metal. One side, the figure of Britannia. The other, a portrait of the King.

He rested it shakily back down, then reached to lift the candle by its holder, and placed it on the desk.

He opened the box's lid.

Pulling out his pistol, Oldenburg opened its pan. The weight of the weapon, a relic from the Civil Wars, caused a tremor in his elbow. He poured in the priming powder, replaced the cover, and blew away the loose grains. He tipped powder into the muzzle and reached again into the box.

After inspecting the ball, an imperfect sphere of lead, he dropped it down the muzzle. Hearing its sibilant slide, the click of its landing, he pushed in the wadding with the scouring stick.

Holding the pistol, Oldenburg listened intently to Pall Mall and Westminster, to the sounds of the morning. The sash window rattled in the wind. He observed the vertical of sky between the curtains. The earlier rain, he saw, had turned to snow.

He lit the match and placed it in the cock. He blew on the match, opened the pan, turned the barrel towards himself, and with barely a pause pulled the trigger.

The explosion sent the ball clean through the front and back of his skull.

At the roar of the pistol, Dora Katherina screamed. Running in from her bedchamber, she saw the powder-charred skin of her husband's face, and his expression stilled at the moment of the shot.

Henry's blood pumping from the wound.

The candle's flame, guttering in the draught from the window.

Britannia looking up from the arm of the chair, impassive to the act she had witnessed.

These impressions squeezed chaotically into Dora Katherina's mind, sending it reeling, bringing her the sensation of a painful shrinking, a narrowing to a point.

Her legs folded. She had to kneel. Her cries were harsh. A vixen's shriek.

She held her hands towards Heaven.

Her beloved Henry was dead.

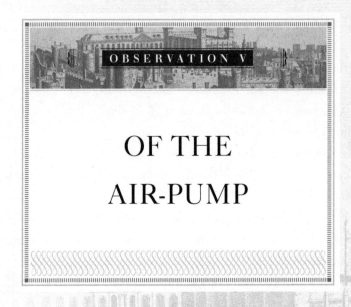

OF THE
AIR-PUMP

ONE OF SIR EDMUND'S HORSES RELEASED a piss stream into the snow, a hot fog rising behind it. The same constable from the Fleet, whose name was Gabriel Knapp, rested his arms over the handles of the sequestered tumbrel, the body of the boy tied on it, covered by a tarpaulin. He summoned the strength for another push. His face shone from the effort of unloading it down from the Justice's dray.

A crust of snow worked into the folds of his coat. The man looked too frail to be doing such business in such weather.

'The Justice is delayed,' Knapp managed. 'He will come later to view the boy. You must carry on without him, as he wants no decay.'

Together, they steered the tumbrel across the snow-covered quadrangle, no more talk between them, following Hooke's footprints.

These stopped in front of a door which Hooke had left unlocked. Harry took the lantern hanging inside, already lit, and led Knapp down the stairway, into the maze of passages and cellar rooms beneath the College.

Suspended over Harry's elbow, the lantern swung before them. The subterranean coolness was different in quality to the outside air: in the separate category of cold reserved for such places, which had never been warm and never would be.

Knapp's face showed no sympathy for the load they carried, but he was the Justice's man, so quite used to the carrying of bodies, Harry supposed. He took a care to keep his own emotions off his face—so what did Knapp presume of him?

Harry led him through a long, low corridor under brick arches supporting the floors above. They passed various doors, signifying their rooms behind. Whatever else the rooms kept inside them, the corridor itself was a storeroom. Along its sides hung various tools and pieces of machinery, and more of Hooke's models and machines. Woods, hides, ropes, fabrics and yarns of all thicknesses, boxed and stacked along the walls, and different grades of papers. Sacks of plasters, minerals, pigments and ores leaned against one another.

With only the single light's illumination, to navigate the tumbrel needed patience and determination. They were careful to avoid a wooden model of the Bethlehem Hospital, fully six feet across. The flying machine, in which Harry had fractured an ankle when making its maiden voyage across the quadrangle, was slung from the wall. Harry and Knapp skirted around its frame, canvas, and the springs that powered its wings.

They went through a solid iron-faced door with heavy studs protruding from its surface. At the top of a short flight of rough wooden stairs, Harry called down.

'Mr. Hooke?'

'I am ready.'

Gently, Harry placed his hands beneath the dead boy and lifted him. The lack of blood made him light. They should not have been so overly fastidious as to bring him on the tumbrel. The effort was more trouble than it was worth.

Knapp followed Harry down the stairs, and the three men stood in a tall narrow cellar room, the floor dug down to give enough height for the apparatus at its centre.

This philosophical instrument left only a tight margin around the claustrophobic room to give the space to work it. Two bulky lamps hung on opposite walls, their glows reflecting off glass and brass.

The apparatus was the *Machina Boyleana*, sometimes the *Pneumatical Engine*, more commonly referred to as the air-pump. Robert Hooke and his patron, Robert Boyle, had used it to investigate the properties of air, and of its absence.

Its base was a bulky frame of oak. Two equilateral triangles at right angles to one another formed a skeletal pyramid. On it sat a hollow globe, fabricated from thick glass. This was the receiver. The thickness of the glass varied across its surface. Viewing Hooke through it, Harry observed a grotesque version of him, his bent form exaggerated, features and limbs stretched into impossible curves.

The top of the receiver was cut away, its lid perfectly fitting the gap. Through this aperture, they could place experimental apparatus. The globe, as Hooke had suggested at the Fleet, was just large enough to hold the boy, and its aperture just wide enough to lower him through.

From the lower part of the receiver, a thick brass tube with a stopcock key protruding joined another brass cylinder. Inside it was the sucker, a wooden cylinder with a thick piece of leather glued to its top, the leather completing the necessary tightness of fit inside the tube. A rotating handle driving a rack and pinion forced this piston up and down to clear the receiver of air.

Knapp coughed, holding out a note. 'A missive for Mr. Hooke,' he said gruffly. 'From Sir Edmund.'

Taking it from him, Hooke gestured for Harry to lead Knapp from the cellars.

Back outside, the constable bade a curt farewell, pulled his montero securely over his ears, and walked to the Justice's dray.

Harry took a lungful of the Bishopsgate air, then returned through the corridor to the air-pump, where Hooke had unwrapped the boy.

❧

HARRY CLIMBED ONTO a small stool next to the apparatus, and Hooke carefully lifted the boy to him. The boy's limbs splayed loosely.

Harry perceived with a jolt how fragile he was.

They balanced him on top of the globe, and Hooke reached up to assist Harry in lowering the legs through the aperture. Harry held them by the shins, feeling they would snap from the pressure of his fingers. The flesh was a soft milky colour. Distaste rose again in his throat, and he castigated himself for it, being careful not to betray his squeamishness to Hooke.

He dropped the boy's feet into the receiver. The knees went in, and then, with a squeeze through the aperture, the thighs and pelvis. He took the boy under the armpits, repositioned him, and deftly finished his stowage inside the glass.

He jumped off the stool, with a steadying hand from Hooke. The slap of his landing reported against the walls of the cellar room, its loudness shocking them both. Each man's concentration on placing the boy into the receiver had transported him into a dreamlike state, in the solitude and silence deep under the College.

With his back following the curve against the glass, the boy's head rested on his knees. His arms extended by his sides, and his hands resting on the floor of the globe, palms upwards, he looked like a beggar appealing for a coin. There was just enough height to the receiver to be able to replace its lid.

Observing the boy's body, Harry became acutely aware of the fabric of his own. Conscious of the workings of his stomach, and the way his lungs pressed the insides of his ribs.

An idea occurred. He was not yet ready to have it scrutinised.

Hooke opened a box containing a smooth grey paste. 'The diachylon. We will seal him inside.'

They spread the diachylon, a blend of olive oil, vegetable stock, and lead oxide boiled together, into the crack between the receiver and its lid. Next, they prepared a mixture of pitch, which they melted on a small stove kept there in the room, with rosin turpentine and wood ash. They smeared it around the stopcock and completed the integrity of the air-pump by pouring oil into the valve containing the cylinder, to lubricate and seal it.

Rotating the handle, Harry drew the piston to the top of the cylinder, then brought it back down the tube with the stopcock opened, sucking air from the receiver into the cylinder. He closed the stopcock, removed the valve, and raised the piston back up inside the cylinder.

They created a vacuum inside the receiver in this laborious way, repeatedly, the pumping becoming more difficult as it vacated the glass. Each man took his turn at the handle. As the air inside the globe grew thinner, the glass began to groan. Soon the handle required the strength of both.

Inside, the boy swayed in protest, with the rocking of the machine as they wound its handle.

At last, a great creak emanated from the air-pump.

'Enough!' Hooke declared.

Hooke inspected the brass cylinder, then the glass, looking through at the huddled figure of the bloodless boy.

'We are close enough.'

❦

THE SNOW STILL fell. Back in the quadrangle, Harry and Hooke shielded their eyes against the morning. Gresham's clock showed it was just half past ten.

'Sir Edmund's man brought a note,' Harry reminded Hooke.

Hooke took the paper from his pocket and studied the seal. It bore the impression used by Viscount Brouncker. He broke it and unfolded the message.

Ordered, that the Services and Apparatus of the Royal Society of London, including Robert Hooke, M.A., Fellow and Curator of this Society, be at the Use of Justice of Peace Sir Edmund Berry Godfrey, that the Boy he speaks of be stored, and that his Dissection be continued at the Convenience to that sayd Justice.

January 1. 1677/8 Brouncker. P.R.S.

'Sir Edmund busies himself,' Hooke said. 'He *is* persuasive. He sends direction from the President.'

'You'd expect Sir Edmund to be busy. It's rare for the President to respond with such speed.'

'I wonder what else Sir Edmund arranges. Still, he has not arrived.'

Hooke locked the door leading down to the cellars, and they returned to his rooms, fatigued after their long efforts with the air-pump.

Leaving behind the boy in the cellar, Harry felt the pull of a subtle shame.

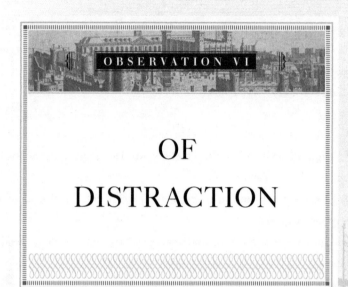

OF

DISTRACTION

THE AUTOMATON'S SKIN, MOULDED IN WAX, was perfectly rendered. The eyeballs had a watery sparkle. His wig was made from real human hair. More hairs, painstakingly transplanted into the brows, ears and nostrils, perfected the illusion of life.

His realism was both unnerving and comforting, a mirror for his audience to marvel at themselves by. Sitting at his desk in a corner of the sizeable library, his right hand gripped a quill halfway between an unfinished letter and a china inkpot, ready for mechanisms to be wound and gears to be engaged.

Three men, other than the mechanical scribe, inhabited the library at

Thanet House. The curtains were closed against the bright daylight outside, the room illuminated by a dozen candles sputtering in ornate silver candlesticks on the table, and more held in candle-branches on the walls, the books' gilded titles glittered along every wall.

The Earl of Shaftesbury, newly released from the Tower, shifted in his seat. The silver tube connecting his bile duct to the bag under his waistcoat, a conduit fitted with a tap to drain his diseased liver, pulled on the skin at its exit.

A heavy peruke matted his hair, making his scalp itch. The wig, descending low on either side of his long head to his shoulders, and his eyes, glassily unreadable, made him resemble an exotic reptile. The slack skin hanging from his jaw enhanced this reptilian aspect, age endowing him with impressive jowls, swinging pendulously as he talked.

Shaftesbury's secretary, Dr. John Locke, looking more like a robin, wore a brown jacket and a rust-coloured waistcoat. The way he cocked his head when listening, and his large, beaky nose, deepened this avian impression. He wore no wig, but kept his hair tied back, showing a high, intelligent forehead. He fiddled with his pocket watch, resetting it to the pendulum clock in the library.

Shaftesbury looked to his secretary for calm advice and logical reasoning. He had often thought of himself as being too feminine, too far the victim of his emotions. Locke provided a more masculine rationality—it was a marriage, of sorts.

Locke had designed and inserted the tube going into Shaftesbury's side, to restore the balance to his humours. A minor discomfort was a small cost to bear. The constant irritability, Locke had explained, was a property inherent in all tissue, independent of the nerves.

The third man, in a military coat of a deep plum colour and French bucket boots, was so still, with a gaze so steady, he might have been a cousin of the mechanical scribe. Pierre Lefèvre owned a thick, simian forehead, a single long eyebrow across it. Shaftesbury was entranced by his economy of motion. His progress into the library had seemed that of a body falling in a horizontal gravity, bringing him to his seat as if pulled by an external attraction. He walked without discernible effort from his muscles, perfectly balanced, with no movement of his head.

His services were as effective as they were expensive.

' . . . his investigators will then find a great deal of mischief as they pan for gold amongst the slurry,' Shaftesbury was saying. 'We have an infiltrator of the Jesuits, a spy within their midst. Titus Oates. An ambitious man, and pliable. He is to be a grand distraction from my revenge against the King.'

Shaftesbury looked pleased with himself, and spread out some papers before him, across a low table by his feet.

Locke, on the other hand, looked disgruntled. He had endured three hapless days deprived of sleep, leaving St. Omers on horseback, riding with Titus Oates to Cap Gris Nez. They had then crossed to Hythe—further discomfort in an old smack, whose every surface speared splinters into his behind. Around the coast, to Foulness Island, on to Gravesend, then the great dockyards at Woolwich. The London air had begun to aggravate his asthma, oppressing his lungs. At a spot between the Board of Ordnance's Gun Wharf and the Royal Ropeyard, they had met with Shaftesbury's man, Uriel Aires, and transferred to a cramped, pinching rowing boat.

Locke then suffered the indignity of being pressed up against Oates, whose bulk threatened the integrity of their boat. Now, after another restless, breathless night at Thanet House—its fireplaces were vindictive, directing their sea coal smoke straight at him—his busy mind full of the months spent in France, the hurried journey at the end of them, and of the grand ambition of Shaftesbury's plan, he was exhausted. The morning had been spent mostly napping. Frustratingly unproductive, for such a busy man as Locke.

'Oates's evidence needs to be neither consistent nor complete,' Shaftesbury continued. 'It gains potency from not being so. I have put together these points for him to remember, purporting to be hastily seen documents, scribbled digests secretly made in fear of being found out. With digression, omission and negligence, Oates's evidence will appear more genuine than events perfectly recalled.'

Shaftesbury mimed this layering of details, one on the other.

'We have the names of Jesuits, in France, and also in Ireland. We know of Catholic families here in London and in the country, holding sympathies for an uprising. They will find it difficult to deflect all the points we prick against their skins, the opinion of the judiciary being so firmly against them. The King will charge Lord High Treasurer Danby to put in motion a search.'

Shaftesbury relaxed a little, the pain in his side easing away from his mind as he revealed more of his plan. He took a sip of his Astrop water, acidulous and cooling.

'You know, I am like a crafty fellow, whose showy manifestations with one hand divert attention from the hidden work of the other. For while everyone looks to the Catholics, Monsieur Lefèvre will busy himself with the killing of the King.'

No reaction from Lefèvre. The magnitude of the Earl's plan seemed entirely unimpressive to him.

Shaftesbury checked for his secretary's response, some fleeting look of disapproval. Locke was now busy writing his spikey, angular shorthand into his notebook. Presumably details of his plan, but the shorthand was a mystery to him, and with Locke you never knew. The less he appeared to listen, the more he seemed to hear. He did not need to record the details, anyway, no matter which form of notation he chose. His memory was prodigious. If Shaftesbury were to ask him, Locke could repeat the whole scheme, with no details missed.

Locke had been in his employ for over ten years. They first met through Shaftesbury's physician, a mutual friend. Shaftesbury had been impressed by Locke's medical knowledge, although he had not yet qualified as Doctor. The mutual friend was soon replaced. His secretary was soon gone, too, as there were few professions Locke could not turn his hand to more competently than those who made a living at them.

A useful man indeed, but strangely secretive, often disappearing for a few days, on his return unwilling to say more than he 'had a little business.'

Shaftesbury could hardly carp at that, though.

About his current subterfuge, Locke, he knew, entertained doubts. But more concerning the means than the end.

Never mind him. A year of planning was time enough.

'Details, details . . . ' Shaftesbury went on. 'Opinions divided as to use of poison or gun. Tell of Oates being shown weapons to kill the King—a knife, some fireballs. Mustard balls. A silver bullet to bring him down. French landings in Ireland. Irresolute priests replaced by more fanatical assassins. More points . . . Catholic whisperings infecting the prisons, the Navy, the Army, lawyers, the guilds, the India Companies, the Royal Africa Company. Jabberings against Protestantism—morale-building stuff, broken open by our interloper—'

'—Call them the Articles,' Locke interrupted. 'Rather than points. It will stick in people's minds better.'

Shaftesbury, who rarely smiled, smiled at him. 'Articles they are, John. The next *Articles*, then . . . The Benedictines in the Savoy, gathering weapons. An attack upon Westminster, and the water companies—plans to poison the supply. Include the names of taverns and coffeehouses where plotters meet with one another—the King seeks to limit these places, so let his suspicions work for us . . . We can add further as we lengthen our campaign.'

He stopped, leaned back in his chair and spread the palms of his hands enquiringly. 'What of Titus Oates?'

At Shaftesbury's question, Locke and Lefèvre shared a look of exasperation. Locke based this sentiment on the journey from St. Omers, spent unprofitably and tediously with the man. Lefèvre had only met him the previous day, time enough to form an impression of the man as a blabberer. Weak, conceited, possibly unstable.

Shaftesbury caught the look between them. 'He comes highly recommended,' he said. 'We wind him up, and he will perform.'

'He is too much the rooster,' Locke said, stifling another cough. 'We need more the mole, able to stay beneath the ground unobserved, until ready to appear.' He sat forwards in his chair. 'Nevertheless, if you have confidence in him. I have found the man who is key to the winding.'

'Who is he?'

'His name is Dr. Israel Tonge. He has already seen the King with accusations against the Catholics. His own fictitious plot. He has written a long history of the Jesuits, too. He knows this territory well.'

'Introduce him to Oates, then, as soon as possible. We will test him and proceed when he is ready.'

Shaftesbury stood, to ease the hurt from the hole in his side. His expression changed for a switch of subject. 'Gabriel Knapp, the constable of the watch, reported to me this morning. He tells me the Justice, Sir Edmund Bury Godfrey, has made our boy his business. Robert Hooke himself was there. With him, an assistant. These two together stored the boy at Gresham's College, inside a vacuum to preserve him. It is the best place, I suppose, until we find the Witch.'

'His air-pump will preserve the boy until then,' Locke agreed.

'If Hooke aids the Justice, would there be a way of quietly sounding him out?'

'I am not close to him, although we are both Royal Society Fellows. My other work keeps me from the meetings. We anatomised a dog together once, at Gresham's. I recall telling him of the boy I dissected who suffered with rickets. I gave him my thoughts on rickets being connected with diseases of the lungs. From Montpellier last year, I sent him my observations of the moon's eclipse.'

'You share the same interests. Barometry and the properties of the air. Anatomy, meteorology, iatrochymistry.'

Locke nodded. 'I have corresponded with him on fuliginos cast out in respiration, use of the philosophical yard as a universal measure, and the swings of pendula at differing latitudes. He is more fully employed in the building of the new London, nowadays.' He paused, knowing Shaftesbury needed reassurance. 'He can have no notion of the boy's use.'

Shaftesbury nodded. 'You know, if the Witch is to be found, I wonder if we may still depend on him.'

Throughout their conversation, Pierre Lefèvre had waited silently, his gaze moving from one face to the other, maintaining the stillness of his head.

For the first time he spoke. 'What do you know of the Justice?'

His voice had an accent difficult to place. French, with an overlay of Dutch, or perhaps Italian, somewhere to the north, or emanating from some part of the Baltic states. He had lived and worked in all these places, and his fluency in their languages always kept this mixture of accents, this unplaceability.

Shaftesbury unleashed a sneer of contempt.

Locke, reflecting on the possibility of complete transmission of meaning between one man and another, answered Lefèvre. 'A man of austerity, and of a melancholy disposition. An intelligent man. He was for Parliament in the Wars. During the Plague, most left London, yet he remained, organising burials and prosecuting grave robbers. He makes his money as a coal merchant. In his work as Justice, there is no hint of abusing his position.'

'He keeps his counsel upon the boy's finding,' Shaftesbury observed. 'It has not hit the London gossip-yards yet.'

'We must have a care, though, especially if he has found allies.'

Shaftesbury thought for a moment. 'There is a way of keeping him from us. Send Oates and Tonge to him, to present their Articles. Sir Edmund is well known for his loathing of papistry. Let him look, then, in entirely the wrong direction, as Monsieur Lefèvre makes his preparations. What do you think, John?'

Locke indicated the mechanical scribe in the corner. 'I think, if your automaton were to write his memoirs, I might not want to read them.'

Shaftesbury raised his eyebrow. Locke had a habit of making his points from a tangent.

Locke smiled. 'He might say of us that we are machines, and only he has understanding.'

Lefèvre turned to stare at him, his face completely blank. Slowly, a grin appeared, showing little narrow teeth. Then he let out a loud, deep laugh.

Shaftesbury frowned at them both. 'I think that means my secretary approves.'

'Which one?' Lefèvre asked, still grinning.

Shaftesbury took off his wig and threw it onto the table. 'Does that close our business?'

When they had left him alone, the pain from the hole made Shaftesbury cry out.

He crossed to his scribe and considered his own body, merging with the mechanical. His human identity extended and altered by the bag and the silver pipe.

Locke was wrong, he thought. It was pain that separated them. The automaton, he thought, will never suffer.

Constant irritability is a property inherent in all tissue.

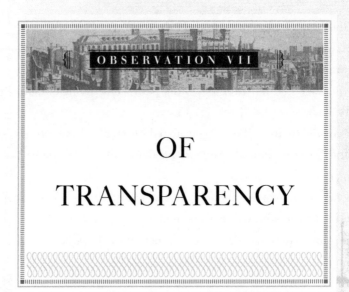

OBSERVATION VII

OF
TRANSPARENCY

IT WAS LATE AFTERNOON BY THE time Sir Edmund arrived at Gresham's. The boy, he saw, was arranged like an exhibit. A curio displayed for a penny a show.

'*Spake I not unto you, saying, do not sin against the child; and ye would not hear? Therefore, behold, also his blood is required.*' The Justice's voice rumbled around the walls of the cellar room. 'I have seen many murders. Whether done hotly or coldly, mostly the method is unimaginative. Either by use of the hand, or some tool. To drain all the blood away is to consider more closely the way of killing.'

The boy's eyes were extraordinary. A rich blue colour—closer to indigo. He turned away from them to look at the two men with him in the cellar.

'This globe will not allow the air to re-enter?'

'It will not,' Hooke replied tetchily, taking the question as a slight. 'We shall maintain the vacuum, to prevent putrefaction.'

'It fits him perfectly.'

'There are limitations to the size of a glass receiver we can make,' Hooke said. 'This is the largest we have manufactured. Grander attempts cracked or imploded.'

Harry pointed through the glass at the top of the boy's legs. 'The holes made after death, if done on these dates written by them, show he was preserved. As we preserve him now.'

'This we surmised at the Fleet.' The Justice's bottom lip still twitched.

'When squeezing the boy into this receiver,' Harry continued, starting to measure mentally the frequency of the twitch, 'I wondered if we returned him from another receiver. One of the same size. One also made of glass.'

Hooke made a tutting noise and sounded peevish. 'He could have been stored in a chamber far larger, one not made of glass. I had myself placed in a box of tin when working with Mr. Boyle, and its air was taken out. It clouded my mind and made me sick, so I banged against its lid. He released me from it.'

'But when all air was taken out, the box crumpled,' Harry argued. 'It could never have been used to preserve bodies.'

'A stronger box could. That this boy fits the receiver is fortuitous.'

'A suggestion, only, Mr. Hooke,' Harry said. Affronted by Hooke's tone, and in front of the Justice, he could feel the colour rising in his cheeks. 'I felt—'

'—You rely too much on your feelings,' Hooke snapped. 'A fault I have noted before.'

Ignoring Hooke, Sir Edmund allowed the possibility. 'The use of glass suggests the need for observation. Otherwise, materials less transparent, and more robust, would be employed.'

'The building of an air-pump requires substantial investment, and no little skill,' Hooke said, 'whether the receiver is glass, or no.'

'Who would sponsor such a philosophical murder?' Sir Edmund asked. 'And why their need for blood?'

Despite his flinty stare at each of them, the Justice got no reply. He turned back to the boy. 'There are other ways of preservation.'

'There are no signs of him being held in liquid, nor of being frozen,' Harry said. 'He was kept in a vacuum.'

Sir Edmund made indecisive, faltering shakes of his head, from side to side. 'I must put off the further study of him. For I am called away.'

'We shall wait on you,' Hooke replied, still bad-tempered, and thinking of President Brouncker's direction.

'This door has a strong lock?'

'And the other doors also,' Hooke said.

Sir Edmund strode from the room, up the short flight of steps, to inspect the ward and sturdy strap hinges of the iron-clad door sealing off the passage. At last, he seemed satisfied.

Diligently, they locked the air-pump room's door behind them, and then the stronger door. It clanged shut: the impact of iron and oak, a shudder of the frame.

Left in the receiver, the boy stared into blackness.

⌁

THEY STOOD TOGETHER in the quadrangle. Soon it would be dusk. The light bled through rips in the cloud, picking up its colour from the thick atmosphere. Oranges and golds tinted the snow-covered rooftops.

Sir Edmund pulled at his lip. 'Mr. Hunt, I have business with Mr. Hooke. I prefer you kept from it until he has considered more upon the matter.'

Still smarting from Hooke's chastisement in the cellar, Harry bid a stiff goodbye to both men. He headed off for his lodgings at Half Moon Alley, in Bishopsgate Without.

Hooke, knowing his walk, recognised his hurt.

The Justice was indifferent to the younger man's feelings. 'There was another such a finding. Another such a boy.'

Hooke looked pointedly at him. He had warned Harry they risked being pulled into deep waters. 'Also drained of his blood?'

'Likewise, it was taken.'

'When was he found, Sir Edmund?'

'One week ago. On Christmas Day.'

'Left at the Fleet River, also?'

'Out east, at Barking Creek, beyond the Woolwich Docks.'

'Have you preserved this first boy, as you require the second?'

'He is pickled, at your new College of Physicians.'

Sir Edmund produced two letters from inside his notebook and passed them over. 'I leave these with you.'

Hooke, looking pained, took them from him.

'Keep these securely,' Sir Edmund instructed. 'The first is a note I have written to you. The second is my copy of the document left with the Fleet boy. It was this endeavour I engaged myself upon today. Why I am here so late.'

Hooke blanched. 'What does it say of the boy?'

'Read these, then consider whether you will help me.'

'Does it tell of the taking of his blood?'

'Read them, please. Good evening to you, Mr. Hooke.'

That man's twitch is getting worse, Hooke thought, watching the Justice go. In his *orbicularis oris*.

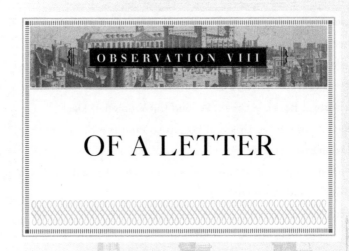

OBSERVATION VIII

OF A LETTER

THE BABBLE OF MALE CONVERSATION. A crowd of students beneath Lincoln's Inn Chapel. Sheltering from the snow in its undercroft, they conferred on the day's lectures, or else their plans on where to drink that evening.

Moses Creed watched them from a high window. They were shadows and silhouettes against the lamplights, as night had nearly fallen. He rubbed a patch into the mist exhaled onto the pane. He kept his coat on. The little warmth from the fire in the grate dissipated speedily in his office on Chancery Lane.

How very young they looked. And eager. He had been eager, too. Imprudently so.

His crime was to have been born too late.

Creed had been a student there. Nearly a decade ago, he realised, feeling a stab from the passing of the years.

He was there when they buried John Thurloe, Oliver Cromwell's Secretary of State and leader of a thousand intrigues, at the chapel he now overlooked.

Thurloe—a totem of the Interregnum, a relic of the time when subjects had usurped their ruler, and Cromwell had reigned—had been preserved by the King on his restoration.

No doubt such a taming suited the second Charles Stuart, Creed thought bitterly.

Creed was bred for dissent. His father had held that bishops' claims to mediate between Heaven and Earth were thinly founded: salvation could be found only within the pages of the Bible. At first Episcopalian, his mother, a believer in the Church and its hierarchy, the King at its apex, had her religion driven towards her husband's by the first Charles Stuart's absolutism.

Both hopeful for the end of monarchy, nevertheless they had shared the same shock as everybody at the brutality of its demise.

Creed was five years old when the anonymous executioner held the King's head aloft. A small boy when Cromwell accepted the Instrument of Government. By then, his father was dead, buried in a field somewhere near the confluence of the Teme and the Severn rivers. Killed fighting for Parliament at the Battle of Worcester.

He wished he knew more of his father. His mother, continuing on their business as glovers, had rarely spoken of him after his death. She was taken by the Plague, in the hard summer of 'sixty-five.

Creed had only memories of half-listened to conversations: his mother with her oldest and most trusted friends, talking of his father's past.

Creed was fourteen when Cromwell died. By the time the second Charles Stuart made his return, he was old enough to understand the depths of his mother's disappointment.

'All kings forget they rule *for* the people. It's a strange fact the people forget this, too. Why else do you think Oliver refused the crown? It taints a man, as he knew full well.'

With the new King came retribution. Creed could not wipe the slate wholly clean, for the chalk always grips to its surface. Moses Creed was known to be Reuben Creed's son.

Listening to the loud confidence of the students below, he remembered when his own capabilities made him believe success was merely a question of opening up for business. Instead, he had never found the preferments and referments he thought would come to him on merit alone.

It took little to convince a client to go elsewhere. A non-committal shrug, the quietest of suggestions.

Creed had lowered his original sights. Now, he dealt mostly with the inferior sort.

Occasionally, he rubbed up against the underworld, a nebulous group with an unsurpassed knowledge of the law. But most of them without the capacity to put one letter after another. This seldom disadvantaged them. Their messages arrived surely enough, without the means of paper, Creed used as a last resort.

Strangely, never from them the troubles he had from the more prosperous when chasing payment.

He indulged a secret sympathy for their codes of morality, and their stern methods of reprisal.

He turned back from the window and looked at the letter resting on his desk. It was one of many letters. And leases. Assignments, affidavits, examinations, warrants, conveyances, indentures. Changes to wills. Disputes.

Such was the substance of his solicitor's life.

Not a single new customer today. No one will come now, he thought, through this snow.

He would deliver the letter.

He looked again at the name of its recipient.

Mr. Robert Hooke.

Creed scribbled a covering note, sealed it, placed it into his green bag, and put some more papers inside too, to give a better appearance of business.

He shut the office door behind him, leaving his fire to burn itself out, and walked down to the street for his habitual hot chocolate at Man's, against Lincoln's Inn Gate.

He would drink his chocolate, he decided, then take the letter to Mr. Hooke's home, in his lodgings at Gresham's College.

Looking up at the Gatehouse, Creed remembered again Oliver Cromwell, who had roomed there as a young legal student himself, sixty years ago.

The Protector had looked down from those windows.

Creed's father had made gloves for Parliament before he joined the fight. Maybe Cromwell himself wore a pair . . .

Although he had thought this thought a thousand times before when making this little journey, Creed still felt a rush of the blood in his heart when he thought it.

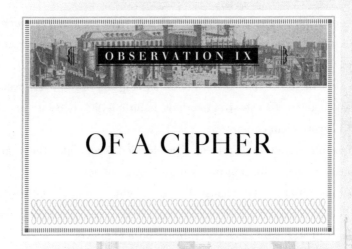

OF A CIPHER

THE JUSTICE'S WRITING SUITED HIM WELL, Hooke thought. The letters formed up into a troop. Evident strength in the verticals, precision in the horizontals. A neat right-hand margin revealed a man who planned ahead.

He lifted the paper up to the candlelight. The pressing of Sir Edmund's nib had left a deeply indented trail across it. Indicative of a forceful character, Hooke decided, rather than an unbalanced one.

Mr. Robert Hooke (Onely).
At His Lodgings within Gresham's College.
Jan: 1 1677/8

Your Abilities surpass mine to gleane Meaning from these Papers.
Their Notation takes the form of a Cypher. I relie upon you, Mr. Hooke, to
divert your most Earnest Attention and provide a Full and Active
understanding, where my owne is Limited and Lame.

You are enough Politick, I think, to understand my shewing this to You,
and onely to You. We will discuss further this Businesse.

Burn this.

Sir Edmund Bury Godfrey Justice of Peace,
from his House at Hartshorne Lane

Swallowing the last of his evening meal, the hare with pease pudding, Hooke washed it down with some claret. He acknowledged the persuasive pull of Sir Edmund's note, and the subtlety that lay behind it. A blend of flattery and exhortation. Sir Edmund was used to getting his way and employed a range of means to do so.

The Justice was a stimulating man. Since Hooke had known him—the daylight hours of one day—he found himself with a boy drained of his blood, the second such boy to be found, and now some enciphered papers.

Sir Edmund's copy of the document left with the boy at the Fleet lay on his desk: sheets of paper, each with a grid of numbers arranged in a square, twelve numbers along by twelve numbers down, each sheet written on one side.

Harry had noticed the numbers when the Justice had briefly shown them the letter. Hooke berated himself for missing the detail.

The cipher brought a misty sensation of familiarity.

It put him in mind to find his box full of silver filings, sold to him at

Bartholomew Fair the previous summer. Licking it improved the memory, the man who sold it—a Mr. Melancholy—had said. Harry had looked at him askance when he bought it, but these things were worth trying. On that same day, they saw the Dutch giantess: an extraordinarily beautiful face, which disturbed his dreams for some while.

Hooke brought his thoughts back to the grids. He held forth often enough about the application of his discoveries and methods, and the merits of the New Philosophy for practical men. With the finding of the boy at the Fleet, and another at Barking Creek, it was an opportunity to demonstrate usefulness. And perhaps receive payment from a grateful State.

He suspected, though, Sir Edmund would lead him into matters he would wish to avoid. Especially if there was truth in his suspicion that this was a Catholic business.

How long would he expect them to keep it? And why the Justice's insistence on burning his letter? Hooke folded it and dropped it onto the fire, where it furled like the petals of a flower closing. He prodded at it with a poker until it broke into cinders.

As he stood by the fireplace, he heard the bangs of Tom racing down the stairs, then the withdrawing of the bolt securing the front door. Hooke had not noticed the knocking and could barely perceive the bolt. A muffled clanking was all.

This chill has affected my tubes, he thought gloomily. I lose my hearing, and my senses of smell and taste, as well as my memory.

Tom's voice called from the lobby. 'Mr. Hooke!'

Hooke looked at himself in the mirror, picking remnants of hare from his sand-coloured teeth. The catarrh in his head did not trouble him so much as his thoughts on assisting the Justice, as he left the warmth of the flames to go downstairs.

Tom had invited the caller in to bring him out of the weather. He stood in the cold lobby, bringing in the even chillier aura of the night. He was a man of about forty years of age, but the manner of his clothes made him seem older—his lack of style noticeable even to Hooke, who cared little for such things.

Gloveless, the man rubbed his hands for warmth, which amplified the unctuous air he had about him. His smile was constant, but lacked warmth behind it, as if he had learned to be pleasant from a book.

He removed his hat, shook the snow from it, and announced himself as 'Moses Creed, Solicitor.'

'Good evening, Mr. Creed,' Hooke welcomed him warily, wondering if he came with a subpoena.

'You are the *illustrious* Mr. Robert Hooke, of the Royal Society?' the solicitor enquired, to distinguish him from a dozen others. 'Creator of the famous *Micrographia*, of the weighing of the air, and of the building of the new London?'

Now Hooke was even more cautious, alarmed by the intensity of the man's obsequiousness. 'I am Mr. Robert Hooke, Curator of Experiments for the Royal Society, and Professor of Geometry here at Gresham's College.'

'It is an *honour*, Mr. Hooke, to meet you. A most skilled natural philosopher, known throughout the kingdom for your prodigious interests and ingenious pursuits!'

'Your words are welcome, and kind.' Hooke raised his hand to stop the solicitor from going further. 'What is it, Sir, I may do for you?'

'You may take this letter, Sir, I am engaged to deliver.'

From a bag slung over his shoulder, Creed took a small letter, bearing a seal of black wax, and held it towards Hooke.

Hooke, disconcerted, took it hesitantly. It had a similar appearance to the letter Sir Edmund had shown them at the Fleet, lifted from the body of the boy.

On it was his name, and the address of his lodgings at Gresham's, written in a remarkably steady and controlled hand.

'Who charged you with conveying this to me, Mr. Creed?'

'I was engaged for my discretion. You understand, I hope, Mr. Hooke.'

'When was it left with you? Will you say that much?'

'I am not one who betrays the terms of his commissions. I bid you good night, Sir.'

BACK IN HIS drawing room, after sending Tom to bed, Hooke asked Mary to prepare him some tea. At his table, he broke the black seal which bore a simple image of a candle and its flame. He opened the letter, diffident in all his movements. For some reason he could not explain even to himself, this letter made him more nervous than all the business with Sir Edmund.

He would not tell Harry: it was an unphilosophical sensation.

More pages covered by grids of numbers arranged in a square, twelve numbers along by twelve numbers down, on one side only of each sheet.

Sir Edmund's writing was orderly, but the writing on these sheets was astonishingly neat. Each number was perfectly sized for its neighbours and perfectly reproduced every time it appeared. It was difficult to discern it had not been printed with type metal. Occasionally, the character of the pen's nib betrayed itself as the ink on it dried, before being re-dipped, and the regularity continued.

He did not think he had ever seen numbers so exactingly done.

Grace called up from the lobby.

'Mr. Hooke, all of London calls on you this evening,' Mary said, putting down his tea.

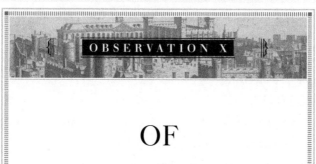

OF
ASSISTANCE

GRACE LED THE VISITOR UP TO the drawing room. The woman wore an enveloping headscarf, whose dryness showed it had stopped snowing.

'Mrs. Oldenburg?' Hooke said doubtfully. Then, when he was sure, 'Good evening to you, Dora Katherina.'

Her resolve crumpled. Seeing her distress, Hooke took her by the hand. He apologised for all the clutter, pulled out a chair from by the table, and poured her a small amount of the remaining claret.

'I have the utmost terrible news, Mr. Hooke,' she said, once she had recomposed herself, taken off her scarf and coat, and was holding the glass he offered to her. 'I come for your help, and your counsel.' Her accent revealed her Irish origins. In her mid-twenties, far younger than her husband—she was only fifteen when she married him—she had long auburn hair and pale, freckled skin. Not for the first time, Hooke thought Henry Oldenburg had a very fine-looking wife.

Dora Katherina took a long draught of the claret. 'Henry committed self-murder this morning.'

'Merciful God!'

'I wish not the manner of his death to become known. I think you, also, would prefer such shame a secret.' She spoke in a monotone.

'How did he do it, Mrs. Oldenburg?' Hooke had his hand to his mouth and looked even greyer than usual.

'A ball shot from his pistol,' she replied. 'I forgot he even kept the thing.'

Hooke sat down heavily, needing to draw himself together. 'We cannot allow this to tarnish his good name.'

Despite her grief, Dora Katherina was clear-headed enough to know he meant the good name of the Royal Society. She had calculated this, and relied on it.

The threat of scandal made Hooke's decision a swift one. 'Your house is secured, and empty?'

'The servants do not live in. None other knows of his death.'

'No neighbours heard the shot?'

'Those we have are out of town for the winter. He was at the top of the house. I'm sure none on the street did. Certainly, none came to investigate.'

Looking thoughtful, Hooke poured her more of the claret. 'I know a man to write the certificate. It shall be our own little intrigue. We did often disagree, your husband and I, on philosophical and pecuniary matters, but the Royal Society owes him much. Will you take me to him? First, I must call upon my assistant, to rouse out the physician.'

He found a quill and paper and wrote out a note. He sanded the ink dry, left Dora Katherina to her drink, and climbed the stairs to Tom's room.

At first thinking he was in trouble for reading instead of being ready for bed, Tom was thrilled by the importance of the mission, made clear by the extraordinary visit Hooke made to his room after bedtime and the solemnity of his tone. The boy took the note, addressed to a Dr. Diodati, along with a small lantern Hooke, after spiking a candle into it, gave to him.

'Speak with no one, Tom, and be as quick as you can. Go with Harry to find Dr. Diodati, and I shall meet you in Pall Mall.'

The boy left him, running off into the dark.

Hooke rejoined Dora Katherina, who waited, looking shrivelled, her sorrow seeming to have made her retract into herself.

The enciphered papers were behind her. Glancing at them, Hooke decided he would not have the time to peruse them. He had to see to Henry Oldenburg, to disguise the manner of his death.

What of the Secretaryship? He would campaign for the vacant position.

And what of the boy left at the Fleet, now preserved in the air-pump? And the other, stored at the College of Physicians, along Warwick Lane?

Hooke tried to push it all from his mind. His life was too stuffed with all the things competing for his time.

He would be too busy to unravel a cipher. There must be no distraction—he had desired Oldenburg's role too much for too long.

Sir Edmund, though, would continue to press for assistance.

Maybe instead he could offer Harry? He had the ability to unravel its meaning.

If only he could remember where he had seen this cipher before . . .

With the press of a headache in his temples, he took Dora Katherina by the arm and led her out of his lodgings, and through the College grounds. They walked along Broad Street until they found a hackney coach to take them to Pall Mall, and the body of the Royal Society's Secretary.

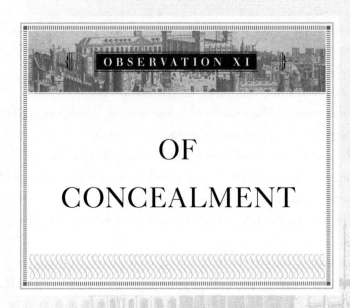

OBSERVATION XI

OF
CONCEALMENT

TOM HELD THE LANTERN, HIS LOW height sending a shadow play of their movements over the ceiling.

Dr. Diodati examined the damaged head of Henry Oldenburg, who still sat in the chair in his study. A blackened hole showed the ball had entered above the hairline over the temple and exited through the opening of the occipital bone, where the spine enters the skull.

It had forced chips of bone and shreds of flesh out with it. These lodged in the sodden fabric and stuffing of the chair—as did the ball itself, flattened against its thick wooden back. Oldenburg's blood misted the wall behind the chair, despite the distance between them.

'We can conceal this,' Hooke whispered.

Dora Katherina brought in cloths and a fresh nightgown, as Hooke had asked her to do.

Harry saw her shudder as she looked again at the pistol. It lay on the floor beside her dead husband, where it had dropped by its scouring stick and powder. Its box was left open, untouched since Oldenburg took the weapon from it.

'Do you wish us to take it?' he asked her.

'Yes, get it out of here!' she beseeched him. 'An evil thing!'

'Husband died peacefully abed,' Diodati said to her. 'That all world know.' He held out his hand. 'Cloths.'

Dr. Diodati was a small rat-like man whose old-fashioned chin beard emphasised the rodent cast of his features. Although his economy with words left few gaps for any patient to interject, he could exude an air of kindliness. He did not look at all worried by the deception Hooke asked him to perform.

Dora Katherina fetched a small china bowl filled with water, and Harry took it from her. At a nod of instruction from Hooke, he wiped down the back of Oldenburg's neck. The middle finger of his left hand shook, which exasperated him. The meat of his body was disloyal, refusing to be governed by his will. He did not want the older men with him to notice his reaction to dead bodies.

Even Mr. Hooke, though, looked rattled by Oldenburg's last choice.

Harry rinsed the cloth through, and the water stained red. Steeling himself, he picked off some larger pieces from the back of the chair, and put them into the bowl. The others, silent, watched his progress, until Diodati withdrew an instrument from his bag and went to assist him. A hollow scraping levatory, made to remove splinters from a skull after trepanning.

Hooke cut around the wound with a small knife. Diodati produced some parrot's bill forceps and excavated more of the shards from the hole.

Harry wiped at the remaining matter in Oldenburg's hair, and asked Tom to empty the contents of the bowl into an oilcloth bag that Hooke had thought to bring with them. The boy was gravely overjoyed to be given such an important task.

'Where are your husband's papers, Dora Katherina?' Hooke asked, searching about the room after they had cleaned some more. 'His correspondences?'

She looked at her husband's colleague, the Curator, in astonishment, having to reach her hand to the wall to steady herself. Her mouth pursed, and her voice went dangerously quiet. 'He tidied them all yesterday, putting them away. He busied himself for most of the day.'

Oldenburg's large oak chest, with ornately decorated wrought-iron bands and a heavy lock securing it, sat under the window.

'I imagine you will be eager to replace my Henry.'

'We will need to peruse and catalogue them for the Society,' Hooke continued, oblivious of her mood.

She flicked a look at the chest. 'The Royal Society may have them when he is in the ground, and not before!' The sudden volume of her anger made them all start, the lantern's light lurching as Tom did. 'I want all of Henry's papers to go to the *Society*. I do not want *you* choosing what can, and what cannot, be published!'

'It may help us understand the reason for his death,' Hooke said, chastened, as at last he registered her upset.

He was unsettled she knew precisely what he wanted: to have first look at Oldenburg's correspondences, and see how his own interests had been reported to others.

More used to Hooke's lack of tact, Harry continued to clean the body, now scrubbing at the burns over the Secretary's forehead. As powder had pushed itself into the skin, their removal was incomplete, but after they plugged the hole with some hurriedly mixed paste made from ingredients found about the house—beeswax, turpentine and some suet, with whitener rubbed over the area—Oldenburg looked acceptable.

They undressed him, cutting and pulling off his bloodstained clothes, which Dora Katherina put into a bag. Diodati held him while Hooke turned the shoulders. Harry dressed him in the nightgown, of cheese-coloured

Irish linen, and, with Dora Katherina leading the way down the narrow staircase, they carried him to the bedroom.

They lay him on the bed and drew the bedclothes over him, so just his face was visible.

Diodati inspected the wounds. With an arrangement of Oldenburg's long, thin hair, and a final polish of the suet mixture's surface, he announced he was done.

After clasping Dora Katherina to him, shaking Hooke by the hand, and acknowledging Harry's help, the doctor scuttled off.

Hooke, staying with Dora Katherina, directed Harry to further clean the study. Tom and his lantern followed, giving Harry the light he needed to inspect every surface in the room, looking for any traces of Oldenburg's self-murder.

When he had finished his scrutiny, and having wiped the chair and the wall, and cleaned the gunpowder blown onto the floor with Oldenburg's last breath, Harry placed the pistol back into its box.

Before leaving, he gave the chest a try, but it was firmly locked. He took the oilcloth bag from Tom, who still clutched it. He saw a large coin, a copper farthing. Not having an extra hand, he put it in his pocket to take down to Dora Katherina.

He then picked up the pistol box and returned down the stairs.

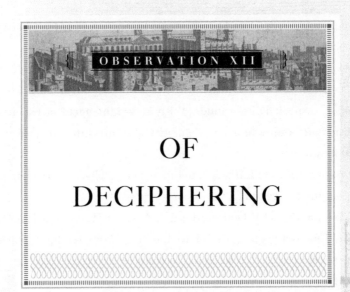

OBSERVATION XII

OF

DECIPHERING

AS THE WATER TURNS FROM GREY to green to black, the last he sees are lines of fizzing air and water, like beams of light following him. The last he feels is the lacing of his skin by the sand, agitated in the churning water. The last he knows is the weight of saltwater in his chest . . .

Harry woke with the convulsive flailing of a drowning man, disturbed by the sound of his landlady climbing the stairs to his attic room. His rapid rise to consciousness confused him, taken from the depths of cold seawater in his dream to the heat of a sweat-damp sheet.

A Norman barge, overburdened with stones to build the White Tower, had overturned, sending its load and its crew to the bottom of the sea, Harry caught in its netting.

In sleep, he had settled on his front, arms stretched forwards over the end of the mattress. His hands were dead. As he shifted, pain prickled the flesh as the circulation returned.

Mrs. Hannam's steps paused outside his door. A strip of candlelight leaked through the jamb. The image of the sinking barge quickly faded. Did she press her ear against it, listening for any transgression of her firm house rules? It would be difficult to smuggle any girl past her, Harry thought, for all the attention she lavished on him.

Or did she wish to break her own rules?

He heard her turn on the landing and go back down the stairs. If she wanted to enter, she had thought the better of it.

Although she often caused him discomfort by her slightly desperate air of trying to please, the thought of her waiting on the other side of his door stirred his humours.

Mrs. Hannam was attractive, in a pinched, underfed kind of way. And who would not be pinched, suffering Mr. Hannam? Harry knew she often went without, for Mr. Hannam languished in the new gaol at Newgate, having instigated a brawl in a brothel, and wanted money from his wife to keep the turnkeys sweet.

Harry sat up, sweating despite the chilly draught seeping through the casement. Pushing aside the blanket, he fumbled for his spectacles, and lit a taper which drooped limply in a small pot of water next to his bed. His tongue had a metallic taste. He took a mouthful of flat ale and rolled it around his gums, running his tongue over his teeth.

Mrs. Hannam must have been curious about Tom's arrival, and his going out to meet with Mr. Hooke. Harry's late return, some hours later, would have done little to diminish her interest.

Harry shuddered at the memory of the old Secretary sitting in his chair. The expression on his face was quite relaxed, looking as if he had dropped off to sleep. That you might shake him awake again—until you saw the hole going into his skull.

An eventful New Year's Day, then: a boy found drained of his blood, his storing to preserve him at the Justice's request, and Henry Oldenburg's suicide.

He took the taper to his desk under the window. He had mounted a board on the wall for the tools hanging from it. Boxes full of materials, stoppered jars, and smoothing papers sat on the floor beneath. On the desk, chosen for its inbuilt and capacious drawers, sat his microscope, his small telescope pointed towards the sky, and his few books.

Also on it, the enciphered letters Hooke had passed to him on their journey from Oldenburg's house.

Hooke had been firm on the need for secrecy. Harry was sure the Justice, Sir Edmund Bury Godfrey, would not be best pleased to find Hooke passing him the matter. Hooke, though, would be concerned with the Secretaryship of the Royal Society, and canvassing support from the Fellows to replace Henry Oldenburg.

Harry, nonetheless, felt pleased Mr. Hooke trusted him and his skills so much.

But what of the Justice of Peace?

Harry distrusted Sir Edmund but had not yet determined why.

Some fact worked against believing him. Something to do with finding the boy yesterday morning, or with the way he had pressed for the boy's preservation, or with the cipher he had later presented to Hooke.

And then Mr. Hooke had received a second letter, looking as if it used the same system.

Harry considered if the writer of the letter left on the boy at the Fleet had written the letter he now held. The one Sir Edmund had showed them owned a similar seal in black wax, although Harry was not close enough to catch the image on it, nor if it had the same regularity of hand.

This one, delivered to Mr. Hooke by a solicitor, had a design of a candle. A simple rectangle, its flame shaped like a teardrop.

Hooke had once described to him a catenary arch, the arch made by a chain suspended between two points, with only gravity and the forces pulling at the ends of the chain working on it. It was Hooke's belief that the eye perceived such an arch as flawlessly harmonic, essentially true. You needed no experience of architecture or knowledge of mathematics to appreciate the self-evident perfection of the shape.

The impression Harry had about Sir Edmund was as if the arch was distorted.

Harry warned himself away from this insidious feeling, towards a healthier scepticism more worthy of the Royal Society: he had to concentrate on what he knew. He had to perceive the facts *as they were*, not press his own emotions on them. Otherwise, he would warp and obscure the true way of things, like a mildewed mirror falsely reflecting the picture of nature.

After viewing the boy stored at Gresham's, Sir Edmund's insistence on speaking to Hooke alone had hurt him. Maybe this suspicion sprang only from his damaged pride.

Wrapping the blanket around his shoulders, Harry sat down on the chair at his desk. He would study the cipher taken from the body of the boy again. He had looked at Sir Edmund's copy of it by the light of his taper when he first came in from Pall Mall. If he had not, a more restful sleep may have been easier to come by.

Harry picked up the letter. The outside paper, which wrapped a sheaf of separate papers inside, was thin and fragile. Delicately, he opened it, and studied again Sir Edmund's writing. The first page:

57	78	58	55	84	78	27	47	86	95	73	79
27	56	86	95	96	67	57	97	106	55	62	98
27	50	56	56	84	56	56	96	114	113	123	65
67	70	94	84	66	55	27	80	66	85	63	98
46	89	67	75	95	87	64	48	88	75	75	89
46	69	87	86	74	89	37	46	76	55	66	55
27	80	66	85	75	88	58	58	88	86	74	87
34	70	86	56	103	67	26	58	65	76	66	88
25	50	64	84	66	55	27	70	56	74	85	89
34	68	97	82	86	88	58	50	86	65	86	87
58	89	76	95	103	87	45	49	75	95	94	59
54	86	88	52	96	78	57	56	77	76	84	55

Harry peeled it from those beneath. The sheets continued, page after unintelligible page of grids, twelve numbers by twelve.

These pages may not conceal words at all, but alchemical signs, or mathematical workings. Or, Harry thought, they may hide anagrammatical texts, requiring further unravelling before it revealed their meaning.

His shoulders sagged. Mr. Hooke expected too much of him. But who could he turn to for help, who would not tell Hooke he had been to them? The mathematicians and cryptologists within the Royal Society's Fellows? Sir Christopher Wren? Sir William Petty? Sir Jonas Moore, employed at the Board of Ordnance? Hooke had asked Harry for his discretion within the Society, to remember their promise to Sir Edmund.

Certainly not John Wallis, the King's cryptographer. He would be far too busy to help an observator, and anyway, he would tell the King. Not quite the discretion Hooke had asked him for.

But could he continue on his own?

Too early for despair. He would attempt the simple, the obvious, and see where this took him.

For the moment he put aside the disheartening thought that the message might be in Latin, or French—or any other language. Counting the incidence of the numbers, he soon realised this cipher was not a straightforward substitution. Their recurrence was too even.

Did these numbers correspond to verses of the Bible, perhaps? King James's? Coverdale's? The Breeches Bible of the Puritans? Latin Vulgate? Old or New Testament? Which Book?

The copy of the King James he owned was battered, much thumbed, not so much by him but by his parents before him. He found little time himself for the reading of it.

He tried to coerce the numbers to correspond to Books and Verses.

After a further hour or so, he had discovered too many correspondences, verses equally beguiling in their possibilities.

He paced about, and then, like a Quaker, he sat silently. He hoped to be filled with inspiration—he would have accepted it from anywhere. None arriving, he rewrote the numbers as letters, each 1 becoming an A, and so on through the alphabet, then stared at the formations of letters he had made to establish if they aligned themselves into words hidden vertically, or diagonally, or backwards.

Had the messenger left his message there, or a keyword to unlock it, leaping from the page, stark in its obviousness, like a night-time beacon fire lit on a hilltop?

Only fragments of words emerged, imposed by his mind on the grids.

A LONE GULL squawked outside, down towards the river. Harry realised the daylight made his taper redundant. He blew it out, and grey smoke curled from its tip. A draught chilled his legs. Their hairs stuck out stiffly, the goosebumps on his skin rough to the touch.

Noises from the street made him stand to look out from his window. This morning it was colder still. The people outside wrapped themselves tighter and in yet more layers than yesterday. Trodden snow along the narrow alley, frozen overnight, made an ankle-breaking impediment.

The commotion came from a group of women helping up another from a fall, her forehead and a hand cut after a crunching landing on the ice. Splashes of red showed vividly where she had hit the ground. She sat, too dazed to enjoy her moment of being the centre of such consideration. Hands pulled at her, her rescuers slipping next to her. Harry watched the excitement. A dance of scurrying hats, from his high viewpoint, as more people rushed to assist.

She was led away by her new-found friends.

Harry, pulling his blanket more closely to him, returned to the cipher.

Another hour of substituting letters for numbers, numbers for letters, of writing out alphabet grids and number grids, encircling or crossing them out, covering sheets of paper to do so. He was little further forwards. He worried away at the numbers, sliding his strips of paper, making further grids of numbers and letters, moving rows and columns. The desk, then his bed as he moved between them, disappeared under paper, and then the floor by his chair.

A knock on the door startled him.

'Mr. Hunt! I have brought you breakfast.'

'Mrs. Hannam, I'm not yet dressed!'

There was no reply, but he was conscious she would be listening. He pulled at his breeches as noiselessly as he could, and opened the door looking dishevelled, but covered.

'Persephone's eggs are remarkably large, and this one is a twin!' Mrs. Hannam did not let go of the tray. He could not take it, as that would have brought her in as well. He looked at the coddled double-yoked egg.

'The Romans broke up the shells of such eggs, to prevent their enemies from making magic against them.' He was aware he tried to impress her. She saw over his shoulder all the papers proliferating over the room.

'You are busy, I see . . . ?' There was a question in her voice. She wanted to talk and had not yet let go of the tray.

'Mr. Hooke keeps me occupied,' he answered. 'This smells good, Mrs. Hannam . . . ?' The question in his own voice at last made her release it. 'I'm obliged.'

'What is all this you engage yourself with?'

'Oh, I translate some mathematical Latin ready for publication. It's dry stuff.'

'You are blessed with an ingenious mind, and the Royal Society is blessed to have you.'

A deep blush spread from Mrs. Hannam's neck to cover her face. 'But one thing I do not understand,' she said shyly. 'How would their enemies recognise a doubly yoked egg from only its empty shell?'

'No, the Romans did it for luck, I think. In truth, it's a while since my reading of it.' Harry wished for something more impressive to follow but could not think of anything to add.

'Well,' she offered after an awkward pause. 'In our own time we have as many curious customs, I'm sure. Like the keeping of a hare's foot.'

'In future times, they'll regard our habits with as little understanding as we have for the Romans, or other peoples from history. Thank you, Mrs. Hannam. I'm starving.'

She caught his meaning and left him to his breakfast. He took it to the window, climbing over his desk to sit on the sill, being careful not to dislodge his instruments, or slip on the papers.

The eggs and bread, with the rest of his ale, slid down easily.

He looked out at his personal view of London, and the blood left after the woman's fall staining the ground.

He would take his workings to Gresham's College, he decided, to see if Mr. Hooke could find the pattern within these numbers, and how he went about seeking the Secretaryship of the Royal Society.

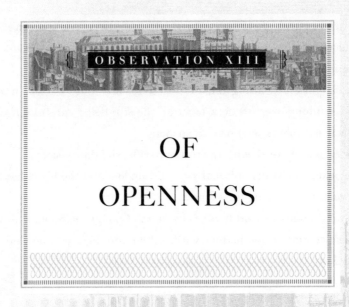

OF

OPENNESS

THE FEW CUSTOMERS CLUSTERED NEAR THE fire, and sought further warmth from their drinks, wrapping their hands around their cups. Hushed conversations. Most read a news-sheet, or their letters, addressed to them there at Garraway's coffeehouse.

Hooke and Harry chose one of the long trestle tables, and took a Muddiman's news-sheet. Hooke ordered a pot of tea between them and negotiated a price with Thomas Garraway for a full pound of the leaves.

'It will calm us after the ordeals of yesterday, and reinvigorate our thinking,' Hooke said.

Harry agreed to take a dish and stifled a yawn. All the sheets of paper with his workings on the cipher weighed down the inner pocket of his coat.

An ample serving girl arrived with two cups and a pot. Hooke showed no signs at all of being tired after his summons to Pall Mall and seeing to the body of Henry Oldenburg. Harry, after a long morning with the cipher, too, bore dark stains of fatigue under his eyes.

'I must gauge opinion before the voting for the new Secretary,' Hooke announced. 'I intend to replace the dead Grubendol.' Grubendol was Hooke's contemptuous name for Henry Oldenburg.

'You'll have the support of all of your New Philosophical Club, Mr. Hooke.' Harry kept back a comment on not speaking ill of the dead.

'Yes, Harry, I have my supporters, who for their own good reasons did not trust the Secretary. Sir Christopher will promote me. Dr. Holder, Theodore Haak, Edmund Wylde, and John Aubrey too will support me. John Hoskins and Sir Jonas Moore also. John Henshaw, Abraham Hill and William Croon, I hope to encourage. Mr. Boyle, I must sound out. He was close to Grubendol, and may own some other idea of his replacement. Nathaniel Grew? I do not know which way he goes. I must tickle him in the ear to draw him to me. He may yet stand against me.'

Gleefully, Hooke rubbed his hands together.

Harry had rarely seen him so spirited. It did not seem to worry him they had disguised the self-murder of his colleague only the previous night. Harry, conversely, kept glimpsing the Secretary. On his journey to Gresham's that morning he spotted him in the crowd, once coming out of a doorway, another time moving across his path. A closer look, of course, showed them to be others, both quite unlike old Henry Oldenburg.

'Wallis will be against me,' Hooke continued, 'as he is against Dr. Holder. They still bicker over the teaching of the deaf mute to speak. I wonder whether Brouncker will persevere as President, now Grubendol is dead.' Hooke reached out and placed his hand on the back of Harry's. 'Also, there is the thorny matter of the Secretary's papers. If I am voted to replace him, I will propose you as being well able to catalogue them.' He sniffed loudly. 'Mrs. Oldenburg was no more obliging when I ventured there this morning.'

'How is the widow, Mr. Hooke?'

'It was a stiff blow to her. She takes comfort that at least on his certificate he died peacefully. Dr. Diodati was accommodating—there will be no raising of the Coroner's suspicions. Grubendol died of an ague.'

'What led him to self-murder?' Harry asked. 'Why see himself off so violently?'

Hooke was little concerned with the manner or motivation of Oldenburg's death. 'He trials the *Great Experiment* . . . Grubendol's departure will make the Society run more smoothly. The matter of my hairspring watch hardened my heart against him. And he displayed great importunity in seeking to create dispute between Mr. Newton of Cambridge and me, concerning planetary motion . . . '

'Mr. Hooke, we must discuss Sir Edmund Bury Godfrey, and the two enciphered letters. And the dead boy from the Fleet.'

'Ah! Yes.' Hooke forced himself to change the direction of his interest, which was plainly difficult to do. 'We have secured the boy away from prying eyes, and we must leave him so until ordered otherwise by the Justice. Let us talk instead of the cipher.'

Harry took the papers from the pocket inside his coat. 'I've worked on it, but progressed little. The pattern's inconstant. Some change alters the relation of numbers throughout.'

'You know the first unravelling may lead to another cipher, and not the final message?'

Harry, his back aching and vision strained, assured him he was aware of the possibility.

'Once revealed, you must make your report of the cipher in straightforward terms for Sir Edmund.'

'I shall aim for a mathematical clarity.'

'Democratic language is the foundation of the Society. There should be openness in all things.' Hooke sounded as if he already campaigned for the Secretaryship. 'Although . . . ' he paused. 'Bring it first to me before Sir Edmund sees it.'

'You've more faith in my capacity to read this cipher than I.'

'You will do it, Harry,' Hooke reassured him warmly. 'Natural philosophers worthy of the name suffer a curious pride, one whose arrogance allows a sharp disappointment at failure. My worry is, your labours will reveal something of the political, in which I would not wish the Royal Society to become embroiled.'

'Openness should only reach so far,' Harry agreed. 'I don't trust Sir Edmund.'

Hooke looked sideways at his assistant. 'His interests are far wider than just this boy. Care is our watchword! Now, let me view what you have done.'

Harry unfolded the papers and spread them across the table. Hooke poured out more tea, its steam vigorous in the low temperature of the room.

'You have shown there to be no single correspondence between these numbers and any meaningful message. An admirable start.'

Taking out his portable writing set, Hooke wrote out the alphabet onto strips of papers, exactly as Harry had done, and proceeded to attack the first page, with its neat grid of numbers.

'If these numbers change sequentially, then their pattern repeats throughout the cipher. It is a strange music, owning its own harmonies and counterpoints.'

'The same grid, of one hundred and forty-four numbers to each page, appears on all pages.'

Hooke placed the sheet down on the table between him and Harry. He looked, jubilant, at his assistant. 'I thought so!' he exclaimed. 'I *have* before seen a similar cipher demonstrated to me!' His face fell as rapidly as it had risen. 'Now where was it? And who showed it?' Hooke became still. 'I am a forgetful dog!' was all he added.

For at least half a minute he sat this way, Harry beside him, hardly daring to draw breath. With a start, Hooke came back to life again, a beaming delight settling on his features. 'Colonel Fields! Colonel Michael Fields. He showed his war codes to a meeting of the Society. Was the event placed into the *Philosophical Transactions* by Grubendol? Sir Jonas Moore at the Board of Ordnance found him out and asked him to Gresham's. This is one of them, I am sure of it. I remember the use of this square, its uniformity designed to keep the formation of words within the hidden message all the more secretive. And the last page kept to the same shape by the addition of drivel.'

'Who is Colonel Fields? Can we trust him with this business?'

Hooke took a long slurp of his tea. 'This cipher depends upon a key-word,' he continued, avoiding the question. 'You form a square with each of its sides an alphabet, twenty-six letters across and twenty-six letters down, then complete the matrix of letters. All simply enough. As de Vigenère prepared his cipher. With each corresponding letter of the keyword, the choice of its substitute is decided.'

Hooke's expression became pensive, regarding Harry as if scouring his face for his thoughts. 'We will not yet speak to the Justice of our workings,' he said, dropping his voice. 'I must first hear more of his search.'

'But why keep them from him?'

'Colonel Fields showed this cipher. That is why I promote hesitation. Fields fought in the Civil Wars, on the side of Parliament. Let us first be sure of our ground.'

'Mr. Hooke, you've not said if we can depend on him. Should I go to him with this cipher?'

Hooke swallowed down the remainder of his tea and slid their workings on the cipher back across to Harry.

Harry, with a premonition of the trouble ahead, took them from him.

'Colonel Fields is most dependable,' Hooke said. 'But would you wish to depend upon such a man?'

OF THE

RED CIPHER

BLACK POWDER FROM hundreds of chimneys and from the fires, braziers and stoves set up to keep the traders warm, dusted the hard, refrozen snow.

Dirty smog coiled around the Black Eagle Brewery, whose smell dominated in a neighbourhood rich with smells. It reminded Harry of stale sweat. The same grimy haze floated between the chimneys of the Whitechapel Bell Foundry, where the bells were cast for Westminster Abbey a hundred years before, and around the brick and tile manufacturers, the glass-blowing houses, sugar refineries, metalworking shops, jewellers, coal stores, tea warehouses, and abattoirs.

On the east side of the Roman Wall, the Conflagration had not reached Whitechapel, so most of the buildings were old, timber framed, and crowded together each side of the High Street.

Harry tried to relax his features into what he hoped resembled ease with this world. As a stranger, he was anxious not to draw attention to himself.

The rattle of carts and drays battered his eardrums. Traders hefted their loads through the crowd with no consideration of feelings or injury, meeting any challenging stares with dissent, jabbing elbows into passers-by who strayed too near. With the clacking beaks and manic beatings of wings, of geese and hens, this raised the human volume. All communication was shouted or screamed.

Squealing pigs surged between the market stalls, beaten by a surly man gripping a stick to encourage them on. They slid on the ice, thumping down on their fattened sides, scrambling to right themselves. The waste from their bowels made a hazard as unpredictable as the glassy shine of the ground.

Harry dodged his way through the crowd, trying to spot Colonel Fields's Anabaptist chapel. It would be easier if he knew what he was looking for. At the top of the High Street, he found himself facing meadows and windmills, and the coppice, a collection of skeletal trees with snow-laden branches.

The remains of the Cromwellian fortifications, the sconce built during the Wars as part of the Lines of Communication, stood before him. But no chapel.

He approached a man dressed in the dark clothes of a Huguenot. The Frenchman sent him back the way he had come, with instructions to pass through an alley just after the Saracen's Head. Going through the crowd again, finding its rhythm, avoiding confrontation, and spotting the garish sign of the tavern—this Saracen's head severed bloodily from his body—Harry at last found the alley.

As he turned into it, the rapid diminution of noise tricked his ears into believing he stood in silence. With the change in sound came a change in light. Fearful of the dimness as he passed through, he broke into a trot. Re-emerging into the comforting daylight he saw crisp snow over a meadow, undisturbed since its fall. He crossed it and climbed over a flimsy gate between flimsier gateposts, then headed towards a roof—all he could see of a building down in a hollow.

Closer, on a slope dropping steeply before him, he observed the building's construction followed the rule of the trapezium rather than the rectangle, and was more a shed than a chapel.

'Is it on fire?' Harry asked himself out loud, for smoke billowed from every seam of the place. Tentatively, he approached the door. Unsteady on its hinges, it stood half open, and he pushed it aside. He walked into the smoke coming from a central fire, gathering under the ceiling, looking for escape since no chimney transmitted it away.

FROM INSIDE THE cloud, he could hear a repeated scraping noise. When his eyes accustomed themselves, he distinguished a man sitting in the parabola of a hammock strung between two posts. Harry was closest to the soles of the man's feet, so the man's head rested on his toes, foreshortened as his body appeared.

Harry advanced a pace to get a more natural view.

'I'm Harry Hunt, Observator of the Royal Society.'

'And I am Colonel Michael Fields. Good morrow.'

Harry realised the Colonel was shaving, a razor rasping at his jaw as he pulled at his skin to stretch smooth the wrinkles of age.

'Mr. Robert Hooke sends me, to seek your help.'

'In all this fog I thought you a phantom.' Fields wiped the blade between his fingers.

The old Colonel was wrapped inside a tattered campaign coat. His head was freshly shaved, with a few nicks on his scalp. It was a sizeable, impressive head, covered with liver spots like islands on a globe. A long scar curled around the back of it, starting above his right ear, whose top was missing.

He had obviously been a strongly built man, but muscle had melted with age. His clothes, once brightly coloured, had faded, only a bright orange scarf relieving their drabness. His trousers were brown. Harry suspected they had once been scarlet.

Beside him lay an edition of the *Souldiers Pocket Bible*, as battered as he was, and an unlit candle—it was tallow, Harry noticed—was stuck to the chair beside him in a cone of melted wax. A horseshoe of other chairs awaited his congregation.

Fields made no effort to leave the sanctuary of his hammock.

'So!' he exclaimed, waving the razor. 'Why do you come here, young man? You want my help, you say—I do not preach again until this evening.'

Harry, his eyes streaming, decided on a straightforward approach.

'You went once to Gresham's College, and spoke there with the Curator of Experiments, Mr. Robert Hooke. You were helpful on ciphers. A cipher you showed has returned again.'

'Returned? Which of the ciphers is this?' asked the old man, disbelieving.

'One using numbers in a grid, their substitution altered by use of a keyword. Each row a dozen numbers along, and a dozen rows to a page.'

'The Red Cipher,' said Fields.

'A red cipher?' Harry repeated. 'Why is it so called?'

'From a soldiering past, Mr. Hunt. From long ago, in the time of the Civil Wars.' Fields pulled at his injured ear. 'I showed it at the College as a historical curiosity only. It was first employed in the Red Regiment of the London Trained Bands. Also, you would shed all of your red blood before giving over the keyword—it was a promise we users of it made to one another. It sounds bluff, now, does it not, such sentiment? Yet such were the times. Used again?'

'Yes,' Harry confirmed. 'If this is your cipher.' He produced the bundle of papers from inside his coat.

'It may, of course, be another system, but the use of twelve numbers along and twelve numbers across gives the appearance of the Red Cipher. You have found out its message?' Fields looked pleased, glad his lesson was learned and evidently useful. His expression fell at Harry's shake of his head. 'Pass it to me.'

The Colonel rested down his razor and bowl on the chair, and spread the papers over his outstretched legs, spending some time sorting through them. Harry stood next to the hammock, the room's atmosphere attacking his eyes.

'Well,' Fields spoke at last. 'A number of your substitutions may be correct, you know—but without its neighbour to guide you, it's knotty to hazard which of them sit prettily. You have no notion of the keyword?'

'None at all, Colonel.'

'Then you won't know its length. That is a way in, as the pattern repeats throughout. You could breach longer messages, certainly, this way . . . De Vigenère, in the last century, employed a similar system.'

'Mr. Hooke believes a de Vigenère square was used in the making of this cipher.'

'Then Mr. Hooke is fallible, for he is wrong!'

Fields sat up straight, making the hammock sway, wanting a better look at Harry. 'We used just *one* alphabet to make the cipher, instead of twenty-six, which owns the advantage of speeding the method along—concealment can be a tedious business. Reach me my pen. Over there. And I have some ink.'

Harry located the pen and ink for the old soldier, and Fields wrote out a grid on the back of one of the sheets Harry had with him:

	1	2	3	4	5
1	A	B	C	D	E
2	F	G	H	I	J
3	K	L	M	N	O
4	P	Q	R	S	T
5	UV	W	X	Y	Z
6	1	2	3	4	5
7	6	7	8	9	0

'This is a simple system!' Harry exclaimed.

'I've not yet added the keyword to this alphabet, to mix the order of the letters.' The Colonel thought for a while. 'So! A suitable keyword, for exam-

ple, might be *Putney*, where we held the debates.' Fields saw Harry's ignorance. 'A historical detail, Mr. Hunt—I would not expect you to know of
them. But let's use this word, *Putney*, as our keyword.' He wrote out a series
of numbers:

41   51   45   34   15   54   41   51   45   34   15   54

'These are the coordinates of the letters in the word *Putney*, which then
repeat throughout the cipher. We add the coordinates of the keyword to the
coordinates of the letters of the message.'

He wrote out more numbers under those of the keyword, then added
the numbers in the first row to the second:

41   51   45   34   15   54   41   51   45   34   15   54

13   43   35   33   52   15   32   32

54   94   80   67   67   69   73   83

'The name Cromwell owns two Ls, each becoming a 32. These, in the
Red Cipher—but only when using *Putney* as the keyword—become 73 and
83, respectively. Cromwell, who was Lord Protector—'

'—I know of Oliver Cromwell, Colonel.'

Fields looked at Harry as if checking he had all of his faculties, was
mentally acute, and so could be trusted he really knew of Oliver Cromwell.
Something in Harry's face convinced him, for his own face broke open in a
blissful smile. 'Good!' he exclaimed. 'Good! Well, likewise, along this bottom line, we have two instances of the number 67. Yet *these* denote both M
and W. Where did you find this? It brings things back, you know . . . '

Mindful of their promise to Sir Edmund, Harry said nothing of the boy
deposited at the Fleet. 'It was delivered to Mr. Hooke, having been left with
a solicitor named Creed, who was secretive about its author.'

'Creed, you say?' the old Colonel asked, stroking the dome of his head.

'Moses Creed. You recognise the name?'

Fields rolled back his streaming eyes, as if he might find the answer to Harry's question on the inside of his forehead. 'I do not know Moses Creed—he is not part of my congregation here. But then, few are. Not many interest themselves in our meetings at present. Would you, maybe?'

'We've a similar problem at the Royal Society,' Harry replied, swerving his question.

The Colonel laughed a hollow laugh, waving the papers at him. 'You can see, it is a simple system, but difficult to break unless you have the key-word. A wartime cipher—robust and worthy, not one to break the brains of the soldiers.'

'I'm obliged to you, Colonel Fields.'

'And so am I to you, Mr. Hunt, for I enjoy this talk of ciphers. It makes me mindful of the man I used to be.'

'The Justice of Peace, Sir Edmund Bury Godfrey, asked us to assist him with an investigation. He came across a similar communication, making use of the same cipher.'

The Colonel gave Harry an appraising look, as if inspecting his buckles for tarnish. 'You know, you must take a care if you are dealing with Sir Edmund. Do you have now the time for an old soldier's tale, to show why I urge caution against the Justice?'

Harry nodded, aware he had said too much. He had been itching to impress. Something about this old soldier made him so.

'Then let me tell you of an occurrence during the Wars . . . '

The Colonel gingerly descended from his hammock and stood by his fire, almost disappearing into the smoke. ' . . . the last of the Wars between Parliament and this new King . . . '

The 'new King' had been on his throne for nearly eighteen years. The old man was about to go off into his reminiscences. Harry willed himself to be patient.

'This will seem as ancient history to you, but bear with me. Bear with me!' Fields warmed himself for a while, then returned to sit on one of the chairs.

'With Oliver Cromwell I travelled to Ireland, attending to the tumults there. We afterwards went together to Scotland, to fight Charles Stuart who is now our King. He had made agreement with the Scots, as did his father before him, promising to root out Episcopacy and implant Presbytery—you understand how expediency rather than Revelation dictates our ways of worship! This Charles decided to move his Scots into England. We fought him at Worcester. There, in September of 'fifty-one, was to be the last battle of all the Civil Wars.'

'But what of Sir Edmund?' Harry asked. 'Where does he fit into your narrative?'

Fields stared at him for a long moment. Harry saw the force of the man. He could imagine him as a young officer exhorting his troops into battle.

'As I say, bear with me . . . So! We were miserably distressed for want of meat, and by tiredness from all the marching. The Royalists set to with fortifying the town and ruining the bridges across the Teme and the Severn, leaving only the bridge closest to Worcester untouched. We were about thirty thousand—far more than those inside the place. At last, we attacked them. I, with Cromwell, stayed to the eastern side of the Severn. Lambert's men crossed at Upton, to the south, using a plank across the hole in the bridge. Dragging great boats with them—up against the flow of the river— Fleetwood's men advanced northwards, to build new bridges with the boats, to let us go freely from one side to the other.'

While Fields spoke, he used his hands in chopping motions to delineate where the opposing forces had mustered. The effect was to keep Harry listening, unwilling to interrupt again.

'The Royalists disliked our plan, and took against the men putting into place these bridges. They shot at them across the river. Cromwell sent three brigades across the Severn, over the bridge of boats. I advanced with these, and we met with some Highlanders. We pushed at them until they desisted. We entered into the town, the Royalists running before us. Bodies lay all around—fallen like leaves from an autumn bough. The noise from men and animals filled the air. A terrible keening hum coming from the men, quite unlike a voice sounding from a throat—more like the organs in their bellies crying out with fear and pain. We chased them as they ran. We overcame them, and cut them down.'

The Colonel's voice became very grave and quiet, so Harry had to lean closer to catch his words. 'It was a slaughter. Their lifeblood covered us. We looked as if we suffered wounds ourselves. When our powder was out, we slashed at them, or cudgelled them, or stamped them with our boots, squashing out their brains from their skulls. We could not keep our feet in all their blood.'

Fields produced a pipe from a pocket of his old orange coat, and Harry noticed the old man's hands were shaking.

'An army is a harsh, self-seeking power. We pushed survivors into the Cathedral, where the stench of their fright was most foul. Many of our men lost their heads and broke up the place. For myself, I would rather hack off my own arm than damage a church window, so I did not participate.'

He searched for his tobacco, struggling to withdraw it from the same pocket. 'Mostly, though, those Royalists inside, we did not kill—they were marched instead to London. The Scots, we sent home to their own country. Many of the foreign mercenaries, and the English, we sent abroad to the Barbadoes, put to work in the sugar mills there, or to cut the cane out in the fields. The King himself slipped away—eventually to reach France from Brighthelmstone.'

Fields concentrated on filling his pipe, and spent some time lighting it, sucking deeply and blowing into the bowl to spark the tobacco.

He at last had it going. 'Have you never asked yourself how it came to be that Charles Stuart escaped away so easily? Despite the rout of his men?'

Harry thought for a moment, recollecting his lessons. 'He hid himself at Boscobel. He was helped by Catholics, who disguised him as a woodman.'

Fields let out a loud laugh which ended in smoke-filled coughs. After he had gathered himself, he waggled his finger at Harry, from side to side. 'His disguise would not have hoodwinked a girl! He went by the name of William Jackson—that is the story Charles Stuart puts about. But it is only half of the story. Perchance you would do well to ask Sir Edmund how the King escaped . . . I surmise, though, you would find him secretive about his war, and guard closely how he helped the King.'

'Sir Edmund assisted the King in his escape?' Harry looked wonderingly at the old man.

'Charles Stuart left Worcester with about sixty men, including Buckingham, Wilmot, Lauderdale and Derby. And Sir Edmund Bury Godfrey. Sir Edmund was a Parliament man, ordered by Cromwell to lead the King away. There is history from above, Mr. Hunt, and history from below. You repeat the history you have heard, and that is to be expected. But, let me tell you, Oliver Cromwell settled that he would not kill a second king, but would instead escort him to France, where he would be out of the way, penniless, and unable to raise an army.'

He sucked at the pipe, and unhurriedly exhaled, merging more smoke into the dense air.

'You must be careful, Mr. Hunt. Sir Edmund Bury Godfrey was the conduit for the King's escape. The Red Cipher was used to arrange it. You must ask yourself: why has it returned?'

OBSERVATION XV

OF
ENTHUSIASM

THIS FELLOW, TITUS OATES, REPULSED HIM, with his fat face, and his fat flesh hanging over each side of his seat, as if liquefying like a burning candle.

This other one with him, too, the little man Israel Tonge, was unpleasant. Perched on his chair, his hands doing a feral dance as he spoke—he seemed possessed by a malignant spirit.

'. . . and the devilish stinks of the papists, with their unholy waters and their cloudy smokes, their blasphemous masses led by snuffling genuflecting monkeys garbed in the clothes of harlotry, their satanic artifices, their Baalish methods, these bladder-puffed-up wily men! Their canting effusions, a landskip of horror so contrary to Christ, their reliance upon the scratching of beads to bring them closer to God, their slavish devotion to

the Whore of Rome, their exorcisms and tricks and conjurations, their un-
trusty deviance and constant bloodthirsty plotting . . . '

'You know, I have not heard anyone rant so madly since the days of Sol-
omon Eagle,' the Earl of Shaftesbury muttered.

Tonge's eyes were the wide eyes of an enthusiast. He was a dreamer of
dreams and a seer of visions, of Jesuits gliding through the air, of their sanc-
tifying of daggers for the killing of Protestants, and their seeking to burn
London again. He had had a living at St. Mary Staining, but saw his church
and most of his parish go up in flames in the Conflagration. The experience
left him scarred and suspicious, convinced that Catholic firebombs put an
end to London and to his living.

John Locke, his eyes half closed, clasped and unclasped his hands impatiently. He had never heard Eagle's famously apocalyptic speeches during
the Plague, and then the Conflagration, but agreed entirely with his employer's sentiment.

After days of Oates, bringing him from France, now he had to endure
Israel Tonge. He was beginning to regret finding him out.

The tiny ranter chose the moment to stand and walk about the Earl's
library, his fingers clawed as if looking for handholds into the air.

Israel Tonge was fifty years of age, uncommonly thin, a head shorter
than Locke and barely reaching Shaftesbury's chest. His long dry hair pro-
truded from his flaky scalp like silver wires. When he moved, a snow-shower
of skin-flakes fell from it, and when he passed his hand through it, he created a blizzard.

' . . . their Romish lies and dastardly machinations against the Protestant sons of martyrs, their extravagances, intolerances, and persecutions of
patriots, their cruelties, malice, and enmity to Truth, their antipathy to
purity and sobriety, their contemptible sneaking away from right-thinkers
as if afraid of God's bright sun. Strawberry-preachers! Text-splitters! Their
faulty benedictional and schismatic aposticals, agends and mannals . . . '

'My father was a chaplain of the New Model Army,' Titus Oates told
Shaftesbury, in his high-pitched, sing-song voice, 'and he did not carry on so.'

Shaftesbury blinked a lizard blink. 'It would have exhausted the troops before any encounter.'

'Tonge is a brainsick Tom O'Bedlam!'

Oates's mouth, a small round hole, had lips that creased together like the strung neck of a bag. His eyes, black and shrewd, were set too close together. His features all gathered in the middle of his face, escaping his enormous chin.

'Dr. Tonge,' Shaftesbury called, and then louder. 'Dr. Tonge!'

' . . . their foul deeds, affronts and afflictions . . . eh?' Tonge's train of vituperation halted at last. 'What's that?'

'Your great zeal brings credit to you, Dr. Tonge, but we progress not in our enterprise. Mr. Oates is to perfect his lines. We have our own plotting to continue. Please, Dr. Tonge, you must concentrate upon the task at hand.'

Tonge's eyes swept the room, an invisible congregation populating it. 'By the powers of the air!' he cried. 'I concentrate upon it fully!'

The man overstretched Shaftesbury's patience. The King had prorogued Parliament, determined to do without it. He took for himself the same powers of his father. The same absolutism and arbitrary way of government. The same way as his cousin French King Louis. It was the papist way. The King's wife and his mistress were both Catholic. So were his brother and his wife. Perhaps the King, too, hid his true religion. He was too close to his cousin. There were rumours Louis paid monies to keep the King able to rule without Parliament.

Mere protest had proved insufficient against him. In Parliament, Shaftesbury had gathered like-minded men around him. His Country Party. A club, the Green Ribboners, had started, with Shaftesbury as its figurehead. The more active liked to style themselves his 'Brisk Boys'. Useful idiots, most of them.

Shaftesbury and Locke had both signed the petition, sixteen thousand names against the continued prorogation of Parliament. They pressed for Exclusion, that his Catholic brother would be kept from his heredity. The King had ignored it.

A heredity justified from God's law, ordained by the Scriptures. The right to rule over the people because of a Royal lineage stretching back to Adam.

Absurd.

His secretary put it well: you cannot inherit fatherhood of the people from your father. You can only gain fatherhood from having a child.

We are all sons of Adam.

Shaftesbury thumped the table. 'You must perfect the Articles, Dr. Tonge, our accusations against the papists, to memorise them. They are detailed and demanding. You are the mouthpieces of our plan. You must be fully prepared before you tell them to the Justice, Sir Edmund Bury Godfrey. Are you ready to continue, Oates?'

Oates poured himself some brandy from the pitcher on Shaftesbury's table. 'I am ready now,' he answered. 'You know, I too am *Doctor*—'

'—Let us continue with our practice, Oates,' Shaftesbury said. 'The evidence we bring against the papists. We must see off these perfidious Catholics, hiding in London like maggots in meat. Article eighteen . . . '

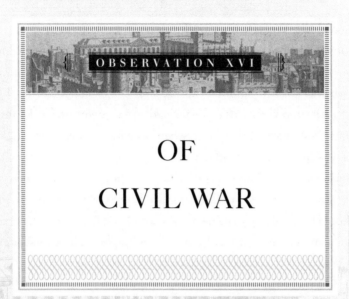

OBSERVATION XVI

OF
CIVIL WAR

AT THE TURN OF HARRY'S KEY, the boy raced to the door. His last jump from the staircase, missing out the bottom three stairs, rattled it on its hinges. Harry tousled Tom's hair as he entered, making it even messier than before.

Sitting in his drawing room, Robert Hooke wrote into his diary. His lines, thirty, forty words long, meandered across the full width of the page, the spaces between his letters so small that to Harry the words appeared as a block of grey.

At his approach, Hooke closed it furtively and pushed it away.

He cast his silver eyes over Harry, looking testy, and dabbed at his nose with a large red handkerchief. 'Sit, sit. Tom, can you prepare the tea as I instructed to you?'

Tom blushed with happiness at the task.

'I must speak with you in seriousness, Harry, about a tender matter.' Hooke's twisting of his pen between his fingers made Harry suspect some reproach was about to follow. 'And you must be candid with me. I busied myself with surveys this afternoon. There are rumours about the town.'

Harry's stomach lurched. As when propelled across Gresham's quadrangle, strapped in Hooke's glider.

Hooke sniffed. 'There is talk of a Devil-boy, found murdered at the Fleet, without his blood, and owning the hooves of a goat. A fearful creature from Hell, waiting to come alive again. King Charles himself keeps it, in his elaboratory at Whitehall Palace, and makes his own dissection. The boy is one of his bastards, with the vices of the father visited upon it, his satanic form reflecting the corruptions of the Court—'

'—I assure you, Mr. Hooke—as I'm certain you believe—I've made no mention of it, to anyone!' Harry had a red blotch of anger on each cheek. He gripped the edge of the table.

'I am sure you would not knowingly reveal anything of the dead boy.'

'I've revealed nothing! Knowingly or unknowingly. Today, I visited Colonel Fields in Whitechapel. Our conversation involved just the cipher, and Sir Edmund Bury Godfrey. I divulged not a thing of the boy.'

'It will be all about London by now,' Hooke said dolefully. 'They tell of sacrifice, of Catholic bloodletting, of drinking the blood and eating the flesh of him.'

'It will vex Sir Edmund, word escaping,' Harry said, struggling to keep a level tone. 'Maybe the eel fisher told of him, as the Justice suspected he would. Or even the old constable there, Knapp, who brought him to Gresham's.'

'You are right. I am sorry, Harry. Others know of this. Word was bound to escape in time.'

A long, weighty silence ensued between the two men. They listened to the bangs and crashes of Tom's scuttling about, setting the kettle and stove, and measuring out the tea.

'You found Colonel Fields?' Hooke said eventually, as a peace offering. 'Was he able to assist you? Did he confirm the cipher's reliance upon a keyword?'

'I did. He was. He did.' Harry had begun to calm, but still suffered a vinegary resentment.

'He was familiar with it?'

'It was one employed during the campaigns of the Civil Wars. He calls it the Red Cipher.'

'Do you have the message with you?'

'The Colonel couldn't unravel the meaning. He said they usually employed a single keyword, for ease of use in the field. There's nothing within the grids of numbers to indicate this word, or its length.'

'Why would it be sent to me without its keyword?'

'Perhaps it will follow,' Harry replied. 'Possibly, you already have it, Mr. Hooke, without realising you do.'

Hooke gestured at all the books and papers in his drawing room. 'I am surrounded by words. How would I ever know which of them unlocks this cipher? It will be clear if it comes, I am sure.'

'Do you think Sir Edmund knows the word?'

'Sir Edmund gave his copy of the cipher to me,' Hooke said. 'You surmise he works upon it, separately, without us?'

'I cannot say, Mr. Hooke, for his undertakings are unknown to me. The Colonel told me of the use of the cipher in a historical matter. Our King's escape to France after the last battle of the Wars, at Worcester.'

Hooke gaped at him, like a lamprey in Enoch Wolfe's box.

'Sir Edmund himself took the King to safety,' Harry added. 'Oliver Cromwell wanted it so.'

'What!' Hooke roared, his eyes bulging in his dismay. 'Say nothing more! Harry, for your own safety, tell not a single soul of it! Forget all you have learned from Colonel Fields. We must end our association with Sir Edmund, and with this cipher. Burn all of your workings—let no one see them.'

'Not to tell him may do him disservice. His interest may be far wider than only this boy. For all we know, he may be investigating a Catholic plot to use the blood from boys.'

'I never took you to be so credulous. I am greatly surprised at you.' Hooke flapped his hands at Harry. 'We helped him at his request. We must now draw back from this, for we are men of philosophy, of natural knowledge, not of politicking. You are a young man, Harry. You do not know what living through the Wars was like. They were supposed to change so much, yet ever since we have all had to assume a second face. The fire dies down. Let it cool.'

'I will keep my silence. As I kept it before.'

'And I will write a letter to the Justice. You wish to help him . . . do not burn your notes. Deliver them instead to him. You know where he lives, along Hartshorne Lane, near Scotland Yard? I shall at last be able to concentrate on the workings of the Society and the Secretaryship. Let us think and speak no more of this—I have no desire to wake up dead!' Hooke smiled thinly at his bleak joke, then looked beseechingly at Harry for his complete agreement.

'Colonel Fields remains alive, and he's known of this for nearly thirty years.'

'You will go to Sir Edmund's house tomorrow with your notes and his copy of the cipher,' Hooke insisted. 'He already knows of the system. He may continue with its uncovering alone.'

'But, Mr. Hooke—'

'—Harry! If you are wise, you will take my advice. Think no more of it.'

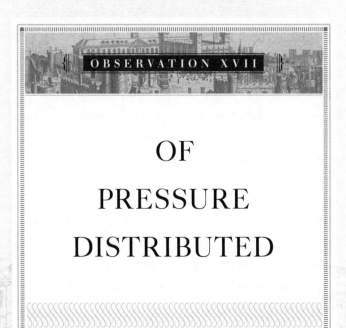

OF
PRESSURE
DISTRIBUTED

THE NEXT MORNING WAS BRIGHT AND warm. The icy skin over the pavement was still hard, but Harry could feel under the pressure of his steps the movement of meltwater beneath it. He considered his footfalls to make a sound similar to the hitting of a stretched copper wire. He committed it to his memory. White cracks branched out from the landing of each stride.

The same thoughts persisted, around and around, and nothing he could do expelled them from his head. The bloodless boy had some connection with the Wars fought more than a quarter of a century ago, before Harry had been born. At least, a cipher used then had resurfaced, as if pushed up through the snow with the body.

Who else knew of the Red Cipher? He should have quizzed Colonel

Fields further. Did Sir Edmund have the keyword? Then why pass the letter left with the boy to Mr. Hooke? Sir Edmund suspected a Catholic involvement. Did he know more, or was it merely his dislike of popery that directed his thoughts?

Schooled by Robert Hooke to accept just the evidence of his senses, to examine first causes without trusting only the word of others, and to make trials for others to repeat and share, Harry's intuition there was something more, something deeper to distrust about the Justice, still troubled him.

Harry took the lower road, Throgmorton Street. It was early, few people yet about. He felt the bundle inside his coat: Sir Edmund's copy of the cipher left with the boy; his own notes to show his working on it; and a letter from Hooke removing them from the search.

He paced towards Holborn, exhilaration quickening in his veins—a mood wrought by disobedience.

Harry had been careful to promise only his silence. However, he knew Hooke had understood a more complete compliance, and his deception brought a flush to his skin.

His walk took him back to the bridge, where the boy had been left.

He made a mental list of reasons he should not just comply with Hooke's wishes.

Firstly: he wanted justice for a small and innocent boy, so gruesomely misused. This was the noble aim, but he knew he had other, less praiseworthy motives.

Secondly: he was no longer Hooke's apprentice—Tom Gyles now had that role—but the Royal Society's Observator. Yet Hooke still treated him as his servant.

Thirdly: he found himself intrigued by the Civil Wars. He only knew of them through the stories of older men such as Hooke. They had made a generation fearful, even men such as Colonel Fields, impressive though he was. Fearful was a disposition Harry was determined to resist, despite his inclination to be so.

Fourthly—this reason was simple resentment—Hooke had accused him of spreading word of the boy.

Fifthly, Harry realised he had a more selfish reason: the freedom of working without Hooke excited him. Of taking responsibility for his own actions, and not simply complying with the instructions of another.

THE FLEET MOVED thickly, a fluid more resembling oil than water. On the bank, the partial melting of the snow had revealed patches of wet mud, dark, almost black. Without Hooke waiting for him, or meeting the Justice, or the dead boy, and with no box of lampreys, the landscape appeared empty and featureless. The sun cast stronger shadows than on that dull, snowy morning, just two days ago, readjusting his memory.

The only sounds were the cries from a couple of gulls, the chatter of a few early risers crossing the bridge behind him, and the flow of the river. No skiffs or wherries yet on the water, although downstream lighters and packet boats nestled against the new quays.

Harry saw where they had staggered about in the mud, although the marks closest to the water had gone after the intervening tides. Their feet had left deep sloughs in the softness of the ground. Snow still lodged in some of their footprints—those away from the strongest sunlight—but most were now empty.

He tracked their arduous journeys from the boy going back up to the quayside to question the eel fisher Enoch Wolfe, and also later trails, presumably of the constable, Knapp, going to load the boy onto the tumbrel, and of Wolfe reclaiming his big box of bait.

Along the bank, parallel to the Fleet's edge, was another trail. It came from the direction of Turnmill Brook, reached where the boy had been left, then returned northwards, upstream.

THE NEW PHILOSOPHY championed a controlled method. Its approach set it apart from the Greeks, the Rationalists, the Idealists, the Schoolmen. In seeking to discredit these old ways of thinking, it needed to offer an alternative, based on observation and experiment.

And yet: did not all the new philosophers rely also on their instincts, on inspiration, flashes of brilliance seemingly revealed to them?

Harry, in his own small way, experienced just such a moment of epiphany. What he saw confirmed his suspicions about Sir Edmund. It proved his anxiety, bubbling up from the darkest, unknown parts of his mind, had been well founded.

Sir Edmund had lied to them.

Along the bank, Harry observed a trail—broken, irregular, almost melted away—of oval shapes, made of compressed, icy snow. Within these ovals, thin lines of unmelted snow formed a lattice pattern. The ovals were, he estimated, about two feet long and eighteen inches wide.

Once, at a meeting of Hooke's New Philosophical Club, he had seen William Wynde describe the shoes of the Eskimo. Wynde had expounded on the way the overlarge soles of their shoes spread out the pressure of each footfall, and the way snow fell away from the shoes' cross braces and webbing of hide strips, to enable them to walk over even the softest of snow.

Only now, this morning, as the snow retreated—the snow compressed under his snowshoes being slower to melt—had the trail of the man who left the boy become visible.

The evidence made it clear: a man wearing snowshoes had walked from north of Holborn Bridge along the bank of the Fleet, deposited the boy, then walked back, *when it had already started to snow.*

Yet Sir Edmund claimed he had not seen him, as had the eel fisher, Enoch Wolfe.

But they must already have been there when the boy was left.

Just before Harry had arrived at Hooke's lodgings, on the morning of New Year's Day, the weather had turned from rain to snow. He remembered the way the raindrops had changed on the lenses of his spectacles, becoming snowflakes. At Gresham's, Tom told him he had only just missed Hooke, so he must have left at the same time the weather was changing.

Sir Edmund claimed he saw nothing of the boy's leaving, but there was not nearly enough time for him to have summoned Hooke from the College, even by messenger on horseback. The distance between Gresham's College and Holborn Bridge was a mile. It had taken Harry less than twenty minutes, even through the snow, to walk it.

By the time Hooke and Harry had arrived, the snowshoe prints had already disappeared, hidden by the further snowfall.

The eel fisher had told them when he arrived with his lampreys there were no marks to be seen, and no one there to be seen. Yet he had supposedly notified Sir Edmund of his find.

Not time enough.

Harry scratched at his chin. Why had Sir Edmund lied to them? And Enoch Wolfe, too?

Any Justice may well have good reason to keep secrets, as he went about his judicial business. Sir Edmund must have recognised the cipher, if the Colonel was to be believed. Maybe he quite rightly suspected who had killed the boy, and Mr. Hooke was wrong to dismiss his suspicions against the Catholics.

Should Harry continue to investigate the death of the boy? Or should he honour his promise to Robert Hooke?

He could not tell Hooke in his current fearfulness, and he had promised him he would withdraw from the matter. He could not confront the Justice with his new knowledge until he knew more of Sir Edmund's activities, and what his search involved.

What best to do?

He would continue his walk, Harry decided. Over Holborn Bridge, over the Fleet, and into Alsatia, to find Enoch Wolfe. Sir Edmund's questioning of him had been brief.

Only then would he act as postman, to deliver Hooke's letter and his own workings on the Red Cipher to the Justice.

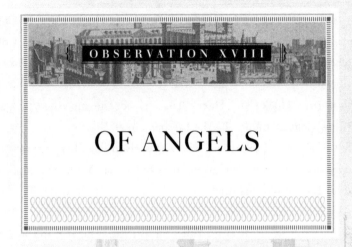

OBSERVATION XVIII

OF ANGELS

SIR CHRISTOPHER WREN'S ST. BENET IN THAMES Street and his St. Bride in Fleet Street, yet to be spired but bells in place, were the nearest and loudest. Temple Church, of the Crusaders, on the very edge of the Conflagration and spared its destruction, and likewise St. Dunstan-in-the-West, were further off, but the notes of their bells rang clear.

It was as if Harry's arrival set them off, an alarm to those who lived here.

The chipped walls and menacing blank windows reminded him of his lack of courage as he had gone through the crowds of Whitechapel. Alsatia's reputation was crueller. A refuge for villains by Royal decree. A Liberty, from the sanctuary offered by the Carmelites of Whitefriars. From the acquiescence of Elizabeth and then James's charter, it made and upheld its own laws.

Hanging signs indexed taverns, inns, coffeehouses, as well as trades. Three pawnshops competed for custom. The signs, like the places they hung from, were dilapidated.

Although nine o'clock had come, it was still quiet. Harry found the peace unsettling. The people of Alsatia seemed to use a different timetable, preferring the night to the day.

Who watched him through these windows as he entered their domain? Which of these facades hid Enoch Wolfe? '*Go down to Alsatia. Anyone there will know me.*' Wolfe's words now sounded like a challenge, their apparent helpfulness mocking Harry's ignorance of the place.

Some starlings, as grimed as their surroundings, scattered past him, the fricative sound of their wings breaking into his thoughts.

He descended through Salisbury Court, and the burnt ruins of Sackville's House. Looking towards the Thames, the Fleet Canal's tangle of masts, spars, and rigging etched the sky. Barques, sloops, and brigantines pressed against the quays, lighters moving between them like drones attending their queens. Blue in the distance, he could see the Fleet Bridge and the prison.

Across the Thames, Southwark still looked threadbare, after more than six hundred houses burned two years before.

A woman's stare. Ensnared by her unblinking gaze, Harry's mind only gradually pulled her husband into focus with her. Their bent bodies and the old fruit texture of their faces instructed him on the negative possibilities of Alsatia. They shuffled, making their cautious way over the dirty melting slush between the paving stones. The old man suffered disobedient tremors, holding his wife's arm to steady himself.

Before Harry summoned the courage to ask if they knew of Enoch Wolfe, the woman turned indifferently away, taking the old man by the elbow to steer his shaky progress.

A tall man, sleeveless despite the cold, revealing arms mapped with veins and sheathed with muscle, walked near. He had a child bouncing high on his shoulders. When Harry approached him, the man changed direction, unwilling to pass the time of day. But after his failure with the old woman, Harry was more determined, and he swerved too.

Unwillingly, the man stopped. The child watched Harry interestedly, resting its chin on the top of the man's head.

'I search for a man calling himself Enoch Wolfe,' Harry told him. The man affected to look as if this information was of absolutely no interest to him. 'Do you know the name?' Harry added this as much to test Wolfe's assertion of his own fame as to find Wolfe's whereabouts.

Harry now saw the girl he carried was young, no older than four, eyes enormous in her round face. She had the same proportions as the dead boy at the Fleet, head large on plump-bellied body.

Watching her quick bird-like movements, Harry thought of the bloodless boy's opposite stillness.

The man flexed his hands as if passing an unseen rope through them. Harry stepped back, thinking himself about to be struck.

Instead, the man spoke. 'Enoch Wolfe! I know the name *Enoch Fucking Wolfe*! But who asks the question?' He put his face close into Harry's, making the girl sway, her feet swinging as counterbalance.

'He told me to find him here in Alsatia,' Harry placated him, reversing a step. 'I'm no friend to him, but neither do I mean him harm. I seek only intelligence.'

'*Intelligence?*' The word was unsavoury. 'Then you must pay. That gabey dildo won't give out, 'less he sees silver first.'

'Will you direct me?' Harry asked, readying himself for flight.

'Angel,' the man told him abruptly, and set off. A thumb stabbed towards St. Andrew's church showed the way.

The girl glanced back, twisting in her seat as they left.

Seeing her, an idea sparked in Harry's mind. As he walked the way the man sent him, he thought on it.

HARRY FOUND THE sign soon enough. Salt and soot streaked the place, and the passage of cartwheels had scarred its bricks. Cards filled its windows, veiled by dirt on the panes, advertising miraculous cures, sure-fire investments, and rooms for renting cheaply.

He took a deep breath and made the stooping walk through the low door of the Angel coffeehouse, arriving into a surprisingly bright and clean room. The only inhabitants, a couple occupying a booth, hardly looked up at him, concentrating instead on their earnest conversation.

The woman—little more than a girl herself—was malnourished. Her bony wrists extended pitifully from the sleeves of her dress. The man also looked meagre, especially so under the generosity of his hat. This he kept on, despite the heat from the blazing fire.

Presuming they were man and wife, they reminded Harry of the old couple shuffling down the street. He thought of a predictive science, one able to foresee the physiognomic outcome of living within a particular place, such as Alsatia, of suffering a poor diet, of experiencing emotions which necessarily had to be contained—as Hooke suggested must be the way of living after the Civil Wars.

He recoiled from these thoughts, flashed into his mind unbidden. The New Philosophy did not limit itself to passive observation. Instead, it sought to improve, alleviate, and ease the burden of living. How best should he continue as a natural philosopher? What need did this thin woman have of Torricellian spaces? How could this couple benefit from his knowledge of barometry, microscopy, astronomy, hydroscopy, machinery, or anatomy?

At this moment of self-doubt, the girl looked up, and at him. Perceiving his stricken expression, she released a slow and beautiful smile. The smile only started with her mouth: her eyes shone, her cheeks radiated friendliness, her forehead wrinkled happily. Her companion also looked across at him, proud and in awe of the beauty of his partner, thin though she was.

Harry could not help himself from smiling back at her, at first self-consciously, but then freely, and at the man with her. Simply from a thin girl's look he found himself happy. Happy at the possibility she represented: that there was a deep seam of fellowship between people.

He walked to a booth close to the couple, peeled off his coat, and dropped it on the table. When he fumbled through its pockets to check his money, it startled him to find the copper farthing from the arm of Henry Oldenburg's chair. He must have slipped it into his pocket in Oldenburg's study.

One of those automatic actions the body does, the brain insensible of its workings. He had no memory of it.

Still cheerful after the girl's smile, Harry spun the coin on the surface of the table. Carolus, Britannia, Carolus, Britannia. They became one and the same, obverse and converse melding the flat disc into an illusory globe, each face bound inextricably with the other.

The coin landed in his palm. Britannia. He knew she was a portrait of some favourite of the King, but could not remember which.

Harry turned the coin over, looking at the King's face. According to the old soldier, the Justice had helped him escape to France, arranged with the use of the cipher. There was not much happened in London without the King's knowledge—or at least the knowledge of his man, the Lord High Treasurer Danby, who kept a network of spies reporting to him.

Did the King know of Harry Hunt? It was as if the face on the coin watched him, following his activity. Harry—unsettled by the notion—looked around him. The couple sat rapt with each other. He could see through to the kitchen, from where he could hear movement, but no one had yet emerged. He peered out at the street through the Angel's dirty windows. Nothing to suggest he was spied on.

He sat here, in the Angel coffeehouse in Alsatia, and the King sat somewhere in Whitehall Palace, or walked around his Privy Garden, or rode out in St. James's Park.

Did the King know of the bloodless boy? If Sir Edmund had not informed him, he would have heard the rumours by now. But if Sir Edmund was there when the boy was left . . .

Why had the Justice lied to them? Why had he insisted they preserve the boy?

Sir Edmund had sent for Robert Hooke to help him investigate the murder of a boy drained of his blood. The Justice had lied about the boy's discovery, but obviously needed Hooke's help, both with finding the facts of his murder and with the cipher.

What had Sir Edmund told Mr. Hooke, after viewing the boy in the cellar? Hooke had kept that information from him.

And why was Wolfe's box so big? It could not have been full of lampreys. Their weight would be too much for a man to carry.

❦

'COFFEE, TEA, CHOCOLATE, betony, sherbet?'

The proprietor appeared from the back of his coffeehouse, flourishing a cloth in front of him as if pestered by flies. He did not wait for Harry's answer. 'Do you read? We have the *Gazette*.' His voice dropped at the end of his sentences, giving his information a mournful slope. 'There is talk of an alliance with Holland, and Spain, and Austria. There could be war against France. The Earl of Shaftesbury has been let go from the Tower. That will please his Green Ribboners, and the Country Party, who look to exclude the King's brother. Tantamount to treason, I say—'

'—Yes, the news, please. And coffee would serve me well,' Harry replied.

'I ask payment first. Thruppence a bowl.'

Harry searched for the correct money and found three silver pennies. He put the farthing away into his pocket to return to Mrs. Oldenburg.

When the proprietor placed the coffee and news-sheet in front of him, Harry reached for his arm, checking his retreat.

'I look for someone—a man.'

'There are better places than here, if that's what you're about.'

'No, no. A singular man. I need to find him, to convey to him a message.'

Harry's cheeks warmed at the man's inference. 'It's in his interest,' he added, seeing guardedness descend.

'Is it? Would it be in my interest, now?' The cloth was pulled taut, and suddenly still.

Harry persisted, despite finding the cloth sinister. 'His name is Enoch Wolfe.'

The proprietor looked puzzled for a second, then made his face go blank. Aware Harry had caught this fleeting expression, he pushed aside further questioning. 'I know not this man.'

'I wonder,' Harry ventured, 'if I may leave a notice in your window, with the others there, asking him to meet me. He's likely to see it, or someone will tell him, as he's assured me he's well known here. How much would you charge for its display?'

The man seemed to be settling in his mind an intricate computation involving Harry's appearance and the fact the man he sought was Enoch Wolfe.

'Five shillings.'

Harry gasped at the price and sensed the same reaction from the couple behind him, who were listening in. 'I have just four.'

'That is all your money?'

'All of it.'

The owner looked as though he would turn him down, then his face relented. 'Four it is, then.'

He watched Harry count out the four shillings in various coins, then placed his hand on Harry's shoulder, pressing uncomfortably on it. 'I saw you with a farthing.'

Unwillingly, Harry took it from his pocket and placed it with the pile of money on the table.

'You were dishonest with me, be it just a farthing. I could end our agreement.'

'I only require the show of a card.'

'So you do. So you do.' With that, the man picked up the farthing and returned it disdainfully to Harry. Beneath his dignity to take it. Then he disappeared back to his kitchen.

The girl coughed, and made to speak to Harry, but her companion silenced her with a look. Deciding to ignore him, she began again, leaning conspiratorially to close the distance between them.

'He knows of Enoch Wolfe, and you are not the first to ask for him. He asked just two shillings then. This Wolfe lives in Alsatia. I am sure he will see your sign. If he answers to it, well, that is something else.'

She spoke very correctly and politely, the way of Quakers.

'I'm obliged,' Harry replied, adding: 'I'm sorry, I have only a farthing.'

The girl looked at him in some surprise. 'We ask not for your money.' Her mildness chided Harry more than if she spoke sharply.

The proprietor returned with a pen and paper.

'Write out your notice, and I shall display it. Then drink down your coffee and go.'

A flicker of obstinacy sparked up, but Harry realised he had no choice but to do as the man required, or he risked wasting the four shillings altogether. He took the pen held out to him, wrote out a note, and drained the rest of the coffee. The proprietor all the while looked sternly down at him.

THE COUPLE LEFT with him, and together they stood outside, watching the notice being added to the collection in the grubby window, fitted into the slot between the loosely fitting pane and the frame. The paper curled away from its anchor. The owner's face loomed forwards behind the glass, stared at them balefully, then withdrew into the dimness beyond.

> *Mr. Enoch Wolfe,*
> *We met at the Holbourne Bridge. Please find me at Gresham's*
> *College, or meet me here Evening Friday 4th Janry.*
> *Mr. Henry Hunt*

'You are Mr. Henry Hunt?' asked the man with the hat.

'More usually, I'm Harry.'

'Happy to meet with you, Harry. I am Invincible Tarripan, and this is my wife Felicity. We await others to join us, for we leave by coach to Plymouth. We sail for the New World, to Prince Rupert's Land.'

'I wish you well in your new life together,' Harry replied. 'It's important I find this Wolfe. Tell me, who was the other man seeking him?'

'I did not mention any man,' Felicity answered archly. 'There were two who asked after your Enoch Wolfe. We had a disagreement concerning them, did we not, my love?' She smiled happily at her husband.

'A disagreement?' Harry prompted.

Invincible answered ahead of his wife. 'They looked to me like young men. We discussed them as you came in.'

'On what did you disagree?'

The couple looked at each other, and Invincible allowed his wife to answer with a resigned shrug.

'Their manner of dress appeared as any prosperous men of the town,' she told Harry. 'Long coats, both of the same colour. A sea green. Perhaps nearer the colour of a turquoise. Swords hanging from their belts. But, I am sure of it . . . ' She looked at her husband, who held up his hands as a shield from what he knew she was about to say. 'They were women. Ladies, more like.'

She turned her beautiful face to look straight at Harry. Even with his confusion at her information, he sensed his tongue go dry.

Invincible looked apologetic. 'Why, though, should any women dress in such a way? They had swords. They were gentlemen.'

His wife dimpled her divergence from him. 'You must allow that I am more likely to discern my own kind. My own sex. And women, you must know, are more acutely observant than men.'

'But who can these ladies be?' Harry asked.

'There, neither of us can help you. We wish you well in your search.'

They took their leave of him and went to look for shelter now that the Angel was closed, Harry becoming just a memory for them as they went to their future together. The grace and generosity of the Quakers struck him, their formal speech reinforcing rather than undermining his impression of their good-heartedness.

If Felicity was right, then who were these ladies dressed so incongruously? And what did they want with Enoch Wolfe?

Lacking the fare for a wherry to Westminster, Harry walked to Hartshorne Lane, to deliver Hooke's letter to Sir Edmund disassociating them from helping him, with the bundle of workings on the cipher.

He took the papers from his pocket, sorted through them, and separated them from the copies he had made.

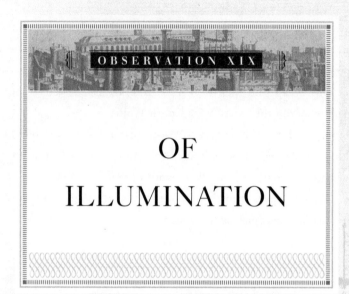

OF

ILLUMINATION

THE SUN'S LOWER CURVE FLATTENED, AS it changed from yellow, to orange, to red. Its underside became ragged, like the teeth of a saw, and the teeth fluctuated, moving like the waves of the sea. The unequal thicknesses of the air inflected and refracted its multiple rays. As Robert Hooke had demonstrated at Gresham's College, it was the same phenomenon that caused the twinkling of the stars.

The leaded panes of the windows, each sitting at a different angle from its neighbour, scattered this last light of the day across the deeply green interior of the Crown Tavern, on Threadneedle Street.

Hooke was yet to arrive.

Harry removed his spectacles, and played with the light shining through them, controlling the way it fell on the table. An almost empty glass of wine, left by a previous customer, served him well as a lens. He splayed his fingers behind it, watching their tips magically appear as if from the air, as it reversed and bent the light passing through.

The serving maid was attending to a man at the next table. She bent towards him, pushing her fleshy breasts at him, laughing with him. This man was much older than her, and despite the warming fire he wore a goat-skin coat.

Harry wondered if he would ever understand the vagaries of the attraction one sex had for the other.

She at last lifted herself away and turned towards Harry, bearing a jar of beer.

She reminded him of Grace Hooke. Grace, though, was clear of freckles or moles, and her teeth, unlike this serving girl's, were all present. They were straight and evenly spaced, and her gums gleamed pinkly. Grace had always been particular about keeping them clean, using soda salts to enhance their whiteness.

When he was Hooke's apprentice, as he rasped, sawed, filed, polished, and carved, Harry had watched her about her uncle's home. Her little pout when concentrating on some task or another. The tunes occurring to her as she hummed them, the murmured music seeming to compose itself, Grace merely following its direction, unaware of its effect on him.

Once, she had asked him to bring down a large pan she was to use for dyeing cloth. He reached for it, and the back of his hand brushed the side of her head, touching her hair. His skin felt as if it burned. She had looked at him, but he could not read her expression. She stayed quite still, and it was only afterwards he wondered if she had wanted him to kiss her. Grace had then smiled and taken the pan from him. Neither of them spoke again of the moment.

Nowadays, Harry visited her uncle on Royal Society business, or to help him with his City surveys, and did not have the excuse to spend such times with her.

He had to desist from such reveries. The papers weighted his coat pocket.

He had made a copy of the cipher left on the boy's body, and also a copy of the letter delivered to Mr. Hooke at his lodgings.

Like the light bent in the atmosphere, or through the window, his spectacles, and the wineglass, the message did not come to him clearly. The elusive keyword was the prism through which the cipher would make sense.

As Colonel Fields had said, it remained a knotty problem. Should he wait for the word to be revealed, either to Mr. Hooke or by Sir Edmund—if he knew it—or else spend time guessing at it, to try to uncover the cipher's meaning?

The papers left on the body must reveal the boy's purpose, surely, and the reason for the draining of his blood. Maybe also the name of his killer. There was also the other document, the one delivered by the solicitor.

Harry had to decipher them as soon as possible, for other boys might suffer the same fate.

There was a murdered boy and a cipher. Sir Edmund wanted the boy preserved. Harry's questioning of the old soldier had revealed the Justice's role in escorting the King to France. The trail of snowshoe prints showed Sir Edmund had lied to them.

Without being able to rely on help from Hooke, who wanted nothing further to do with the business, he had to continue deviously.

He had left a message with Enoch Wolfe, the eel fisher—a man sought also by others, possibly two women, as Felicity Tarripan had told him in Alsatia. There was the old constable, Gabriel Knapp, who must know where Sir Edmund was at the time of the boy's leaving. But if Harry tried to find him, word would reach Sir Edmund.

What best to do?

Candlelight and the fire in the grate were now the only sources of illumination in the room. The stars appeared, and from force of habit he named them as he saw them: Polaris, Sirius, Procyon, Rigel, Castor, Capella, Aldebaran . . .

ANOTHER LIGHT, FAR brighter than any of the stars or candles in the room, approached him through the Crown. A lamp, the power of its flame's illumination increased by mirrors and lenses, caused all in the tavern to shield their eyes, and look aggrieved at the source of their discomfort.

Behind it walked Robert Hooke, late and seeming vexed. The recalcitrant lamp had a self-fuelling mechanism, the oil fed to the flame using a counterpoise, and the candle was held by a spring. All of which made it problematic. Circumspectly, Hooke placed it on the table between them, opened the chamber, and snuffed it out.

'My improved design!'

'Good evening, Mr. Hooke.' Harry's eyes grew accustomed again to the easier light of the room's candles. 'Your lamp's notably bright.'

'The ancients knew of such methods. I have refined them. Archimedes made use of mirrors for setting on fire the enemy ships in the siege of Syracuse. Aristophanes described glasses and spheres to converge the rays of the sun. I have shown this lamp today at Gresham's, at the Cutlerian lecture.'

'Was the lecture well attended, Mr. Hooke?'

'What do you think, Harry?'

'By your expression, I would say not.'

'One person only came! And I believe *him* a spy sent by Cutler to check whether I perform my lectures dutifully. I will publish the talk—eight diverse ways to construct such self-feeding lamps! Eight! I hope more will read of it than troubled themselves to come to the demonstration. The man—an ill-mannered fellow, and rough looking—spoke of the rumours. He wanted to talk of the Devil-boy being held at Gresham's. A portent of a Jesuitical design upon our kingdom, so they say. Grace came in, luckily enough, and put the fellow off his tittle-tattle. I remember he wore a goatskin coat.'

Harry turned to look again at the serving girl and the man she flirted with, but both had gone, the seat the man occupied now empty. Had he not also worn a goatskin coat?

He looked back at Hooke, trying to dismiss a rising apprehension. 'These rumours spread like a blaze. Might it be, he came for someone else, not Cutler at all? Sir Edmund Bury Godfrey will crave intelligence, as you've let go of his search.'

'Sir Edmund would summon me himself. You are in danger of wandering off into invisible notions.'

'Have you had word from the Justice?'

Hooke shook his head. 'You said nothing to him of the Civil Wars at your visit to Hartshorne Lane?'

'I said nothing. In truth, Mr. Hooke, I hold the same fears of being entangled in his business as you.'

To tell Hooke of his detour to the Fleet, and of the prints there across the snow, would be to tell him of his deception. He would also leave his visit to Alsatia unmentioned.

Hooke, satisfied with Harry's answer, tried to attract the attention of the Crown's owner, Thomas Blagrove. Blagrove was busy serving from behind a high, sturdy table stacked with jars, jugs, lidded decanters, pitchers and bottles. Behind him, an open trapdoor led down to the cellar and his impressive stock of imported alcohols, spirits and tinctures, and brews of his own devising. He was something of an experimentalist himself, letting favoured customers sample drinks imported from the corners of the world, as well as his own preparations, educating them in matters geographical and of the palate.

Blagrove came over to their table.

'Your recommendation, Mr. Blagrove?' Hooke asked.

'I have a bracing Japanese wine, made by the fermenting of rice. It has an immediate effect on the head.'

'I have heard of this drink,' Hooke replied, 'but have never yet tried it. There is a Chinese drink, a variant perhaps, called shamshoo. Your proposal has much to recommend it, but let us instead begin with some claret. Our troubles with the French have not dried your supply?'

'I have a man,' was Blagrove's inscrutable reply. 'It gets ever more costly, though.'

'We will have some.' Hooke answered for both of them. Harry assented by remaining silent, although he would have tried the rice wine.

When Blagrove had poured each of the men a glass of his best Bordeaux, Hooke took a mouthful. '*In vino veritas*, Pliny tells us,' he said, 'and, to a certain measure, he is right. But also, *At the last it biteth like a serpent, and stingeth like an adder.*'

He noticed Harry had not yet taken any of his drink.

'Are you well, Harry?' He studied his assistant. 'You look unusually pale.'

'It must be the last three days, Mr. Hooke. They've had a strong effect on me. The boy. The business with Mr. Oldenburg's death. This cipher from the Civil Wars.'

'I have steel wine at home, which will settle you. You must try to forget it, all of it, and return to your usual work. The business of the Royal Society will occupy your mind. Your equilibrium shall quickly return.'

Hooke's expression was both worried and encouraging, and his silver eyes required his agreement.

Harry managed a weak and brave-seeming smile.

Hooke then occupied himself with the oil-feed mechanism of the lamp, adjusting some slight deficiency with his pocketknife.

Harry watched him, glad he was not expected to engage in further conversation.

The next day, he decided, he would go to the solicitor, Moses Creed, to find out what he remembered of whoever left the cipher for Robert Hooke with him.

'There!' Hooke exclaimed. 'I think I've fixed it.'

OBSERVATION XX

OF THE
ARTICLES

AT HIS HOME AT HARTSHORNE LANE, Sir Edmund Bury Godfrey sat at his writing desk by the window. On it lay the bundle of papers Henry Hunt had delivered, including the letter from Robert Hooke bemoaning his inability to continue assistance. Too stretched, Hooke claimed, with other matters concerning the Royal Society.

Hooke did not commit himself so far, Sir Edmund noted, as to refuse the further storage of the boy. What had so enfeebled him?

More rumours of the Devil-boy found at the Fleet. Only this afternoon he had heard tell—given to him as most solemn testimony—of a crowd of naked onlookers dancing around the boy as his blood was taken out, and they all drank from it.

Not much dancing possible on that mud, he thought.

Now, two more men came to give him evidence. They sat in the two chairs before him, one of them over-filling his, his bulk putting strain on it. The other man with him was small, and apparently unable to control the movements of his knees.

Most of their testimony came from the podgy unattractive man—this Titus Oates—who had a miniature mouth with a high unmanly voice coming from it. Everything that came out of it was so extraordinary, so inflammatory, so libellous against so many people.

It must surely be fabrication.

But Oates was curiously persuasive.

All he had got from the other man—this Israel Tonge—was a stream of nonsensical ranting, the silver wires that sprouted from his head shaking as he whipped up the enthusiasm of an invisible audience. It was as if by talking Tonge remembered who he was. If he were to stop, it would be an end to him. His form would disappear into the silence.

Who was this mountebank with his merry-andrew?

'You put a sombre matter to me, Mr. Oates and Mr. Tonge—'

Tonge's hair shook again, his hands shot up into the air, and his frail body followed them out of his chair.

'Oh yes, Sir Edmund! It is beyond dispute, and shows clearly the evil, malevolent schemes of these plotting, blaspheming mischief-makers. It will shine a Holy light upon them, bright enough to blind their Catholic eyes!'

'The kingdom finds itself in grave peril, Justice,' Oates added, his fat hands folded across his lap.

'Peril is always grave, Oates. Sharpen your point.'

'Please, Sir Edmund, I am *Doctor* Oates, a doctor of divinity—'

'—Pray silence, Oates! Your allegations are profound and awful. You describe treasons against the King and his family, and felonies against houses and towns. You name perpetrators of these deeds, many of the highest quality, who will be damned by your evidence. Is this really to be your testimony?'

'We must apprehend and disarm these devilish plotters and contrivanc-
ers, these popish offenders who combine and multiply over His Majesty's
Kingdom, else the sacred governance of our nation shall be disrupted!'

'Yes, yes, Tonge. Calm yourself.' Sir Edmund rolled his eyes
heavenwards.

'Titus Oates has uncovered weighty matters, matters which cannot be
ignored, matters which are fatal to His Majesty's person, or else we risk
being forever undone!'

'May I rely on your testimony?' Sir Edmund shouted, to block Tonge's
flow.

'You may hang your great black hat on it, Sir Edmund!' Tonge responded.
'Every word in our deposition is the truth, vouched for by this brave and
plucky man.' He pointed at his partner, although he was immediately next
to him and directly in front of the Justice. 'Titus Oates! Titus Oates it was
who gathered the information. Titus Oates, forced into dirty subterfuge to
uncover this wickedness, at much risk to himself in so doing.'

'I have endeavoured,' Oates interceded modestly, 'to mix with the Jesuits to learn more of their plotting. I have become as one with them, in order
to more completely expose their calumny—'

'—Their counterfeiting subterfuges!'

'My only object throughout these undertakings has been to detect and
defeat the conspiracy against His Majesty.'

'Titus Oates played a role, the better to insinuate himself amongst the
sinful Jesuits! The idolatrous Church of Rome commands its soldiers to kill
His Majesty. Titus Oates has braved their wicked company to find them out!'

Sir Edmund thumped his desk. 'Keep a hold of yourself, Tonge, for your
constant movement is distracting. You have unambiguous news of this?'

Oates and Tonge both nodded affirmations.

'We have our evidence with us,' Oates said. 'We have the narrative of
this horrid plot. We have . . . our *Articles*.'

'And how, then, is His Majesty's killing to be undertaken?'

'By shot,' Oates replied. 'A silver bullet for his heart. I have seen the
plans and met the perpetrators. I work only towards his safety. I think not

of my own reward.'

Sir Edmund stretched out his arm and grasped Oates's great chin. 'Then you are wiser than you look. A silver bullet, to be sure! And where is this to be done?'

'They linger within the Park,' Tonge replied, looking nervous as the Justice pushed his companion's face away. 'It is well known His Majesty is careless of his safety, and makes an easy target.'

Sir Edmund inspected them both, the fat one and the mad jack-in-the-box.

Oates was apparently uncowed by the Justice's roughness, his face open and earnest. He reached inside a pocket and withdrew a set of notes.

'We have all the details here, Sir Edmund. Forty-three separate Articles describing the heretical plans to bring in popery.'

'Are further persons of quality involved?'

Oates placed a look of great pain on his face, as if the forthcoming information caused him hurt to reveal. He hung his head and spoke to the floor in a hushed voice. 'Lord Petre knows of the assassination, but it troubles him dreadfully to keep hold his tongue. I wish it were not so.'

No flicker of dishonesty, nor hint of a false note. Oates was a picture of steadfast sincerity, a man doing his duty, telling what it sickened him to disclose.

'I myself have faced danger,' Oates continued, 'and been threatened. Israel Tonge, here, appears in documents, his name encircled in green, meaning he is a target as well.'

Tonge turned to Oates in amazement. This was the first he had learned of his happenstance within the pernicious Catholic pages. 'Do you perceive their impiety?' he demanded of the Justice, dodging to one side as if from a flying Jesuit.

'This is a base business. Mr. Tonge, *Dr.* Oates. I shall pass the details of your testimony to the King. I cannot dismiss stories of assassination, however unlikely they sound. It will be fully investigated. Do you understand my meaning? Fully. Do you now have anything to add, or to deny?'

'Why, only more to add, Sir Edmund,' they answered together.

Oates shifted to pass him the papers, stretching open the arms of his chair. At the wood's moan of complaint, Sir Edmund feared for his furniture.

'Every word written here is true,' Oates declared.

Sir Edmund rubbed his lower lip, which troubled him. 'There is one thing I do not yet understand. You say the Jesuit John Grove started the fire at Southwark. I was there. I helped put it out. I saw with my own eyes Grove assisting. Why should he set a fire, only then to extinguish it?'

His visitors looked at him with sympathy, as if he released his grip on reason.

'Why, to allay suspicion,' they said, again together, like children chanting a nursery rhyme.

❧

AFTER THEIR TESTIMONY, Sir Edmund stood for a while outside his home, watching them go off in the dark towards the Strand, Oates dwarfing the tiny, dancing Tonge, his lantern dancing with him.

Hartshorne Lane was quiet. The last of the snow had refrozen, the wheel tracks forming hard ruts.

Sir Edmund returned inside, back up to his office, and sat for a while reading through the deposition left by his informants, spreading yet more papers over his desk.

Despite his unwillingness to believe these extraordinary claims, there was so much detail to them. It made their story the more plausible. You could not choose the quality of your witnesses. And no self-respecting conspiracy would use a crackbrain such as Tonge to do its bidding.

He must inform the King.

But how were the bloodless boys employed in this Catholic plan? How did the Catholics make use of the blood taken from them? Did friend or foe leave their bodies to be found? Oates made no reference to the boys in his testimony.

As well as the deposition from Oates and Tonge—the *Articles*, they called them, self-importantly—he had two copies of the cipher in his own handwriting, done laboriously on the day of finding the Fleet boy. One of them he had given to Hooke, then returned by his assistant, Hunt. He had the covering letter from Hooke.

Also, he had some pages of Hunt's endeavours to reveal the message. How could these false starts be at all helpful? He saw Hunt had attempted to unravel it using a de Vigenère square.

He had no chance to get near with that.

He fumbled in his pocket for a key, unlocked the drawer in his writing desk, and took out the original letter, the one left on the Fleet boy.

He stared at the system of numbers and began to write in his notebook.

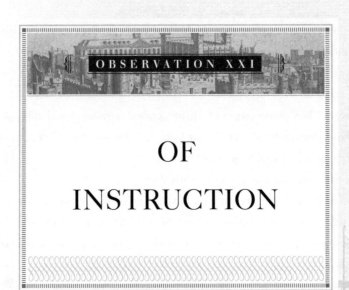

OF

INSTRUCTION

THE HOLE IN HIS SIDE WAS inflamed and raw, pulled at by the silver tube. He would ask John Locke to look at it, for as well as the pain the wound wept unusually, the liquid seeping into his shirt. He could feel it sticking the material to his flesh, tugging as he moved.

Shaftesbury looked up from his book, John Milton's *Paradise Lost*, disturbed from reading of the angel Raphael's talk with Adam by the entrance of his man.

John Locke looked up too, from writing in his book. Lefèvre contemplated Shaftesbury's automaton and did not stir.

Uriel Aires, Shaftesbury's coach driver with the goatskin coat, brought with him a fraught-looking Enoch Wolfe.

Wolfe was transformed from when he was at the Fleet. Shaved, hair freshly powdered, resplendent in a wheat-coloured suit, anyone who saw him then would be hard-pushed to identify him as the unkempt eel fisher.

'Mr. Wolfe.' Shaftesbury motioned him to sit. 'For what do we pay you?'

As Wolfe sat down, Shaftesbury stood up, still holding his book.

'I have had no report from you!'

His sudden shout made Wolfe cringe in his chair. Shaftesbury's spittle landed on his cheek, and he dared not wipe it away.

'I charged you with the fetching of the boy, but you were too incompetent. And you have since been neglectful of your reports.'

Wolfe's voice shook as the Earl leaned towards him. 'That was not my fault, my Lord. I never heard Sir Edmund . . . the mud . . . the snow—'

'—I've already had those excuses! I await your report!'

'I rely upon a network of spies, my Lord, each of them verified one against the other before I present their intelligence to you.'

Shaftesbury dropped his voice, almost to a whisper. 'That is well, Mr. Wolfe, all very well. I wanted *your* intelligence, that was all. You know, most men have a higher notion of their abilities than their actual worth. I, myself, am prone to conceit. We need such self-delusions to keep our spirits up, as a mechanism feeds on grease.'

He studied Wolfe's face, observing the physiological changes as fear made blood leave the cheeks. 'Although, if I require new footwear,' he continued reasonably, 'I do not pay the bootmaker for trying his best. I expect the leather to meet the sole, be well stitched, and resist the entry of water.'

Wolfe had to stifle a choking sensation and a desire to prostrate himself before the Earl.

'You had one thing to tell me, Wolfe, and that was your failure to find the Witch.'

'My Lord, he seems to be nowhere in London. I have looked. I have asked. You may well use the same people—everyone in London sells information—but my reports to you result from much enquiry. They are proficiently done.'

Shaftesbury put one end of *Paradise Lost*'s spine against the side of Wolfe's nose and rammed his hand against the other, as forcefully as he could.

The nose cracked. Blood spattered from it. Wolfe let out a shriek, and sat huddled, holding his head and sobbing.

'Take a care you do not drip on my carpet,' Shaftesbury warned him, sitting himself back down.

Locke, judging Wolfe would need his nose resetting to regain its previous shape, led him out of the library.

'Uriel!' Shaftesbury spoke as if he had not just committed violence. 'What intelligence did you glean from Mr. Hooke?'

'Nothing of use at all. I spoke to him of the rumours of the boy found with goat's hooves and asked if he gave them credence. His reaction, I would say, was fearful. He told me he knew of no such thing. Another, a girl, disturbed us, so I could not question him further.'

Aires made no show of deference to his employer. They had known each other for over thirty years. Aires, then with Parliament's troops in Dorset, had served under him after Shaftesbury changed sides from the Royalists. The Earl—then plain Anthony Ashley Cooper—had noticed him for his youth, loyalty, and bravery. He had used Aires as a messenger, and then, when the Wars were over, kept him in his retinue.

The youth had long disappeared, but the rest remained.

'The talk of Devil-boys is all around London,' Shaftesbury said. 'Hooke must have heard it. It is in the news-sheets as a sign of Catholic invasion. We know Hooke still stores our boy, for I have Gresham's College watched constantly. What I cannot let happen is for Hooke to dissect him.'

'I could get more from him, if we require less discretion.'

'That will not be necessary. We must watch him, though, for he has his assistant nosing into our business. He went to Whitechapel and spoke with Colonel Fields.'

'I warned Michael Fields before.' Aires looked as if he relished the memory. 'When *he* nosed into our business.'

'The assistant was seen at the Fleet, where the boy was left, there again this morning. He is young. He wears a brown leather coat. And spectacles, too.'

'Then I spied him inside the Crown Tavern, talking with Mr. Hooke after the lecture.'

Shaftesbury picked up a small piece of paper and held it for Aires to inspect. 'This same assistant went to Alsatia, seeking Enoch Wolfe.'

The paper he held was Harry's note asking to meet with Wolfe, left in the Angel's window.

'He is busy.'

'His name is Henry Hunt. He has written it on his note. Titus Oates has been to the Justice, Sir Edmund Bury Godfrey, this evening, and is to give further evidence to the King. We must not allow any interference. Hunt wishes to meet with Enoch Wolfe. We will ensure that he does. Monsieur Lefèvre will be there also.'

Lefèvre turned round from the mechanical scribe.

Shaftesbury crumpled up Harry's note and threw it into the fire. 'You understand what I want?'

'I do,' Aires replied. 'This assistant will also.'

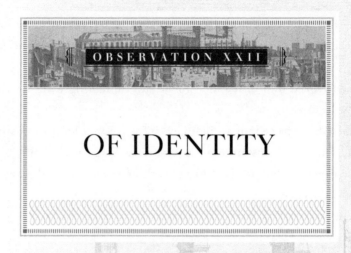

OBSERVATION XXII

OF IDENTITY

HARRY CHECKED THE TIME ON HARRIS'S clock on St. Dunstan-in-the-West. It was a quarter past ten in the morning. Put up in gratitude for the church's escape from the Conflagration, the clock rang out every quarter, and the sound of its bell, clanged by the pagan giants Gog and Magog, followed his back.

The snow was now atolls of refrozen slush. Grip could be found in the gaps. The morning light was flat, coming through a mist obscuring the horizon and fading the roofs and each end of Fleet Street.

Harry turned up Chancery Lane to Lincoln's Inn, and in through the red brick archway of the Gatehouse. Surrounded by the jumble of old buildings housing the solicitors, barristers, and clerks of the Inn, he asked for directions. A careless wave sent him across the courtyard, past the Hall, and through a passageway, to a sign needing some care, the dirt of years obscuring much of the name. After wiping it with his hand, he interpreted it as pointing up to the *Office of M. Creed, Solicitor.*

The stairwell was dark, its few windows high and small, its walls wanting new plaster and paint. Pushed and heaved by its shifting joists and beams, the tall narrow building twisted like the breaking of a neck. The stairs never turned at a right angle, and each tread had its own way of lying. The boards of the corridor, once the stairs had been done, were similarly chaotic.

Along the very top storey Harry found a door marked '*M. Creed*'. It was one of several identical doors, doubtless leading into similar small offices, only their nameplates setting them apart.

Answering his knock, Moses Creed did not welcome Harry in, but instead blocked the doorway. A fusty smell emanated from inside. Harry had a glimpse of a room piled high with documents tied with green ferret string or red tape. Large ledgers and ancient law books leaned in from the walls. Under layers of thick dust, rarely handled, they appeared to have settled into their shelves, as if sweating their contents through the pores of their leather.

It reminded Harry of Robert Hooke's rooms at the College: a portrait of a life.

Watchfully, as if worried Harry would stop him, the solicitor shut the door and locked it, leaving them both standing in the corridor. Although shorter than Harry, Creed gave the impression he looked down on him, achieved by pushing his head far back.

'Mr. Creed? Mr. Moses Creed?'

'Mr. Moses Creed, I am.'

The solicitor looked to be about forty years of age, but presented himself in the manner of a man far senior, his dress and attitude suggesting he inhabited a different scale of time.

Harry got straight to the point with a lie.

'You delivered a letter to Mr. Robert Hooke at Gresham's College, on the evening of Monday, the first day of January, three days ago. Sir Edmund

Bury Godfrey, the Justice, has engaged our assistance. He asked me to question you, concerning the appearance of the person, or persons, who brought you this letter.' Harry's sentences reached towards his own idea of a legal man's rhetorical mode, and he told himself to desist. 'People . . . '

Creed aimed his gaze along the length of his nose at Harry. 'And you are?'

'I apologise. My name is Henry Hunt. I work with the Royal Society.'

Creed made a derisive scoffing sound. 'If that be the case, your concerns are natural philosophy, experimental learning, the weighing of the air, navigation at sea, and so on . . . not solicitors engaged as little more than postmen.'

Creed started walking the way Harry had come, so the younger man followed him back along the corridor.

'You could say the same of the Justice of Peace,' Creed continued. 'What would he want with me? If the rumours are true, the Catholics kill our children and take their blood. He will be more busy finding them out, I imagine.'

'Sir Edmund sought the help of Mr. Hooke.' Harry tried to ignore the solicitor's discourteous tone. 'I help Mr. Hooke. Sir Edmund requested I ask you about the letter's sender.'

'Sir Edmund himself? Not Mr. Hooke? Ah.' Creed stopped. Harry waited, both of them standing at the top of the stairs, Harry thinking maintaining his silence might prompt Creed to talk sooner.

It did not.

'Mr. Creed?'

Very eventually, Creed responded. 'There can be few people in London who do not know of Mr. Hooke's name, of his reputation, and of his prodigious interests. It was an honour to meet *him* the other evening, if only to deliver a letter.' He sniffed at Harry, insultingly, then started off down the stairs.

Harry, who had never been sniffed at before, clenched his teeth to stop an ill-considered retort. He waited for the solicitor to say more, but he did not, until they reached the first landing.

'I do not yet understand why a letter I delivered to Mr. Hooke is of interest to the Justice,' Creed said over his shoulder.

Harry hesitated. What best to say to this unpleasant man, whose laborious way of giving out information must only injure his business? Harry could tell Creed suspected he was bluffing by how he picked at his story. Soon, he would realise Harry had no permission from Hooke to be here, and no authority at all from Sir Edmund to ask these questions.

'A letter came into Sir Edmund's possession which used a cipher. The letter you took to Mr. Hooke used the same way of encipherment. Sir Edmund, naturally enough, requires Mr. Hooke to help him.'

Creed regarded Harry with a faint smile, enjoying the younger man's annoyance. 'It *came into his possession*, did it? A mysterious process you describe. There are others Sir Edmund would go to for help with a cipher. Those who dedicate themselves to their elucidation. John Wallis, for example, who once worked for Cromwell and who now works for the King. Those at the Board of Ordnance, who also work for the King. Or Danby's men, who work for Danby.' He chuckled. 'Why, it would be like using a razor to chop wood to have such a man as Hooke attack a cipher.'

'Nonetheless, Mr. Creed, it was to Mr. Hooke the Justice came.'

They walked out into the cold, and the solicitor rubbed his hands. He led Harry towards the Chapel undercroft, and they steered between some students coming the other way.

'Do you have a letter of authority from Sir Edmund? I see no obligation to answer you.'

'I can get such a document, if you need one,' Harry said hurriedly. 'The Justice's house on Hartshorne Lane is not far.'

Creed thought for a short while, snorted, and then gave Harry a shrug of permission.

'My question, then, Mr. Creed, is who brought Mr. Hooke's letter to you?'

'There was insistence upon anonymity.'

'Yet you accepted this commission.'

'Payment is an effective form of introduction.'

'You had no notion who it was?'

'None at all.'

They were underneath the Chapel, the stone arches reaching over them.

A most frustrating man, Harry thought. Again, he tried the tactic of quietness to draw further information. Again, the tactic failed.

'Mr. Creed?'

Creed shot him a testy look. 'I acted upon instructions. I delivered the letter to Gresham's College.'

'His appearance was . . . ?'

'As any young man. A little like you. Perchance, squarer in the face? Broader. Taller. Very little like yourself, then, considering more fully.'

'Young?' Harry could feel the blood rising in his cheeks, as annoyance became irritation.

'Young. Yes.'

'Was there one on his own, or was there another with him?'

Harry's question sparked a change in the solicitor as impressive as it was unexpected. He became—most startlingly to Harry—*enthusiastic*.

'The way you ask shows you think there were two, yet I made no indication that two there were. Your assumption brings about your question!'

'I make no such assumption,' Harry replied hotly. 'Though I've had a pair described to me, elsewhere, on another matter. Were there two together?'

'There *were* two together! One spoke, and one was silent.'

Harry felt defeated, as if Creed had scored a point against him in a game whose rules he only dimly understood.

'Perchance, Mr. Hunt, the couple you heard of in your *other matter* were the same men here. What intelligence do you have of them, so we may assure ourselves they are the same pair, or no?'

Harry thought of the conversation outside the Angel coffeehouse, recalling Felicity Tarripan's smile as she told him her observations of the pair seeking Enoch Wolfe.

'Well, to start, did they wear sea-green coats?'

'Between a green and a blue? They *did*, I remember.' Creed's enthusiasm increased further, his face becoming more animated, and his eyes seeming to shine.

'Did you see any of their other clothes, beneath the coats?'

'I did not, unfortunately. Their coats remained buttoned throughout our meeting. I remember, for it was sunny and warm, most unusually so in December. My window allows the light in generously—especially late in an afternoon—which was the time of their arrival. I should have offered them employment as curtains.'

Again, he made his scoffing sound, a rattle of mucus at the back of his throat.

'Can you remember anything else that distinguished this pair?' Harry asked, tiring of Creed's superior manner.

Creed laughed at him as they crossed the courtyard, taking Harry back towards the Gatehouse and Chancery Lane. 'Oh, I find it difficult to tell one young man from another. A *young* man does not hold a deal of difference in his appearance to any other. An *older* man, on the other hand, has a face to set him apart. The alteration from youth to old age is the reverse of that of a stone being washed by a tide. This would smooth over time, its roughness polished, its edges lost. We, conversely, grow rough, lined and cragged with age. What will you look like at fifty, I wonder? This would be a skill worthy of your Royal Society, to present a history of what a man has done, or to predict what he will do, using solely the evidence of his face. Perchance, the project is already underway. A taxonomy of wrinkles and sagging skin.'

'An interesting notion, Mr. Creed,' Harry said, reminded of his thoughts on the couples, old and young, in Alsatia. 'Have you enquired about Fellowship?'

Creed emitted a short, loud guffaw. 'I have not.'

They reached the great oak doors of the Gatehouse, and Creed stopped just through them, out on Chancery Lane. 'A man's mode of dress, of course, is another consideration. The clothing *you* wear does not differ from ten thousand others. In fact, I would say, you dress to immerse yourself in the congruence of the throng. Young men of the middling sort dress as if Oliver Cromwell still ruled. The rich dress as they please, but then, one dandy too is indistinguishable from another, under his wig and whitener. The older man owns distinguishing features in abundance. Younger men seem to disappear as you look at them.'

Creed mimed a candle's flame being snuffed out, his fingers tracing the imaginary smoke rising.

Harry was indignant. 'There are enough clues amongst the young to set them apart, if you have the will to observe. You believe there are no differences, therefore you do not perceive the differences.' He became aware he risked rudeness. 'I apologise, Mr. Creed. I am too blunt.'

An unyielding tone entered Creed's voice. 'I meet with men more blunt than you are ever likely to be, Mr. Hunt, and have long ceased to resent such egalitarian talk. It is a gentlemanly pursuit to seek offence where none is meant. It is quite right what you say. We do train ourselves to look for certain things at the cost of missing others. I am sure you are no less guilty than most.'

'I have one last question for you, Mr. Creed. Do you consider it possible the men who came to you were, in fact, not men at all, but rather, ladies?'

'Ladies! *Females?*' The solicitor clasped his hands joyfully in front of him.

'Mr. Creed?'

'I had not considered it, so I am startled by your question. But, yes, *conceivably*, they could have been.'

Creed went south towards the Thames, disappearing into the fog, chuckling to himself.

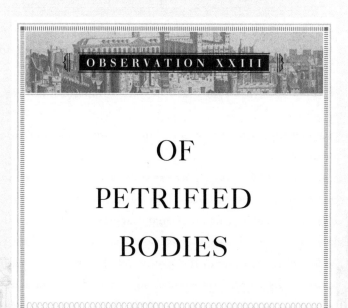

OF
PETRIFIED
BODIES

ROBERT HOOKE STOOD IN FRONT OF his cabinet of fossils, swaying gently, contemplating them—as he often did when really thinking on something else. They were a reminder of his childhood, spent scrambling across the cliffs and the sands near Freshwater on the Isle of Wight, where the sea and the frost break the cliffs away over unimaginable expanses of time, the fossils scattering over the beach.

He inhaled deeply from his pipe, hoping the smoke would clear his lungs of the thick matter within them. He felt the Portuguese bhang slide down his trachea, seeming to stretch his bronchi, and imagined his alveoli, the small, thin air sacs that cluster like balloons, rising eagerly to claim their share.

Something had blocked the way of his thoughts, but he did not know what it was. Some stray inkling, maybe, of which his waking mind was unaware.

He studied a tooth-shaped fossil, trying to imagine the rest of the creature.

His cabinet represented mutability in place of stasis, and an ancient rather than a youthful Earth.

Instead of a fixed Creation, a diversity of creatures had lived, and died, to be replaced by other, newer forms of life. Hooke saw the evidence: erosion of the cliffs, which had loosened their material and then deposited them, to consolidate into layers. These distinct layers held fossils of different creatures, not found in any other of the layers, and of no similar creature now alive. He had fossils of creatures whose design showed they could have only inhabited the seas, which were discovered high up in cliff sides. Even up on mountain tops.

Such change must happen by degrees, over great expanses of time.

He must take a care. The prevailing view held the terraqueous globe to be as the Deluge had left it, ignoring such trivial things as volcanoes or earthquakes. He had only to look at the repeated dredging of the Fleet Canal to know this was fallacious. After heavy rain, the grating at Turnmill Brook had given way, and mud and silt washed all the way down to the Fleet Bridge, to a depth of three feet.

His fossils were explained away as tricks of nature, formed at the same time of the Creation, which Bishop Ussher decreed to be in 4004 BC.

Natural laws are God's laws, and so must concord with the Scriptures.

Hooke did not wish to fall foul of religious authority.

He did not wish to fall foul of *any* authority.

Another puff from the pipe. He was cheered by his refusal to continue helping Sir Edmund. He had expected more resistance. Used to the pressure from the Royal Society on his time—his constant work and experimentation for them, despite their lack of gratitude or recognition of the strain that it put him under—he was surprised Sir Edmund allowed him to put down the matter.

Hooke was glad, too, Harry was no longer involved. He showed much promise. An able Observator. Perhaps one day he would become Curator of Experiments for the Royal Society.

He did not want anything to endanger his assistant's progress.

By suggesting Harry let loose word of the boy, he had caused him much injury. From where did this tendency to hurt those closest to him come from?

Hooke sometimes believed himself still to be the boy climbing on rocks, listening to the crash of waves against them, sprayed by salt from the sea, crushing fossils as he went.

GRACE CAME DOWN from her bedchamber and entered the drawing room quietly, wanting to gauge her uncle's mood before disturbing him. She saw him standing by the cabinet, one hand out to steady himself, the other grasping his pipe. A sweet, cloying smell filled the room.

'Uncle?'

Hooke's eyes rotated slowly towards her, their eyelids half closed.

'Uncle?' Grace repeated. 'Did you not hear the knocking at the door?'

Hooke tilted his head back, to shake the stupor from his brain. 'I did not, Grace. My ears . . . this chill . . . my head is brimful . . . would you see who calls?'

Grace went down the stairs as another set of knocks sounded from the door. She opened it to find the head of a horse looking at her, but then it swung away, replaced by its rider. A young man held out a sealed letter. His breath steamed in the cold of Gresham's quadrangle. He looked admiringly at her, at her long blonde hair and clear skin, and the half-smile on her perfectly symmetrical face.

'A missive from Viscount Brouncker,' he managed.

She went as if to take it, but did not pull it from him, and he did not let go. They stood for a flirtatious second, connected by the paper. With a laugh of thanks, she took it and shut the door, returning to Uncle and his fossils.

Having watched her from the door of his drawing room, Hooke frowned at her. She should not risk her reputation with messengers. After the saga with Sir Thomas Bloodworth's son, a setback to his plans, he still hoped she would marry a man of high station. Admiral Sir Robert Holmes, he knew, had thoughts.

Hooke was too interested in the contents of the letter to worry about the prospects for his niece for long. He took it to his table, broke the seal, opened it up, and then let out a cry of triumph.

'Eureka! Brouncker says I am Secretary! I have replaced old Grubendol!' He rushed to Grace and hugged her to him. 'Yet to be ratified by the Council, but they will follow his direction. And Harry is to undertake the search of his papers! Where is Mary? Where is Tom? We must celebrate this news!'

Instructing Mary, who appeared at the noise of Hooke's rare gusto, to fetch some wine, and Tom to help her with the best glasses, Hooke cleared a space on the table, and Grace brought chairs from various parts of the room.

Another knock, though, harder, louder, more officious-sounding than the last, interrupted Hooke's joy.

Again, Grace answered, but this time an older man pushed his way straight past her and strode up to the drawing room.

'Mr. Hooke. The King orders your attendance, at once, at the Chelsea Physic Garden. We have a boy, drained of his blood.'

OF THE
CHELSEA PHYSIC
GARDEN

LIKE EVERYONE, ELIZABETH HANNAM HAD HEARD the rumours sweeping through London of the Devil-boy. Now another had appeared. Young Tom Gyles confirmed it.

She could not wait to tell all of this new portent.

The instruction to watch her lodger, given from the thin lips of the Justice, had made Harry an object of suspicion. Now, she was certain Sir Edmund had charged her to protect him, as a young man important to the King.

She thought of the news Tom had brought, her discourse to Harry on the qualities of gooseberry interrupted by an almost lunatic threshing on her door.

'All Mr. Hooke told me is this,' Tom had said. 'They have found another boy! You are to go to the Westbourne, at the Chelsea Physic Garden!'

'But Mr. Hooke wishes no more of this business,' Harry had replied.

'The King,' Tom announced grandly, 'says otherwise.'

⌇

THEY HASTENED TO Bishopsgate, Harry with a large portion of Mrs. Hannam's sweet marrow tart in his pocket, Tom skipping on ahead.

Hooke waited in the College quadrangle, huddled in his grey coat. Grace stood with him. The heightened colour of her face from the cold, and the moisture of her breath condensing in the air, made Harry feel the same tightening in his chest as when he laid eyes on Felicity Tarripan in the Angel, and the same drying of his tongue.

'Come! Come!' Hooke greeted them unhappily. 'We will find a waterman for the journey to Chelsea. Thank you, Tom. You are to stay here.'

Harry watched Tom go back inside Hooke's rooms with Grace, Grace turning to wave. He was fond of the boy, of his willingness to perform his errands, of his dreaming of the day when he would go to sea full of his knowledge of navigation, learned from Mr. Hooke.

Crossing the quadrangle, Hooke's voice lowered to a guarded whisper. 'Harry, I really am not well. I've had a most dreadful night, bursting with cold, although this morning I puked a little, which eased me. Some syrup of poppies and some bhang—judiciously taken—steadies me.'

Harry made sympathetic sounds, but hurried Hooke on. Gresham's College had escaped destruction, but once on Bishopsgate Street and Grace Church Street, all the houses soon turned to new, rebuilt to the post-Fire regulations.

Down Fish Street Hill, past Hooke's Monument to the Great Conflagration, and the church of St. Magnus the Martyr, where the workmen dismantled the last of the scaffolding. Then to Coldharbour and the Watermen's Hall.

Hooke's nostrils did look sore—to Harry's concern—until Hooke reassured him. He had been snuffling the juice of beetroot.

'Sir Edmund's persuasiveness knows no bounds, it seems,' Hooke said.

'Has he convinced the King to ensure you continue with the search?'

'It must be the Justice, surely?' Hooke did not seem interested in his own question, grumbling the whole way down to the river.

Between the houses built on the waterfront, they were met by the sickly smell of the Thames. They followed a high-walled alley, narrow and murky, its steps greasy as they descended. It was not the remains of the snow making their journey precarious, but the effluent matter from the City. Discharged into the river, it stuck to every surface around them, making them reluctant to stretch out their hands for a hold.

Emerging onto the quayside they could see the Morice waterwheels, the replacements of those burnt, beneath the first two arches of London Bridge. Harry could hear their wood straining as they turned on their axles, pushed by the surge of the water. The pumps, made from the trunks of elm trees, driven by great wooden cogs, had force enough to propel the water through the conduit pipes as far up as Cornhill.

Hooke's hunched back provoked the watermen to shout out 'Oars!', recognising a frequent customer. All his surveying of London made him a regular visitor to the river.

Clambering into the first wherry, both men gripped its rails, unsteady on its high seat.

'We go to Chelsea, to the Physic Garden there.'

The waterman pushed them off, skipping into his vessel gracefully. 'Yes, Mr. Hooke. Chelsea stairs it is.'

THE WATERMAN TOLD them his name was Kill-Sin Abbott. 'Puritanical parents, God bless their memories.' The whole way west, they listened to a relentless commentary on the advantages of travel by river rather than by hackney coach—'. . . all that rattling which shakes up your innards!'—with particular ire for the sedan-chairs—' . . . Joggling and jiggling, it cannot claim gentlemanly dignity, can it?' A thought struck him. 'What of ladies, carried in such a way? Jounced about, it must be damaging to them, it can only be damaging.'—and of the grievances of the watermen against the lightermen for not restricting their services to goods being taken to and from vessels—'They're *lighter*men. You smoke the difference? They take our trade brazenly. We are the *water*men.'

Harry's eyes wept from the wind, the cold air loaded with drizzle. He pulled his coat as tightly around him as he could, retracting into its leather to protect himself from the malicious chill.

Their wherry, rocking over the peaks of the water, sticky foam splashing their faces, took them past the warehouses of the Hanseatic League's Steelyard, the busy Queenhithe dock, the entrance to the Fleet Canal, and then Alsatia.

Harry still kept back from Hooke his visit there, and his searching for Enoch Wolfe.

A gull, well fed and sheeny, landed on the rail, and watched them intently.

Another spy, Harry thought, clapping his hands to send it away. They are everywhere.

'We take *people*, they take *cargo* . . . ' Kill-Sin continued reasonably, as if coaxing a child to swallow tough mutton. Harry and Hooke nodded their agreement from time to time, staying silent. For when Hooke tried to engage him in a more considered discussion of the economics of ferrying passengers about the metropolis with only a single bridge across the Thames, he was met with a resolute disparagement. Only Kill-Sin's innate civility stopped him from using water language.

Around the bend of the Thames. Scotland Yard, Whitehall Palace with its Banqueting Hall, and the towers of Holbein Gate. The Abbey, the Hall, and Parliament House, their massive roofs dark against the sky.

The waterman's sinewy arms took them on. Past Vauxhall and the New Spring Gardens, quiet except for the sounds of birdsong and the wind riffling through the leaves of the plantation, the sibilant noise carrying over the water to them.

They reached the mouth of the Westbourne.

'Chelsea stairs it is!' Kill-Sin repeated, concluding the trip as he started.

MIST ROLLED ACROSS the undulating ground, gathering in its folds, bleaching greens to greys. The air became one with the earth. They forgot the idea of solidity. Stepping onto the grass from the water stairs brought a jolt to misled senses to find the ground unyielding. It was in fact a thick, tough material, which crunched under them in the cold. The passage of the wind slid it about in pewtery ripples.

They approached the low wall of the Physic Garden. Set up by the Worshipful Society of Apothecaries as a training ground, it was neatly laid out for simples, herbs, roots, and flowers. A pale imitation of its spring and summer lushness, its January display looked bare.

The immense glass conservatory appeared ahead, visible through the branches of a pair of Lebanon cedars. The heat from its stoves, circulating beneath the brick floor, steamed the panes.

'You could poison Westminster with the contents of this garden,' Hooke told Harry, cheering a little.

Beyond the conservatory, they could see a black-clad figure sitting astride a horse. His mount, also, was black. Sir Edmund Bury Godfrey did not return Hooke's wave, although he stared straight at them.

As they crossed the distance between them, the Justice looked even more severe than Harry had seen him before.

'This boy lies there,' Sir Edmund said by way of greeting. He indicated down to the river.

The Westbourne was far narrower than the Fleet. Carved by movement of water and wind, rather than by any design of Hooke's, lengthy grass grew over the edge, demanding a close approach to observe where dark earth met water.

Walking to this edge, they looked down onto another naked dead boy, lying in a clump of lungwort. His head rested against the roots of a birch tree pushing its way through the bank.

They looked for footprints in the mud. Harry studied the ground for the traces of snowshoes, but there were none.

Sir Edmund dismounted and took out his portable pen and ink set from a saddlebag.

The earth, saturated from days of snow and the hovering mist, gave way when Harry scrambled down. His rapid descent disturbed a nearby lapwing protecting her nest, feigning to have an injured wing. Harry jumped at the bird's shriek of outrage.

Wiping mud from the seat of his trousers, he gazed at the boy, who looked older than the one at the Fleet: four or five years old, this one, but he was just as small.

Eyes a nondescript grey, their corneas not yet clouded over.

'Drained, too?' Hooke called from above him.

Harry studied the puncture holes and felt the dried texture of the skin.

'Yes, Mr. Hooke. With similar dates by the holes. Also, there's a cut across his chest, stitched to close it again.'

Sir Edmund squatted as close as he could to the crumbling bank, recording their findings into his black notebook.

From up on the level of the Physic Garden, the sound of another horse reached them.

'Good morrow, Mr. Hooke. And to you, Sir Edmund.' The new arrival looked down into the Westbourne. 'And to you, Harry.'

They knew the man well, for he was a Fellow of the Royal Society and a regular member of Hooke's own, more intimate group, the New Philosophical Club. He was Sir Jonas Moore: plump, with oddly transparent skin, which revealed the plentiful flesh and vessels beneath, like an illustration of the workings of the human body. He was famous for his draining of the Bedford Level, mapping the Thames from Westminster to the sea, and for overseeing the building of the great mole at Tangier.

With Hooke, he had helped survey London after the Conflagration, and they collaborated on the Fleet Canal sluice. Harry had prepared a tides table for him and made him a telescope, for which Sir Jonas still owed nearly three pounds.

The King employed him as Surveyor-General of the Board of Ordnance, at the Tower of London.

He slid from his horse, a fine-looking blood bay, looking unused to being carried by such transport.

'The King ordered I should meet with you here, to be shown the boy. He asks that we take him to the Palace—God's blood!' He had caught sight of the boy, and his swearing earned a reproving tut from Hooke. He walked nearer the edge to see more.

'If you hold the tree's root, it is an easy climb down,' Hooke told him, having seen Harry do it.

Harry helped Sir Jonas as he joined him by the water.

The lapwing complained again. 'The Tiddy Mun,' Sir Jonas observed. 'He follows me here, as he follows me since my work in the Fens.'

Harry's manifest confusion encouraged Sir Jonas to explain further. 'The Cambridgeshire bog-dwellers tell the legend of the Tiddy Mun, whose voice is the cry of the lapwing. He commands the mists and the water.'

'The others were the same,' Hooke interrupted Sir Jonas.

Others? Harry shot a look of enquiry up at Hooke. This was the first time he had spoken of more than one boy. Hooke spluttered into his hand.

'This boy is not decayed,' Sir Jonas observed. 'Has the cold stopped his rotting?'

'Slowed it, true enough,' Hooke told him.

'But if you observe the boy's eyes, they are fresh,' Harry said.

Hooke peered down from the bank. 'This frost would damage them. I do not believe he was left here before this morning.'

'You know best of such things.' Sir Jonas said.

'There was a gap of one week between the other findings,' Hooke told him. 'This comes sooner.'

'Do you make surmise upon this frequency?'

'I cannot distinguish patterns within so small a number. You, being more mathematical, may care to do so.'

Sir Jonas waved the suggestion aside, sharing a grim amusement with his friend. 'You keep the other boys preserved?'

Sir Edmund answered. 'The first found is pickled at the College of Physicians. The second is at Gresham's College, in Mr. Hooke's air-pump there.'

So, two other boys, then, Harry mused. What else did Hooke hide?

'Your famous air-pump!' Sir Jonas said. 'We are to study this boy in the King's own elaboratory. Then, I wish to view the other boys.'

Harry, readily, and Hooke, reluctantly, signalled their assent. Sir Edmund was more reticent even than Hooke.

'Good!' Sir Jonas exclaimed, noting Harry's reaction against those of the older men with him. 'We will lift out the boy from this place. Put him over my mount. I will happily walk the distance back.'

Sir Jonas climbed out of the riverbed, assisted by Sir Edmund pulling him up. Harry lifted the boy from his cradle among the roots of the birch, and off the covering of lungwort. He offered him up, and Sir Edmund and Sir Jonas took the body from him, to strap him over the saddle of Sir Jonas's mount.

'Come, and we shall leave this bird with her nest in peace,' Sir Jonas said.

'Give up your coat, Harry,' Hooke said, when Harry had climbed back to them. 'Cover this boy.'

OBSERVATION XXV

OF INGENIOUS PURSUITS

OLIVER CROMWELL'S HEAD, BOILED AND TARRED, still rested on its spike after all these years. He looked peaceable enough, Harry thought, as they went past Westminster Hall. Although blackened from the weather and London soot.

The Lord Protector had the perfect vantage point to survey the capital which once was his.

'I knew him,' Sir Jonas said, noticing Harry's attention. 'He was against the draining of the Fens, being from those parts, and spoke against the scheme. During the Wars, I prepared a model of a New London for him. He was for liberty of conscience, with which I could never disagree.'

IT WAS THE nature of Charles II's court that people wandered freely about its grounds, walking through the Privy Garden and past the buildings of the Cockpit, the Banqueting Hall, and even Whitehall Palace itself, without challenge.

Sir Jonas Moore and Robert Hooke were frequent visitors there, and the few guards they saw waved them through. At the King Street Gate, Sir Jonas explained to two servants what was to be done with the boy, and they took him and his horse away.

The four men walked through into the Privy Garden and past its pyramidical sundial. It had nearly three hundred dials, all made ineffective by the day's thick mist.

Entering the Palace, they walked through a long gallery, Sir Jonas leading them rapidly on.

Reunited with his brown leather coat, the condescending stares they received, and the fact every inhabitant of this place was dressed richly and had the expensive smell of cleanliness rising from them, made Harry feel he stood out like a spot against the sun.

Sir Jonas took them on through another gallery, where they could hear the noise of a crowd and the clatter of sword blades. More servants admitted them through a lofty doorway.

Inside the room Harry found himself in, everything was red. The walls, the silks, the leathers, the hangings, the carpets, the furniture. An edge showed a flash of gold, a corner a glimpse of silver, but red wholly dominated. The sole painting was a fiery depiction of Eos, goddess of dawn. Its light threw red over its landscape, drenching it in violence.

The King resided on a long duchesse brisée, also red, with gold eagles embroidered across its fabric. This was placed on a platform to improve his view and raise him above his subjects.

Surrounding him, being careful not to obstruct his vision, courtiers shouted encouragement to two masked figures practising their fencing across the width of the room. Both employed thin light swords, their tips foiled with leather. The speed of the blades created a swoosh of sound with each thrust, their arcs leaving trails as if painting the air behind them. The audience swayed and shouted with a fervour suggesting bets had been placed.

Harry wondered if each combatant was near the limit of his ability, for their swordplay was so quick, each parry and riposte so expertly done. He was sure one or other must soon get injured, even using blunted points. The taller of them moved more languidly, seeming to keep perfect balance as he deflected the other's thrusts. Harry judged him the better of the two. As one attacked, the other defended, and he realised they played by some system, as neither lunged at the same time, although the rules were too subtle for him to fathom exactly the etiquette of the bout.

The finish, too, was mysterious: the taller of the pair held up a hand, signalling the conclusion of their duel. They both turned to the watching King, took off their masks, and then curtsied.

To Harry's astonishment, long hair spilled from inside the masks they wore—one had blonde, the other black—and as they lifted themselves, he saw the faces of two ladies. Both were out of breath and flushed from their efforts. Harry recognised at last the outline of female forms under their shirts and breeches.

Enthusiastically clapping them, the King noticed Sir Jonas, stood up, and beckoned. When Hooke, Harry, and Sir Edmund stayed where they were, he waved to them as well. Harry suffered an even keéner self-consciousness as he passed through all the courtiers, as everyone gawped at them.

King Charles II was tall, over two yards high. On his platform, he towered above them. His dark skin, a throwback to his Medici forefathers, being slightly pocked, gave him a leathery appearance. Lines cut deeply between the muscles of his face, making his features emphatic. The royal nose was large, long and sharply boned.

Despite its oddness, Harry considered, the King's face had a liveliness and friendliness which made it attractive.

He wore an imposing full-length black peruke, a dark blue Persian vest pinked with white silk, and a pale-yellow sash and stockings.

The two fencers still stood by the platform. The King introduced the taller of the pair to the Justice, the Curator, and the Observator. 'The Duchesse de Mazarin, Hortense Mancini.'

She smiled at them all, a flash of perfect teeth, her black eyes resting for an extra second on Harry.

Felicity Tarripan, the Quaker at Alsatia, making her way to Prince Rupert's Land with her husband, was beautiful. Grace Hooke was beautiful too. Hortense Mancini, though, had quite another style of beauty: severe, dramatic, aristocratic. She had black hair, and olive skin unconcealed by whitener. Only her lips, dark red, showed the use of colouring. This alone distinguished her from the other courtiers in Whitehall, who covered themselves in so much powder they became uniform. She was in her thirties, but even so, Harry considered, she was exquisite.

Once more she looked at him—he could not believe his good fortune—then she begged her leave. Instead of granting it, the King turned back to the men, and raised a complicit eyebrow.

'The history of a nation is decided upon a woman's whim. Hmm?'

The Duchesse smiled at his comment, then turned the same smile at the men with him, bedazzling them all. When she left them, the King added, *sotto voce*, 'I proposed marriage to her, during my days in France. Since I was too poor, she would not have me. Now, she's married to the richest man in Europe, but she has refused him, too.'

Anne Lennard, Countess of Sussex—the King's daughter and the other fencer—did not wait for an introduction, merely nodding at them, then moving away through the crowd.

The King watched the departure of his daughter as if wanting her to glance back, but she did not. When the King was not speaking, Harry realised, when his face fell into repose, a solemnity settled over his features. Was this a truer reflection of his character?

After a sigh of discontent, the King led them from the room.

They followed his elegant walk along a corridor. The royal walk he had struggled to disguise, Harry knew, when escaping after Worcester, trying to pass himself off as a woodman.

The King opened a door himself, despite the leaping headfirst of a doorman, and ushered them through.

❧

HARRY WAS IN the King's elaboratory.

Spread over the main table were details of a ship, the *Experiment*: two hundred tons and eighteen guns, designed by Sir William Petty of the Royal Society and remarkable for its double bottom, two keels running parallel beneath its hull. The King invited them to admire its sweep. Knowing none of them were sailors, he showed them around the drawings, naming and describing the *Experiment's* functions, and the relationship between cordage and sails. He spoke of the science of working a ship, the sails acting on it with reference to its centre of rotation, the wind acting on the sails, and the water on the rudder.

He showed them Sir Christopher Wren's lunar globe, a unicorn's horn—which they all knew was a narwhal's tusk—ferns in a glass alembic releasing mysterious bubbles into the water, an alligator's skull, a mouldy armadillo, and further curiosities in the royal knickknackatory. A *lumbricus latus*, taken from the guts of a man, some four times the length of its host and with over four hundred mouths, coiled in a preserving jar. Also, a large piece of red volcanic rock, sent to him by Edmund Halley from St. Helena. Little clue remained of its violent expulsion from the earth.

The King's talent at putting others at ease—attained, people said, from his escape and his long stay in France, where he had become used to mixing with the lower sort—did not work on the Justice. Of all of them, Sir Edmund was quietest, and the constant wiping of his mouth showed some agitation. He only spoke when addressed, and an ungracious chill emanated from him, affecting the natural flow of their conversation.

Harry wanted the opportunity to ask him about the morning at the

Fleet River, on New Year's Day, and the falling of the snow. Why had he concealed his knowledge of the snowshoe prints? It would be better to speak of it when they were alone. The matter of stretching his promise to Hooke beyond its elastic limit still stood.

The King showed a painting of the *Royal Escape*, originally called *Surprize*, the little coal brig which completed Charles's dramatic flight to France, renamed and brought into the Navy.

Harry thought of Colonel Fields's story. He stood in the same elaboratory as Sir Edmund, the man who helped the King flee from Worcester. Sir Edmund obeyed the order from Oliver Cromwell, whose head was displayed just outside. Harry also remembered the copper farthing, which he still had in his pocket, and the uneasy intuition he had had, feeling watched by the portrait of the King on its face.

The King led Hooke away to examine the Curator's own gift to him, a clock using Hooke's balance-spring mechanism, still keeping the royal time.

Harry took the chance to view an object he had seen before, when it was first received by the Royal Society. Smuggled to Henry Oldenburg from the Dutch Republic when the hostilities began, it sat in its own glass case.

He studied the wax-injected veins and venules running through its fabric.

It was the uterus of a woman in labour with her child. Childbirth had killed them both. Dr. Swammerdam had dissected and preserved it. It looked as fresh as when they died, the waxes and oils imparting a healthy lustre. Harry imagined the child pushing its way out, refusing to believe its entry into the world was being denied, desperate to fill its tiny lungs for the first time with air.

It was not difficult to understand the King's interest in it. After all, he was a man fascinated by women—some said he preferred their company and even their conversation to that of men.

It was no secret the Queen, Catherine of Braganza, had been pregnant three times. All ended in miscarriage. It led to much talk against her, people openly saying the King should remarry. The contrast with his fecund mistresses could not have been starker. He had thirteen acknowledged children—four of them by his mistress, Barbara Villiers. Who knew how many more secret children he had sired, or how many women he had been with?

The King refused to leave his wife, however, and sternly discouraged such talk. He had taken a great disliking to the Earl of Shaftesbury for saying so: it was one reason Shaftesbury had found himself in the Tower.

Harry, looking at Swammerdam's preserved exhibit, pictured the boy inside the air-pump at Gresham's College. The fancy struck him that the machine was a brass and glass womb, made by the hand of man, and so a crude facsimile of nature's work.

'The truest microcosm,' the King confided, arriving at his shoulder, 'is the womb of a mother. Hmm?'

They turned at the swinging open of the elaboratory doors, as the body of the boy found at the Westbourne, was carried in and laid out on the King's table.

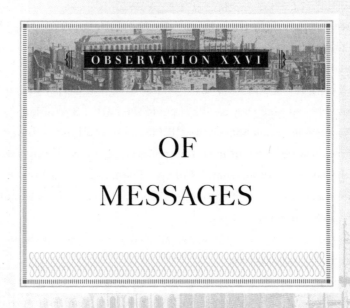

OF

MESSAGES

HOOKE SUGGESTED THE IDEA: HARRY PERFORMED the autopsy.

Determined to ignore the trembling in his unruly finger and his own queasiness—the procedure was no different from his practising on dogs and cats—he used the King's anatomy tools to reopen the cut across the boy's chest.

He released the breastplate, previously cut away from the ribs, and announced the heart had been taken.

'*The Lord shall send upon thee cursing, vexation, and rebuke,*' Sir Edmund said, appalled by the cavity Harry revealed.

Splashes of candle wax on the boy's belly suggested the draining of his blood and the removal of his heart took place at night or in a darkened room. It was the same expensive wax Harry had unpeeled from the boy at the Fleet.

There were two puncture marks, with precisely written dates next to them. This boy, too, must have been preserved, and judging by the oldest date for three months or more. He looked small for his age, possibly chosen to enable the preservation of him in a glass receiver, as Harry had thought might be the way with the boy now stored at Gresham's College.

One of the puncture marks, though, showed evidence of healing.

'He was drained through a pipe when still alive,' Harry noted.

The four men looked at one another, all aghast at the thought of this boy's last days.

Sir Edmund wrote all of this into his notebook.

HAVING FINISHED THEIR study of this boy, the King asked Sir Edmund for a full account of the others. The Justice spoke of the two found at Barking Creek and the Fleet River, and of their preservation. Harry noticed he omitted to mention the Red Cipher, and Hooke did not offer the information either.

After his report, the King turned to Hooke. 'Now, Robert, are you willing to aid Sir Edmund once more? We cannot have boys found murdered, and without their blood, being left about London.'

Hooke's expression, and the way his eyes looked everywhere but at the King, showed he was not willing at all. 'I can be of little use, surely, Your Majesty. My skills are peculiar,' he answered.

'I believe that you, and Harry here, can assist Sir Edmund greatly,' the King replied. 'It would match the principles of my Society to do so.'

'The many threads of this matter require a dextrous unpicking,' Hooke persisted.

'You could also say,' Harry submitted, 'these threads may be tied to make their unravelling an easier task, like in a cunning-man's knot.'

'Whereas a man killed with a single blow and left in the street leaves few clues behind him!' Sir Edmund was visibly buoyed by Harry's unexpected support.

Hooke's exasperated look showed Harry did not help extricate them from the matter.

'Valiantly said, Harry! Hmm?' The King clapped as he said it. 'Good fellow!'

'You may guide each other,' Sir Jonas pressed Hooke. 'Your knowledge of natural philosophy makes you useful.'

Hooke considered Sir Jonas's words dejectedly. 'You profess too much faith in our experimentalism.'

'I am convinced of its usefulness,' Sir Edmund said, 'as you both have demonstrated. Although if I were as exacting as you, I should never catch a single malefactor.'

'Some parts of nature are too large to be comprehended, some too little to be perceived,' Hooke replied. 'Our most solid definitions are imperfect, only expressions of our misguided apprehensions, not the true nature of things themselves—'

'—You talk too generally, Robert!' the King interrupted. 'And reckon too little of your way of setting about the world. Your protests are *hyperbolical*, as Monsieur Descartes would have it. We are all of us imperfect, and so must strive against our imperfections. So, let us together consider anew this investigation.'

Hooke looked defeated and performed an unhappy dip of his head.

'Sir Edmund?' Harry, seizing his chance, half raised his hand as if for a teacher in a schoolroom.

The Justice regarded him expectantly, grateful for his new ally. 'What is it, Mr. Hunt, that you desire to say?'

'How was your being at the Fleet contrived?'

Sir Edmund's expression faded to a frown. 'I received a letter the night before, asking to meet with me there at first light. It spoke of Jesuits infiltrating London, meeting at Holborn Bridge.'

'Who sent this letter?' Sir Jonas enquired.

'There was no name on it. Maybe another, unconnected with the boy, required the meeting. The constable there turned the curious away. The sender was one such refused.' It sounded as if Sir Edmund tried to convince himself as much as the four men he addressed. 'You feel the boy was left for me?'

Harry's pulse quickened. Afterwards, he would answer to Hooke. 'I wonder why you kept from us you saw the boy being left there.'

The Justice gave Harry an obdurate stare. His approval of this assistant had vanished.

'I returned to the Fleet again, two days later,' Harry explained, 'when the snow was almost melted. It showed the way of setting down the body.'

The displeasure in Hooke's eyes made them seem like balls of metal.

'I'm sorry, Mr. Hooke, I've not spoken of this because of my promise to you.'

'You must enlighten me, Sir,' the Justice said. 'For I saw no such a thing.' His eyes blazed, boring into Harry. Harry knew Sir Edmund had perfected this inspection over years of dealing with men far tougher than him.

'There were clear tracks left, of frozen snow. The snow above, being softer, had melted away to reveal them. They showed the progress of a man wearing snowshoes.' Harry refused to flinch from Sir Edmund's gaze, although the muscle of his thigh had started its wobble.

'Snowshoes!' Sir Jonas exclaimed. 'But used to traverse the mud.'

Harry nodded. 'Their wearer couldn't know he'd use them on snow until it began to fall.'

'Unless the man who bled the boy knew it would snow then,' Sir Jonas suggested.

Hooke looked sceptical. 'I have made observations of the weather all my life. I could not have told you exactly when it would begin to snow.'

'But the time of the falling snow is significant,' the King said.

'I remember the moment, Your Majesty, on that first morning, when the rain changed to snow,' Harry said. 'It was before I reached Gresham's College. Sir Edmund had already sent a message to Mr. Hooke. By the time I reached them at Holborn Bridge, the snow had settled, covering the bank and the prints.'

'And you believe I was there before it, and before the body was left.' Sir Edmund wiped at his mouth again. 'But I sent no such summons to Gresham's! I did not expect Mr. Hooke to be there. I arrived as the snow fell thickly, met there by Gabriel Knapp, my constable, and the man Enoch Wolfe with him.'

'I remember I did not speak to you, Sir Edmund, of the message brought to me,' Hooke said.

'Do you recall anything of the messenger, Robert?' the King asked.

'It was still dark, Your Majesty! The weather stopped me from going out to him. Such men are invisible! One thinks only of the message they bring.' Hooke reconsidered. 'I have the impression in my mind of age. He was an elderly man.' The realisation came: he had been pulled inexorably into another's design. 'I was required to be there also.'

'Sir Edmund, did you not speculate on Mr. Hooke's presence there?' Harry said, despite the dark expression on the Justice's face.

'I did not think to question my good fortune!' Sir Edmund exclaimed. 'I was too much preoccupied with the murdered boy.' The Justice's expression moderated, softening. 'There are aspects of your search, Mr. Hunt, of which I know nothing. You have kept them from me, since the falling snow led you to think me implicated in the murder of the boy. You must believe me. I seek the man who so wickedly murdered these boys. It is a part of the Catholic plot against the life of His Majesty, I am sure. The letter I had on New Year's Eve spoke of it. Also, I have had two men come to me, named Titus Oates and Israel Tonge, attesting to an intricate plan to kill the King. I know not how the blood of boys is to be used, but I believe it for some portent that the papists will recognise as their signal. We must look to the treacherous Catholics.'

'You are a capable man, Harry,' the King said. 'Impressively so. You will all of you share your knowledge together, for apart you have only befuddled one another.'

With this praise from the King, Harry dared to press the Justice further.

'You have a cipher, left on the boy's body, which requires a keyword. Does its sender believe you have it?'

'I have speculated that he will reveal it to me.'

'What did you know of the cipher before you passed it to Mr. Hooke?'

Hooke's anxiety was palpable in the way he investigated the surface of the rug they stood on.

'Inside, I saw numbers, nothing more,' Sir Edmund said.

The Justice saw Hooke and Harry exchange one of their looks. His eyes narrowed at the thought they did not believe him. 'It is familiar.'

'I know its use,' Hooke said. 'It was a method employed in our nation's Wars, on the Parliament side, to conduct Your Majesty to France. This is the reason I returned it.'

'You gave scant cause for giving up the task,' Sir Edmund said. 'I wondered upon it.'

Hooke screwed up his face. 'If you had told us of the system, we would not have wasted so much time on it.'

'I did not have the keyword. I thought you able to break into it, without its origin becoming known—'

'—It is true, there was some outside help to get me to France,' the King interrupted. 'The legend is more attractive, hmm? Who told you of this, Robert? It is an aspect of history never revealed.'

Harry answered in Hooke's place. 'I went to Colonel Michael Fields, Your Majesty, in Whitechapel. He visited Gresham's once, to show his ciphers.'

'That old rabble-rouser?' The King was incredulous. 'Still alive?'

'He told me of Oliver Cromwell's assistance to you.'

'It suited us all. My bread was baked. I desire you not to bandy this about.'

'We will not, Your Majesty,' Hooke answered, and then corrected himself. 'I am sorry, Harry, for I answer for you. You are your own man now, and so must answer for yourself.'

'I shall be quiet, too, Your Majesty, on the matter,' Harry affirmed.

The King looked satisfied with their promise. He turned to Sir Edmund. 'You must go now to meet with Lord High Treasurer Danby, to discuss with him Titus Oates and Israel Tonge. He will subject their evidence to a more close scrutiny, pull at its weft and warp to find if it comes undone. If their story of a Catholic plot becomes known, with these rumours of blood-drained boys, it will unsettle all of London. It takes but a little to stir up the mob. There is a danger the innocent will fall together with the guilty—if there be any guilty.'

'I do not concern myself with the innocent,' Sir Edmund assured him. 'The innocent have nothing to fear. That there is a Catholic plot, I have no doubt. Of what Oates and Tonge know of it, we shall find. That these boys herald it, I am certain.'

Sir Edmund left them, bowing low to his King.

The King watched the Justice's retreating back. 'Jonas, Robert, Harry, we will observe the other boys. Robert, as we go, you may entertain me with stories of weighing the air, and whatnot.'

OF
ADMISSION

THEIR JOURNEY, BY COACH, WAS NOTABLE for the conversation between Robert Hooke and the King.

Hooke spoke of his trials to send a whisper the distance of a furlong, and his hopes to multiply that tenfold—'Why, we could have the whole of London speaking to one another in an instant!' the King cried—and of conveying sound as swiftly as the passage of light through the air, along extended wires. He described signalling machines utilising towers and telescopes to relay messages across the country. He spoke of the movements of brush-horned gnats, their limbs and muscles making them like little automata, and of the vital function inherent in their fibres—the flapping of wings relying on some signal from brain to muscle, like tiny gunpowder trails through their bodies.

Hooke went on to explain the propagation of light corpuscles through the æther, original and connate properties of coloured lights, and the phenomenon of refrangibility, in which the least refrangibile rays tend to redness, and the most to a deep violet. His enthusiasm, reversing his earlier mood, as he discussed the wonder of all colours on being compounded producing purest white, and mentioning his correspondence on the matter with Mr. Isaac Newton of Trinity College, Cambridge—' . . . a capable man, though we disagree on some particulars.'—became infectious, and it was a jovial party arriving at the College of Physicians despite the reason for their visit.

The room they went into held specimens displaying disease or injury, and also deformity, growth God had ostensibly forsaken. Thin sheets, like winding sheets, placed over its windows, diffused the light.

This boy, found at Barking Creek on Christmas Day, sat in wine vinegar and seawater.

The liquid made him white, even more bleached of colour than his bloodless body actually was. His hands pushed against the glass, their palms compressed flat on the inside of the jar. Deterioration from being in the river was evident, unlike the boys at the Fleet and the Westbourne. He was a similar size to both of them, and a similar age to the boy left at the Fleet, being about three years old.

Dates written by the punctures into his legs showed he was first bled over six months before.

'An imperfect form of preservation, Your Majesty,' Hooke observed. 'Is it necessary to keep him?'

'Sir Edmund keeps the boys, as evidence,' Sir Jonas answered for his King.

'Have not his parents come forwards, to report their child missing?' Harry asked, wondering which man might answer him.

'It is a sad fact, Harry,'—it was the King—'there are many children in London whom no one would miss. Perhaps this boy is one of them, for no alarm has been raised.'

'Surely an autopsy, properly detailed and reported, is all the evidence required?' Hooke asked.

Sir Jonas shuffled awkwardly. 'I ordered Sir Edmund to preserve them.'

Harry and Hooke looked at each other. That was why Sir Edmund had been so adamant on the boy's preservation in the air-pump.

The King regarded Sir Jonas, weighing if he should make further enquiry of his Surveyor-General in front of the two natural philosophers. He could sense their questions rising.

He made his decision. 'Robert, Harry, take me to the other boy, the one at Gresham's College. Sir Jonas, you may return to the Tower. I shall meet with you there later.'

Sir Jonas bowed deeply, and left them. Harry observed a dark blue vein throbbing in the King's forehead, and realised Sir Jonas had offended him: it would seem by his order to keep the boys preserved.

The King took a deep breath to recompose himself, and then, when he was ready, smiled at them. He ushered them out of the specimens room. An orderly, dumbstruck by the presence of his Majesty, bowed and locked the door behind them.

Hooke, as they left the College of Physicians, designed by him and recently completed, instinctively studied the wall. He wiped his hand over its surface, noting the atmosphere's effect on it. It already darkened from London's fumes. Satisfied with the stone's resistance to the smoke, he paced after the others waiting by the King's coach.

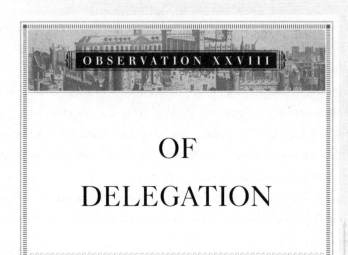

OBSERVATION XXVIII

OF

DELEGATION

WHEN THE KING HAD ENSCONCED HIMSELF in Hooke's drawing room, Mary had to be restrained from dusting around him. She looked on, horrified, as he pushed at tools and springs and weights to make space for the royal posterior. He balanced on Hooke's oak chest, one leg elegantly crossed over the other, surrounded by the clutter of the room. He took off his hat and peruke, revealing short grey hair and an unexpectedly round head, which for Tom turned him into quite another person.

Tom boiled tea for the King. He scalded himself in his carefulness, concentrating so hard he shook, and he proudly showed Harry the pink patch of skin on his hand. He also gave Harry a note, delivered there to Hooke's lodgings: Enoch Wolfe would meet him at the Angel. Harry ignored Hooke's squint of enquiry.

Mary scurried this way and that, convinced the lack of tidiness would permanently unhinge the King's mind. The name Robinson would be despised throughout London, although she had pleaded with Mr. Hooke to let her clear the room on so many occasions. Oh, injustice! Oh, shame!

After the King's refreshment, Grace serving the tea and receiving lingering looks of approval, and a conversation between the men regarding the forty genera of John Wilkins's *An Essay towards a Real Character, and a Philosophical Language*, the King was taken down into Gresham's cellars, through the long corridor, and to the air-pump.

***

HE STARED AT the boy for a long while, pressing his hand against the glass receiver. The boy, he saw, had eyes of an unusual blue.

'He will not decay?'

'While we keep the integrity of the seal, Your Majesty, the boy shall remain just so,' Hooke replied.

'In that case, let him stay here, Robert. It is the best place until we choose what to do with him.'

'In the talk about London of a Devil-boy, they mention Gresham's as the place of its keeping.' Hooke's fearful expression showed his continued aversion to being involved.

'I have heard the same at Whitehall. The Court is as full of prattlers as the City.' The King looked out to the corridor. 'Double up the locks on these doors. Let no one enter.'

'Why does Sir Jonas wish these boys to be kept?' Harry asked, then remembered himself. 'Your Majesty.'

'That I must ascertain. He has done so without my knowledge. I am sure he has reason enough. Meanwhile, keep this boy here, where he is safest, until those who know him best may identify him.'

The King took his hand from the glass and pulled Hooke close to him. 'You *will* help Sir Edmund?' he asked.

'I have much Royal Society and City business to attend to,' Hooke complained. 'I fear my affairs press too much.'

'These murders are a City business, Robert, and, by the curious nature of them, they are Royal Society business too. I could make it my business and command you.'

'Perhaps Harry and I may share the work. You have seen his capacities already.'

The King looked visibly relieved at what he took to be the overcoming of Hooke's resistance. 'And what of the mysterious document left on this boy? The use of a cipher gives it the complexion of a philosophical matter. This must appeal to you, Robert. Hmm? You know the system, for it was a cipher used in the Wars, by Parliament. The Colonel has shown you the way. You simply need to find its keyword.'

'Harry, are you willing to renew your efforts with the cipher? You will need to take back your copy from Sir Edmund.'

'I will not, Mr. Hooke. I made another.'

The sound of the King's laughter filled the cellar room. 'He *is* his own man, is he not, Robert!' He clapped his hands together, and gave Harry a satirical bow. 'Harry, I have known you not yet a day, and you have impressed me more than most men in a year. I shall be thankful for a speedy translation. Bring it directly to me, and we will then inform the Justice.'

'You are happy to do so?' Hooke asked Harry.

Harry admired the way Hooke had made great play of resistance, eventual acceptance, then swift delegation.

His own curiosity, and the wishes of his King, made his decision an easy one.

'It shall please me to help, Your Majesty, as far as my capacities allow.'

They left the cellar room, and the boy in the glass, locked up the doors behind them, and walked back out to the quadrangle. The King, sweeping his hat on as an exaggerated goodbye, climbed into his coach.

'The King guesses at the identity of the boys,' Harry said, as the coach pulled out of the College. 'He said, *keep this boy here, where he is safest, until those who know him best may identify him.* Sir Jonas knows more, too. And the King wants first look at the cipher.'

Hooke's eyes closed as if his improved lamp shone into them. He shrugged, then nodded his head. A mixture of signals.

He linked his arm with Harry's, and together they walked back to his lodgings.

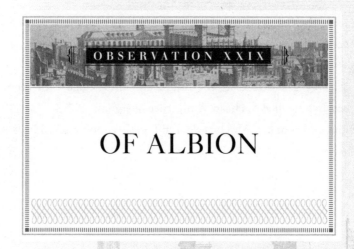

OBSERVATION XXIX

OF ALBION

COLONEL MICHAEL FIELDS KNEW WHAT IT was to taste the earth, and to have its coldness pierce the marrow of his bones. To feel the fear as a cannonball flew, furrowed the terrain, searched greedily for its victim. To grasp a knife as it vanished into another man's flesh, as if the spirit of the blade led the hand, hitting rib but sliding on, through tight muscle into lung.

He knew what it was to watch the light become dull in another man's eye—the tightest contract of all.

What did these men know of life lived rawly?

Under the Gatehouse at Lincoln's Inn, his bald, liver-spotted head on thick neck slowed almost imperceptibly. Decision made, his momentum resumed.

These solicitors drew things out. Every argument had its equal and opposite. Every statement led to a hundred more. They punned in Latin, and laughed at their own cleverness, enjoying the fruits of expensive education.

He did not despise them, for they were men like himself, but he would not accept the system they represented. They were the progression from Norman law—an inhumane justice, an imposition on the common run of humanity.

He desired the universal adoption of the English tongue, to give back the law to the people it should serve.

Michael Fields stemmed from Albion.

He had lied to Hooke's man, Hunt, from the Royal Society—so careless of the story enveloping him—when he asked about Moses Creed. He rubbed at the scar on his forearm, a lump of pale senseless skin where the pipe was inserted. Blood-brothers. All had willingly agreed to their covenant. They followed the same teachings, the same men: Overton, Walwyn and Lilburne, whose words had wrought such change in them.

Fields had experienced the void within him filled as he listened to the Levellers' creed. The sovereignty of the people stood as their aim: government by agreement of a people equal under God, men and women, all to enjoy the fruits of their equality.

Tens of thousands of Londoners had signed the Leveller petitions. Forty thousand signatures for the Large Petition alone. Ten thousand had signed a female-only petition, the Humble Petition of Diverse Affected Women. Solidarity had spread through the population with the speed of an infection. A glorious, life-affirming epidemic passed from one to another by mouth, by the Word.

He saw the sign showing the way to Moses Creed's office. He snorted derisively at the solicitors walking the corridors and clattering down the stairs, carrying their bundles of documents. His scorn alarmed one or two, but those practising close to Creed knew his visitors tended towards a different cut.

Fields had been glad to receive the Royal Society man's visit. It had re-awoken his passion for the Good Old Cause.

The Red Cipher, used again, was the signal.

He jogged up the irregular flights of stairs, but slowed towards the top. He had forgotten he no longer owned a young man's lungs. Breathing heavily, he reached the solicitor's door.

It opened immediately.

'Yes?' the solicitor asked, suspicious. This man looked to be a villain. Such was his lot.

'You are Mr. Moses Creed?' gasped the villain.

'I am. You are?'

'Fields.' It seemed Creed had met his match in brevity of introductions until the Colonel continued.

'I met you when you were a child, Mr. Creed—I knew your parents well. I am happy at last to meet the man.'

'And what is it I may do for you, Sir?' A muted recall stirred in the solicitor's mind.

'Your father, Reuben, often spoke of you—and of his love for you—when we served together in the Wars. His separation from you caused him pain. Your mother, Abigail, too, spoke of you, loving you as much.'

Creed realised water had gathered across the rims of his eyes. He blinked it away and swallowed.

Seeing his distress, Fields embraced him, pulling him tightly to his chest. Creed found the smell of his old campaign coat—leather, sweat, grease, and tobacco—comforting. It reminded him of childhood.

'And I tell you what you may do for me, Moses. Listen to the how—and the why—your father died.'

OBSERVATION XXX

OF

CORRESPONDENCE

LET THEM TAKE THE PAPERS. WHAT were they now to her? His correspondences *were* her husband. Her Henry. In them he lived on, but they
were worthless if not with the Royal Society. He had lived for the Society,
and, for all she knew, had died for it as well. Let them have them and glean
from them what meaning they could. Through Robert Hooke, and this boy
with him, through their learning, Henry's work would continue . . .

Hooke and Harry took care not to disturb Dora Katherina's thoughts,
not attempting any meaningful conversation. Both felt dispirited, affected
by the melancholy of the evening, and chilled to the bone. The fire in
Henry Oldenburg's study was empty. The rain hitting the roof above them,
slapping on the tiles and smacking onto the ground outside, made it difficult to hear, so little was said between them all.

Dora Katherina passed Hooke a small silver key, saying nothing, only a last token gesture of reluctance—a little pull back—as she let it go. They listened to her go down to the warmth of her living room.

The two men stood together silently, looking at the chair in which they had found the Secretary, its back suspiciously stained. Their cleaning would not have been enough if anyone had looked for signs of violence. Was there still a faintest of smells from the discharge of the pistol? The senses could deceive. You would never notice if you did not know it was fired, Harry decided.

Harry inspected Oldenburg's small library, scanning the books, three hundred or so, observing only what he would expect in such a man's collection. Philosophical, mathematical, theological, historical and political. They would not take long to catalogue.

Hooke held up the key. 'Let us delay no further.'

They went to the chest and Hooke offered the key to the lock. The mechanism, old and worn, released after an indirect twist rather than a turn.

Harry lifted the lid, revealing the chest to be full of paper. Hundreds of letters sent from all around the globe. In different hands, time and again, Henry Oldenburg's name presented itself, broken seals showing the marks of their senders. Some bore the scars of their journeys. Crumpled, torn, or stained by saltwater. Others looked much as they did when first folded. Some showed spots of ironmould, indicating old communications. Oldenburg's own, too, the duplicates of letters sent, were stored in the chest.

All of them to be read through, catalogued, and placed with the collection at Gresham's College. Unlike the cataloguing of Oldenburg's library, this was days and days of work. Harry mentally sized the task ahead, guessing at its time of completion.

'Grubendol was an industrious soul,' Hooke observed. 'I say that for him.'

Harry pulled at the first layer of bundles, imagining the miles of ink in Oldenburg's chest, and the roods of paper—acres, even—and all the hours the Secretary must have spent sitting in this room, spinning out replies and their copies, no sooner one reply completed than another one demanding response.

Unfolding the first few to hand, he saw the places they had come from: one from Antwerp, another from Buda, a third from Lyon. A fourth, whose reply must have taken the best part of a year to reach its destination, came from Vera Cruz.

I have never left London since I came in as a boy, he thought, stroking the texture of the far-travelled papers.

'It would be best to sort them here, and list the chest's contents,' Hooke told him. 'Then, we can make Dora Katherina a receipt for them.' Hooke's voice went quieter. 'Also, we keep curious eyes away from these letters while we search them.'

'What do you hope to find, Mr. Hooke?' Harry had to raise his voice over a crescendo of rain, thrown by the wind, battering the roof and the windows. Hooke waited for it to ease before he answered.

'I wish to peruse the letters from Huygens regarding my mechanism for the watch, and those from Mr. Newton, in the dispute over the motions of heavenly bodies. I never believed Grubendol behaved straightforwardly in these matters. Be vigilant when you read these letters, Harry. I return now to Gresham's. I leave you my lamp—it will be dark soon. Toil not for too long. After the rigours of these past few days, you look as though you need some rest. And besides, you have the cipher to work at.'

As Hooke's footsteps sounded his departure, Harry sensed the oncoming silence as a physical thing filling the room, as if the æther pressed harder on his eardrums. He stood by Oldenburg's armchair, resting his hand on its back. A sharp loneliness, as biting as the cold, made him feel an unfamiliar ache in his core.

He crossed the study to its window overlooking St. James's Park. From this vantage point he could view the road to Chelsea, where the boy at the Physic Garden was left. He could also see the buildings of Whitehall, where he had spoken with the King, and towards Hartshorne Lane, although rooftops hid Sir Edmund's house from view.

London was a city of views, and of windows looking out at them, their lines of sight criss-crossing like the system of nerves in the body. Could nothing be done in London that was not also seen? Was it possible to walk unobserved through its streets, to keep one's business hidden? Who knew he was here today, other than Robert Hooke and Dora Katherina? Who watched him, to check on his progress—or to hinder it?

These ideas of being observed—since seeing the King on the coin—were intruding too much on his usual flow of thoughts. He warned himself against them. Delusions of persecution were like an infection.

He withdrew a small book from his pocket to begin his cataloguing. He sat in Oldenburg's chair—not the armchair where the Secretary had last rested, but the one at the desk, looking like a captain's chair on a ship. This was how Oldenburg must have sat, able to reach his shelves of books, to stretch to the chest to open it and store his correspondences, all without leaving this desk.

He took one of Oldenburg's pens—a new one, not wanting to disturb one Oldenburg had used—and sharpened it with Oldenburg's knife. He wrote headings into his book: number, sender, place of origin, date of letter, subject, date of reply, matters arising, and a column to reference other correspondence. He left room for more columns should he need them.

He pulled out a first handful of letters from the chest, to open, appraise, and record their contents. He noted the senders, seeing Spinoza, Newton, Leibniz, Boyle, Huygens, Flamsteed, Malpighi, Leeuwenhoek, and Wallis. With the reading of them, and cataloguing them, three hours soon passed before he returned to the chest.

LOOKING INTO IT, he saw the corner of a darker, larger bundle, through a gap between the letters resting on it. Intrigued by its appearance, he pushed these to one side to uncover it.

It was a large package wrapped in grubby sailcloth, roughly stitched to secure it, and oiled to seal it against weather. Wrapped on a diagonal, the points of the cloth came together at the centre of its uppermost face. The stitches were further sealed, an unsteady wax line following their pattern.

Looking at it closely, Harry saw that originally the cloth had been neatly stitched. Opened, then sewn again, more approximately. More hastily, maybe. Did the old man Henry Oldenburg close it up again? His unsteady hands could be the reason for the waywardness of the wax lines.

Harry lifted the package out from the chest. It was weighty. He put it on the desk and studied it. Running his fingers over its edges and corners, he could feel the bumps of knots under the sailcloth. Papers tied into sheaves with string.

A letter, sewn into the fabric. He broke the wax, a bright scarlet colour, bearing Oldenburg's seal, and unfolded the paper.

The Eminent Mr. Robert Hooke
To be sent 1st Janry. 1678.

It was the Secretary's handwriting. But Henry Oldenburg had not released it to Hooke.

Instead, he had put it in this chest and fired a lead ball into his head.

Under the scarlet wax Oldenburg had poured was a smaller patch of black wax, which Harry exposed by patiently scraping away Oldenburg's seal.

It had the symbol of a candle and its flame.

A growing unease, like a vibration from the earth, went through him.

How were the bodies of three boys, the Justice of Peace, Catholic plotters, the suicide of Henry Oldenburg, an old soldier, the Red Cipher, two ladies dressed in sea green, Sir Jonas Moore, and the King all conjoined? What were the links in the chain, and from where did it hang?

Within this package might be the answers.

He was reluctant to break into it. It had no postmark. He could understand why the sender had not relied on the Post Office to send it to Oldenburg: such a package would draw attention to itself. The Lord High

Treasurer Danby's spies would assiduously untie it, break its seals, read its contents, and then reseal it. Only the closest inspection would reveal they had ever tampered with it.

Or else, everybody named in it would find themselves arrested.

Harry considered if he should take it straight to Hooke, as Oldenburg had not. Was he obliged to do so? He was there to catalogue the Secretary's papers. He would not be returning the other letters in this chest to their senders.

He decided to open it up, using the small knife to help him, separating strings from wax, letting loose the bundles of papers within.

A letter, in Oldenburg's untidy hand, was uppermost. He had written it on the morning of his death.

> *Pall Mall 1st Janry 1677/78*
> *Mr. Robert Hooke,*
>   *I, Henry Oldenburg Secretary of the Royal Society of London for the Improving of Natural Knowledge, doe give unto you our esteemed Curator and Honoured Friend this quantity of papers.*
>   *This creature is fallen from what he was, miserabilis homuncio, so I doe give over the Enterprize of their decypherment.*
>   *The sin of our first parent, Adam, in eating of the forbidden Fruit from whence proceeded all Eternal punishments, is the cause of all our Miseries. His Disobedience and Pride are mine also. I can no longer continue with it, nor can I destroy the Endeavour of such a Man who saw so far. By leaving them for you Mr. Hooke, I follow the wishes of the Writer of these works.*
>   *I am at the end of my Useful life. I am desirous that some Use be made of these, by that Man who is the wisest of all in that Solomon's House, the Royal Society.*
>   *I am, for little Time longer,*
>   *Henry Oldenburg*

Flicking through the bundles of paper in the package, Harry recognised the same grids, twelve numbers by twelve, as the Red Cipher.

An extraordinarily neat hand. The numbers so regular, it seemed impossible a human hand could have created them.

Harry left them still tied, reread Oldenburg's words, and spent some while more thinking what best to do.

Judgment reached, he reassembled it, placing its different parts meticulously as he had found them, tied it with some of Oldenburg's string, locked up the chest, and said his goodbyes to Dora Katherina.

With the package concealed in the pocket inside his coat, he headed unwillingly off, leaning into the fierce rain.

It was time to meet with Enoch Wolfe.

It was not the weather making him hesitant. The thought of going to Alsatia, at night, filled him with fear.

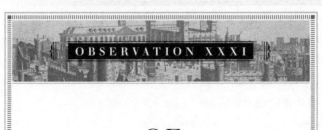

OF NOCTURNAL CREATURES

THE ANGEL CREAKED ON HIS CHAINS, his sign swinging in the wind. Rain sprayed onto him, gathered along the bottom of the board, and fell as a stream on the rough and muddy pavement.

Harry had avoided trouble, mindful to keep his head down, as he walked through Alsatia. Some men had shouted after him but he had ignored them, and they did not pursue. They threw something, but wildly, and he did not turn.

He peered in through the window of the Angel coffeehouse, rubbing at the wet glass with his sleeve. His note, he saw, had gone, leaving a gap among all the cards and papers. Hopefully, Enoch Wolfe had not forgotten, and would be there to meet him.

Inside, Tobias Turner, the proprietor of the coffeehouse, sat alone smoking his pipe in one of the booths, reading a pamphlet by the light of a candle.

Harry backed away from the window, avoiding the sign's cascade even though rainwater already soaked inside his collar, and went towards the door. He readied himself to disturb the proprietor. The man was brusque—Harry could imagine his displeasure at having his reading interrupted.

He extinguished Hooke's bright lamp from consideration, not wanting to blind the man at his door.

As Harry raised his hand to knock, he heard the rattle of a coach's wheel bands, iron on cobbles.

Harry turned at the sound. A coach-and-four, moving steadily up the lane towards him, a lantern hanging next to the driver lighting its way. It was glossy black, its surfaces silvery in the rain.

As he craned forwards to see more clearly the driver, a man huddled in a goatskin coat, the coach slowed and came to a halt. Its wood, leather, and iron all made their individual groans and grumbles. The coach's door was exactly opposite Harry, as if waiting for him to step in. Its window was perforated tin.

The driver made no movement in his seat. Although they were now quite close, and shared a soaking from the weather, there was no nod of acknowledgement from him. He stared in front of him, reins held loosely between thick fingers.

The attitude of the man, his silence and indifference as he waited—for what?—made Harry catch his breath. The driver was small but strong-look-ing, older than he had first appeared, with a whey-coloured face his lantern could not impart colour to.

Harry thought he recognised him, but it was more the coat he remem-bered. From the Crown Tavern, its wearer talking to the serving girl.

There was a click, the door of the coach swung open, and another man appeared from its interior. Harry glimpsed him as he walked, abnormally smoothly, through the lanternlight.

The man had a flat plane of bone at the top of his nose, the curious shape of his skull pushing his eyes wide apart. One long brow stretched over his forehead. He wore French bucket boots and an officer's coat.

The driver jumped from his seat, taking down the lantern and a grappling hook attached to a long length of rope.

Inside the Angel, Turner snuffed his candle out, turning the window into a mirror. The darkness inside threw a broken picture of the street onto the windowpanes, reflecting between the notices wedged against them.

Harry turned to the disappearance of the light and saw the reversed image of the man from inside the coach. He was being stared at. The man's gaze held his, challenging him to turn. Harry could not. Instead, he stood transfixed to the flat show of events behind him. He could feel his tongue sticking to the roof of his mouth. His limbs were heavy, as if the blood in them had doubled.

He could not take his eyes away from the man's peculiar face.

After a long moment, the man turned away with a contemptuous air that made Harry feel dismissed as only trivial. He disappeared down the narrow alley between the Angel and a warehouse. The driver in the goatskin coat followed him, vanishing just as rapidly from view.

Harry turned from the window and allowed himself to take normal breaths.

'Who are those men?' he said out loud.

'Too many strangers in Alsatia,' a deep voice slurred, spreading fumes of strong drink.

Harry turned to see he was being studied through one natural eye, belonging to a tall African. A patch with an eye painted on it covered the other, a crude copy drawing notice to the loss instead of concealing it.

The man fumed over Harry again, and sloped off, antagonism apparent in his stiff-legged stride.

Shivering, Harry wiped the rain from his face and hair. He took a deep breath and crossed to the coach. Its horses waited patiently in the road, untethered. They stood obediently for the driver's return.

He inspected the vehicle, walking around it. He pulled open the door. The coach was empty, with only the bare furniture of its interior.

He looked along the alleyway for the two men, but there was no sign of them.

Back at the window of the Angel, he tried to discern any movement inside. No sign, either, of the proprietor.

He tried the door of the coffeehouse, finding it locked against him.

He walked into the dark alley. There was no way into the Angel from the side of it, no doorway or low window. There was only another ominous alley behind. He took a few uncertain steps into the blackness. He could distinguish nothing, and there was nothing he could hear.

He could not understand how the men had got inside.

He would leave the questioning of Enoch Wolfe until the daytime. He walked no further into the forbidding nothingness in front of him, but turned back on himself, hurrying at a trot to the lane.

⌒

'HENRY HUNT!'

The front door of the Angel was open, and Harry saw the proprietor, Turner, beckoning him urgently.

'You will not see Enoch Wolfe now.'

'You said he would meet me.'

'Others come for him.'

'Who are they?'

'Who are you, to pose such questions? You would be wise to fear them.'

'Wolfe is not the simple eel fisher I first took him to be.'

'Eel fisher?' Turner laughed drily.

A loud smashing of glass from way up above them cut his mirth short. From upstairs came the sound of running. Someone at the top of the house.

The two men stayed still in the doorway for a moment. Turner was first to react. He walked cautiously towards the noise, going back inside his coffeehouse, pushing Harry out of the way.

After a longer moment of indecision, Harry followed him, stumbling in the darkness up the narrow stairs.

A loud creak above stopped them both.

On the stairs they could see nothing. Harry could not even discern Turner's back, although he was less than an arm's reach away. Harry's heart thumped as he listened, and his ears probed the gloom for the tiniest sound: a boot, or the scrape of a weapon.

From downstairs there was a bang as the front door blew shut. Both men froze, until, ahead, Harry sensed Turner take a cautious step up. He followed, ordering his unwilling feet to move.

They could hear a man's sobbing. It came from an attic room, another flight of stairs above them. They went slowly, warily, Harry close behind Turner, upwards to the top of the house.

On the last steps, under their boots, they felt the crunch of broken glass.

As they reached the upper landing, where the frame and glass of a small window lay scattered over the bare floorboards, there was a scream—high-pitched like the squeal of a boar—from inside one of the rooms.

From below them there came another noise, a loud impact, and another, then something broke open the front door.

They had two choices: to carry on up, or to return downstairs. Harry thought of a third: to stay just where he was.

Again, Turner acted first, deciding to push open the door to the room with the sound coming from it.

Harry followed, unwilling to be left alone in the darkness.

Against the bedroom's window, he could make out the silhouettes of three men. One was perfectly still, despite the thrashing of the man he held.

Behind them came the sound of feet thumping up the wooden staircase, and Sir Edmund Bury Godfrey's lantern swung into the room, the Justice holding onto it grimly.

His light showed the man with the single eyebrow holding Enoch Wolfe the eel fisher, who wore a suit and had a metal shield over his nose. The man gripped Wolfe's neck, holding him up off the floor, his arms outstretched to avoid Wolfe's frantically kicking feet. The man's grip was so tight Wolfe could only emit gagging noises.

The driver of the coach—the wearer of the goatskin coat—stood with his arms folded, with his eyes locked solely on Harry's. He ignored Turner and Sir Edmund, and the murder being carried out beside him. He had a benign expression, as if giving Harry a gift. This look shocked Harry as much as the sight of Wolfe being held by his neck.

They seemed to be doing this for him.

For the first time, the man holding Wolfe made a move, bending his head forwards. They heard a bubbling sound, and the rasp of air escaping from a ripped throat.

Wolfe's kicks slowed, and he quietened. He slackened, and became limp.

The coach driver still stared only at Harry. Wolfe's killer, too, stared at him.

The murderer dropped the body and spat out Wolfe's Adam's apple. The lump fell to the floor and rolled towards them.

There was blood on his lips and chin. He produced a handkerchief, and fastidiously wiped it away. Still, he stared at Harry.

His face was so blank it chilled Harry, Turner, and Sir Edmund equally.

The Justice turned and ran. Harry and Turner took an astonished look at each other, then chased after him, following back down the stairs. Sir Edmund's lantern swung wildly in front of them, making each step seem to veer crazily beneath them.

Sir Edmund charged out through the broken door of the coffeehouse, making strange mewling sounds as he went.

Harry slipped, crashing to the bottom of the stairs, his back hitting each tread as he fell. The wall abruptly halted his descent. He slumped to the floor, groaning. Behind him, Turner grabbed him to lift him, and thrust him through the exit from the back of the Angel, into a muddy yard with some chicken coops.

'Go on! Over the wall. Keep on up the hill. A path follows the back of this row.'

'Was that Enoch Wolfe?' Harry asked him, disbelievingly. Smartly dressed, and with the noseguard, the man had looked quite different.

'He feared for his life! That is why he wished to meet with you.'

'Who killed him?'

'You saw! A monster! He seeks his son, the Devil-boy!'

Turner's face was wild, his eyes black holes in white circles. He raced away, going off in the opposite direction, leaving Harry alone to fend for himself.

Harry managed to get over the top of the wall, sliding down the other side. He staggered on the uneven ground, pain shooting up his shins. He cried out, but immediately stifled his noise, frightened the killer would hear him.

A dog barked, a high-pitched yapping. Harry crawled away from it, hoping someone had tethered the animal, trying to ignore the hurt in his shins and at the base of his spine. He bumped into a rickety framework of planking, some kind of fence or shelter, and caught his coat on a nail. The leather pulled him, and he tripped, landing on his back again.

The rain had stopped while he had been inside the Angel. The clouds were parting, and some dim moonlight reached through a gap between them. Harry stayed for a moment where he was, looking up at the sky, for the air had left his lungs, and also for the comfort of seeing the moon, familiar and soothing amid the savagery of Alsatia.

The murder he had witnessed, and the sight of the Justice fleeing instead of trying to intervene—Sir Edmund had not even drawn his sword—left Harry numb, and unable to think. His mind could only manage to picture the lump rolling on the floor, and the coach driver's eyes, fixed on his.

The dog's barking quietened. Harry could hear no other sounds. His fear, and his trembling that came with it, began to subside. He picked himself up cautiously and made a laboured way along the narrow path, as fast as he could despite his injuries, desperate to put distance between him and the nightmare behind. His own footsteps seemed unnatural to him, not knowing where the next step would send him on the stony ground.

He went through Alsatia, back towards the safety of Holborn Bridge. All the way, he listened out for the sound of coach wheels on cobbles.

Only once he was there, well away from the Angel, walking on the main thoroughfare, did he relight Hooke's lamp.

OBSERVATION XXXII

OF A WITCH

THE BROWNS AND REDS AND GREENS of the covers of all the books, with the glittering golds of those with titles on their spines, made it seem a splendid autumn day in the library. The curtains were drawn back, and bright morning light poured in. Despite this, candles burned everywhere about the room.

Pierre Lefèvre noticed John Locke studying him quizzically, and stared back. It was Locke who cut the invisible lines joining them, made uncomfortable by the man's intensity. Also, Locke saw it as an unwinnable game, and therefore unproductive.

Lefèvre transferred his stare to the mechanical scribe's, no sign of his minor victory discernible. He seemed to find succour from the machine's refusal to give way.

Locke reached for a copy of Hobbes's *Leviathan*, describing the relationship between the multitude and its representative sovereign. He thumbed through the book, leaning with an angular elbow against its shelf, reading of the State of Nature.

For Hobbes, the State of Nature presented only fear. In it, people lived solitary lives, with selfishness forced on them. They lived in a constant State of War, since no one had force enough to impose their rule over others. Giving such power to a sovereign was a bastion against this fear.

Locke's was a more heavenly view. Surely the State of Nature was one of goodwill, where people had lived together in peace, assisting one another? They lived in liberty, to live as they saw fit. Not free to do as they pleased, though, since if all are equal, they must abide by laws which maintain their equality.

The purpose of government, therefore, was to protect the natural rights of the people, as enjoyed in the State of Nature. If it did not do so, it could not have legitimacy. A sovereign without equality as their aim was contrary to natural law.

A magistrate is given a sword to protect the people he serves, not to use against them.

Other than the turning of pages and the occasional cough or tut of disagreement from Locke, the library was quiet. No sounds reached them from outside, or from the rest of the house. The books insulated the room, their great weight of pages pressed together between their covers, some extending two feet from the walls.

A door set into the bookshelves opened behind them. They saw the long, jowled face of the Earl of Shaftesbury.

Behind him was Locke's elaboratory. A great glass-fronted cabinet, reaching almost to the ceiling, stored his knickknackatory, the objects of interest collected on his travels. Much of his equipment was still covered by dust sheets, as he had left it before travelling in France. After his return to Thanet House, Locke had not yet had the chance to use it, with all his coaching of Titus Oates. His work to find a method of breathing underwater had been interrupted. He wanted to return to his meteorology, too. He had recently taken delivery of one of Hooke's self-recording weather clocks, and was eager to use it.

Quietly, Shaftesbury shut the elaboratory door behind him. He was without his peruke and there was a distance in his eyes. After a massage with oils and a smoke of opium and tobacco, Shaftesbury felt more at ease with himself, the hole in his side unusually painless.

Lefèvre glided to the window and pulled at the long curtains, closing the gap between them. The motes of dust disappeared as the shaft of daylight did, and candlelight regained supremacy in the room.

Shaftesbury, nodding his thanks, indicated to them where to sit. Lefèvre appeared magically in his chair. Locke closed *Leviathan* and brought out his notebook, anticipating more elements to the plot.

'John. Monsieur Lefèvre. I have excellent news, news to assist my design. I have learned from my man Smith, who lurks about Whitehall, that the Duchess of York's Secretary, Edward Coleman, has sent communications to the French, begging for their aids and assistances. If she is to be our Queen—if her husband inherits—this is fine ammunition against her.'

Locke rested his chin on the edge of his notebook. 'We manufacture meetings between Coleman and Oates, place him at our imagined Consult, and we have first proof of plottings against the King from one close to him.'

'Coleman seeks money only, but it is as damning. The false wrapped entirely in the real, and all delivered as one.'

'We may send Coleman promises from friendly parties that they will reward his efforts. These alone will hang him.' Locke said these words as if to test Shaftesbury's will. Although he knew full well if the plot gathered more momentum, Coleman's death would not unduly worry the Earl.

'Write them,' Shaftesbury commanded.

Locke nodded. 'And I shall brief Oates.'

'I have more for our Articles, too. I desire Oates to swear he overheard of the firing of Southwark and Limehouse Hole by Jesuits, and to have seen plans to set afire Wapping and Westminster. And plans to slit one hundred thousand throats in London—how the Catholics would go about it. Reminisce of the St. Bartholomew's day massacre. Remember fondly Catherine de Medici. Hark back to the Gunpowder Plot. All as bloodthirsty as you wish.'

Shaftesbury closed his eyes, apparently drifting to sleep. The other two waited for him to stir. Eventually, his eyes still closed, he spoke.

'Monsieur Lefèvre, thank you. Henry Hunt will now steer clear. Sir Edmund Bury Godfrey, too, it sounds, was unmanned. You may concentrate on your assignment to kill the King.'

He turned to Locke. 'But still, we do not have our boy.'

'Still, we cannot find the Witch,' Locke replied. 'He has concealed himself, or else he has left London. All our intelligencers search for him. Aires wears out the wheels of your coach in gathering their reports. For now, the boy is safe at Gresham's.'

'You know, if the Witch is not to be found, should we look instead to Robert Hooke? Would he agree to help us?'

'Too faint-hearted, I think. Although, there are means to encourage him.' Locke sneaked a look at Lefèvre.

'There is another alternative, of course, who I believe owns the necessary artfulness.' Shaftesbury looked searchingly at Locke, but his Secretary was only prepared to offer him an equivocal shrug.

Shaftesbury sighed. 'Tomorrow, then, after Oates and Tonge have met with the King.'

He left Locke and Lefèvre in the library, bidding them both a curt goodbye.

Locke watched him go, wondering if the news of Edward Coleman would play out as the Earl thought.

Lefèvre was back by the automaton.

'Do you think he listens to us?' he asked Locke, staring at it.

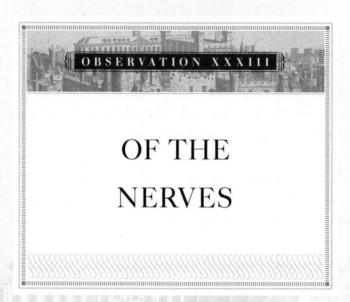

OF THE
NERVES

THE BRIGHT SICKENING COLOUR OF ENOCH Wolfe's blood. And the blood drained from the boys. The Red Cipher returned. Titus Oates and Israel Tonge, and their stories of London overthrown.

Sir Edmund had spent the night wandering the streets of London, a distracted figure, his heart sick and his head full of Catholic murder. He had ended up east, past Blackwall, and the route he had taken was mazy. He doubted he could repeat it.

Again, he saw the gristle from Wolfe's throat, rolling—repulsive—across the room.

The killing of Wolfe so brutally showed the menace of the Jesuits.

He was sickened by his own cowardice, too. He should have tried to prevent the murder. Instead, he had frozen, then he had run. There was no mitigating his shame in pretence he could have done nothing, being out of his jurisdiction in the Liberty of Alsatia. His moral duty to stop the monster overruled that.

But the monster's stillness had been satanic.

The monster, and the boys at Barking Creek, the Fleet, and the Westbourne were portents of a hellish conscience.

Everywhere, he heard the rumours. They showed Catholic malfeasance beyond any sensible doubt. Listening to more of the secrets of the plot laid out before him by Oates and Tonge, like a landscape revealing itself from the crest of a high hill, Sir Edmund knew they proved his suspicions to be true.

Why this papist need for blood?

Jews were accused of taking human blood to bake their matzo bread, although he did not believe it. The few Jews in London, allowed back in Cromwell's time, were respectable and eager to assimilate. And besides, such use of blood was against their teachings.

In the papist travesty of the Eucharist prayer, bread and wine are changed into the body and blood of Christ. Sir Edmund did not believe in transubstantiation, and would never believe it. He had robustly dismissed this superstition at many a dinner—it meant a Catholic must piss the blood of Christ back out. And what about the wafer? Such false notions could only sensibly be dismissed.

The wine retained the appearance of wine, though, even after its transformation. Was blood being drained from boys for some new Jesuitical rite?

He wiped some spray from his face and stared at the waterman taking him to Hartshorne Lane stairs, to gauge if he sensed his timidity. Prudently, the man avoided his look. The Justice took comfort from the waterman's blatant existence, and his vigorous arms pulling at the oars of the wherry.

The reappearance of the Red Cipher had been a hard blow. With the King's life in danger, he must be resolute—but the pressure in his skull felt as if the gold band around his hat contracted.

An idea struck him, and it chilled his heart.

Robert Hooke took the blood from these boys.

Hooke's skills were obvious, his knowledge was prodigious, and he had the air-pump. And what of his assistant, Hunt, also proficient with the apparatus? Did they work together?

Hooke and Hunt had told him they were done with the search. Hooke had told him by letter, and Hunt had told him face to face.

Hooke wanted no part in the leftovers from the Civil Wars. Even at the King's command, his uneasiness had been obvious to all.

Henry Hunt was duplicitous throughout. He had admitted as much at the Palace.

Was Gresham's College the place he should search, as the heart of this wicked enterprise?

He had sought aid from the very last people in London he should have! How foolishly he had trusted them, holding too much regard for Hooke's reputation about the town.

No, no, it made no sense.

In the absence of certitude, his mind assailed by doubts, he allowed fantastical thoughts.

Go back to the very beginning, start again . . .

Sir Edmund had wavered between whole-hearted trust and deep-seated suspicion since he had met the pair. He wished he knew their true colours.

He, though, had kept much from them, and could not expect openness in return.

Only Titus Oates and Israel Tonge sought to help him freely.

They told him of Jesuits secretly armed, ready for rebellion. The Catholic powers abroad gladly aided such a coup. Had there not been incendiarism enough to convince? Southwark had seen such a fire. Another one recently at Limehouse Hole. How many other times had the lucky finding of fireballs, moments before their discharge, saved the Righteous?

There never came a rising from below. A river has its source from above. The Catholic nobility and gentry must have more careful checks put on them. The use of an air-pump to store the boy, the fine candles . . . All pointed to money. When the mob stirred, a Justice should look for those who gained by its anger. Those desiring profit would sponsor an irreligious uprising.

Perhaps even French King Louis had an interest.

Informed by the Angel's owner, Tobias Turner, of Enoch Wolfe's willingness to meet with Hunt, he had gone to Alsatia too, having his own questions to put. He had seen Shaftesbury's man, Uriel Aires—well known to him—driving Shaftesbury's black coach-and-four, and that beast with one long eyebrow emerging from the coach.

So, whatever purpose the Jesuit conspirators kept it for, the Earl of Shaftesbury procured the blood for them. Even from inside the Tower, the Earl had arranged it. With all his suspicions though, Sir Edmund knew he had no evidence against him. He would need the King's authority to question such a man.

Yet Shaftesbury hated the Catholics, missing no opportunity to stir opinion against them.

Wolfe had discovered the boy at the Fleet. It was too coincidental he was slaughtered.

These worries gnawed at Sir Edmund: contradictory, incoherent. Enlarging within the great spaces of his imagination, growing ever fatter as he became more fearful.

He took off his hat and cradled his head in his hand, stroking his temples to quieten his mind. He could feel his thoughts unravelling. His reason, the tool of his trade, was overstretched, through confusion, through lack of direction. He had to regain control of himself, and on his investigation, or else it would undo him.

Everywhere he looked he saw only problems, questions, transgression, delinquency, conspiracy.

He tried to believe Hooke's story of being summoned to the Fleet by a messenger, but what if Hooke himself was the anatomiser? The murderer of boys?

Hooke had been there because he left the boy . . . Did Hooke and Shaftesbury work together? Shaftesbury had the money for the enterprise. Did Hooke's assistant, Hunt, manufacture the story of prints left by snowshoes, to divert his thoughts away from their own experiments?

They performed many strange trials at Gresham's College.

Think of the doors leading off from the long corridor down in the cellars, behind them vast containers of blood, great glass globes full of broken infants, their eyes moving in ghastly agony. Conduits—tubes made of pig guts or some such material—leading from one boy to another, blood coursing through them. A repugnant peristalsis. All of them swaying and swelling under the impulse of blood pumped through them, their hands outstretched, pleading for an end to their suffering . . .

Sir Edmund filled with dread. The sentiment diffused through him like black ink dripped into water.

Stop with these thoughts, Edmund, stop with them.

THE WHERRY REACHED the turn at Westminster, where the river flowing from the south swerved lazily east. Sir Edmund forced himself to think of something else, looking at London from this point on the river. The waterman saw the twitch on his face, the effort of will to do so.

The usual landmarks as he approached his home: the bell tower of St. Martin's, the four towers of Northumberland House, St. James's Park rising on the hill behind, the rows of trees along the line of its canal. He looked over the low buildings of his own coal and wood stores, as the wherry travelled against the water's flow to his own wharf at the end of Hartshorne Lane.

Did anyone wait for him here, or around a bend in an alley? Or behind a door—ready to fling it open into his face and stun him helpless, knock him to the ground?

He paid the waterman double the fare for the information he had learned of nothing untoward by his property, in this part of St. Martin-in-the-Fields. No rumours of a threat against him.

Sir Edmund climbed from the vessel and walked listlessly to his house, a long narrow building of red brick. He stayed to the middle of the roadway, looking left and right.

Hartshorne Lane, leading from the river to the Strand, was busy with people. Usually, he walked through them like a great flagship surrounded by its flotilla, impervious and separate from those around him, all motion and purpose. This morning, his face was pale, and his eyes darted everywhere. Those who saw him thought he looked as nervous as a cat in a kennel. He gripped the hilt of his rapier in its scabbard, the weapon poking out behind him from under his coat like the Devil's tail. They scurried away from him, keeping well clear, wondering what it was he expected.

They, too, had heard the rumours.

Many tiny alleys and courts led off from Hartshorne Lane. Sir Edmund looked down each of them, into every corner and hollow, behind every crate and box and cart, walking on the balls of his feet, ready to run. Whether towards or away, he had not decided. The early morning sunlight flung shadows across his path and sent bright stars into his vision. He squinted into the light, pulling for the shade afforded by the brim of his hat.

He walked about the outside of his house, trying to look in all directions at once. He stared up at the windows for the smallest sign of movement, checking no one skulked behind the low wall surrounding it, turning to see if anyone crept behind him.

Still watching around him, he went to his outbuildings, to ensure no one had tampered with the locks.

Long and squat, the store for his coal was strongly built, and secure for when he held the coal back, working with his allies at the Woodmongers' Company to keep the prices high. The dust dispersed over the ground and across the walls of the structure, the stained bricks surrounding the doorway looking as if an explosion had blasted black powder from inside.

He hefted the large door made of rough thick planking. Locked. No sign of being tried by a jemmy or blade.

The yard in which he kept his wood, with its stacks of planking kept apart on blocks to dry with the air moving freely around them, and sagging tarpaulins suspended over them to keep off the weather, afforded perfect cover for any Jesuit assassin. Here, the gloom cast by the tarpaulins was almost impenetrable.

Sir Edmund drew his sword, holding it in front of him, feeling his way into the shadows with its point. He circled each of the stacks, moving aside some timbers to reassure himself no one hid under them.

Nothing. He entered the narrow passageway to the side of the house.

More shadows. Damn this strong light. Away from Hartshorne Lane, only silence.

Who came after him, who taunted him with these signs, and infected his head with girlish nervousness? He would go indoors and check his weapons. He could at least defend himself while in his own home. He would stay there for a day. Try to rest. He was fraught. He had gunpowder, pistols, and muskets—enough to start his own insurrection, should he so choose.

Left in the gap between his front door and its frame was a letter with a black wax seal, impressed into it a design of a lit candle.

He slid the sword back into place on his belt.

Breaking the wax and pulling open the letter, he saw it had just one word written on it.

He unlocked the door leading into his house, and went through.

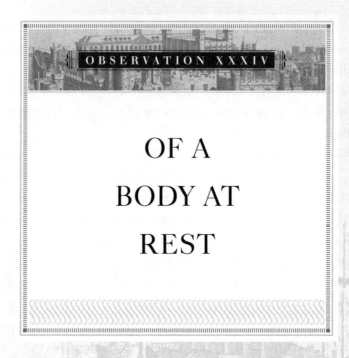

OBSERVATION XXXIV

OF A BODY AT REST

HARRY FIRST STIRRED WHEN THE BELLS of St. Ethelburga-the-Virgin sounded for the one o'clock service. He had missed the whole of the morning, sleeping on. No dreams had troubled him. He wondered if he even moved a limb.

He lay for a while in his bed, thinking of nothing.

When he sat up, the pain from his tailbone made him cry out. It brought back the memory of Alsatia. As if his mind worked to keep it from him, he had not thought of it.

He turned onto his belly, wriggled to the edge of the bed, and placed his feet on the floor. The weight through his shins reminded him he had fallen over a wall, after witnessing Enoch Wolfe's throat being bitten away.

Harry could see the monster's teeth, each one outlined by dark blood. The monster had stared at him as he held the struggling Wolfe. And the other man with him, the driver of the coach, had also stood and watched him.

Why had they not watched Turner? Or Sir Edmund, when he arrived? Why had they made no move towards them?

It was a show. They had been confident the killing of Wolfe would stun their audience. It had even worked on the Justice, who had been the first to run.

Or, more like, a ritual.

Reaching for the chamber pot from under his bed, Harry convulsively puked into it, until only a thread of thin liquid remained. His throat and nose burned from the taste, and he washed it away with some beer. He wiped his eyes with his sleeve, then reached for his spectacles.

He had slept in his breeches. Cautiously, he pulled them down to inspect his legs. One shin did not look too bad, a dark yellowy-green spreading down from his knee, and its skin was not broken. It did not feel too sore, either, although he would not want to bump it. The other shin, though, had turned black, the bruise from his fall following the line of sharp bone. He touched it and winced, pulling his hand away. He touched it again, more firmly. The pain of his press brought tears to his eyes, but he continued his finger along the length of the bone, seeking a notch or a line.

It did not seem to be broken. It looked spectacular, even worse than it felt. He had been lucky not to shatter it. His heel, too, was sore. He also had a cut in his hand from a stone, the congealed blood crusting it over.

He took the little mirror he kept by his bedside and used it to observe his coccyx. He pushed at it, each side. Not too damaged, just badly bruised.

He would rest today, he decided. As soon as he had settled on this decision, he heard a voice tell him: *Three boys are dead.*

He started, disquieted, and looked around his room, but no one was there.

It had been a man's voice. Not Hooke's, whose nasal tones he knew so well. An older man's voice. Not Sir Edmund's. Not Colonel Fields's. Not anyone's he could remember.

It was a voice from his imagination, he realised. The voice of his conscience. Maybe it was the voice of his older self. It had been so clear.

Three boys are dead.

Enoch Wolfe was also dead, murdered by a monster. A bestial man.

Why had Wolfe been killed? Had he been sent to collect the boy, as the size of his box of lampreys suggested? The girl riding on the man's shoulders in Alsatia had given him the idea: Wolfe carried the box to take the bloodless boy away from the Fleet, lampreys only covering its top.

Was Wolfe killed, then, because of his failure to take the boy from the Fleet?

Where was the boy to be taken?

To the monster? Did this monster kill the boys? Did he feed on their blood?

Was he the one who wrote on them, noting the days he took blood through the holes he had made? The wearer of the Eskimo snowshoes? The one who wrote out the Red Cipher in a letter left on the Fleet boy, and in a letter delivered to Robert Hooke?

Whoever drained the boys used expensive candles, presumably to provide light for the procedure. The coach carrying the monster had been expensive too. If Harry's notion was true—Hooke disagreed with it—that glass receivers of air-pumps preserved the boys, then this, too, required money.

But why were the boys not worked on in daytime, when there was plenty of light? Harry could not think further than only the night was possible, or convenient. Something ruled the daytime out, but what?

According to Sir Edmund, Catholics conspired against the King. The Justice had spoken of the threat at the Palace, having evidence from two men named Titus Oates and Israel Tonge. An armed insurrection, and the King's life in danger.

Was the preservation and experimentation on boys using air-pumps funded by Catholics?

Harry wondered if Sir Edmund had been right all along.

Did Oates and Tonge know of the blood taken from boys? The King had sent Sir Edmund to the Lord High Treasurer Danby, to examine their evidence. Harry supposed he would hear soon enough if it was true, for the news-sheets were full of papist insurgency, and would be quick to report new proofs.

A collection of aches, Harry hobbled to the table by the window, and the package from Oldenburg's chest.

What about the two in sea-green coats? Who were they? They had also looked for Enoch Wolfe in Alsatia, and taken the enciphered letter for Mr. Hooke to the solicitor, Moses Creed. Were they, as Felicity Tarripan had thought, ladies?

There were two possibles he could think of straightaway: he had watched them fencing at the Palace. Two ladies with swords, who dressed like men. This train of thought took him nowhere, although the Duchesse, he knew, was Catholic. Plenty of women dressed like men, if their work demanded it. Among the gentle class, though, it was rare. But Wolfe disguised himself as an eel fisher if occasion demanded, so identity could be changed at will.

They certainly had money enough for an elaboratory, air-pumps, and a fine coach. Did they sponsor these philosophical murders?

It was absurd. Ladies—a Duchesse and a Countess—would send servants to Alsatia for such a man as Wolfe.

The Countess was the King's daughter. The King himself experimented on the boys, as in the rumours spreading across London. In his Whitehall Palace elaboratory.

Stop with these thoughts, Harry, stop with them.

HE MUST KEEP to the maxim of the Royal Society: seek the truth from what is known, and what can be shown to be true.

What was the relationship between the boys? The connection between them?

All young, obviously. And innocent—Sir Edmund would take this to be a Catholic requirement.

Small—so they could be stored in glass receivers. Sir Edmund had agreed this meant a need for observation, otherwise glass would not be used.

When at the College of Physicians, they had not studied the boy found at Barking Creek closely enough. Harry needed to look at him again. When he visited there with the King, Mr. Hooke, and Sir Jonas, they had left the boy in the jar, and spoken generally of the search into the killings.

Sir Jonas had made his admission to the King. Harry also needed to question Sir Jonas. But what if Sir Jonas had no wish to be asked? Not even the King had known of his order to Sir Edmund to keep the boys preserved.

Harry sat tentatively down at his desk, positioning his coccyx over the back of its seat, and ran his hands over the package, feeling its rough sailcloth.

He knew he had to do something, even if he could not leave his lodgings. He could work at the cipher again, while he was sore.

The old soldier, Colonel Fields, had told him of the Red Cipher from the Civil Wars, and of the King's escape to France. The Colonel did not say—and Harry had not thought to ask—who else knew of the cipher, and who might use it, all these years after.

Fields might know of the monster, if he too used the Red Cipher.

The cipher, used again, left with the bodies of boys drained of their blood. Harry corrected himself: only with the boy at the Fleet. Was there something special about this one, particular boy? If so, then what set him apart from the others?

To guess at the cipher's keyword would be fruitless. Even if the word was English, that was still all English words to choose from. And there were many other languages it could be. It could be more than one word. It did not even have to be a word: it could be a collection of letters put together randomly. His chance of success was miniscule.

His mind still full of questions, Harry decided he would leave the package alone.

Instead, he took some smoothing paper, and used it to work on some wood he had, it not yet quite suiting the mechanism it housed. The repetitive action calmed him as he considered the events of the last few days, and how he should continue.

What best to do?

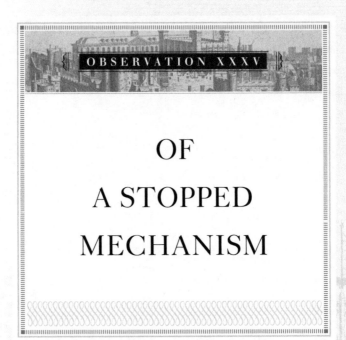

OF

A STOPPED

MECHANISM

THE FOLLOWING MORNING FOUND THE OLD constable, Gabriel Knapp, clinging to a narrow buttress under an arch of London Bridge, the nearest to the north bank. Spray drenched him. Water poured from his montero.

The Morice waterwheels, three times his height, which powered the great pumps delivering water to the City, dripped with slime. Their blades trawled filth from the river. Their smell made bile rise in his throat.

Looking at the water made Knapp feel himself transported upriver, going up against its rush. Curling like the backs of maddened porpoises, the waves owned a compelling attraction, enticing him to join them in a last, fatal leap. This lure made him grip more tightly the slippery beam above him.

As it crashed through the gaps between the wooden starlings supporting the bridge, the Thames deafened him. Shaped like the prows of ships, the points of the starlings knifed through the flow. Forced between them, the water rocked the whole structure.

Knapp's foot slipped as he inched along the step, and he pulled himself further into the fiction of protection offered by the stone curving over him.

Two other watchmen stood on the bank, refusing to follow him out along the beams leading to this narrow shelf.

The waterwheel was still, deliberately stopped. The cause of its halting hung above him.

Knapp wondered how he would ever pull it away. He beckoned again half-heartedly to the watchmen, knowing they would not help him. They had watched him set off on his hair-raising scramble, across the timbers supporting the wheel, to get to this spot.

Gresham's College, where he had delivered the dead boy, was no distance.

'Gresham's!' he mouthed and pointed north along the line of Fish Street. They stared at him, confused. Although just yards separated them, the thrash of the waves whipped his words away. He crooked a finger, and with his other hand pointed to it. 'Hooke! Hooke!'

Enlightenment spread across their faces. 'Gresham's!' they called back. 'Hooke!'

'Yes!' And then quietly, directed at himself: 'Old fool!'

The watchmen ran off, glad to be away from the bridge, and away from the water.

The wet stone was too treacherous to move further along, but Knapp could not muster the courage to take himself back. Hooke would bring the younger man Hunt with him, he hoped. They would assist him. It would have been better to bring a boat for the purpose of removal—but no water-man would relish tying his wherry to the starling.

Knapp tried not to watch the water.

Instead, he looked up at the body of a man, whose back arched over the topmost blades of the wheel. Someone had jammed him into the mechanism.

Knapp gazed into the upside-down face.

The wait for the watchmen's return seemed interminable. Knapp's ear-drums rang from their constant battering. He tried to think of ways to take the dead man down from his perch. Most he rejected as too whimsical, es-pecially as he doubted he could propel himself, either forwards or back-wards, from his own place of transfixion.

The inverted figure above him, with his black camlet coat hanging and his arms spread out beseechingly, looked as if he flew down to take him from this dangerous spot.

'I should have served you better,' Knapp said to him, sadly.

~

FROM ST. MAGNUS THE Martyr, Harry had to push his way through the crowd gathering at the Morice waterworks. He limped, his falls in Alsatia making him wince, shins and tailbone still sore, heel tender, pain now stiff-ening a shoulder. Robert Hooke scuttled beside him, wondering what had made Harry so unwieldy in his walking.

Harry had been about to tell Hooke of his nightmarish visit to Alsatia, and of witnessing the bestial murder of Enoch Wolfe, but the watchmen coming to Gresham's College, demanding their aid at London Bridge, had interrupted him.

Through the network of beams, the constable was only partly visible. More easily seen was the man hanging from the wheel. The crowd swayed up and down the quayside, fluctuating between a better view of the consta-ble and a better view of the dead body. Some people positioned themselves higher up the hill, by the Waterman's Hall, to view more over the crush. Some even climbed the tower of the waterworks.

One waterman took a brave group of onlookers out on the Thames, row-ing against its flow to keep position. Animated gesticulating from them conveyed their excitement at what they saw.

'Held there by nails!'

The story took a hold of the crowd. 'Like Christ himself! The Jesuits are among us!'

Harry and Hooke pushed through them, leaving their fetchers, the two timid watchmen, behind. By a telepathic understanding the crowd let them through, aware they had something to do with the unfolding drama.

Hooke tugged at Harry. 'I will go to St. Magnus!' he told him urgently. 'The men there work to finish the inside. I shall seek their help.'

'They need tools to release him from the wheel, Mr. Hooke.'

Reaching the bridge, Harry saw Knapp, whose face was an ashy colour. As Harry looked at him, the old man's foot slipped. He recovered his balance and hugged even tighter the wall of the arch.

Harry knew he must help him. The dead body was more firmly situated, in no danger of being swept away by the river.

He searched out a route across the jumble of beams. He had to get to the constable before he fell—he could not wait for Hooke's return with the workmen.

A first wary step from the safety of the bank, testing how slippery the timber was. It offered no friction at all for his boot. The distance to the far side of the arch, and to the stone ledge holding the constable, seemed impossible to traverse. Harry's woollen glove held the beam more effectively, so he bent to take off his boots. He put them down regretfully, not expecting to see them again, for they would disappear into the crowd.

Stepping out once more, the rough material of his stockings provided more grip on the wood. This seemed safer, but in the cold his toes at once became numb. Shards of pain stabbed under his toenails.

He sidled onto the beam. The safety offered by the bank soon seemed far away. The excited babble of the crowd—they marvelled at his decision to do what none of them would have done, and they wondered who this slight youth was to go to the aid of the old man—merged with the reverberation of the water. By the time he brought his other leg up, and gone further along the beam, their voices had disappeared altogether.

Now all Harry could hear was water. Below him, the Thames raced through the arch. His feet refused to shuffle. He clutched the end of a purlin above his head and slid his hand in front of him, until the weight of his body forced him to shift his feet to adjust. Traversing the beams and rafters this way, gradually, little by little, his hands leading his reluctant feet, he reached a vertical spar, round like a ship's mast. The spar extended the height of the arch. The way around it was blocked by the machinery behind.

He was now closer to Gabriel Knapp than he was to the bank.

'Mr. Hunt!' Knapp's panicked face bobbed out from the wall. 'Go back! I was foolish to venture so far. Leave me to my fate.'

'How did you pass this spar?' Harry shouted back.

Knapp forced himself to remember. 'A strut adjoins it! Projecting out, below the surface of the water. I fell and chanced upon it. But what will you gain by reaching me? We will then both be marooned on this spot.'

'Mr. Hooke summons help,' Harry replied, attempting assurance.

He searched for the support, dropping so his leg entered the Thames. The water snatched it and banged it against the wood, cracking painfully his anklebone, making him bite his lip. He tried again. This time he located the little ledge of timber below the surface. He scraped a strand of slime flailing from it, then rested his weight onto it. He encircled the spar with his arms—his hands almost touched behind it. Knapp, he was sure, whose arms were longer, would have been able to clasp his hands together. Harry could not, and the lack of safety almost brought him to a standstill. He could not believe the old man had got so far.

One . . . two . . . three. Go! On around, straining to maintain the almost-circle of his arms, his right foot scrabbled its way to the next beam. He performed the move smoothly, misleading the crowd on the bank, who cheered him on, thinking him braver and more skilful than he was.

He inched further towards Knapp, who watched him frantically, his conviction that Harry would fall too evident. Harry reached the wheel and looked at the cogs and the mechanism of the pump, trying to work out a way of climbing up and then across the wheel.

He summoned the courage to take the long stride onto the side of the wheel, over the rushing water, and reached for one of the blades.

There was no way of getting to Knapp without his weight pressing the dead body between the top of the wheel and the beam it passed under. He pulled himself up and traversed the length of the blade. He had to avoid the inverted body, stepping carefully over it, and he descended the other side of the wheel.

The gap between the wheel and the bridge was crossed, a second tall spar circumnavigated in the same way as the first. His feet, the cold eating its way through them, sensed nothing. He had to watch them to check their hold, before transferring his weight. His upper body shivered violently, and he had trouble keeping his hands on the beams.

At last, the journey was done. Harry pulled his knees up onto the little stone ledge alongside Knapp. The constable extended his hand to help him up, and they stood together, both too frozen and frightened to enjoy any sense of triumph.

'Mr. Hunt, you are a brave fool, but a fool.'

'Will you return with this fool?'

Knapp looked at him miserably.

Now Harry looked up, and into the face of the dead man.

It was the Justice of Peace for Westminster, Sir Edmund Bury Godfrey.

His mouth was wide open as if he shouted to them to get him off from the wheel. His eyes were bloodied, and looked accusingly at the two men with him. A gash went across his ear. His skin was bright red and mottled with dark purple bruises.

His body was caught where the waterwheel ran under the arch, a blade sliced into his back. The beam above crushed his belly. Sir Edmund quivered spasmodically as the force of the water vibrated the wheel.

His neck had a deep weal from a ligature, and Harry could observe where a knot had pressed into the flesh.

'I knew Sir Edmund for over thirty years,' Knapp shouted over the noise. 'He escaped death so many times I thought he would live forever. But we are all of us mortal.'

'Mr. Hooke summons help from builders. They shall assist us, and release Sir Edmu—'

A scraping sound stopped him. The end of a thick rope descended past them, from a window way above, overlooking the side of the bridge. Appearing like a phantom from the sky, a small man wearing the worn clothing of a carpenter dangled from it. Harry recognised him from the building site of St. Magnus.

'A rope would have been simpler for us both,' Harry told the constable.

'The deuce on this place!' the carpenter said as he landed next to them. Sawdust clogged the pores of his skin. 'You've got more stomach than brains, eh!'

He unravelled the knot from his waist and considered them. 'I shall tie you on first, constable.'

He secured Knapp expertly, and gave the rope a couple of pulls to signal readiness. It tautened, pulled by brawny arms from the bridge. Knapp stepped on the blades as he ascended. The wheel turned a degree, until stopped by the blockage in its mechanism.

Knapp kicked himself away from the underside of the arch and disappeared from view.

The carpenter looked shrewdly at Harry. 'Wager your heart's panting, Mr. Hunt! What you want with rescuing Heavyrakes here?'

A practical man, he looked up at Sir Edmund matter-of-factly, thinking of his removal from the wheel rather than the wrong of his murder. He looked up for the rope to be lowered back to him.

'Better people than the Justice to go about salvaging. Let the Devil take him!'

'Mr. Latham,' Harry managed as his reply, shivering ferociously, 'can you cover him before you take him up? We would not want it yet known Sir Edmund is dead.'

'We?' Latham asked suspiciously. 'You and Mr. Hooke, you mean?'

'Mr. Hooke. Most of all the King.'

Latham looked unimpressed. 'I will do it for Mr. Hooke. I give not a fig for the King.'

AT THIS END of the bridge, nearest the City, a large three storey building replaced the jumble of houses lost in the Conflagration. As the weight of construction to post-Fire regulations would be too great for the old stone to bear, it was made from timber. Wider than the bridge, great joists supported it from beneath. Its various shops and works had their backs projecting over the Thames.

Harry, following Knapp, was brought from the Morice waterwheel through the rear window of a tannery. Gathering like filings to a lodestone, people pressed against its front windows, and banged on the door, demanding to know more of the papist leaving of a dead man on the wheel.

The tanner had locked and bolted his door, and looked fearful for his windows.

The rumours of nails and crucifixion had taken hold.

Spanning the road, the building's top storey created a gloomy tunnel, lit by lanterns day and night. All bridge traffic through it was at a stop. Carts and carriages backed up on Fish Street, as far as Monument Yard.

Robert Hooke tried to be authoritative, and calm the crowd, but they only hushed when the body of the dead man appeared feet first through the window.

Those able to glimpse the action through the tannery shouted their commentary to those behind.

Sir Edmund's coat was tied to cover his face. Latham, the carpenter, looked pleased with himself, having worked to release Sir Edmund by cleverly disengaging a cog and cutting away part of the blade. His proficiency had earned claps from the crowd on the quayside.

Hooke ordered the Justice to be carried away to Gresham's College, and the tanner gave over a handcart, irked by the disruption to his business, impatient to get them gone.

When the tanner unlocked his door, and the Justice, pushed by workmen from St. Magnus, emerged, calls of 'Another Protestant martyr!' went up, and 'Where hide the papists who murdered this man?'

'This is hopeless!' Hooke decided, meeting the crush. 'Return him inside.'

The workmen, needing to fend off the onlookers, who pulled and tore at Sir Edmund's clothes, manoeuvred it back into the tannery.

The tanner protested they trespassed in his property. Hooke's reputation, and the looks from his burly builders from the church, persuaded him to stay hospitable.

'Until we have an escort, or the crowd dies away,' Hooke assured him, the watchmen having taken Knapp through the crush to get him dry and warm, and to fetch reinforcements.

The tanner went to lean resentfully against his door, leaving only Hooke, Harry and the small group of builders with Sir Edmund. Noble Fisher, their foreman, directed his men to stand at the windows, to defend against the crowd if it tried to force its way in.

The room was full of skins, in piles or stretched on frames. Most were cut, some bore the outlines of their original wearers. The stink of tannin made the men choke.

Harry removed his breeches and socks, took one of the skins from a pile, and used it to dry his legs. He had no sensation in them even as he rubbed at them. To stop his shivering he wrapped himself in more of the skins, doing his best to ignore its smell, and the tanner's enraged stare.

Now a chance to look at the body. They studied Sir Edmund's long black coat, his black woollen trousers, his waistcoat with silver buttons, his shoes, belt, and his rapier. The buttons each had a design of a three-masted schooner under full sail.

'No common robbery, and has not been made to look so,' Hooke observed.

'He's without his notebook,' Harry said.

'I never saw him without it. It may have been taken.'

'Or it fell into the Thames from his spot on the wheel.'

Hooke swabbed river water from Sir Edmund's face with his handkerchief. He studied the dark and mottled skin.

'Does he rot?' Fisher asked, interested.

'This is not the sign of putrefaction,' Hooke answered him.

'I saw him the night before last,' Harry said. 'He was a lean man. Putrefaction takes time in such men to show.'

Hooke studied the dark ring of bruises around Sir Edmund's neck. 'He was brought here after death.'

'Captain Huff was not stuck in the wheel to kill him?' Latham's rough hands rubbed together from a grisly enjoyment.

'Hit about the ear, and his neck was pressed. The Coroner's Office will say the same. An autopsy will find the fullness of it. Will you turn him for me?'

Fisher, with Latham, lifted Sir Edmund onto his front, and at Hooke's direction pulled off the coat and shirt to reveal his back. Hooke indicated the pattern of lividity, where the blood had settled. 'You see the shoulders are pale where he pressed on them? When he died—or shortly after—he faced upwards. Will you dress him again? Let us not study him further in here.'

Until the watchmen returned, all they could do was wait, with the clamour from outside, the shaking of the tannery from the force of the Thames, and the noise of the waterwheel below them, free to turn again.

When the watchmen got to them, they brought soldiers of the King's Foot, who had been making their way to the commotion at the bridge.

One of the soldiers, a tall, ginger-haired captain, gave Hooke a half-salute.

'The King will meet you at Gresham's College, Mr. Hooke. You are to study the body there, with him.'

'Looks like you are to be Coroner, Mr. Hooke,' Noble Fisher told him.

Hooke's face showed little enthusiasm for the role.

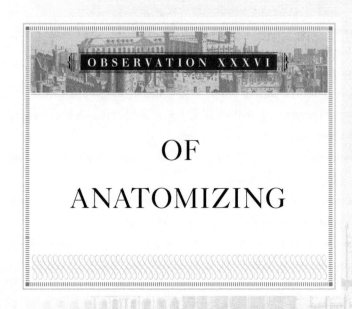

OBSERVATION XXXVI

OF
ANATOMIZING

MORE CALLS OF 'PAPISTS!'

Never a single papist, Harry thought, as they picked their way through Cornhill to get to Gresham's. He walked beside the tanner's cart, trying to promote circulation of blood through his feet. He had lost his boots, so walked in his soaking wool stockings.

The red-uniformed soldiers, sent from the garrison at the Tower to get London Bridge unblocked, made their weapons conspicuous, showing the business ends of their pikes to the more fervent of the crowd.

Up Bishopsgate Street a procession formed, and a tense atmosphere overtook them all. The mood had turned ugly against such Romish outrages in their city.

If they found out it was the Justice of Peace for Westminster, Sir Edmund Bury Godfrey, who had been splayed over the Morice waterwheel, full hysteria would break out.

It was a relief to be back in Hooke's rooms. After an hour or so, the noise abated, and the crowd melted away back into London, after the entertainment of the dead man's recovery.

Some of the soldiers still stood outside, guarding the entrances, their pikes impaling the sky.

MARY HAD KINDLED the fire as fully as the little grate would allow, Tom feeding in the coal, and now she busied around providing cordials and brews.

'Why should you climb out onto the wheel? The recovery of the body was straightforward. Why did you follow the constable?' While he found fault, Hooke wrote in his diary, playing with a sequence of letters. 'I am exasperated!'

Wrapped in layers of Hooke's blankets, Harry looked like a giant pupa ready to hatch. At last, his shivering had stopped.

Hooke pointed his pen accusingly. 'You expose yourself to danger, despite my wishes and against good sense. Wandering across the Morice water pump, ignoring the threat of being swept away into the Thames? From where do you find such disregard for self-preservation? It is not from me, I avow. I instructed you to leave off Sir Edmund's search, yet you persisted. Do you wish not to see old age?'

'In truth, Mr. Hooke, events push themselves on me.'

'Nonsense!' Hooke looked angrily at him. 'You bring them on yourself. And you have lost your boots!'

Harry took a bowl of steaming liquid from Grace, who gave him a look of—could it be?—admiration. Hooke's chiding continued, but Harry thought only of this look from her. Not just admiration, he decided. More of complicity. She had often faced such lectures from her uncle.

'You are a fool, Harry!' Hooke banged down his pen. 'No man's life is worth more than another's, but I would be very sorry to have you lose yo—'

Tom interrupted. 'Mr. Hooke! The King arrives!'

'Thank you, Tom. We will be there presently.'

Hooke put down his pen. He had rearranged the letters of Sir Edmund Bury Godfrey's name:

I fynd murder'd by rogues.

❧

HIS EXPRESSION SEVERE, the King arrived at the College in a plain carriage, drawn by two equally nondescript horses. Only Sir Jonas Moore was with him. The soldiers of the Foot guarding the College saluted them, but first had to be told by their captain who they were. Neither man had dressed formally, choosing quiet clothes for their visit.

Hooke and Harry took them into the College, along a corridor leading to the anatomy room. Harry limped along silently in a borrowed pair of Hooke's stockings, Hooke's shoes being too large to wear, and Tom's too small.

The walls of the corridor were a dark salmon colour, with a faded floral pattern on the peeling flock paper. The King walked over a threadbare carpet which wanted replacing. The interior of the College, to his surprise, had become shabby.

Portraits of Gresham's Professors and original Fellows of the Royal Society punctuated the walls. A portrait of Hooke—which at first the King did not recognise, as he looked healthily pink and wore his best peruke— was one of the last they went by.

Through the windows, they could see the red uniforms of the guards, patrolling the covered walkway around the quadrangle.

The cellar room housing the air-pump was dedicated to one purpose. The room they entered was similarly focused. One central object dictated its use: a black marble slab, sloped on two hefty trestles. Grooves chased into the marble's top followed its perimeter, aiming for a wooden sink, for the blood draining from them.

Stored on the walls, racked ready to hand, were Hooke's instruments. Dismembering knives and saws, incision shears, razors, scissors, lancets, extractors, and probes lined up next to one another. A large chisel and mallet, a pair of stork's bills, and a set of strainers were placed by a polished brass basin, along with various sizes of sponge and a blood porringer.

Sir Edmund waited on the handcart, having been brought in by soldiers. A calico cloth covered him, apart from his feet, hanging stiffly over the cart's end.

Harry thought of callous Procrustes and his bed, his victims shortened or lengthened to fit its length.

The King signalled his readiness for the anatomising to commence.

Hooke put on a simple leather apron and passed another to Harry.

Harry pulled away the cloth and embraced Sir Edmund to lift him from the cart. Their faces touched. Harry's living warmth jerked away, repulsed by the coldness of dead flesh. He placed his shoulder under the Justice and used the strength of his back to lift him onto the slab.

His movements surprised the King and Sir Jonas, for the Justice was far broader and taller than this assistant's slight frame. All the carrying of machines and tools at Hooke's bidding had made him stronger than he looked.

Made difficult by the obstinate rigidity of the corpse, Harry took off and folded the coat and suit.

'Sir Edmund is inflexible,' the King remarked. 'As he was in life.'

Hooke answered him. 'Do you perceive this all-over redness of him? I believe he was exposed to heat, which rigidifies him. Cooked bodies tend to stiffen, then remain stiff.'

'Not *rigor mortis*, then? He underwent a trial by fire, hmm? Most assume a Catholic conspiracy. The man Sir Edmund told us of, Titus Oates, came to me this morning, and another one with him—a strange cricket of a man—and told of the plot against me. I am to be brought down with a silver bullet! The wound does not heal, supposedly. The news of Sir Edmund's death will feed the frenzy.' He looked at Sir Jonas. 'This is a ticklish thing.'

Once Harry finished undressing Sir Edmund, he put all of the clothes and the pair of shoes into an oilskin bag.

They noted the contusion on the left ear, and the line around the neck, and redness of the flesh.

'It looks as though he has just emerged from a deep hot bath,' the King said.

Where his chest was crushed in the mechanism of the Morice water-wheel, his broken ribs showed through.

'Turn him, Harry,' Hooke instructed.

Turned onto his front, a darker hue presented itself: blood drawn by gravity to the lowest parts of the body. This lividity showed the Justice had lain on his back after death. Pale patches on his shoulders and buttocks showed where his weight had compressed the flesh, forcing his blood from the vessels.

At Hooke's signal, Harry turned the Justice over once more.

'Do you see these further red markings?' Hooke asked, pointing them out the King.

A rash extended from the ankle of each leg to high up on each thigh. Harry lifted the legs and confirmed it was only on the fronts of them.

'This is bumpy, like a mild pox,' said the King, exploring with his fingertips. 'Could it show boiled water poured onto him, as rough questioning?' He sounded hopeful.

'These are the marks left by the touch of stinging nettles,' Hooke replied. 'The infectious juice arises through a tube in the leaf, from a bag at the base of each point.'

'There's more of the same on the backs of his hands,' Harry noticed.

Hooke regarded them closely.

'A curious arrangement. I suggest he had his hands like so.' He showed them by pressing his two clenched fists together. 'Leaving the backs of the hands exposed to the sting.'

'Like a man wearing manacles,' Sir Jonas suggested.

'No marks on his wrists to suggest manacles,' Harry said. 'But why else would he hold his hands like that?'

'He ran through nettles,' Hooke said, musing aloud, 'without breeches, his legs exposed to their stings. If walking, nettles would spring back after his progress, to sting the backs of his legs. He displays no such marks. He held his hands curiously, touching together, in front of him.'

'Making his escape, perchance?' the King suggested. 'Running, not walking.'

'His killer may have forced him through the nettles,' Sir Jonas said. 'Not a means of murder I have heard.'

The King looked doubtful. 'Could the nettles have killed him, Robert?'

'Diverse plants have the power to kill from a brush to the skin. The juice from nettles may be gathered. In sufficient quantity, conceivably, it may infect the fluid or vital parts of a person.'

'Would he have died, though, from the nettles' stings?'

Hooke shook his head. 'Unlikely, Your Majesty. I doubt it owns sufficient pungency. Some, though, are more sensitive to poisons.'

He produced a small instrument from his pocket. 'This I made using Leeuwenhoek's method, melting the end of a glass rod to form a small sphere. It achieves a powerful lens.'

Hooke held the little microscope to one of Sir Edmund's wrists. After studying it, he motioned to the King, who peered through the glass, then passed it to Sir Jonas.

The hairs on Sir Edmund's wrists appeared as thick, smooth cylinders, and they observed the individual flakes and fissures on the surface of his skin.

Also, long fibres attached themselves to the hairs.

'A wide band of material, very fine, was used to bind him,' Hooke told them. 'The fibres have remained. Observe they are different in colour to those of his shirt, which are grey and white, being bleached cotton.'

'Much finer,' the King said. 'Are they silk?'

'When magnified, silk fibres look round and hard, transparent and reflective. These are flat, with a brownish hue. They are those of a fine lawn cloth.' Hooke took the microscope from Sir Jonas, and passed it to Harry, who studied the exposed arm. 'It is this material which tied the man.'

'A fine lawn?' Sir Jonas asked. 'As a priest might wear?'

'Sir Edmund, had this body not so unhappily been his own, might assume Catholic practises, following the furrow of his thinking. He deemed the fine wax on the bodies of the boys might show a priestly hand, indicative of liturgical candles. We cannot assume this shows popery. The lawn cloth fibres equally signpost Anglicanism. Perhaps they release themselves from the sleeves of a Protestant bishop, rather than a Catholic priest.'

The King allowed a merry expression at the picture of his bishops tormenting the Justice so, but looking back at Sir Edmund on the slab his face turned serious again. 'Still, we know not the manner of his killing. Or if he is a victim of murder at all.'

Deep in thought, Hooke's silver eyes looked over the table, then through and beyond the wall in front of him. 'I think the all-over redness of him shows the way of it. We have a superfluity of signs. His was a complex death.'

❧

'DO WE COMMENCE with the cutting, Mr. Hooke?' Harry prompted. Twitching again, the muscle in his leg annoyed him, and revulsion thickened his tongue. He was determined not to show his queasiness.

Hooke gave Harry an almost imperceptible nod of the head and took a leather sheath from its place on the wall. He withdrew a knife, half a yard long and tapering to a malicious point, serrated along the middle third of its edge. The tool was manufactured for him, of best London steel, to suit his own demands.

He rapidly opened two incisions to form a large crucifix across Sir Edmund's torso. He cut the first incision across the lower part of the breastbone, reaching from the left side of the broken rib cage to the right. The second reached from the throat down to the pubic bone, a neat curl of the slit avoiding the navel.

'Over the years I have refined my methods, though I am nowadays more used to incising dogs and porpoises.'

He peeled the tissue from the chest, twisting the point of his great knife to release strands of the more awkwardly sticking flesh. He blinked at

Harry, who pulled the large flaps to each side, exposing the ribs and the strap muscles of the front of the neck.

The King observed, as Sir Edmund had, that as these two worked they communicated silently, Hooke directing Harry using these small nods, blinks, and tiny lifts of his hands. Harry answered in the same style. It was like watching a private language, or a language for the deaf. Although he viewed the opening of bodies with distaste, the King enjoyed watching their proficiency. Hooke's frailty disappeared, and he became as agile in his actions as the young man. Their easy movements, he thought, the certainty and economy of them, resembled the motions of a clock.

Working through the front of the throat, Hooke set about the windpipe and larynx. 'There is some damage. No obstructions remain within.'

'His blood is as red as a cherry!' The King exclaimed.

'I have seen such redness before, Your Majesty,' Hooke answered. 'In people burned in fires. The last time after the Southwark fire two years since. I watched it from the Fish Street pillar, with Grace, and we overlooked its progress through the evening. Yet as we can see, there are no burns on Sir Edmund's body, no singeing of the hair, branding of the skin, nor roasting of the parts.'

Hooke cut out the breastplate, and pulled at a section of lung. 'Full of bubbly liquor.'

Hooke lowered his knife into Sir Edmund, twisting it, and repeated the motion a little further over, angling the tool slightly. 'The diaphanous medium of the air, when made sufficiently hot, produces the action of light, or fire. Something inside it, a volatile, nitrous spirit, tends to the violence of burning. When heating wood within a closed vessel, a vessel inhibiting the access of air, it is not consumed. Instead, it moves to become charcoal—'

Hooke held up Sir Edmund's bright red heart.

'Is this really where we feel our most subtle thoughts and passions?' the King asked. 'Our sense of grace, our knowledge of religion and sin?'

Hooke, his knife held before him, considered the question.

'William Harvey, famous for his *De Motu Cordis*, showed the heart to be for moving the blood about the body, and then about again. It can be explained as a pump. When, however, you study the heart to find hate, or charity, or a predilection for sin, it becomes an altogether more enigmatic organ.'

Hooke placed the Justice's heart on the bench beside him. 'Your Majesty, I shall cut open the stomach.'

Sir Jonas and the King shifted back, as near to the wall as they could. After a while, Harry opened the window.

'There is something strange within . . . '

Hooke took out a dirty ball. He placed it, too, on the surface of the bench, and proceeded to straighten it out.

It unfolded into a rectangle. With the flat of his knife, he wiped the surface of what revealed itself to be a piece of paper.

On it was written a single word:

CORPUS

'He swallowed the cipher's keyword,' Harry observed.

'He knew he was about to die,' Sir Jonas said.

Hooke held up the paper. 'It is not Sir Edmund's writing. I remember his hand from his copy of the cipher.'

'And hardly the neat writing of the cipher from the solicitor,' Harry added, seeing a messy, shaky scrawl.

The King looked puzzled. '*Corpus*? Meaning body? A dead body? The body of Christ? Or a body of work?'

'Was he killed for this word?' Harry asked them. 'Did he hide it from his persecutor?'

The other men offered no answer.

'See if any more such messages inhabit him,' the King commanded.

Despite their further investigation of the stomach and bowel, and slitting along the length of intestines, no more pieces of paper were to be found.

Hooke nodded again to Harry.

Harry folded some sacking under Sir Edmund's head to lift it from the marble. Hooke cut over the crown of the head from behind one ear to the other, a shear of toothed steel on bone. Harry gripped the edges of the flap and pulled it over the face, his forearms straining with effort. Then he pulled the flap at the back down to the nape of the neck.

The dull sheen of the top of the skull was exposed. With a handsaw, Harry worked around its equator and pulled the top away. It released with a sucking sound and the grating of bone on bone.

Eventually their work, and the unpalatable odour of the body, and the sights and sounds of the head being scooped, forced the King from the room. The pinkness of the surface of Sir Edmund's brain upset him. Most repellent of all was the rawness—the very meatiness—of the edges of the separated scalp.

The remaining three men looked after him, and then at one another, with some curiosity. The King had witnessed violence and death many times in his life. Was it because the body was his Justice of Peace for Westminster, the man who had assisted him in his escape to France, that he suffered this attack of squeamishness?

They could hear him outside, pulling in heaving gasps of the smoky London air.

Its coolness and relative freshness invigorated him. Recomposed, he returned inside.

Hooke held up his wet knife and showed it theatrically to the King. He used the razor-sharp blade to shave the fine hairs from the back of his own wrist. 'This can be a superior tool of enquiry than the mind, Your Majesty, even if it means getting the hands dirty.'

'Are you well again, Your Majesty?' Harry asked, pleased it was the King who had succumbed to his feelings, and not him.

'I have recovered, Harry, thank you.'

'I shall return the head to its right relations.'

'I should like that of all things.'

Harry refitted the top of the skull—reminding the King of the lid of the air-pump's receiver—and pulled the flesh of the head back together. He stitched the scalp with some waxed twine, clamping the two edges together with his left hand and sewing with his right. Sir Edmund's fractured ribs gaping open like a great mouth, he replaced the breastplate as best he could. The long incisions across the torso received a simple blanket stitch, which left the fatty edges meeting in long undulating lines.

He draped the linen to cover the body, set to with cleaning the floor beneath the slab, which was slippery, then wiped the top of the bench.

THEY LEFT THE dissecting room, the body of Sir Edmund still lying on the slab, and crossed the grounds of the College. The church bells of St. Martin Outwich pealed one o'clock.

'Keep him here, Robert, secure at Gresham's,' the King commanded. 'I must speak with my Council, to decide how we let loose the news of Sir Edmund's death. He will be fetched shortly. I rely upon your discretion.'

Leaving Gresham's with Sir Jonas in his simple carriage, the remainder of the Foot following and taking their pikes with them, the King did not glance back.

'He leaves the keyword with us, to reveal the meaning of the cipher,' Harry said.

Hooke looked up at the sky despairingly. 'Again, we are expected to keep secrets.'

'The King's life is threatened. When the news spreads it was Sir Edmund on the wheel, it will provoke more outrage against the Catholics.'

They walked towards Hooke's lodgings, Harry wondering what the documents left on the boy, those delivered to Mr. Hooke by the solicitor, and the package from Henry Oldenburg's study, held for them, now they had the keyword.

'Harry, look there,' Hooke said, pointing down at the threshold of his lodgings.

There, placed neatly, side-by-side, stood Harry's boots.

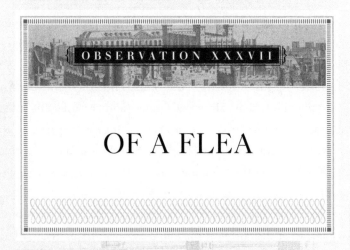

OBSERVATION XXXVII

OF A FLEA

COLD FRESH AIR AND THE SOUND of the bells of St. Butolph's came in through the library window. Shaftesbury sat reading Robert Hooke's *Micrographia*, studying one of its illustrations: Hooke's engraving of a flea.

He waited for the bells to finish, and Aires waited with him.

'Do you have news of the Witch, Uriel? If no, then I have given up on him.'

'No news at all. Not for want of trying.'

'I do not doubt it.' Shaftesbury motioned to Aires for him to sit and pushed the still-open book towards him. 'We have been too cautious of the name of the Royal Society, and of its Curator Robert Hooke, to do what should already have been done.'

'It owns little more than its name. When I went to its meeting room for Hooke's lecture, I thought Gresham's College a dingy, threadbare place. Mr. Hooke, likewise, is unprepossessing.'

'The powers of his mind are acute. This is his *Micrographia*. An astonishing and ingenious book. He reveals to us another world, one invisible to the eye, living under us, around us, and on us. It gives us pause for thought, I think, when we are busy colonising the New World, but we cannot command a flea. We suffer their company or kill them. There is to be no parley with them.'

Aires scrutinised the engraving. 'I would say that to a flea we must appear as gods, with the power of life and death over them. And as fleas suck at ours, Christ's blood is sucked, too, by the Catholics.'

Shaftesbury smiled at this. 'You must share your thoughts with Dr. Locke on the religious observance of insects. You know, I have gone too softly. I supposed that to witness Enoch Wolfe's death would discourage Hooke's assistant. It would most men, I think. But Henry Hunt is far from discouraged. For today he climbed across the Morice waterworks and helped retrieve a dead man.'

'The gossip is, the man on the wheel was Sir Edmund Bury Godfrey. The Justice.'

'My thoughts, too. He was seen about London, looking perturbed, and has been missing since yesterday morning.'

'Do you give more licence with Henry Hunt than you gave me before?'

'Like Mr. Hooke's flea, this little busy creature bites and pierces the skin, leaving it inflamed. You have every licence. Take Lefèvre with you.'

When Aires had left, Shaftesbury turned to his automaton. 'And then, I think, we must take back our boy.'

OF
LETTERS
DECIPHERED

HARRY HAD BECOME A MACHINE, SO absorbed in his task to uncover the meaning of the enciphered letters he forgot the world outside. He had not noticed the morning come.

Using the keyword *corpus*, he had deciphered his copy of the letter found on the boy at the Fleet.

Sir Edmund Bury Godfrey,
this 23rd day of December 1677

If you read this it means that I am dead. This is that therefore which goes before, a document of posteriority. My worldly reputation now is of no matter. With tranquillity I leave all that behind me.

Impudence makes me wish for a right settling of all things after my death. At least this letter can be offered as a gesture towards that right way of things. Here I am concerned with why I did die. In this last Letter I do not dissemble, and offer no strategy from my Grave.

I have incurred the anger of Heaven. I chose to live wholly in opposition to God, by the chusing of my actions.

I cling not to a Protestant dismissal of Purgatory to ease my burden.

A man is given two Paths, and two Lights light his way, and he is given two Guides to lead him. One path leads to God in His Creation and the doing of his Will through curing bodily affliction. This path is illuminated by the Light of Nature. The other way is a more exalted Path. It is a calling to heal men's Souls through the preaching of the Word of God. Its Light is the Light of Grace.

The Light of Nature is the Light of the Mind. The Light of Grace is the superior Light, the Light of God, which is the Light of the Holy Ghost. All things are within the two Lights, without which there would be nothing, and no knowledge of them.

The Child has to learn himself how not to fear the Dark. It is beyond the powers of rhetorick to teach him. Nature and Experience only convince him that to enter a blackened Room need not terrify. Likewise, we cannot be given experience of death, to learn its Nature, and so no reasonings can perswade us to pass happily unto it.

We begin to die from the day we are born. Yet I find it small comfort that Death represents our natural Estate. Now in the face of it I tremble in my Marrow, and offer myself,

Daniel Whitcombe,

To the Mercy of God.

Harry stood up from his table with difficulty, suffering from his falls in Alsatia and his clamber across the Morice waterwheels. He looked out from his window across the walks of Moorfields. A fine drizzle misted the air, and everything he could see looked colourless and dreary.

He had also deciphered his copy of the letter delivered to Robert Hooke by the solicitor.

Mr. Robert Hooke,
this 23rd day of December 1677

Sir: My guiding Principle was Discovery. I directed my Time on God's Earth towards worldly concerns, with a singular interpretation of Usefulness.

I worked as Chymist, Operator, Mechanic, Natural Philosopher. Call them what you will. I studied Physic, Anatomy, Geometry, Astronomy, Navigation, Horology, Astrology, Statics, Magnetism, Chymistry, Alchemical and Natural Experiments, and knew them each and all more completely than most who profess themselves Virtuosi.

For the last year my Employments, taking me away from my usual Course, have stayed me upon one main Stream, and so I have not wandered to follow mazy Tributaries. I have uncovered much, whose Foundations lie on excellent, diverse, substantial and noble Experiments. I have worked secretly, without recourse to Intelligence or Society. I leave with you the flesh of these Findings. You will ascertain quickly enough the reason for my secrecy and avoidance of the Clubb.

God has made this great Machine and placed us within a most inconsiderable part of it, and allowed us to survey his Creation through reflections of a Glass, darkly: our limited Senses and Capacities. I presumed to penetrate the depths of Nature, to polish the Glass, and to understand the whole Constitution of the Universe.

I leave my Observations with you. You are able to decide how my Work shall best be used.

Daniel Whitcombe,
Natural Philosopher

Who is—or was—this Daniel Whitcombe, making such claims for himself?

I have incurred the anger of Heaven. Was he the murderer of the boys, and the taker of their blood?

Would Hooke know of the name Daniel Whitcombe? Harry could not recall mention of it, although Hooke knew half of London.

Looking at Hooke's new building on Moorfields, the Bethlehem Hospital, Harry wondered if these letters showed a lunatic's ravings. No one could have worked secretly, and alone, on so many areas of knowledge, and known them *each and all more completely than most who profess themselves Virtuosi.* Such a skilled experimentalist would have needed to communicate with other natural philosophers, to share ideas. Otherwise, he would merely repeat the same trials, and the mistakes, of others.

Daniel Whitcombe's grand claims could not be true.

But the package, using the same Civil War cipher and in the same meticulous handwriting as the enciphered letter to Mr. Hooke, was with Henry Oldenburg. Maybe Whitcombe had not needed to attend meetings, or correspond with other natural philosophers, if Oldenburg had sent him accounts of their experiments in his correspondences, and those published in the Society's *Philosophical Transactions.*

Harry dressed, and placed the deciphered letters in the pocket inside his coat.

He must take them to Mr. Hooke. And he must tell him of the murder of Enoch Wolfe.

Pulling his boots on, he was still troubled by their return.

When Sir Edmund had gone to Gresham's College, to the air-pump in the cellar, they had discussed if the boy was preserved in glass to allow for observation. Ever since, Harry had been dogged by the idea he was being watched, as if in a similar receiver. The way the murderer had watched him as he killed Wolfe, and the coach driver next to him.

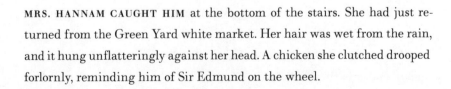

MRS. HANNAM CAUGHT HIM at the bottom of the stairs. She had just returned from the Green Yard white market. Her hair was wet from the rain, and it hung unflatteringly against her head. A chicken she clutched drooped forlornly, reminding him of Sir Edmund on the wheel.

Suddenly light-headed, he grasped the bannister to steady himself.

'You look exhausted, Mr. Hunt. Should you venture out? The weather is too cold, and this drizzle brings a melancholy with it.'

'I must go to the College. I've pressing business there.'

'I hope you're not short of time, for everywhere there are soldiers. They stop everyone. I was questioned twice. A fine thought, me and my chicken Jesuitical assassins!'

'Because of the rumours of a plan against the King's life.'

'And more. A dead man was recovered from the waterwheels under London Bridge. There's talk he was the Justice of Peace, Sir Edmund. The last to see him near his home heard him muttering of the Catholic plot. I pray he's safe, for he's a one who protects us.'

Before Harry could think of the best response for her, some safe and reassuring remark, there came a booming knock at the door.

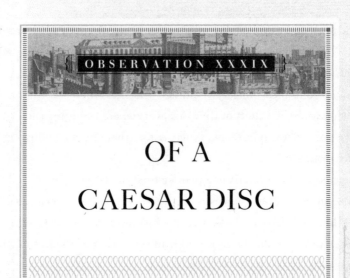

OBSERVATION XXXIX

OF A
CAESAR DISC

HARRY STOPPED MRS. HANNAM, HOLDING HER BY the shoulder.

Certainly not Tom's knock, and the circle of his landlady's friends would not bash at the door so forcefully. In more serene times, Harry would not think twice about going to answer it. After the bloodless boys, the murder of Enoch Wolfe by a monster, and then recovering Sir Edmund from the Morice waterworks, Harry had become far more wary.

He stepped down into the narrow hallway and placed himself in front of Mrs. Hannam.

The knock came again, even louder.

'Mr. Hunt! Are you in there?'

Harry recognised the voice.

He hurried to the door before the old soldier could launch another assault.

Coming in, Colonel Fields clasped Harry firmly by the hand. Unshaven, a beard extruding into the world, he had a stubble of hair surrounding his head, the top left bald and shiny.

'It is good to meet with you once more.' Fields followed Harry into the hallway, filling its width. 'So! You have your boots! I wondered if the soldiers at Gresham's College might have off with them.'

'It was you who returned them, Colonel?'

'I watched your endeavours clambering over the Morice water pump, to take the body from it.'

'I'm obliged.' Harry ignored Mrs. Hannam's dumbfounded expression, and her sudden letting go of the chicken.

'I did not call upon you then—there were a great many soldiers about. Whose was the body you found? And who came to look at him at the College?'

'Mrs. Hannam. This is Colonel Michael Fields. May I speak with him here?'

'Of course.' Mrs. Hannam's voice was tremulous from the news her lodger was the man who had climbed out onto the wheel. 'Talk away!' Then she caught his meaning, and went to the door of her parlour, and urged them in. 'Are you hungry, Colonel? I shall search out what food there is.'

'When a man does not know where his next meal is, he is always hungry, Mrs. Hannam,' Fields replied gratefully.

Mrs. Hannam found herself curtsying, before she could correct herself. Feeling a warm flush over her face, she fled off to the kitchen.

'A handsome woman, Mr. Hunt!' Fields had a way of stating things that if you disagreed you would think twice before speaking up. 'Is she a widow?'

'Her husband is in a debtor's gaol.'

'Ah . . . life owns a way of disappointing most, does it not?'

Harry waited until she was out of earshot. 'Colonel, we don't know who the dead man is, and I can't divulge who came to Gresham's.'

'The King came to Gresham's College.' Fields winked at Harry. 'With Sir Jonas Moore. I shall answer that question for you—I respect your duty to stay quiet on the matter. I imagine also the man's identity is known. I shall not insist upon an answer, for we are friends. Although I have my suspicions. The Justice of Peace, Sir Edmund Bury Godfrey, for example, is a good candidate for the man affixed onto the wheel.' He inspected Harry closely. 'You have a card-playing face. It is no matter—I am here for quite another reason. We last met in Whitechapel and discussed the Red Cipher. Have you advanced at all, to reveal its meaning?'

The Colonel would be a useful ally. As for what kind of enemy he would make, this old soldier turned Anabaptist preacher, it was difficult to decide. There was certainly more he could say on Daniel Whitcombe's use of the cipher.

Harry made his choice.

'I have.'

'You found its key?'

'Yes. The word was *corpus*.'

Fields looked immensely satisfied.

Harry took out the papers from his coat, resisting the urge to produce them with a flourish. 'These are two letters from a man calling himself Daniel Whitcombe. Either a boastful man, or else the greatest natural philosopher who ever lived.'

Fields clapped his hands, resounding in the small room they were in. 'With Daniel Whitcombe,' he said, 'there is an aspect of both.'

'You know him, as a fellow user of the Red Cipher.'

Fields nodded. 'As well as your boots, I have another gift for you. I have kept it for many years, as a memento. It shall live a more useful life with you, I think.'

He produced a small cloth bag with a drawstring around its neck and took out what looked to Harry like a flat plate.

'It is a Caesar disc. The one I used when a soldier.'

Made of brass, it was in fact three flat rings, fitted concentrically, one inside another. On two were the letters of the alphabet, and on the third, inner ring, were numbers. By turning the discs, the two alphabets and the numbers could be shifted by any number of steps, until it returned to the starting position.

'Easy to use, and easy to carry. Sturdy and simple. A perfect instrument for the field!'

Perceiving Harry's reluctance to take it, Fields placed it into his hands.

'Have it! And I shall tell you more of Daniel Whitcombe.'

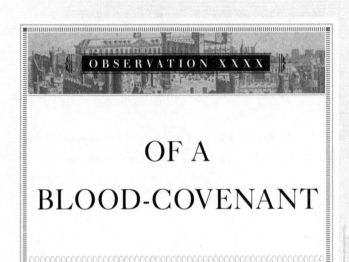

OBSERVATION XXXX

OF A
BLOOD-COVENANT

THEY SAT IN THE SIMPLY FURNISHED parlour, each with beer and some cowslip tart.

'So! You have questions, Mr. Hunt,' the old soldier stated, as he finished reading the letters.

Harry found Fields's bluff manner entirely trustworthy. The promise to Sir Edmund not to speak of the boys seeming no longer binding, he had passed the letters to him.

'The first of them being, what do you know of Daniel Whitcombe?' Harry said.

Fields stood to take off his coat, which he folded and placed on the small table in front of him. 'Daniel served under me, in the Wars which split this nation apart. Now, I told you before—when you came to me in Whitechapel—that I did not know the solicitor, Moses Creed.'

Fields rolled up his shirtsleeve to reveal a still-powerful forearm, and stepped towards Harry, looming over him. 'However, I *did* know of him, having met him when he was a child. I apologise for the lie. I knew his father, Reuben, very well. We—Reuben Creed, Daniel Whitcombe, and I—all of us three, were for a time inseparable.'

Fields turned his arm, revealing to Harry his scar, a whorl of pallid skin. 'We even made a blood-covenant with one another.'

'Using a pipe, Colonel?'

'A quill, I think—it was hurriedly done. Inside a tent by Lostwithiel, in Cornwall. A juvenile enthusiasm, you may say, but indicative of our bond. Daniel supplied the method. He was a field chirurgeon, his skills unsurpassed.'

Fields lowered his arm and replaced the sleeve. 'Reuben was a glove maker before he was a soldier. He became useful to Daniel in the stitching of men together. I told you of the last battle, at Worcester. Before that encounter, there had been ten years of struggle.'

He sat down again, very upright, his mind back in the Wars allowing his body his younger self's vigour.

'So, I was with the London Trained Bands. These London regiments became a stout and trustworthy force, often called upon when Parliament had need—though they never liked to stray far from home.'

'And was Daniel Whitcombe with you?' Harry asked. 'And Reuben Creed?'

The Colonel looked at him kindly. 'No, no. Not yet. I did not meet with Reuben until I fought at Edgehill, near Banbury, by the side of the Roman Fosse Way. We faced a charge from their horse—it was the Prince Rupert who laid into us. My company, in amongst it, drew back . . . '

Fields's face darkened, and Harry suspected his talk of 'drawing back' hid the true situation: that of a frightened mass of men spinning away from the oncoming horses, fleeing from the shaking of the earth.

'Reuben moved through our men, pacifying them with his calmness—so very contrastingly with the majority. This is how he first came to my notice. The matter went to push of pike. The King's standard bearer was killed, and the Royal standard captured.'

'I've read of this, Colonel,' Harry said. 'It was Sir Edmund Verney who held the standard. His dead hand had to be cut from it, so resolute was he.'

Fields raised his cup above his head. 'History from above, and history from below.' He brought the cup back down, spilling some of his beer. 'It has the air of myth about it. It is difficult to follow what happens on a battlefield. It is such a busy place.

'Anyways, after—now firm friends with Reuben—we faced the Royalists at Chelsea Fields. It was a stand-off, nothing more, but it gave us great heart. We spent the winter fortifying London. Men, women—children, even—worked to build up the Lines of Communication, their walls and sconces, and to dig the great ditch. Even on Sundays they worked! Eleven miles of fortifications ringed the City, the earth wall eighteen feet high.'

Fields took a great bite of his tart, washed it down with half his beer, and sighed his approval. 'Then, we went to relieve Gloucester, the place besieged by the Royalists. I was by now a captain. Reuben was loath to leave his wife—and his new son Moses—both of whom he loved greatly, but what choice had he?'

Harry assumed the question rhetorical, and quietly compared this story with his own little life, one untouched by such turbulence.

'I cannot impart how cruel those times were. Conflicts, seemingly endless. Both sides feinting different directions, like a pugilist showing one fist, only to hit with the other. I lost many of my friends. To see the corpses of men, who just before had been animate and brave, can only be thought repugnant. To have a man burst in front of you makes you wonder about the nature of Creation itself.'

Fields very deliberately looked at Harry, watching what affect his words had.

'At Alton, we fought the Royalists—using the icy roads at the time of a night-frost to advance rapidly—and we surprised them in the town. Reuben led the way into the church there, and threw grenadoes in to kill the Royalist commander. I spent the following spring in London, recuperating from a wound.'

Fields ran a finger along the scar running over the back of his head.

'A combination of a musket ball and the chirurgeon's work to remove it. Which did more damage is moot—I am pleased to inform you I am still alive!'

Harry smiled nauseously at the old man's joking of a ball fired into his skull.

'Do not look so pasty-faced on my account, Mr. Hunt. I was fainted away from the chirurgeon's cutting. I remember not a thing of it.'

He raised Harry's deciphered letters. 'That was the first time I met the author of these, for it was Daniel Whitcombe who cared for me, stitched me up, and healed me.'

The old Colonel opened his mouth wide, pulling at his lips with his fingers, and presented his front teeth, slightly shorter than their companions, tapping at them hard. 'I lost mine when hitting the ground from the force of the ball. It was Daniel who found suitable replacements, taken from a dead man lying in the field. The roots took hold—they remain to this day as firm as any of their companions.'

Fields searched for his tobacco in a battered leather-covered box, an old cartridge box hung from his belt. He spent some time pushing the tobacco into his pipe, looking at it doubtfully as it was damp from drizzle.

After a couple of fruitless tries at ignition, he continued on. 'So! We then went to relieve Plymouth. After being defeated there, we were set upon by Royalists—beaten and robbed, and stripped of our clothes, which in the rainy weather was cruel treatment. I was sadly diminished in body and spirit, and endured a fever lasting some two months. Again, Daniel cared for me, and he brought me through. By now, Reuben had started to help him—preferring the work—and his skills with sewing were prodigious. It was about this time we three brothers of the blade became brothers-in-blood—as I have said, and shown you the scar.'

Fields sucked stoically at the pipe, still trying to get his tobacco to catch.

'The next occasion I saw battle was at Naseby—a great victory for us—but our Sergeant Major-General, Sir Philip Skippon, was wounded. A ball passed through him, yet he fought on, clutching his saddle and pale in the face. It was Daniel who plugged the hole in his side, with Reuben assisting him.

'By the following year Charles Stuart gave up Oxford, and we had taken Bristol from Prince Rupert. The other Royalist strongholds were quick to follow into our hands. Basing House, at long last, Dartmouth, Torrington, Chester, and we then won a battle at Stow-on-the-Wold. Exeter and Newark surrendered, and the first War was over.'

He waved his unlit pipe in the air, in celebration of the memory.

'We returned then to London. Us three, and Reuben's wife Abigail— Moses Creed's mother, therefore—became interested in those calling themselves the Levellers. We followed John Lilburne, a Lieutenant-Colonel in our army, and also a man named William Walwyn. Their speeches stirred our hearts. My eyes were unpeeled of a misty covering, which had before obscured the world from me, from seeing it in its right relations.

'At this time the Royalists' King, the first Charles Stuart, was captured— but he soon escaped, fleeing to the Isle of Wight. There, he made promise to the Scots that if they helped him, he would make theirs the English religion, and would suppress any who dissented.'

'Mr. Hooke's told me of the King's time on the Isle of Wight, at Carisbrooke Castle. Mr. Hooke was then a boy. I believe his father met with the King there.'

'Mr. Hooke was then a boy . . . how time races along, for to me it seems freshly as yesterday. Yet I find myself an old man. Time is given out to us in mean and miserly portions.'

The tobacco still refused to light, and with the constant trying to coax it to life Fields broke the tube of his pipe, the clay snapping in his grasp. He threw it into the fire with disgust.

'So! There was the first Charles Stuart on the Isle of Wight, and in the meanwhile we met at Putney, to debate the future of the country and the kingship—Do you remember my mention of the word *Putney* at our first meeting? I used it as a keyword to show the working of the Red Cipher.'

'You instructed me on how it changed the name of Cromwell into numbers.'

'Just so!' The Colonel looked gratified. 'Having won the War, none of us knew what to do in our victory. The execution came soon after. I saw Charles Stuart's head held aloft—and still I believe it was just to see him off so violently. It showed our resolve to turn from the old way of despotism, and cheered us after our years of fighting.'

'Yet the Wars did not end,' Harry observed.

'No, they did not. His death solved little, for, unlike me, most opposed it—and, we had more foes to fight outside our borders. We went to Ireland with Cromwell, to stop their rebellion. The Irish fought savagely, being a barbarous people, and also, we stood on their soil. Think how hard we had worked to protect London, building defences around the whole of the City. In Ireland we met with resistance as stiff. At Wexford, Reuben, upon the scout for us inside the town—disguised and passing himself off as Irish—unfastened the gates for us. Once inside, we were unrestrained, and we put them to the sword. At Clonmel, the Irish defended themselves well and cleverly, building a hole we fell into when their wall was breached. They killed about a thousand of us, slashing at us with scythes and poking with their pikes and partisans. The three of us took a care to escape that hole.'

Fields faltered. His head and his limbs started shaking vehemently, his hands clasping and unclasping. 'Do you surmise Mrs. Hannam has more of this tart?' he asked, once the spasm had passed. 'I believe it the finest I have tasted. Some more beer, too, for I am out, and this talking brings a thirst with it.'

Dutifully, Harry went out to look for Mrs. Hannam, and she was happy to return to the Colonel, who thanked her for the provisions.

'A handsome woman, is she not?' Fields remarked, when she was safely out of earshot, having returned to her kitchen singing to herself. 'Narrow in the flanks, but handsome. Where was I?'

'In Ireland, Colonel,' Harry answered gently, noting the Colonel's continued upset. His memories had made him blanch, and his hands still shook agitatedly. 'At Clonmel.'

'So! You may imagine how happy we were to return from there. We went then to Scotland. On the way we lost many through sickness and shortness of rations—about a quarter of our force. All the while Daniel applied himself, saving many, with Reuben assisting him. By the time of Dunbar we were wearied, but their discipline was poor—and so we beat them. Cromwell had little time to relish his win, however, for he succumbed to the curious Scottish air, which pulls a man down into his misery. Daniel came then to *his* notice, for Daniel it was who tended to him.

'When we returned to England, we were pleased to do so, for Scotland is a dismal place. It was then that Daniel and Reuben were taken from me, on Oliver Cromwell's orders.'

Fields chewed ruminatively on his new slice of tart. 'You see, Daniel had got to know Cromwell well, and impressed all by his chirurgy. Reuben had killed the commander at Alton, and opened the gate at Wexford, and impressed all by his bravery. He assisted Daniel, more and more becoming a healer, regarding his dexterity as God-given. God seemed to cover their heads—That is why they were selected for covert work, naturally enough.'

'Both he and Reuben were employed to convey the King to France,' Harry said.

'Yes, the second Charles Stuart. Cromwell thought them the best of men to safeguard him.'

'What happened to them? Their mission was accomplished.'

'I shall tell you the thank-yous they received. One stretched from the branch of an oak tree. I saw his body hanging there, by where the Severn and Teme rivers meet—not long after the Battle of Worcester. The other, I know, was stopped at Brighthelmstone, taken to be Royalist, and sent to the Barbadoes as a slave. I found out years after, having thought him dead, too.'

'It was Reuben Creed who died, and Daniel Whitcombe who survived.'

'A long time ago . . . After Reuben died, I loved his wife, Abigail, who shared my admiration of the Levellers. She would never have me, though—loving the memory of her dead husband too much. I never sought another—loving her too much.'

'Reuben was killed because he knew of the subterfuge of the King's escape.'

Fields nodded and stroked the bristles over the dome of his head. 'A brutish act—a wasteful act, too, for he was a man of great skill, and great bravery. He was killed for what he knew. He was killed, but someone decided that Daniel should live, and that he should continue with the King on his journey to France. At Brighthelmstone, though, he was captured by our own Parliament forces, thought to be a turncoat, and shipped to the Barbadoes.'

'You heard nothing of him since?'

'I made my own investigation. I was warned away. I heard of his use in the reaping of cane and the making of sugar—on the Earl of Shaftesbury's plantations. I thought I saw him, once, years ago, at the place of the old Charing Cross—by the pillory there. It was rumoured he performed the trepanning of Prince Rupert, to alleviate the hurt from a wound to his brain.'

'Where has Whitcombe carried out his experimental and philosophical trials? Who paid for him to do so?'

'These questions I cannot answer,' the Colonel replied. 'If the body upon the Morice waterwheel was not that of the Justice, then you can ask him. I am sure he would know.'

'In truth, I cannot ask him, Colonel.'

The Colonel barely paused at Harry's tacit disclosure. 'Did Sir Edmund tell you of the keyword before he died?'

'It was revealed at the autopsy of his body. He'd swallowed it, written on a piece of paper.'

'So! He supposed he would meet his death.'

'Did Daniel Whitcombe have reason to kill Sir Edmund?'

Fields shrugged, and swept crumbs off his lap. 'Oh, he had reason enough—as did I, I suppose. But the Wars were a long time ago. We all did things that would be thought reprehensible in peace time . . . ' Fields trailed off, looking into space.

'Reason enough, Colonel?'

'Sir Edmund obeyed his orders, given to him by his commanders. In this case, by John Thurloe, who was Cromwell's Secretary of State. And Thurloe acted on the orders of Cromwell himself. That is why I never blamed Sir Edmund for Reuben's death.'

'Sir Edmund killed Reuben Creed by hanging him from a tree.'

'Yes, Sir Edmund killed him. An unnecessary insurance, I believe, for Reuben could have been trusted with the secret of Cromwell helping the present King's escape. Thurloe was ever a careful man.'

'Did Whitcombe at last take revenge against the Justice, do you think, for the death of his friend?'

'Why would he now, if he has been in London for so long?'

Harry needed a moment to consider. 'I wonder if, instead, he's now dead too, as his letter to Sir Edmund says.'

'I thought him dead before, Mr. Hunt. He returned.'

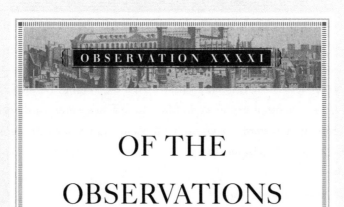

OF THE

OBSERVATIONS

DAYTIME MERGED SEAMLESSLY INTO EVENING, THE gloom of one re-placed by the gloom of the other. The rain still fell outside. Harry listened to it spattering on the roof, making a sleepy sighing sound.

Other than the rain, and the occasional crack of a beam as the warmth from the fires left the house, all was quiet. After his visit from Colonel Fields, Harry had gone to bed early, in the late afternoon, but the throb in his tailbone and the tenderness of his shins and ankle made sleep impossi-ble. He also had a sickening headache drilling the bone above his eyebrows.

Accepting defeat, he lit a candle and went to his table, and to the pack-age he had found with Oldenburg's correspondences.

Meticulously, he unwrapped the sailcloth from its contents.

Four piles of papers, each neatly tied with thread. He spread them out over the floor of his room.

Each pile had a title page, uniform in colour and size, bought from the same paper seller. Their titles swam in front of him, but he made himself focus. He would attempt the work. Maybe the aches would subside.

Using the keyword *corpus*, and the Colonel's Caesar disc, he soon revealed the title of each pile:

Observations Historical

Observations Philosophical

Observations Habitual

Observations Propagational

The top sheets contrasted with the various sheets beneath, whose edges rippled, a mixture of weights, hues, and sizes. It appeared Daniel Whitcombe had brought together his researches, noted on papers bought on different occasions and from various makers, by theme, like in a commonplace book.

The writing on them was small, with extraordinarily regular lettering. The hand of a skilled chirurgeon, Harry thought.

Threads further divided each of the piles. Harry untied *Observations Historical.* It was some effort to unpick the knots, and eventually he tired of trying to loosen them, and took a small knife to them. He released ten sheaves of notes, and, from under the main title page, a short explanatory letter.

With the help of the brass Caesar disc given to him by Colonel Fields, he revealed the hidden description.

History describes mankind's rules or institutes, concerning Duties, Sins, or Indifference in matters of Religion, or things that are commanded, forbidden or permitted by their Municipal Laws. It describes the Opinions or Traditions to be found amongst Mankind, concerning God, Creation, Revelation, Prophecies, and Miracles.

The ten bundles beneath this sheet were headed: *Observations of Religions*; *Observations of Institutions*; *Observations of Sin*; *Observations of Indifference*; *Observations of Divine Law*; *Observations of Civil Law*; *Observations of Offences against God*; *Observations of Miracles*; *Observations of Obligation*; *Observations of Atonement*.

Harry did not open any of these. Instead, he piled them up next to him on the floor and went to the second, far larger, pile, *Observations Philosophical*. Again, when he cut it open, under the top page was another single sheet. Below it were eighteen more bundles, each with their title sheets of the same paper. Harry deciphered Whitcombe's note on the contents of these bundles.

> *The knowledge of Things. Their Essence and Nature, properties, causes, and consequences of each Species, must be divided according to the several Orders and Species of Things. So far as we have the true notion of Things as really they are in their Being, so far we advance in Real and True Knowledge. Having a true, clear, and distinct Idea of the Nature of Anything, because we are ignorant of their Essence, takes in their Causes, Properties, and Effects, or as much of them as we can know.*

Harry read the top sheet of the first of the smaller bundles he had freed. It was titled *Observations of The Light of Grace*. The next was headed *Observations of The Light of Nature*, followed by *Observations Concerning Experience*; *Observations Of Astronomical Magic*; *Observations Of Theological Cabala*; *Observations Of Medicinal Alchemy*; *Observations Of Water*; *Observations Of Fire*; *Observations Of Air*; *Observations Of Breath*; *Observations of the Soul*; *Observations of the Body*; *Observations of Animals*; *Observations of Minerals*; *Observations of Vegetables*; *Observations of the Heart and Blood*; *Observations Of Homunculii*; and the last; *Observations of Miscellaneous Species*.

The largest of the bundles was *Observations of the Heart and Blood*, easily a hundred sheets, followed in size by *Observations of The Light of Grace*, *Observations of The Light of Nature*, then *Observations Of Air*, *Observations*

Of Fire, and *Observations Of Water.* The other bundles were far smaller, suggesting these were subjects more peripheral to Whitcombe's studies.

Blood, the heart, grace, nature, air, fire, and water. These would seem to be at the centre of his interests. Unless, rather, this was work Whitcombe had been directed to do, in his 'employments'.

What was Daniel Whitcombe's design?

All Harry had was like the fragments of a shipwreck. He did not yet have enough to envisage the whole ship.

He brought his attention back to the letter addressed to Sir Edmund, to Whitcombe's interest in the Light of Nature, and the Light of Grace. Paracelsus, he recalled from one of Hooke's lectures given at the Royal Society, discussed the two Lights. Descartes wrote of them as well.

Harry looked at the biggest bundle left by Whitcombe, *Observations of the Heart and Blood.* Its title showed his knowledge of William Harvey, echoing the title of Harvey's work, *Exercitatio Anatomica de Motu Cordis et Sanguinis in Animalibus*, published some fifty years before.

Harry piled the bundles up, again not opening them, and turned to the third section, *Observations Habitual.*

> *Things we do find amongst other People fit for our imitation, whether politic or private Wisdom. Any Arts conducing to the Conveniences of Life.*

This third collection of notes had their top pages labelled *Observations on Wisdom; Observations on Private Knowledge; Observations on Universal Languages; Observations on Substance; Observations on Nourishment; Observations on Medicines; Observations on Mechanical Motion;* and the last was *Observations on Perceiving.* The largest pile of these under *Observations Habitual* was *Observations on Mechanical Motion.* Harry put all these aside as well.

The fourth pile, *Observations Propagational,* a thick gathering of bound papers, almost as large as *Observations Philosophical,* was divided by Whitcombe's careful tying into just two sections.

He cut open the parcel and translated Whitcombe's note.

The propagation and transplantation of the Natural Products of the Country, fit to be traded for some useful Quality they have. Any advantageous Commerce. And these Notes concern Practice or Action.

The two headings for each section were *Observations on Production* and *Observations on Trade.*

Harry lay back on his bed in the dim light afforded by his flickering candle. He tried to think of all these piles pushed over the floor, and all their titles, to make room in his mind for the receiving of them, to better retain their details when he resumed with his deciphering. He pictured Whitcombe's themes as objects in a room, jostling one another for space, leaning against one another untidily. He envisaged himself picking them up, moving them around, reorganising them into neat piles. All this helped his memory, a trick learned from a reading of Cicero.

The scope of Whitcombe's miscellany made him question where to start. The thickest pile was the notes on *Observations Philosophical.* This coincided more closely with his own interests in the natural, the mechanical, and the philosophical.

In his letters, Whitcombe wrote of provoking God, of presuming to penetrate the depths of nature. He described his work as a natural philosopher, an experimentalist, a mechanic, an observator: yet much of the material in the package concerned history, trade, political intelligencing, and religious moralising.

Harry was not an antiquary, a merchant, or a clergyman. He would start with what he knew.

He reached for the *Observations Philosophical,* and cut the threads tying the pile's uppermost bundle, *Observations on the Light of Grace.*

It was now eight o'clock in the evening. He had arranged to meet with Colonel Fields later, at Whitechapel. Another hour on the deciphering, and then it would be time to go.

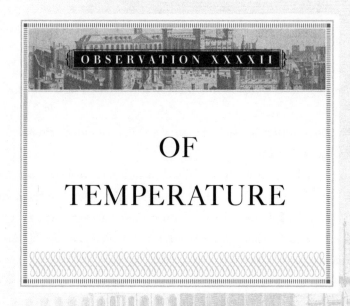

OF

TEMPERATURE

AT HOOKE'S LODGINGS, TOM GYLES CROUCHED on the kitchen floor while Mary prepared a goose, gathering up the plucked feathers. He collected them to glue onto his next project: a machine with flapping wings, powered by clockwork.

Mr. Hooke had promised to assist him that evening with the completion of his model of the moon. Together, they were to suspend it over the College quadrangle, on a rope tied from Hooke's observatory across to the repository in the opposite gallery.

Hooke, though, had been waiting for the King's men, who at last came for Sir Edmund. More soldiers of the Foot brought a discreet dray into Gresham's, and they had loaded the body in the darkness.

After the days of excitement building his model, as the time of its suspension grew near, Tom felt a curious lack of elation. He had felt unwell since returning from the market, sent there on a mission for Mary to find eggs and black pudding. He had had a fright there, too: between the stalls, a man obstructed him, then punched him in the arm as if he had been at fault.

When Mary had finished plucking, he stood up stiffly, a film of sweat on his face. He moved away from the heat of the fire, holding the feathers in his arms, and went up the stairs.

It occurred to Hooke, who was preparing some spirit of *sal ammoniac* to take as a purgative, that Tom seemed subdued. Usually, he would be telling the boy to be more careful, stop annoying Mary, stop asking him questions when he was busy. Instead of the usual thumping of him going up the stairs, it was a slow trudge. The calm should have been welcome. Instead, Hooke found it disturbed the stream of his thinking.

When Tom returned down from his room, having deposited the feathers there, Hooke looked more closely at him. The boy's face was still damp with sweat, and a flush on his cheeks made Hooke pat the chair next to him, for Tom to sit down.

'You may rest until Mary brings dinner.' Hooke sounded forced and overly cheerful.

Mary spoiled Hooke's attempted unconcern by coming to inspect Tom herself. Gripping him by the chin, she studied his reddened, moist face.

'I can feel the heat coming from him. Look at him, Mr. Hooke! The child cannot feel at all well, bless the lamb.'

Tom pulled himself away from her grasp. 'My back aches. I am sore.'

'Your joints, are they the same?' Mary asked.

'Stiff too.' Tom stood up, sullen and miserable.

'Then you must go to your bed.'

'Mary, will you prepare a broth?' Hooke said, overruled by his housekeeper. 'I have some Aldersgate cordial, too, which will cool him. Continue with the goose later, when Tom is abed. I shall call upon Dr. Diodati presently. He is a capable man. He will make Tom better.'

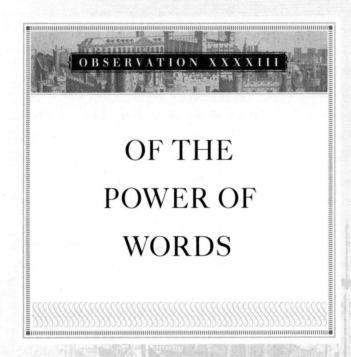

OBSERVATION XXXXIII

OF THE POWER OF WORDS

THE CROWD PADDED SOFTLY ALONG CABLE Street, their lanterns and flambeaux mimicking the night sky, in which a million points of light shone, separated by the reaches of space. With the starshine came a pitiless cold, making Harry wish he had come more wrapped. His teeth chattered, despite his leather coat and a thick felt cap loaned to him by Mrs. Hannam, whiffs of her husband still clinging.

They walked towards the meadows by Knock Fergus. The lights flowed around them on either side. There was no talk among the people, just the noise of feet and the occasional slap of a freezing hand against another.

Harry, with Hooke's improved lamp sending out its powerful light, saw Moses Creed waiting for them, and Fields welcomed him with a tight embrace. Moses Creed gave Harry a perfunctory handshake. Harry, likewise, was not delighted to meet the solicitor.

The Colonel led them on, rejoining the stream of people.

They followed the line of a flint wall reflecting the lights from its edges. Fields guided them to an iron gate halfway along it, where a barrel of whale oil burned brightly, extending tongues of flame as tall as a man. Here, the lights converged, as the people funnelled through the gateway into a large courtyard.

Harry could hear the sounds of a crowd, but it was the noise of hundreds of people speaking calmly to one another, rather than shouting or jostling. A man stood at the gate, greeting Fields with a grasp of his hand.

The place they entered was built on a square, and the arrangement of its buildings, looking like run-down outhouses leaning together, gave it the feel of a farmyard. Hanging lanterns and torches sent scoops of light across the sea of heads. Everyone stood looking towards a makeshift stage, with a canvas roof and a single chair at its centre.

Most of these heads were grey-haired, elderly, at least fifty years old. Harry felt out of place, and foolish. He wondered if Creed felt the same, for the other man, although fifteen or so years older than him, was similarly outlandish. Nobody showed them any suspicion, though.

In fact, Harry was conscious of nothing more than an immense goodwill shared throughout the crowd. Except, it was not a crowd: it was an audience, ruly and quiet, gathered to listen.

Some had brought food, and they shared it out. If one had brought bread and a neighbour had meat, they combined, and a third offered beer. Others had blankets with them, and these too were shared, and draped over the shoulders of the watchers. Despite the proximity of bodies there was no pushing, even as more people flowed in through the gate. Some sat on chairs brought with them, at no risk of being unbalanced.

Harry, with Fields and Moses Creed next to him, was towards the back of the crowd, but the slope of the ground meant he could see across all the grey heads to the stage. He was grateful for the warmth from all these bodies pressed together. He experienced the growing expectancy travelling through them all, as the various conversations around him died down. He saw Fields and Creed beside him hold the same expression as everyone else. A rapt concentration, intent on witnessing the precise moment they gathered and waited for.

Harry could not comprehend why, for nothing seemed to have changed, and nobody had mounted the stage, but all of a sudden there was the creak of ageing limbs as everyone craned for a better view. It was like the turning of a school of fish, done before realisation the moment had come.

Onto the stage, accompanied by an elderly woman, shuffled an even more elderly man. He used a stick to support himself, and the woman held his arm.

'It is, isn't it?' a woman in front of them asked her companion.

'It is.'

Harry recognised the old couple on the stage. He remembered them from Alsatia. The old man's tremors, seen when seeking Enoch Wolfe at the Angel, were quite gone.

Harry looked across at Colonel Fields, whose eyes were moist with emotion.

A man as old as the century, who had seen the last Tudor and three of the Stuarts, pulled himself straight to look at them all.

It was William Walwyn, the Leveller.

HE GAVE THEM all a shy smile at being welcomed by so many. A spontaneous outburst of clapping greeted him back.

The clapping receded, the strange logic of an audience dictating its length.

'I am sure there was no man born marked of God above another,' Walwyn began, his voice unwavering and clear, cutting through the night. 'For none comes into the world with a saddle on his back. Neither any booted and spurred to ride him.'

The people acknowledged the creed of the Levellers, and again Walwyn waited until their applause died down. Fields, like many standing with him, openly let the tears fall, down his face and onto his old campaign coat.

This was what Fields had fought for, for all those years. This, for him, was the way, the truth, and the light.

It was listening to Walwyn more than thirty years ago which led him to challenge all of his deepest-held beliefs, beliefs soaked up unthinkingly from his parents and peers. Beliefs concerning government, property, the church and clergy. Of the way he conducted himself among his fellows.

Walwyn spoke of communism, of establishing equality between men and women, of a universal toleration between the sects and religions. Whatever is erroneous, he said, will in time whither and perish.

Walwyn even refused to condemn the Catholics, saying they should keep their altars, priests, and their Pope, as long as they were loyal to their sovereign, and lived quietly together with those who preferred other forms of worship.

Fields remembered his reaction when he first heard the Leveller's words. The shock of hearing such a militant tolerance had given way to the excitement of a profound realisation: the striving to be a good and compassionate man had little to do with ceremony. A Jew, a Hindu, or a Muslim had a clear idea of their place within the world, and who was Michael Fields to disparage them?

William Walwyn spoke again.

'Love is the balsam that, often and well rubbed in, may cure your gangrene, and though at first your distemper may cause you to loathe it, yet take a little and a little of it, use inwardly and outwardly, constantly, and you will find your disposition to alter, until you become a strong and healthful Christian.'

Harry, although he listened to the sermons at his Anglican church, expected to do so on a Sunday, comprehended he believed in nothing. Nothing he took to be true had been hard won. He had been content to assume a customary religion.

He was no better, no different, to a superstitious man of the woods worshipping Jack-in-the-Green.

Custom drew most people into their religion. It was far easier not to resist this pressure, ever running with the stream, following the fashion of belief. Within this elderly multitude listening, eagerly accepting the message of Walwyn's words, Harry was surrounded by so many who could not just follow the religion of the times, but instead sought the true word of God.

Harry could see the solicitor watching the old Leveller, spellbound. Creed had his hand raised to his mouth. His eyes were wet, too. The man on the stage—old now, but his spirit still burning brightly, his righteous anger still channelled to the cause of his fellows—was the man his father, Reuben, had believed in.

This was why Fields had brought Moses Creed here. For him to know his own father.

'Look about you!' Walwyn's voice became louder, more forceful, and all the people in the crowd simultaneously swayed closer, pulled in by the power of his voice.

Walwyn paused. His silence made the crowd breathless, as if high on a mountaintop where the air was scarce. They willed him to continue.

When he did, there was a collective sigh.

'We have many, nowadays, who are doubly unjust and think not of it. They are favourable in examining themselves, and severe towards others. They ought to be severe towards themselves, and favourable towards others! It is a fault not easily mended. It requires a greater power of religion to do it than most have yet attained. Either renounce the name, or let your practice demonstrate you are a Christian!'

Again, a crackle of applause from the crowd. Walwyn did not need to pull them away from their own beliefs. He was too subtle a man to try. He simply described what they knew to be true. What they saw every day.

'He who is glad of his neighbour's defamation would not be sorry at his ruin. A slanderer would be a murderer, but for fear of retribution. Therefore, every virtuous man should shun a slanderer, as he would shun a serpent.'

It was a bright light he shone on them.

How far they had failed. Their responsibility was not to any authority, but to themselves and one another.

Harry heard clearly why Fields was so in thrall to this man, why the

Colonel had asked him to come with them. It was as if by the clarity of his words, expressed with a freedom from zeal, Walwyn unleashed the powers of nature to entice everyone there.

'If I have all faith, and have not love, I am as sounding brass, or as a tinkling cymbal. If faith works, it works by love. Let us all therefore walk in love, even as Christ loved, and gave himself as an offering and a sacrifice for us.'

Colonel Fields had brought Harry here so he could understand more of the Levellers, and the beliefs which sustained him, Daniel Whitcombe, and Reuben Creed through the horrors of the Civil Wars.

⋦

THE SMELL OF sugar in the air, from the warehouses stretching down almost to the Tower, put Harry in mind of Whitcombe's being taken as a slave to the Barbadoes, on the Earl of Shaftesbury's plantations. How had he made his return? His letters spoke of his employments—employed by whom?

Whitcombe wrote of two Lights, the Light of Nature and the Light of God. Why had he needed to write a last confession to Sir Edmund Bury Godfrey? To atone? What spiritual hold could Sir Edmund have held over him? Had Whitcombe betrayed the Justice somehow, perhaps after the Battle of Worcester?

But if Sir Edmund killed Reuben Creed, surely the guilt was his?

Why, if Whitcombe had been in London, had he never approached his old comrade, Colonel Fields? Did shame prevent him?

Torchlight and lanternlight reflected from the tears on the Colonel's cheeks. Moses Creed, at the Colonel's other shoulder, eyes trained unwaveringly on William Walwyn on the stage, looked as though he had run for a distance, his breaths coming hard from his lungs as clouds of vapour.

As for Harry, though, Walwyn's words did not touch him.

The voice spoke to him again: *What hope have you? You have no faith and no love. You are not even a tinkling cymbal.*

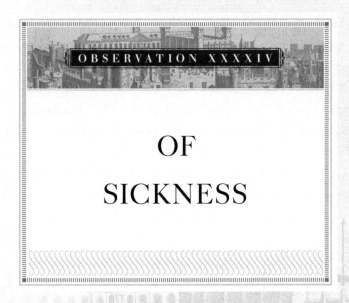

OBSERVATION XXXXIV

OF

SICKNESS

ROBERT HOOKE'S NOSE DRIPPED IN THE cold. The ground was frosty, making his journey precarious. Wishing he had not loaned his best lamp to Harry as he slipped again, he called on Dr. Diodati at his house on Puddle Dock Hill.

Hooke's various ailments had forged a relationship profitable to both—pecuniary for the physician, remedial for the natural philosopher. Like steel wine, Theodore Diodati was an acquired taste, but no less restorative. Hooke admired the economy of his means of expression, and doodled ideas of universal languages based on it. He knew others were not so taken, and that the lack of a soothing bedside manner would never bring the most fashionable to Diodati's door.

Despite the lateness of the hour, Diodati agreed to return with him. Once they were back at Gresham's College, Hooke led him up to the servant's bedroom.

Tom lay with his face pressed into his pillow, his hands clenched over his head.

'The sickness worsens quickly,' Hooke told Diodati.

The doctor examined Tom, observing red eyes, a nose swollen and running, and a rash forming over the skin. He pulled the sheets up to Tom's chin, and led Hooke out to the landing, beyond the boy's hearing. Mary waited there, pale and frightened.

'Measles,' Diodati told them.

'Not the smallpox?' Hooke asked him anxiously.

'Measles.'

Hooke looked at Mary, his mouth a thin-lipped O, in his relief at the diagnosis.

'Should we let blood?'

'Four ounces, arm, boy small.'

Diodati returned to Tom, who did not notice him and did not stir as he produced a bowl and a lancet from his bag. 'Cloth.'

Hooke sent Mary, who sobbed with the relief it was not the smallpox, as she had thought—'though the measles was quite grave enough, poor lamb,'—to fetch some linen.

When she returned, Diodati pressed the point of the lancet into Tom's flesh, making him cry out pitifully. The cut produced a steady flow. By a skilled pinching of the wound, the doctor directed Tom's blood into the bowl. The boy lay still, not moving his arm away from the cutting.

'Good, Tom, good,' Hooke told him, stroking his forehead. 'Brave child.'

Satisfied he had taken enough blood, Diodati made a compress with the cloth, and gently wiped Tom's arm until the blood thickened at the cut.

'Again, morning,' he told Hooke.

When Diodati had gone, Hooke and Mary sat with Tom, whose raw and swollen throat prevented him from talking. Instead, he made low animal-like sounds, deep from his belly.

Hooke tried to soothe Mary, promising if Dr. Diodati could not help, then there was Mr. Gidley, the chirurgeon, also Dr. Whitchurch, and old Dr. King. There was also John Mapletoft, Professor of Physic there at Gresham's College.

'Any of these alone would save Tom,' he assured her. 'All together, they will certainly pull him through.'

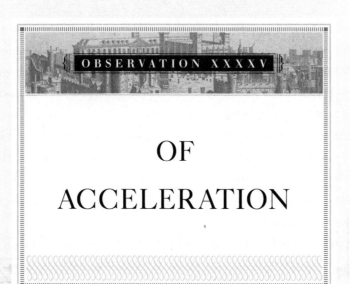

OF
ACCELERATION

THE PAIN IN HARRY'S ANKLE, CRACKED on the beams of the Morice waterwheel, troubled him most of all, especially after the long duration of William Walwyn's speech. He walked stiffly, all aches and sores, watching for loose stones which could trip him. Sending its forceful beam into the darkness before him, the weight of Hooke's lamp pulled at his arm, and Harry swapped it from one hand to the other.

The show of the constellations in Whitechapel was snatched away. Clouds had returned over London, bringing a fine rain which froze as it hit the ground. The way was treacherous underfoot.

Harry welcomed the visibility the lamp gave, but wished it did not draw so much comment, or so many covetous looks. It might be taken from him—he could imagine Hooke's displeasure.

Away from the shared generosity of the Levellers, he was back to the incivility of the London night. He took off his spectacles and folded them inside his pocket. There, he had his bunch of keys, and he held them inside the pocket, between his fingers, ready to pull them out. It was the nearest thing to defence that he had.

After going through Aldgate, he decided to take the better-lit Leadenhall Street rather than Wormwood Street, the darker and more menacing route by the Roman wall.

He would go to Gresham's College. Hooke would undoubtedly still be up, as was his habit.

Harry wanted to speak to him of the *Observations*, and of their author, Daniel Whitcombe. And of the Colonel's news, that Sir Edmund had killed Reuben Creed, which might be the reason for his murder. Harry had still not told Hooke of Enoch Wolfe's murder.

He concentrated on the sound his feet made on the pavement. He could hear the irregularity of his step caused by his limp, and he whiled away his journey by endeavouring to make the pattern of his strides more even, and watching his feet in the pool of lamplight thrown over the frost.

A ghost owl screeched behind him, from near the synagogue.

By the turn to African House, Harry heard another noise, at first faint and then getting louder, and it took him some time to realise it was the sound of tramping feet. He saw a patrol further down the way, their pikes held upright, led by an enormous man dressed as a curate, whose features all crowded into the centre of his face. Harry slowed, wanting not to be noticed, and he watched them all assemble outside a house. An officer pounded on its door. It opened to loud complaints coming from the man inside.

Harry was shocked to witness them ended by a hard cuff from one of the soldiers.

This astonishment, and the curious sight of a church official leading soldiers, stayed with him for all of the length of Leadenhall Street, until another sound reached him: the clatter of coach wheels on cobbles.

There was little to separate its sound from that of other coaches going by—maybe an inkling he had heard that exact sound before—yet he turned.

Going under the light of a torch mounted high on a wall was the same glossy black coach-and-four which had taken the monster to Alsatia, being driven by the man in a goatskin coat.

The coach expanded in his vision, inflating like a sinister balloon. The horses paced implacably towards him, their heads dipping and rising like mechanical hammers.

He needed the safety of Gresham's College.

He broke into a run, trying to ignore the pain in his ankle and shins, but the slipperiness of the ground meant he lost his footing, his leg shooting out sideways, painfully twisting his knee.

The clopping of the horses' shoes increased in tempo, but he dared not look around to see if the driver had urged them on. He had to find a turn too tight for the coach and hope it passed on by. His heart pumped hard. A rushing sound started in his ears, unhelpfully, making it more difficult to discern the progress of the coach-and-four.

He turned into Lyme Way, finding a dark narrow alley heading to the markets. Behind him, the horses stopped. In the fish market, he slowed, his breath steaming in the cold. He stayed by an arched doorway, pressing against the door which had a sheet torn from a pamphlet pasted to it.

The Saviour of the Nation, it said.

No more sounds from the coach. He tried to convince himself he had not been spotted, that the driver had been just going about his business, but still he found himself waiting. His breathing returned to a more normal rate, but the sweat on his back was cooling, making him shiver.

Harry persuaded himself to go on.

By the bare stalls of the hide market, footsteps followed behind. He swung the lamp but could see no one there. The footsteps stopped as he did. He wondered if he should extinguish it—he knew the landmarks in the dark well enough—but the distance to Gresham's was not so far.

He went on, more hurriedly. The steps did not start up again.

In his mind, Harry saw the face of Enoch Wolfe at the moment his neck was bitten away, and the stares of the two men with him.

Then he heard running, getting louder, coming towards him. His heart lurched, as if loose inside his chest. He turned, going instead for the direction of the Thames, hurrying as fast as he could on the slippery ground and his injured ankle and knee, wincing at each stride.

Keep the monster away from Gresham's. From Hooke, Grace, Tom, and Mary.

He hoped to conceal himself in the maze of alleys off Fish Street Hill.

Into a passageway with rubbish strewn along it, stinking of rotting vegetables. A dead cat, its body deflated, fur matted and bloodied, kicked out of the way against the wall.

Harry opened the lamp and snuffed it out. He found some steps down to a basement doorway. He wavered for a short while, thinking what best to do, and then, tentatively, he descended, extending each foot into the blackness, depending on its cover to keep him from being found, worrying he would be unable to escape should he be discovered, that he would be trapped in this little ominous space.

The running stopped. There was laboured breathing and the crunch of halting boots at the level of the street. The glow of a lantern played over the rough surface of the bricks above him, the frost on the wall reflecting its light.

He pushed himself down, further down, into his dark corner.

Then, the light went out.

'Fuckster!'

Harry heard the lantern being shaken, his pursuer trying to bring it back to life.

Crouching down in the hole, Harry waited. The man's lantern had gone quiet.

A dark shape. A hand grabbed at him, finding his ear, pulled him out of his crouch and off his feet. Harry smacked down on a hard step, his forehead hitting it, bouncing off it, sending white shoots of pain through him. His fall smashed Hooke's lamp. He swung its twisted frame out at his assailant. It connected with some part of him, for a harsh bellow sounded out, and the hand let slip of him.

Harry scrambled up off the ground, trying to shake the hurt from his head, and ran up the flight of steps, treading over his attacker who had fallen across them. The man's body recoiled from his weight, and he let out a loud grunt of pain. Harry almost lost his footing, but he reached the top of the stairs.

He raced down towards the river, as fast as his sore body could take him. The man was running after, still cursing, but falling behind.

Harry, convinced the monster from the Angel coffeehouse looked to bite him too, searched for more cover, somewhere else to hide, but these streets were so constricted and straight he was sure he would be seen.

He headed to Hooke's Fish Street pillar, the Monument to the Great Conflagration. It was kept locked at night, but Harry had the key in his bunch for when he went to assist Hooke with experiments.

He tried one key, then another, frantically working through them, unable to see which was which. At last, he found the right one, and opened the door to the dark void inside.

❧

HE TRIED TO push the door shut behind him, to lock it against his attacker, but with a great leap the monster crashed against it, forcing it back. Both of them sprawled on the floor.

Harry was first up. He twisted away and sprinted up the steps, following their tight spiral inside the column of the Monument.

He ran, his ankle forgotten, with the boots of the man behind him resounding on the marble. Harry used one hand to push against the curving wall, sliding it along the stone. He knew the tightness of the spiral and the pitch of the staircase. He sensed the reports of each bootfall behind him drop further back.

With pain burning his legs, he started to pace himself for the long climb of the steps. When he looked down, he saw only black. The muscles of his thighs and back screaming at him to stop, he followed the coil taking him up the column, winding ever higher, and away from the monster.

When Harry reached the final step, then ventured out onto the narrow balcony surrounding the top of the column, he slipped on the freezing rain. He gasped desperately for breath, lungs feeling as if they burst through his ribs. In the back of his throat was a taste like blood.

The rooftops of London looked far away and below. The Thames was a malevolent black ribbon. The spire of St. Olave's threatened oppressively. The welcoming lights by Gresham's College were mockingly unreachable, separated from him by a hellish beast who bit throats.

Under the Monument's great copper urn, with its flames reaching out, Harry tried to think of some plan. There was nothing up here to aid him, and no place to conceal himself. He realised he would have to meet the monster face to face.

Who could it be who so chewed his victims, and who came for him now? His opponent had made no attempt to speak to him, had not shouted after him, except for his curses and his one grunt when trodden on.

Harry squatted against the wall, holding the longest key of his bunch like a stiletto, wondering if he would be able to push it into the monster. He held Hooke's broken lamp, preparing to swing it again.

The rain ran from his hair and into his eyes. He wiped at them, staring fixedly at the narrow doorway for a bestial head to appear. With his spectacles inside his pocket, his view was blurred.

He waited.

Boots crunched on the top steps, and heavy breaths approached.

Aim for the eyes, with their strange lack of feeling, a single brow across them . . .

The monster emerged through the little door, his feet slipping too on the balcony floor. The silhouette of his head turned each way. He chose the opposite direction around the platform, away from Harry.

Harry let him go further, judging he must have reached the other side of the column. Enough distance between them to creep down the stairs.

As quietly as he could, Harry made his move, relieved he would not have to stab him. He had not breathed since the monster's entrance onto the balcony. He did not allow himself to exhale, enclosing the air inside his raging lungs, as the steam of his breath would be visible.

As Harry bent his head to go through the low door, his opponent must have sensed him.

The scrape of his boots on the stone, and more loud gasps.

Managing to engage a wrist, the monster jerked Harry back from the door and swung him out again onto the balcony. Harry was forced into the railing, and his lungs emptied from the jolt, but instead of letting himself be stopped by the bars he continued to turn, taking his foe by surprise.

Harry pulled him after and unbalanced him. The monster, taller, hit his back against the top rail, and skidded on the icy floor, falling to his knees.

Harry swung Hooke's lamp frantically, but missed. He tried to return to the doorway, turned too hastily, and slipped again. He fell sideways to the floor, losing the lamp and his hat.

He rolled, then crawled on the ice, desperate for grip and the safety of the stairway, but his attacker had managed to rise.

The monster pulled Harry up by his hair.

Harry cried out as the roots separated from his scalp. He jabbed backwards with his key, and must have connected, as a roar came from behind. Even so, the monster managed to get a grip of Harry's arm, as well as his hair. Harry tried to jab again but could not free himself.

The monster twisted his wrist, painfully, and forced Harry to drop the bunch of keys. They fell with a jangle to the platform, and bounced away, dropping to the paving below.

Harry kicked out at the frame of the open doorway, close enough he could push back from it with his leg. They both pitched backwards and hit against the rail.

His attacker hit it harder, the impact releasing his hold.

He made a grab at Harry's coat, but his flailing found no purchase on the wet leather. Harry pushed into him and up with his shoulder, using both legs to push himself away from the wall.

The monster went over the rail.

Harry saw a hand catch one of the vertical bars, wrapping itself around it, and then the other hand, more slowly appearing, as it was all the monster could do to reach. Both hands then slithered down, knuckles bone-white as the thick fingers sought desperate purchase on the wet iron, to keep from the abyss below.

After a second to consider, Harry put his arms through to hold on to the monster's hands, to rescue him, clasping his wrists, but the freezing rain made it impossible. He could feel his hold starting to slip.

He looked into the monster's face, near enough to focus on him, watching his realisation he was not to be saved.

It was not the monster. Not the murderer of Enoch Wolfe, but the man who had accompanied him to Alsatia. The driver of the coach, in the goatskin coat.

He was older, fifty or so. A tough-looking man. An old soldier, maybe. Blood from a deep cut from Hooke's lamp streamed down one side of his head.

He locked his eyes onto Harry's, as he had done in Alsatia.

Harry felt the man's weight release from his grasp, and saw him drop away, slowly at first, then faster, accelerating as gravity demanded, and disappear into the darkness.

The man made no sound. Harry would have expected a cry, but he went uncomplainingly to his death.

From two hundred feet above, Harry perceived the body hitting the ground as a vibration through the Portland stone of the Monument.

HEIGHT HAD NEVER worried him. Now, after his forehead hitting the step, and his exertions to climb the stairway inside the Monument, followed by the struggle to avoid, to fight, and then to save the man chasing him, Harry felt bilious and faint. His view across London from the Monument's balcony, blacks and silvers in the moonlight, had a nautical roll. The rain's coldness made the skin on his forehead feel ready to split.

He was not certain he had done all he could to stop the man from falling. He had thought him a monster, but still the thought sickened him.

Below him, at the base of the column, people and their lanterns clustered around the body, which rested on its front, arms outstretched like an angel's wings. A quadrant of blood from the ruined head had sprayed over the paving of Monument Yard.

The black coach-and-four waited there. Wolfe's killer looked up at him from the dead driver's seat. From this distance, he looked more like a man than the monster he had become in Harry's imagination, but Harry could still distinguish the thick forehead with the single eyebrow across it.

From the crowd gathering at the body a chant of 'Papists!' started up. Some saw the coach, and questioned its driver, taking him to be suspicious. When he warned them off, his accent was definitely foreign. They started to rock the vehicle.

The man produced a musket, and they stepped back. He turned the coach, still levelling his weapon at them, leaving his partner to them.

At last feeling steadier, Harry picked up Hooke's dead lamp, and Mr. Hannam's hat. He descended the twisting stairway in the dark.

He emerged from the Monument, into the light cast by the people who had run to the loud smack of the man hitting the ground. Gathered by the broken corpse, they watched Harry curiously as he walked through them.

Among them was a pair dressed in long sea-green coats.

Felicity Tarripan, the Quaker, would have recognised them, and taken them to be female.

Harry, too, would have known them if he had seen them, for they were the ladies he had witnessed fencing together at Whitehall: Hortense

Mancini, Duchesse de Mazarin, and with her the King's daughter Anne Lennard, Countess of Sussex.

'It was a pickpocket chased me to the top of the pillar!' Harry shouted at a threatening, suspicious-looking man.

Roman Catholic malefaction had already been assumed. The crowd heard what it had wanted to hear.

'A pickpocket' became 'A papist!'

Harry started in with the chant as the idea took hold. 'Papists, yes, it must be!'

'Jesuit!'

'With a foreigner!'

'Insurgents!'

Taking advantage of the wave of Protestant zeal, Harry manoeuvred himself to the edge of the crowd, waving his fist and shouting.

'Papists! There are papists amongst us!'

When he had gone further up Fish Street, almost to where it became Grace Church Street, the Duchesse and the Countess followed after him.

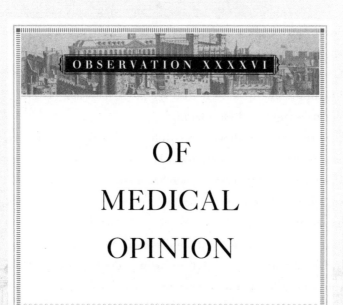

OF
MEDICAL
OPINION

SEEING HOOKE'S TROUBLED FACE, MR. GIDLEY, PEAR-SHAPED and port-stained, agreed to accompany him to Gresham's, even though it was early in the morning. Hooke described the symptoms his apprentice exhibited. Gidley's face became graver as he heard.

'Dr. Diodati is an excellent physician,' he told Hooke, locking his door behind them. 'A credit to his trade. And yet . . . ' He frowned from professional difficulty. He did not share the satisfaction of most chirurgeons at uncovering the mistake of a physician, and besides, Hooke's obvious worry and the perilous state of the boy made such pettiness doubly ignoble. 'I must diverge from his understanding of the sickness. You say the boy pissed blood?'

Hooke confirmed it: Tom had.

Hooke had a folding umbrella with him, to his own design, and the two men sheltered from the rain beneath it, walking together.

'The way you describe it, Mr. Hooke, is more indicative of the smallpox. Bleeding in the smallpox is a mortal symptom, habitually fatal. Let us hope Dr. Diodati is right, and I am wrong.'

They turned from Broad Street into Gresham's, where Harry, without his keys, waited in the quadrangle. He had his landlady's husband's hat pulled low over his forehead. No one had answered his knock.

'Ah, Harry,' Hooke greeted him morosely. 'Tom is gravely sick, and we fear it to be the smallpox.'

Harry had walked to Gresham's from his lodgings sore, stiff, and with a collection of tender bruises. All his pains were forgotten at Hooke's news, replaced instead by an urgent concern.

He walked deferentially behind the older men, the deciphered letters and the first of Daniel Whitcombe's *Observations* inside his coat.

They all went solemnly to Hooke's rooms, then up the next flight of stairs to the servant's bedrooms, where they were met by Mary, a paler version of herself, and also Diodati, there since daybreak. The two men, physician and chirurgeon, bowed to one another.

'Pissed blood, you say?' Gidley repeated, looking at Tom's huddled figure under the bedclothes.

'Did,' Diodati said.

Hooke's eyes darted left and right.

Gidley lifted back the bedclothes. 'I have no doubt. It is variolous.'

Harry's heart seemed to double in weight.

'You know,' Gidley said gently, 'there is little a physician, or a chirurgeon, can do for the smallpox. Only nature will decide whether he may live, or whether he may die.'

He asked Diodati to join him, and together they discussed Tom's symptoms, and if either heating or cooling medicines might at least assuage them. Tom was fast asleep after a morning of being bled by Diodati, so they spoke quietly, being careful not to disturb him.

Gidley turned to Hooke. 'It is the smallpox. Without question.'

'Sorry, Mr. Hooke. So sorry,' Diodati said.

'The boy is irrecoverable,' Gidley said, as they left together. 'It would be a miracle beyond our doing if he were to survive.'

Harry, too, said his goodbyes to Hooke, the deciphered bundle of papers he had with him left unshown. With a squeeze for Mary, who could not control the shaking of her shoulders, he left them, to limp disconsolately back to his lodgings in Half Moon Alley.

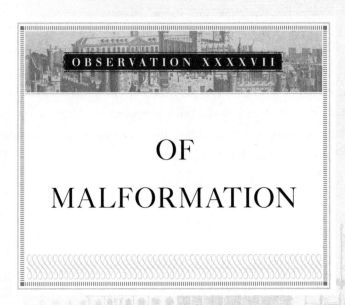

OF

MALFORMATION

'THE ASSISTANT KILLED URIEL?'

The shock of this news, and the pain from the silver pipe, made Shaftesbury's words over-emphatic.

'You should have let me dispatch him when I dispatched Wolfe,' Lefèvre said.

They were in John Locke's elaboratory. On its large table lay an array of armaments: pistols, swords, grenadoes, vicious-looking knives of various lengths, and a spiked glove.

Lefèvre also had a steel contraption made to fit along a forearm, with a long thin blade—more like a skewer—loaded on a powerful spring. A magazine stored more blades to fit the mechanism, a leather sheath yet more to reload it.

He adjusted, cleaned, and oiled this apparatus as they talked.

Locke observed Lefèvre and speculated whether he took pleasure in carnage, or if he committed violence disinterestedly. Did such a man feel emotion by the same gauge as others? Apparent calm could hide the most turbulent of spirits.

Locke was over by the window tending to a collection of weather instruments he had set up on the balcony. This included his new weather clock to Hooke's design. He had high hopes for this, for it promised to automate the laborious business of recording at least some of his observations. It recorded wind, time, and barometric changes with a pen and a paper scroll.

He also had his older instruments: a gauge to measure the strength and quarter of the winds, a sealed thermometer graduated according to his own decimal degrees of expansion, a hygroscope to measure moisture, which relied on the sensitivity of the beard of an oat. Also, a wheel barometer, its tube filled with quicksilver, and a large weather gauge, its glass receiver self-emptying.

Locke also liked to record the weather's effect on his own body. His lungs were a constant guide to the quality of the air. The bones in his feet gave him intimations, too. Any colds or agues he suffered were written down along with the prevalent weather, and other details such as the quantity of insects, or the sweating of marble. All these observations he made onto sheets specially printed for him, columned and headed to his own requirements.

'Wolfe was the more pressing concern,' Shaftesbury answered Lefèvre. 'He wished to tell everything. So, we silenced him . . . but yes, Monsieur Lefèvre, now I lament that you did not.'

'Most men would have left off, after witnessing the demonstration.' Locke commented, looking out at the darkening sky.

It had stopped raining overnight, but the heavy bank of cumulonimbus loitering over London showed plenty more was on the way. The low pressure of the air shown by his barometers was worrying. The sulphurous, stinking miasmas that enveloped the city were gruesome for his lungs.

He wanted to cough just at the thought of them. 'Uriel found out, to his cost, that Henry Hunt is resilient to the direct approach.'

'Yes, John, he did,' Shaftesbury answered sadly.

'He wanted to take him,' Lefèvre said. 'He told me to stay back.'

Shaftesbury idly picked up a blade. 'Perhaps he wanted to prove to himself he could still do such a thing.'

'I shall do what Aires could not.' Lefèvre directed his blank, challenging stare at the Earl.

'I know fully you are able!' Shaftesbury barked. 'That is why we employ you, for your capabilities. And why we so amply pay you.' He turned to his secretary at the window. 'John, is now the time to unleash Monsieur Lefèvre at the assistant?'

Locke looked as pained as his employer. He took no pleasure in such acts, although sometimes it was a proper means to an end. They had moved to a State of War.

'Without the Witch you have no chance of success. You must also kill the King, if you are to have your way.'

'You have doubts.' Shaftesbury had noticed Locke's use of 'you' instead of 'we'.

Locke left his instruments and walked across the floor's black and white tiles to the table. Shaftesbury raised an eyebrow expectantly, knowing a lesson was on its way.

'When I was in France,' Locke said, 'I was taken to look at a boy who had bony growths extending from his fingers and toes. Not his nails misgrowing, but the phalanges. His mother allowed me to measure them. Some were as long as three hundred grys of a philosophical foot.' He placed his hand consolingly on Shaftesbury shoulder. 'A misdirection of the natural growth.'

Shaftesbury shrugged his hand away.

'God allows such malformation,' Locke continued. 'He allows people crippled in brain or body. He allows abortments.'

'I see what you are about,' Shaftesbury said stiffly. Locke was the only person he allowed to speak so directly. 'You know this always was a personal matter, too.'

'We are centaurs,' Locke replied. 'Going only where our horse legs take us.'

Shaftesbury's eyes filled with tears. 'But I ask you, John, should we kill Hunt too?'

Locke leaned his elbows on the table, and clasped his hands together as if in prayer. 'And I answer you. The King first. The assistant after.'

Shaftesbury passed the blade to Lefèvre. 'It shall be at the Procession.'

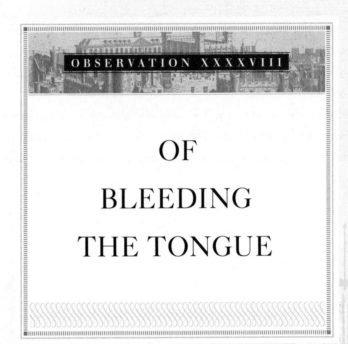

OF
BLEEDING
THE TONGUE

STARING UPWARDS, TUCKED TIGHTLY INTO BED by Mary to prevent him from kicking away the layers of blankets, Tom lay completely still.

The whites of his eyes had turned red.

Mr. Gidley, returned to Gresham's later that morning, pulled away the bedclothes and prodded the boy. The rash had become firmer, and had spread down from Tom's face over his neck and chest, pimples multiplying over the surface of his body until they joined in large patches of raised skin. Tom looked as though he had been beaten where the blood collected under the skin.

Gidley withdrew his bowl and an evil-looking needle from his medical bag.

'I can ease his suffering by a bleeding from the tongue. Palliative only. I pretend not that it will cure him.'

Gidley asked Mary to hold Tom's mouth open. She was pleased to do something for the boy, but she grimaced when the point went into Tom's tongue.

'Hold him forwards, Mr. Hooke, so he does not choke.'

Tom's breathing became irregular as he panicked at the sensation of his tongue's root being pulled. The bowl filled up, the chirurgeon so well practised little blood spilled. When satisfied by the amount, Gidley stopped the blood's flow with a press of his fingers. 'About seven ounces,' he informed Hooke. 'No more.'

He stood and motioned them back down the stairs.

In Hooke's drawing room, he told them there would be little longer to wait.

'All you can do now is to make his last hours as comfortable as can be.' He pulled on his coat to leave. 'Mr. Hooke? May I speak with you outside?'

They went together out across the quadrangle until Gidley considered they were far enough away from Mary, not wishing to cause her more upset.

'Have you surveyed the boy's arm?'

'His arm, Mr. Gidley? I have not.'

'I saw a lump which does not resemble a pustule. It shows the sign of injection.'

'Injection?' Hooke repeated, looking disbelievingly at him.

'You know of the Chinese way, of mothers warding off the smallpox? Fluid from a pustule is mixed into the child's blood, then scraped into the skin. The Turks do it, too. They believe it helps them in staving off the disease in later life, although how many of their children they kill by this method I cannot guess. Tom has been deliberately infected.'

Hooke could not speak, the doctor's information taking his words from him.

Gidley shook his hand, both as consolation and as goodbye, and left towards Bishopsgate.

Hooke groaned, the sound seeming to him far away, as if heard from another's throat.

Why was he to be punished so? He had wanted no part of this. The use of injection, and obvious medical expertise—used not to cure but, despicably, to bring to an end a boy's life—was surely indicative of the same man who had drained the boys found at the Fleet, the Westbourne, and Barking Creek.

Who would be so cruel as to take the life of an innocent young boy to warn him away? It would have taken far less to stop him.

It was his assistant who had continued. Was it Harry being warned? Or, even, was it Harry who was to have been injected?

Harry had gone back to the Fleet, where he had seen the prints of snowshoes, despite his personal promise to leave off the matter. Harry had disobeyed him by working on the cipher after he had instructed him to return it to the Justice, even making his own copy to do so.

And now, Sir Edmund was dead, murdered and left stuck on the Morice waterwheel.

By the time Hooke was back at his front door, after his slow walk across the quadrangle, his question to himself had been answered, and the idea had become a certainty. The injection was meant for Harry, administered instead mistakenly to Tom, when Harry went ahead with his searching, unmindful of the dreadful consequences.

'Some strong waters, please, Mary,' he said, weakly, once back inside. 'Anything we have. I am aghast.'

It should have been Harry, he was sure. To his great shame, Hooke caught himself momentarily wishing it were.

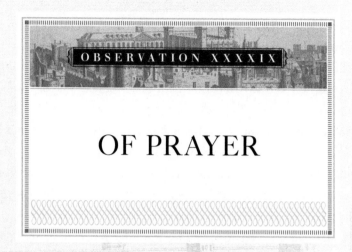

OF PRAYER

BLACKENED PATCHES NOW COVERED HIM, AS if drawn over with charcoal. All afternoon they saw to him, administering caudles and broths. They washed the sweat from him and brought boiling water for him to inhale its steam.

Hooke bled Tom again, another seven ounces. Mary held his tongue, and Grace stroked his hand.

Tom's mother, Hannah Gyles, came to visit her son. He did not seem to realise she was there. She hummed songs softly to him through the cloth Hooke had given her to tie over her mouth. She sang the lullabies she had sung to him when he was an infant. Although afraid of the pustules covering him, she held his hand and smoothed his hair.

Later, as the evening came, she returned to feed the others of her family.

Tom bled from his nose and throat, but he sat up in bed, desperate to talk. They could not understand what he was trying to say, his throat so constricted he could only form unintelligible sounds. The boy wept from frustration.

Hooke held him until he calmed and fell asleep. He laid Tom back on his bed, tenderly pulling the sheets and blankets up over him.

After their meal, a sad supper of cold meats and potatoes, Harry arrived to see Tom, and the four of them went up to Tom's bedchamber with more broth. Harry kept the woollen cap on, to hide the lump on his head.

Candlelight wavered over the sheets around Tom's chest, soaked a deep red colour.

Tom opened his eyes, which oozed with blood, and gave a sketch of a smile to them through his discomfort. Hooke squeezed his hand for a while, telling him of his mother's visit, and talking of Tom's considerable help to him as his apprentice, their experiments together, promising to help Tom with his moon and his glider, when he was well again.

Tom managed to lift himself a little further up the bed but could not sit up. Grace adjusted his pillow to support him.

'What happens to a body after it is dead?' Tom said the words clearly, although his shivering made his voice tremble.

Mary clutched him to her. 'Is this the miracle?' she cried. 'Tom, you will be well again!'

'The soul is taken to the Kingdom of Heaven, which is the best of all places,' Hooke replied to Tom's question, his heart lifting.

'It is not this cold in Heaven?'

'I do not believe there is anything in Heaven to cause you unhappiness. It is as warm as you require. Mary, would you find him more covers.'

All the blankets in the house were already spread over Tom's bed. Mary went and stripped the sheets from her own and put these across him. Grace followed her example.

'And mine also, Mary,' Hooke instructed his housekeeper.

When the two women had gone, Hooke brought Harry closer to the boy. Harry stroked Tom's hair, and tears filled his eyes, as if to protect him from too stark a sight as Tom Gyles so ill.

When Grace and Mary returned, Tom, buried under the pile of sheets and blankets, managed some of the broth Hooke spooned to him.

'And I will see him in the best of all places?' Tom became agitated. Harry clasped his hand.

'Who, Tom? Who will you see?'

'The boy in the cellar room.'

His legs kicked out under the covers, as if swimming away from the thought of the boy trapped inside the air-pump's receiver.

To calm him, Hooke talked of angels, telling him of the archangel Michael. Of Jacob's dream of the ladder between Earth and Heaven, the angels standing on it. Of the angels who witnessed the birth of Adam. Of the angel who told Abraham, as he prepared to kill Isaac his son, that his faith was shown, and his son would be spared. He told him of the seven angels who guarded God's throne.

Little paroxysmal motions shook Tom's body. Eventually, he settled himself to go to sleep. Hooke, Harry, Grace, and Mary continued their watch over him, still hoping for the miracle of his recovery.

They knelt by his bed, and held hands, praying as fervently as they ever had.

'Our Father, who art in Heaven . . . '

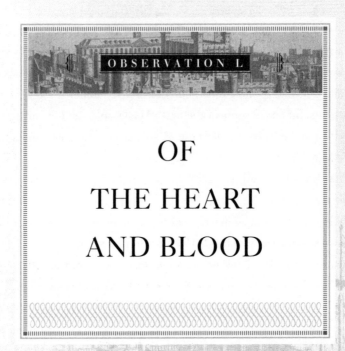

OF
THE HEART
AND BLOOD

THE FRAME BANGED THUNDEROUSLY, THE PANES rattled, and the rollers under the sash cords complained with their habitual squeak.

The pages rustled, lifted by cold morning air from the open window.

Harry raised his spectacles to ease his nose. His forehead was aching, the bruise vehemently purple and sickly yellow, lined with blues and greens like veins in a decadent cheese.

He sat in his room, at the little table, Daniel Whitcombe's papers and his own covering its surface, spreading across the bed, and covering the floor.

Whitcombe's long, repetitious *Observations* gradually revealed their meaning to him as he worked on. The window was open, to keep him awake. A relentless rhythm of deciphering—the reading aloud of the next

number along the page, the clicking rotation of Colonel Fields's brass Caesar
disc, the noting of its position, the flexing of his knotted fingers, the computation, the writing of the next letter. After a while, no longer needing it, he
put the Caesar disc aside, knowing the substitutions it would give.

He ignored the aching of his neck and shoulders, and the way the letters blurred in and out of focus. He willed himself on, despite the increasing
frequency of his mistakes. Using the same letter from the keyword *corpus*
twice in succession, or missing out letters from the cipher, throwing out the
sequence of substitution, reduced the next few letters to gibberish. He had
to find his way again, trace the source of his error.

It seemed an apt self-punishment, a form of penance, to continue with
this task. It eased him, more selfishly, quieting his conscience.

When Grace and Mary had gone to fetch blankets, Hooke had shown
him the mark on Tom's arm. He had pointed at it silently, lips pressed together, silver eyes staring into his.

Hooke had not said another word to him.

Once more Harry picked up his pen, his hand shaking, the tip of his
finger concave where the pen pressed against it. All night he had been deciphering the pile of papers, *Observations Philosophical.*

The first bundle he had chosen, *Observations of the Light of Grace*, had
proved to be a long discussion, relying heavily on the works of Aristotle and
of Thomas Aquinas, and including much Biblical quotation, especially of
the Old Testament, as to whether without grace man could know any truth
at all, could wish or do good, or merit everlasting life.

Harry uncovered a preoccupation with sin and guilt, and a self-lacerat-
ing tone. As in the deciphered letters, Whitcombe's unhappiness was
evident.

Having laboured through this first pile, Harry had ignored *Observations of the Light of Nature*, fearing even more of the same, as he also left
*Observations Concerning Experience, Astronomical Magic, Theological Ca-
bala* and *Medicinal Alchemy.*

Instead, he had chosen to study the pile entitled *Observations of the
Body*, which, in great detail and with less recourse to existing philosophies

or self-pity, set out meticulous programmes of microscopical study and anatomical method applied to a whole chain of being, from the fine structure of a gnat's wings to the hollowed bones of a bird's skeleton, a detailed autopsy of a lion, and studies of human anatomy, both male and female.

After musing on where Whitcombe might have got a lion, Harry selected the largest of all the bundles, *Observations of the Heart and Blood.* A hundred or so sheets, it was these pages which rustled in the icy draught from the window. *Observations of Water, Observations of Fire, of Air, of Breath, of the Soul, of Animals, of Minerals, of Vegetables, of Homunculii*, and the last, smaller bundle making up *Observations Philosophical, Observations of Miscellaneous Species*, all remained untouched. They were pushed under his bed, resting on the same rough canvas cloth which had wrapped them when they were stored inside Henry Oldenburg's oak chest.

Observations of the Heart and Blood explained Whitcombe's experimental trials endeavouring to understand the circulatory apparatus, and the blood and lymph flowing through it. The heart, the arteries, the veins, and the capillaries between them: all were studied and described in fatiguing detail. It showed the movement of the vital spirits in the blood away from the heart, to the lungs, and returning to the heart again. The differences between venial blood and arterial blood, explaining that the florid colour of arterial blood was due to the nitrous salts in it, after its mixing with air. Air volatilized the blood, to nourish the body. The route of the blood as it did so, and cleaned in the kidney, was described. The work of the liver, and the effects on the body of damage to it. It explained the blood moving through the heart, and the growth of new blood vessels, and how this stopped with age— unless the body was wounded, when it worked to repair itself.

It included an account of Whitcombe meeting with William Harvey during the Civil Wars, when Harvey had been Charles I's physician. They had met on a cold day, and discussed the blueness of their extremities, as the blood stagnated because of the chill. Distant from their hearts, the blood's vitality was lost, demonstrating the crucial nature of the pumping action of the heart to provide heat to the blood. Without this continual motion, it would congeal.

Harry uncovered Whitcombe's trials of the dissection of living animals, opening their chests, revealing their hearts moving, then resting, to move again. As the animals died, their hearts beat more deliberately—a benefit to Whitcombe, more easily able to perceive their motions.

Observations of the Heart and Blood also showed Daniel Whitcombe's desire to comprehend the mysterious processes and energies animating a body, and the measureless difference between dead matter and living.

He imitated the heart's structure with models and reproduced its function with machines. Its pumping action was easy to copy, but his attempts to use such a pump to enable a creature to live all ended in failure, as size proved an insurmountable problem. Unless he kept the pump outside the creature, which stayed attached to the machine. This tethering had been unacceptable: Whitcombe sought a freely moving subject. At smaller sizes, though, the power of his pumps diminished, until too weak to propel blood around the body.

Whitcombe abandoned his experiments with mechanical pumps, and instead transplanted hearts from one animal to another. But these had all died, either during the chirurgy or soon after. It was as if the new organ repulsed its recipient body, seeking to kill it off. He had dissected pigs, convinced the similarity of a pig's heart to a human heart would enable him to keep a human alive, although he never attempted—at least in these *Observations*—to place a pig's heart into a person.

Toads, frogs, snakes, eels, fish, cats, dogs, pigs, and wolves: nothing was spared his attentions. The heart of an eel beats without auricles, and if cut up the different pieces continue to pulse. Even if skinned and disembowelled, an eel can still move. Zoophytes, such as the sea anemone, have no hearts at all. Their material and structure fascinated Whitcombe, as he sought to endow the human frame with this same ability: to do without a heart.

Harry was struggling. Whitcombe's numbers, and his own letters of their decipherment, squirmed on the page, stretching and compressing, deflating in on themselves, to then reinflate. The lines of writing undulated, like observing the last rays of the sun through the evening atmosphere, as he had done in the Crown Tavern when awaiting Robert Hooke.

He rubbed his head gingerly, exploring the damage to it. A patch of skin where his hair had been pulled was raw, and weeping moisture.

Just a bit more work, before he went down to find Mrs. Hannam, to ask if she had anything for a late breakfast. He would have wished for bacon until reading of Whitcombe's experiments.

He opened the window a little wider, took a deep inhalation of icy London air, then sat back on his chair, its joints flexing as they took his weight.

He started on the next page of numbers, to turn them into more of Whitcombe's account of his studies into blood.

The next part of Whitcombe's *Observations* revealed itself laboriously, turning from numbers into Harry's own careful lettering. A transformative alchemy. One by one, the letters accrued, forming yet further words, the meandering sentences having to be made sense of, and needing to be organised, as the Red Cipher allowed for no punctuation.

One by one—thirteen in all—he uncovered the next of Whitcombe's experiments. All of these trials furthered the knowledge of blood. All sought the replacement of a defective heart. All sought the revivification of a subject whose heart had failed them. All thirteen required the use of human blood, and the use of human children.

Thirteen children, all boys, had been dissected, studied, transplanted, infused. Some had been stored in an air-pump, kept so more trials could be performed. None of these boys had survived the procedures. Most—but not all—were dead before Daniel Whitcombe set to work on them.

Thirteen children: twelve of them, Harry realised, reading on, used to heal the other.

To bring him from the dead back to the living.

Harry put the papers down. At last, aching, exhausted, he knew for certain.

To help him consider his discoveries, he absent-mindedly picked up a file, and rasped at some metal he had on his worktable. The fit was not yet quite right.

He knew why the boys discovered at the Fleet, at the Westbourne, and at Barking Creek, and ten others besides, had been drained of their blood.

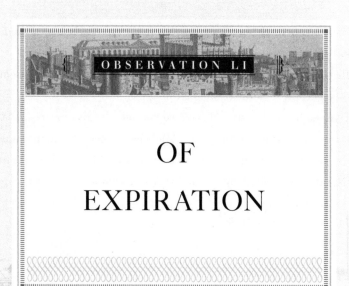

OBSERVATION LI

OF

EXPIRATION

THE MIRACLE DID NOT HAPPEN. THEIR prayers were not answered.

At fourteen minutes after noon, with a muffled rattling sound in his throat, Tom Gyles died.

Mary took off all the stained blankets and sheets. Grace folded Tom's hands across his chest. One of his eyes stayed slightly open from his last look at them. Robert Hooke gently squeezed it shut.

Tom looked as if he still shivered from the cold, his features contorted and pinched. Hooke coaxed the muscles of his face, stroking them, massaging them until Tom's expression relaxed.

Grace cried silently, her mouth pressed into her hands.

Great bellows of grief overwhelmed Mary.

Hooke hoped his words of Heaven and the angels had brought some comfort to Tom before he died.

He went down the stairs, sat at the table in his drawing room, and poured a glass of restorative steel wine.

That such vitality should have so completely disappeared, that all of Tom's noise should be so completely silenced, placed Hooke into a numbed shock of misery. The pain of Tom's death attacked him, filling his heart.

He sat, surrounded by all of his instruments, books, drawings, and models, and he sobbed.

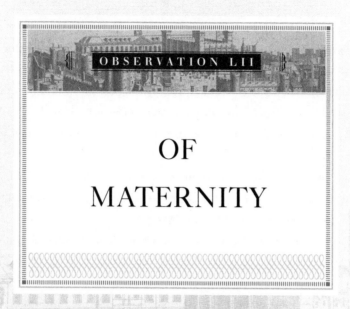

OBSERVATION LII

OF

MATERNITY

THE FOLLOWING MORNING, HOOKE WENT BY the brothels of Love Lane and into Silver Street. He passed St. Olave's, ruined in the Conflagration and being rebuilt, but did not spare it a glance. He carried his umbrella, and the rain splashed from it in a jittering circle around him.

Everywhere there were soldiers, but none of them stopped him, either recognising the famous natural philosopher, or realising he was not to be bothered.

He was there to acquaint Hannah Gyles of the arrangements he had made. He summoned the strength from somewhere to complete his mission, but he was so weary. Everything in him felt heavy.

He had put everything in order for the funeral, to be held that evening, then met with the Society Council at Gresham's repository. There, they had confirmed Viscount Brouncker's message. The overwhelming motion of the Council had been to accept him as Secretary *pro tempore* after Henry Oldenburg's death, and for him to write the Journals, as yet without payment. There had been several assurances the position would become fully ratified, and his campaigning would soon be properly rewarded.

What had meant so much to him just days ago now seemed entirely trivial.

A crowd of children played outside the door as he approached, and he waded through them. They stared at his long, wet nose and his hunched back, and his eyes which had been crying.

Hannah stood awkwardly in her kitchen. Hooke wished he could show more affection to her, hug her to him, but instead for a difficult moment they stood apart, both frozen by their separate griefs.

Tom had been one of many, yet his mother collapsed in her sorrow, her knees giving way from under her. Now, Hooke could go to her, and they held one another without any thoughts of self-consciousness, and they were, for a short time, unaware anything existed outside this small dark room with its rickety chairs, its bitter-smelling smoke from a fire made of willow logs, and the only thing of value a small silver candle branch.

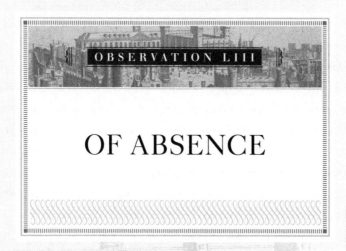

OF ABSENCE

'COME AND STAND BY THE FIREPLACE, Harry, and warm yourself.'

Mary lethargically stirred the coals, sending sparks into Hooke's drawing room. Shadows around her eyes, and a tightness of her features, showed her suffering. Over the flames she hung a large iron kettle, filled with water from the Bishopsgate pump.

'Mr. Hooke has me making tea, for he expects the King again,' she continued, her voice flat, when in happier times it would have been loud in her excitement. 'His Majesty must like Gresham's better than his Palace, even though Mr. Hooke will not let me rid this room of all this *stuff*. How can any monarch endure such a space?'

Harry fidgeted with the cuff of his coat, not answering her question, knowing it was half-heartedly posed.

Wearily, Mary lowered herself for a rare sit on one of the chairs by the fireplace. She put out a hand to take his. 'You are cold, like an icicle!'

'Has Mr. Hooke said why the King returns?' Harry asked her.

'To look at the air-pump, he told me. With the threat against his person, it is a wonder the King ventures forth at all. It is to be kept a secret— Mr. Hooke left me in no doubt of that. Mr. Hooke is an ingenious man, Harry, but it wonders me that His Majesty should seek his company here. More than ever since news of the popish plot. A man named Titus Oates has revealed it. It is said the King has been given poisoned wine, which he thought looked tainted, and so he dipped it into some bread, and fed it to one of his dogs, which then fell down stone d—Oh!'

The King might be poisoned here at Gresham's, in Hooke's lodgings, and she would be blamed. She would go into the history books as the house-keeper who did not take a care to mind the King's life, when he had come to visit. The name Robinson would forevermore be taught to children as a lesson against heedlessness and neglect.

'The King is well looked after,' Harry reassured her. 'Soldiers are every-where in London, seeking out those against him.'

Mary looked gratefully at him. 'Have they stopped you too? Praise be for men such as Oates. If he had not come across this devilish business . . . I have heard him called the Saviour of the Nation.'

Mary noticed the bundle of papers Harry had with him, and she blew her red cheeks out as if playing an invisible trumpet. 'Mr. Hooke will not have a mind for your business, Harry. He has done little since poor Tom left us for Heaven. He only sits and stares into the fire. This morning he has gone to Hannah. Otherwise, he has never left here, not even for a coffee-house.' She placed the back of her hand on Harry's cheek. 'Get closer to the fire.'

There was a loud knocking at the door, and a loud call of 'Robert!'

'I shall bring the King inside,' Harry said, standing and smoothing down his clothes.

Before he left Mary, he was careful to put his papers away in a drawer under Hooke's worktable.

Opening the door of Hooke's lodgings, Harry saw the King was on his own. There were no soldiers with him. Not even Sir Jonas Moore, who had come with him on his last visit to Gresham's.

The King wore a plain dark coat, scuffed boots, no wig, and a pleased expression.

'Your Majesty!'

'You expect a squadron with me, eh, Harry? Well, let me tell you, I am *not* the King! For even my own guards did not recognise me! Therefore, I *cannot* be their King. I have gone through two blocks of the road. I even announced myself to them as William Jackson, to see if they knew their history.'

'You come in the guise you used escaping to France, after Worcester, Your Majesty.'

The King clapped Harry on the arm. 'Danby forbade me to leave Whitehall until this Catholic design is all finished with—one way or the other, I suppose—and so the *King* rests in his chamber. *William Jackson*, however, is out and about the town!'

'Come inside, then, Mr. Jackson. We await Mr. Hooke's arrival.'

'You do not, Your Majesty, for I am here.' Robert Hooke's hunched form was behind them, in his grey coat and a hat. His silver eyes were edged with pink, the blood vessels prominent, giving him the appearance of an albino. 'This is a sorry business, and I will be glad to have done with it.'

'I have arranged a coach for the boy,' the King said. 'It shall be here presently.'

'Welcome news,' Hooke replied. 'It has made me fretful keeping him here.'

'Let us then prepare the way for his removal, Robert, and take him from the vacuum.'

Hooke turned around and led them towards the cellars, back across the quadrangle. He had hardly acknowledged Harry—the merest of nods—but expected him to follow.

Harry stayed quiet, and did not suggest they delayed for Mary's tea, although Hooke looked chilled through.

After the boy was collected, Hooke might become more receptive to him. More willing to listen to his story of Daniel Whitcombe's work with the infusion of blood.

~

WHEN THE THREE men reached the door to the cellars, they found it already unlocked, and slightly ajar. A dark slit showed the way down to the subterranean level below them.

'One of the other Professors must be down there,' Hooke told the King, doubt apparent in his voice. 'The lantern which usually hangs here has been taken.'

'No one else has the key to the heavy door, Robert? The one which blocks off the way to your air-pump?'

'Only I have that key, other than Mr. Boyle, who rarely comes to the College.'

For the first time, Hooke looked straight at his assistant, speaking to him as if he ate wormwood. 'Will you bring a light from my lodgings?'

Harry went back across the quadrangle, thinking that Hooke could not even bear to say his name. Mary let him in, as he had lost his key from the top of the Monument.

Suddenly fretful, a quiver working down his spine, he went to the drawer under the worktable. The package was as he had left it, not five minutes before. Reassured, he found a lamp, and lit it with a taper Mary fetched for him. It was a poor relation to the fine lamp he had broken against his assailant.

He returned to Hooke and the King, both waiting at the cellar entrance.

He passed Hooke the lamp. They descended the stairs and went along the low corridor. The King's head brushed the cellar's roof, and he had to stoop going between the boxes and sacks, the models and various bits of apparatus, and past Hooke's flying machine.

What they saw next brought them up short. The sturdy iron-clad door, which usually sealed off the end of the passageway leading to the air-pump room, stood open, hanging eccentrically from one hinge. Scorch marks on its surface showed the force of gunpowder, and a line of black along the floor led to where someone had stood to ignite the charge.

The three men looked at one another, wondering if they should go back, to safety, or advance, to the boy and the air-pump. Was the King's life in danger? Was the person—or people—still down there, in the dark of Gresham's cellars?

'Such a sound would have been heard, surely?' the King whispered.

'The charge must have been precisely measured—just sufficient to break open the door. I heard nothing, walking into Gresham's. Did you, Harry?'

'I arrived only a short while ago, Mr. Hooke. And Mary mentioned nothing of an explosion.'

The King advanced cautiously, his arms stretched out to either side, to keep the other men behind him.

The door into the air-pump room also hung open, its wood splintered, attacked with an axe around its lock. The lock had been wrenched from its mortise and lay on the stone floor.

The King still led the way, walking vigilantly down the few steps into the room. There was no one else inside awaiting them.

Rasping underfoot, tiny shards of glass lay scattered over the floor. In the centre of the cramped space, the air-pump's receiver was obliterated. There remained a few daggers of glass, forming a wicked collar, protruding from its mount. The body of the machine was bent, its brass cylinder smashed, the timber frame axed and ruined.

The bloodless boy was gone.

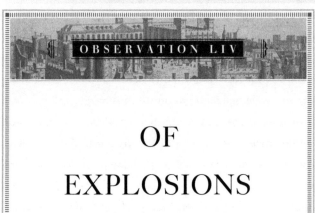

OF EXPLOSIONS AND FIRE

HOOKE'S SHOCK, SHOWING ITSELF IN A speechless opening and closing of his mouth, vacillated between its causes: the violence carried out against the apparatus—a singular abhorrence expressed upon it—and the taking of the boy.

'Who else knows of the placing of the child in here?' the King demanded, looking as stunned as Hooke.

'Only Harry and I know of it,' Hooke answered. 'And you, Your Majesty. Did Sir Jonas know? Sir Edmund knew, and Sir Edmund's man, who delivered him here.'

'Knapp,' Harry added. 'The same man who tried to take the Justice from the wheel.'

'No one here at the College?' the King asked. 'None of the Gresham Professors? None of the Fellows?'

'Sir Edmund swore us to secrecy. I lament ever becoming involved at all,' Hooke said.

'And,' Harry remembered, 'Viscount Brouncker, the President, authorised assistance to the Justice. That aid included the storing of the boy.'

'And who else has the key?'

How easily and effectively the King asserted his authority when he wanted to. His tone of voice hardly changed, yet became utterly commanding.

'All the Professors have access,' Hooke replied. 'And the College grants permission to let our rooms to others.'

From far off, muffled by the bricks arching over their heads, the sound of a door's closing reached them, and the turning of its lock.

'Someone has secured the outer door,' Hooke explained to the King. 'They cannot realise we are down here.'

Another sound became audible. Nearer, sharper. A curious fizzing sound. Harry could not think what it was.

The King recognised it all too well. 'Burning gunpowder!'

'Ah, yes,' Hooke agreed, still distracted by his thoughts of the broken air-pump. 'You are righ . . . ' His voice trailed off, as at last he comprehended what was happening.

Harry had already jumped up the few steps and outside the room, and he swung the heavy iron-faced door across the cellar's passage. It took seconds, but in his mind far longer—too long. The door almost broke free of its remaining hinge but stayed on enough to close it across the corridor. He leaned against its weight, ensuring as best he could it fitted into its frame. He raced back, pushing Hooke back down the steps.

As Harry attempted to close the air-pump room's door, a great movement of air seized it from his grasp. It leaped back open in a wild arcing motion, then crashed into the wall behind. The iron-clad door flew by him along the corridor, spinning, launched along the passageway as if made of thin board. It smashed against the end wall, one corner hitting first, sending brick fragments flying from its impact.

It happened slowly: Harry's thoughts were running so fast he had the time to watch the door float past him, as if it passed through water.

A blow, and then a suck, then a vortex of wind sent the fragments of the receiver's glass whirling up from the floor. The three men covered their heads with their arms, trying to protect themselves from the angry air, glass slivers held in violent suspension.

After the initial detonation this all happened at once, in an instant, and strangely silently, Harry thought, not realising his eardrums were shocked and useless. The sting from his lacerated forehead and the backs of his hands did not register, attuned as he was on the immediate needs of survival. His leather coat prevented a further slashing.

The blast had extinguished the light from the lamp. They called out to one another, to check they still lived. They fumbled for each other in the absolute darkness, all deafened, each seeking comfort he was not the only one to survive.

'Mr. Hooke!' Harry shouted. 'Are you injured?'

'Just cuts, Harry.'

Harry held on to his arm tightly. 'The powder was a distance away, lucky for us. Your Majesty?'

'By God's grace, I am alive.'

They each shook glass from their hair. The King picked out a glass splinter from the back of his hand, licking the blood at the wound.

Then, another sound. With their hearing so injured, it reached them as if through a wall of earth, but loud enough to make them understand their danger was far from over.

It was the sound of combustion, the crackling of flame. It was the sound of all the materials stored along the corridor, the rolled papers, the stacked woods, Hooke's models and the piled fabrics, beginning to burn.

The fire gathered momentum as it enrolled new recruits to its cause. An invading army of heat, the blaze devouring everything in its way.

Harry got himself to the door. Orange reflected from his spectacles. These two glowing circles let Hooke and the King perceive the difficulty they were in.

A monstrous black smoke hugged the arched ceiling of the cellar passageway, as if gripping between the bricks to pull itself towards them.

❧

'WE CANNOT GO forwards through that!' Harry shouted at the others.

'So, we must instead retreat,' the King shouted back. 'How long will this door last?'

'The iron door would withhold if only it were not so broken,' Harry answered. 'This inner door will not last against the fierceness of the fire.'

'Then all we can fight for is time. It may burn itself out. We must close that door.'

Fire filled the corridor, timber boxes collapsing as the flames ate them away. The wooden Bethlehem Hospital was ablaze. Hooke's flying machine—the canvas disappearing in glowing bites across its length, the spindles of its delicate frame folding in on one another—fell from the wall.

The King pulled his shirt out from inside the waist of his breeches, and ripped a strip from it to place over his mouth. Harry followed his example, even able to regret the tearing of his shirt. The iron-clad door, blown off its final hinge, thrown ten feet from its place, was fearsomely heavy. Harry picked up one side of it, and the King seized the other, and they dragged it back. They leaned it against its twisted frame, but its sheets of iron had buckled and the timber inside them was splintered. It would be a modest barrier to the advancing flames. Already the metal began to warm.

They left it. A meagre return for their efforts.

Back inside the cellar room, they all coughed from the smoke. Hooke was the worst affected, but he managed, as Harry closed the inside door— the one barrier between them and their immolation—to gasp: 'The diachylon!'

'Yes!' Harry, exultant, scrabbled across the floor, reaching in the dark for the box of paste they had used to seal the air-pump. After ripping his hands again on more glass, his fingers knocked against the hard sides of the box. He then continued to search, running his hands over the walls, seeking the bucket of water used to cool the air-pump's brass cylinder.

He did not find the bucket with his hands. Instead, he kicked against it, resting at an angle against the wall. He reached into it, to find if any water remained. Just about a quarter had stayed in.

His heart was racing, the pulse in his neck feeling as if it would burst through. He carried the bucket to the door, desperate no more of the precious water would spill.

The King lent his height to the pushing in of the diachylon paste along the top of the door. Hooke frenziedly filled the sides and around the broken mortise, and Harry ran a line of the paste between the door's bottom edge and the floor, fighting for mastery over his shaking hands. When the corners were finished, he soaked the little water left into the wood, pressed more of the paste from the box along the seal to reinforce it, and pushed a last wad into it, blocking out the finger of fire-cooked air reaching at them through the keyhole.

After the hectic actions of sealing themselves in, awaiting the fire's approach brought a strange, dead time, in which all they could do was listen to the groaning of the iron plates of the outside door. The darkness pressed against them. It was eerie, making Harry feel as if he floated in space. He touched the rough wall by him to feel its reassuring solidity. The smoke already inside their room tasted bitter.

They sensed the intensity of the heat building, hotter and hotter, the sweat running down inside their clothes. Sitting helplessly in the dark, Harry, trembling, became aware of all the injuries he had sustained, every ache and soreness piercing through him.

From the blackness, a hand reached for him, taking his, and gripping it tightly.

Harry and Hooke hugged one another, their differences forgotten.

Harry clung to his mentor. Hooke stroked Harry's hair, just as he had comforted Tom Gyles in his last hours.

The King sat apart from them, his knees brought up to his chin. It did not seem a very royal way to go, he thought. Roasting carried a taint of indignity about it. He ran bloody fingers over his scalp, and wondered why it was that at moments like this he was at his most calm.

They listened to the amplifying crackle of the flames, waiting for the final breach of the wooden door to signal their end.

They waited.

They could hear the constant rustle and crackle of approaching fire coming from the corridor, and the thumps and rattles of the spilling of materials onto stone, as the sacks and boxes holding them burned away. Further crashes came to them, as more of Hooke's constructions collapsed, falling to the ground, consumed by flames.

The noise of iron incessantly ringing in their damaged ears clanked and echoed the length of the corridor. It was as if they were trapped inside a vast, old, cracked bell.

The sucking noise of the diachylon paste being expelled from the gaps between the door and its frame told them there was no hope. The men shrank back, pressing themselves as far into the imaginary safety of the walls as they could, as the iron door ruptured with a huge, shocking, crashing noise.

Their last desperate tries at saving themselves had been in vain.

Harry felt tears falling, and was surprised to find they were his own, as if it should be the most unusual thing to cry at the moment of death. It took this sensation of wetness on his cheeks, seeping from his stinging eyes, to realise he did not want to die. In his light-headedness from all the smoke, he could consider his realisation as if from a distance away, feeling apart from himself. He wiped at the tears, turning the dust on his fingers to a gritty paste. He rubbed it between his fingertips.

You do not want to die. It was his own voice, he was sure of it. But different. Aged. More experienced. The voice of his older self, allowed to live after this moment. Harry listened to him regretfully, knowing he would never meet this man, who spoke so kindly to him.

'I do not want to die.' He said it aloud.

Hooke squeezed his hand weakly, his strength almost gone.

The door landed onto the cellar room's flagstones with a resounding echo, followed by a swirl of angry sparks and the inrush of black, choking smoke.

They each took a last breath, holding it in their lungs even though they knew it was now too late for them all. Their end was to be there, in the darkness of the cellar, invisible to one another, Hooke's air-pump destroyed about them.

It was Hooke who first let go of the air inside him, and his intake of breath filled his chest with the smoke.

To Harry, the sound reaching him of the iron plates of the door buckling was subdued, distant, stifled by his damaged eardrums. His head was fantastically weighty, impossible to keep from falling onto his chest. Sleep sought to take him off, into infinity. Everything seemed distant, far away . . .

❧

. . . A DIM UNDERSTANDING appeared to him, slowly becoming firmer. A leisurely comprehension.

Not the sound of the iron door buckling he could hear, clattering, jangling, and sibilant. It was the sound of metal buckets, water being splashed from them, and boots clambering over the iron plates and the remains of the machine strewn over the floor.

This realisation came at the same time as his recognition of the sound of voices, bellowing excitedly, calling out for survivors.

The light from several lanterns spilled into the room, their beams jerking about, seeking into the shadows, reflecting from the smashed air-pump.

From behind the lights Mary Robinson's face appeared, black with soot, a handkerchief over her mouth, her wide eyes fearful of what she might find. She saw the huddle of Hooke and Harry together, with another man she knew to be the King, although he appeared far removed from his usual dignity. When confronted by their silence, she burst into wails of despair.

More faces appeared, almost wholly obscured through the haze of smoke, as equally grimed from their fight against the fire. Grace was with them, too, clutching a bucket.

When Grace saw Harry, she ran to him and pulled at his hands. 'You must go now, Harry!' she shouted into his face, slapping him when he closed his eyes, his head slumping again.

'Grace,' he said to her, slurring her name, hardly able to speak from the effects of the smoke. 'I don't want to die.'

'These fumes will kill you yet.' She hoisted him up and pulled his arm across her shoulders.

Mary bent and lifted Hooke clean off the floor, draping him over her back.

Grace, with the help of the King, who was less affected by the smoke, got Harry up the steps, half pushing and half carrying him from the cellar room. Mary followed close behind with her load of the lifeless Hooke.

They staggered back through the corridor, the objects which had lined the walls now black and skeletal remains. Some of them still glowed in the ash, threatening to re-ignite. The people parted in front of them, bravely continuing to douse the remaining flames, buckets swinging their way from hand to hand.

Outside in the quadrangle the line of firefighters formed a buzzing swarm of celebration around them. Those still in the corridor, now starved of their supply of buckets, began their return to the daylight to join them.

Grace and the King carefully lowered Harry to the ground, where he crouched on his knees, coughing up black liquid. A pattern of lines streaked his face, like the veins of a leaf. His tears through the soot.

Mary placed Hooke down. The King sat next to him, his head between his knees, great coughs shaking his frame.

Harry dragged in gasps of cold London air, drawing it far down into his lungs. Even London air, he found, could taste sweet. He had thought he would never smell it or breathe it again.

Cheering and hollering contagiously spread through their rescuers, but this died down as the awareness took hold that Hooke was still, and unconscious.

Harry crawled to him, still coughing, and crouched beside his inert body. His anxiety, as he pushed at Hooke's chest, and tried to breathe life back into him, conveyed itself through the crowd. They sidled back, becoming sombre.

Harry felt for the pulse of life in Hooke's neck, and found just a remote throb in his carotid artery. Blood still flowed, Hooke's weakened heart pushing it feebly on its journey around him.

The King kept back, face hidden behind his torn band of shirt, sitting to hide his height from the crowd. He, too, was concerned for his Curator, but did not want the crowd to fuss about him, or for word to escape he visited Gresham's College. Without his wig, and covered with soot, he was unfamiliar to them all. And, in times like these, no one would expect the King to be in such a place.

Harry's pressing of Hooke's chest brought only a weak flicker of purple eyelids and a faltering movement of his hands. Harry, and then Grace as she joined with his endeavours to save her uncle, kept at him, both desperate for him to breathe more strongly. After a seemingly endless series of pumps and thumps to the older man's chest, trying to massage the life back into it, they slowed, then stopped.

Hooke hardly moved, his signs of life so faded. Mary—with a scream at them they must not give in—took over, and pounded Hooke's ribs, but still, he did not respond.

Harry looked searchingly at Grace, who fixed her eyes on him. His eyes were a startling white against the smoke-black of his face.

His look implored her to trust him.

Harry motioned to Mary for her to stop. He placed the palm of his hand firmly over Hooke's mouth and nose.

After a long moment of being deprived of air, Hooke's lungs reacted, and with a great coughing up of smoke and a spume of grey saliva from his mouth, he stirred, struggling against the pressure of Harry's grip. Harry let go of him, and stood up, the relief his efforts had revived his one-time master, and his closest friend, making him want to stretch to the sky.

After yet more coughs, and even more liquid from his lungs, Hooke's eyes snapped open. He stared at them all in confusion. As recollection of what had happened came to him, he managed at last to sit up. Grace wrapped her arms around him, sobbing her tears on his shoulder.

The crowd, still clutching their buckets, were exultant. They had thought all their efforts had been in vain, but the illustrious Curator would live.

The King edged over to Harry. 'Well done, Harry. Well done!' he exclaimed. 'Robert is dear to us both. I too would have wept if he had been taken from us.'

He leaned forwards and—to Harry's astonishment—kissed him on both cheeks. He kept his mouth by Harry's ear. 'You will not divulge my identity, will you? I do not wish it known there has been this try at assassination. I begin to believe Titus Oates. There *is* a damnable and hellish plot against me.'

'Yet, Your Majesty, you were not nearly killed.'

'I was not?' the King said, mystified.

'The King is safe in Whitehall. It was William Jackson nearly dead in the fire.'

'I see what you are about.' The King tried a cackle, which became a series of splutters. 'Do you think, rather, that Robert Hooke, my Curator of Experiments, was their quarry?'

'I too have had my life threatened. I have sought after the killer of these boys, and a boy, Mr. Hooke's apprentice, was killed in my place. By injection of smallpox. Furthermore, at the top of the Fish Street pillar, I had to fight off a man who chased me there.'

'So you are being pursued, hmm? You must watch yourself, for it would be a shame to lose a man with your talents. I shall arrange protection.'

'I think this fire, and the taking of the Fleet boy, concerns another matter, one stemming from Oliver Cromwell's use of a man named Daniel Whitcombe. He is a natural philosopher and experimentalist, whose interests coincide with Mr. Hooke's.'

Harry coughed some more, then continued. 'Whitcombe made experiments on boys. He wrote of his work in a series of papers, called by him his *Observations*. The cipher he used, to keep his trials secret, was the same used to assist your escape to France. Sir Edmund found the cipher's keyword, and at the last made sure to communicate it to us.'

Harry's speech ended in yet more coughing up of the soot-filled liquid in his lungs.

'*Corpus*,' the King recalled, banging him on the back. 'Tell more of this to me later, Harry, when you are well. I remember Daniel Whitcombe. He was to be my physician, should I have need of him. Everyone called him the Witch. Oliver Cromwell gave him the name, so he said, after Whitcombe had cared for him. An easy nickname, if you think about it.'

The King shook Harry's hand, then, more gently, Hooke's, showing he was ready to leave. 'With the pasting of us in, you saved my life, Robert.'

Thanking everyone graciously for his rescue, assuming an elaborate accent which some took to be Welsh, and planting further royal kisses onto an ecstatic Mary's cheeks, he saw his chance to slip away, as the crowd's embellishments of the story of the rescue became ever more ornate, and more loudly expressed.

The tale was told many times over. Of Mary's watching Harry through the kitchen window as he returned to the cellars. Of her hearing footsteps out in the quadrangle a few minutes later, expecting to see Hooke and Harry, and instead spying two figures running. A flash of sea-green coats, and the idea they carried something—she could not be sure what it was. Before she had time to decide she didn't much like the look of them, a great bang rattled the cups hanging from their hooks on the dresser, and shook the sash windows. The very ground seemed to shiver—she never had a sensation like it, nor did she want to again—and when she crossed to the door of the cellar a tongue of flame almost caught her apron as she unlocked it. It would have set her ablaze like a martyr in Mary's time.

At this point of her story, other voices broke in, their own accounts interweaving with the housekeeper's, as they told of hearing the great bang, and coming into the College from Broad Street and Bishopsgate Street, the panicking horses kicking at the walls of the stables, and Mary begging for help.

The population was an effective firefighting force through necessity. Their familiarity with fire made them expert in deciding cause. The conviction shared among them all: it was undoubtedly the work of papists.

Returning to Hooke, who was now washing himself down at the water pump, still coughing from the inhalation of smoke, Harry observed a flush of colour on his normally pale skin.

'Mr. Hooke, you have the same redness which affected the Justice. We must get you inside, in the warmth, and you must take your rest. When you're revived, I'll tell you of the writings of a man named Daniel Whitcombe, detailing his trials requiring the blood of boys. I shall also tell you of the murder of Enoch Wolfe in Alsatia, and of a fight at the top of the Monument.'

Hooke, his chest still heaving, gave one of his silent nods.

With Grace and Mary supporting him, they returned to the safety of his lodgings.

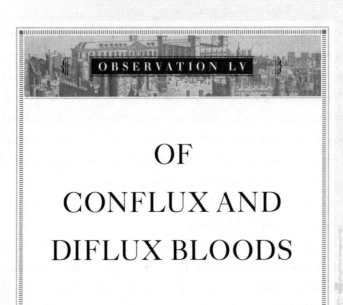

OF
CONFLUX AND
DIFLUX BLOODS

REDNESS FADING, becoming his more customary grey, Robert Hooke sat by the fireplace, a blanket over him at his housekeeper's instruction.

'You need liquid, Mr. Hooke,' Mary said, pouring tea for him. 'The fire is still inside you, and wants putting out!'

Harry sat at the table, extracting pieces of glass from the back of his hands, his hair, and from the leather of his coat. As he spoke, he placed them into a pile in front of him. Grace sat next to him, from time to time looking at him as if he had turned into somebody else, somebody far distant from the mild boy she grew up with.

She was repulsed when Harry described the death of Enoch Wolfe, whose throat had been ripped away by a creature more demon than man, and shocked by the story of Harry's brawl at the top of the Fish Street pillar.

Hooke winced as he listened. 'You have become very secretive.'

'I've hardly had the chance to tell you,' Harry replied. 'Tom was ill, and today we went to the boy in the air-pump and found the cellars open. And then we were busy with explosions and fire.'

'Tom was poisoned, Harry. *Murdered.*' Hooke coughed violently. 'A sickness was injected into him, which was surely meant for you. You have not been mindful of my wishes, nor of the safety of those around you! I counselled against your involvement in this, when you first told me the Colonel's tale of the King's escape.' Hooke wiped at his blood-shot, smoke-filled eyes, and his voice quivered with emotion. 'A young life has been lost.'

'How could I have known Tom would be killed?' Harry asked, his own voice as tremulous. 'I wish I was injected in his place.'

Hooke bit his tongue, not wishing to say something he would regret. He sipped at the tea held out by Mary, who was fretting next to him. The drink was too hot, his mouth sensitively raw after the fire.

'You know Tom was like a brother to me,' Harry said. 'I miss him most of all things. Please, Mr. Hooke, you say I am secretive. Let me speak, then, of what I know.'

Harry stood, angry and tearful, and took out the pile of papers he had placed in the drawer. He passed Hooke his deciphered *Observations*. He sat back down, and Grace shot him a sympathetic look.

She listened intently, her hand to her mouth, as he repeated Colonel Fields's story of his blood-brothers, Daniel Whitcombe and Reuben Creed, ordered by Oliver Cromwell to assist in the King's escape. He told them of Whitcombe's skills as an army chirurgeon, of his being taken into slavery in the Barbadoes, and of Creed being hanged from a tree outside Worcester.

'Using the keyword *corpus*, it was an easy thing to read Whitcombe's letters. He prepares for his death, and leaves instruction to pass his work to you. The letter to Sir Edmund speaks of two Lights. At first, I didn't understand it. I think Whitcombe finished with his trials after seeing he had turned away from the Light of Grace, immersed as he was only in the Light of Nature. He sought absolution. I also deciphered his work on blood and its infusion, from within a package left with Henry Oldenburg. It was in the chest. I found it there as I began to catalogue the Secretary's correspondence.'

'A task you have neglected,' Hooke said bitingly.

'The deciphering's taken all of my attention. I bring with me part of Whitcombe's papers, called *Observations of the Heart and Blood.*'

'After William Harvey,' Hooke noted.

Harry nodded. '*Observations of the Heart and Blood* details the workings of the heart, and the uses of the blood. Whitcombe was procured children for his trials. Boys. He had no use for bodies dead from age or disease. Nor those of criminals hanged or shot, nor of suicides, as we are allowed to dissect. He required healthy young bodies, uncorrupted. He describes his methods to extract and infuse blood from one body to another. He calls this commixture.'

Harry noticed his own voice was rising, getting higher, betraying his excitement at Whitcombe's findings, even though the cost of discovery had been so considerable. He continued, finding a more measured pitch. 'The Royal Society took sick men looking to be cured, and injected blood into them, to learn the restorative effect on their humours. Those who died added little to our investigations, as they may have died anyway, or they may have continued to live. We persuaded one healthy man, Arthur Coga, to accept the blood of a lamb. Mr. Coga was lucky. Daniel Whitcombe shows, by the laws of chance, he was far more likely to die from the taking of another man's blood.'

Hooke stared unhappily into his fire. 'The Society stopped all such trials on learning of Professor Denis at the Montmort Academy, and his failures to cure the sick. Men died agonising deaths from blood being infused into them.'

Harry picked at another fragment of glass lodged under the skin on his wrist. 'The reasons for Denis's failure weren't studied enough. Whitcombe discovered four categories of blood. He found that some, on being introduced one to another, clot together. The red parts of the bloods bind, to make it useless, harmful to any body it is infused into. He calls these conflux bloods. The new blood with the old results in convulsions and, if the quantity is sufficient, in death. A diflux blood does not do this, so continues to flow freely.'

'If a diflux blood had been used, Professor Denis's patients could have been saved!' Hooke said, at last becoming more animated, less stern towards Harry, with the possibilities of a new science opening up before him. 'Are the humours constant across these various bloods?'

'Whitcombe tried to separate them, but could find no part in the blood which could be filtered away to bring changes of character. His subjects remained as sanguine, choleric, melancholic, or phlegmatic as they had ever been, as far as he could measure.

'He also studied the function of the liver, with its properties of sanguification. He identified boys with diflux bloods, and tried to convey one liver into the body of another. But he failed. He supplanted hearts also, but didn't succeed in continuing a life. The boy found at the Chelsea Physic Garden was such a death. The chymical circulation between the heart, the spleen and the liver, in imparting the vital spirits to continue around the body, is, Whitcombe says, beyond the power of a man's understanding. It must be left to the province of God.'

❧

HARRY SUCCEEDED IN removing the last of the glass in his wrist, a long sliver which pulled at his skin.

'There's much self-hatred in Daniel Whitcombe's pages. The *Observations* form a confession of his guilt.'

'He became sensible to his own conscience,' Hooke said.

'At first, he hardened himself to his emotions, determined to avoid squeamishness. He used the dead, and then the living, to investigate the workings of nature. Our common state is death. Life is the exception, a brief visit to this temporal world. It was but a small step, taking life, to further his discoveries. Confronted by failure, though, he became sickened by the stealing of bodies, and of the kidnapping of children.'

'Why would he set about such trials?'

'His object was to infuse blood into a child. A special child. He calls him the 'recipient boy', and those used for their blood, the 'emittent boys'. He experimented on them. Some while they still lived, wanting fresh blood.'

'Who is this special child?'

'He never says his name, nor who wanted him saved.'

'Saved? Saved from what, though, Harry?'

'Why, saved from death, Mr. Hooke. He is a dead child. Daniel Whitcombe sought to revivify him.'

'Impossible!' Hooke's drink spilled as he thumped his fist on the arm of his chair. 'Bring him back to life? He is mad! Go to the King, Harry, and tell him all. Then be done with it.'

'Others think him sane. I think the experiments are meant to continue. The boy left on New Year's Day was kept at Sir Jonas Moore's command. He knows more of them, I'm sure. The Fleet boy was the special child. The dates written on his body prove it, for they correspond with the dates of experiments described in the *Observations*. He received infusions meant to revivify him. His faulty heart was to be replaced.'

'Whitcombe met with the same limits of size of glass receiver as I did,' Hooke mused. 'He thought to watch the boy if he came back to life, to take him from the vacuum.'

'We surmised the boy, having his blood taken, had been murdered for his blood. In truth, he waited for blood to be given. Twelve other boys were used, Daniel Whitcombe searching different methods, testing different ways. The recipient boy was preserved for a year or more, as he worked on them.'

'Who employed him, then?' Hooke asked. 'What callous, murderous mind would think one life worth the cost of so many?'

'His *Observations* don't say, Mr. Hooke, as far as I've read them. My conjecture is this: Daniel Whitcombe went as a slave to the Barbadoes, where he worked on a plantation owned by the Earl of Shaftesbury—Shaftesbury, until recently imprisoned in the Tower, put there for his constant arguments with the King. The news-sheets say he was released on New Year's Day, the same day we found the boy at the Fleet. If Shaftesbury came to know of Whitcombe's skills, surely he would have taken him from the manufacture of sugar?'

Harry looked apologetic, knowing Hooke would not like his next piece of information. 'I do know who found the emittent boys for Daniel Whitcombe, or at least ordered them to be so. But I think he, too, at the end, didn't believe one life outweighed others.'

Hooke had already guessed what Harry was about to say, and said it for him. 'It was Henry Oldenburg, the previous Secretary of the Royal Society.'

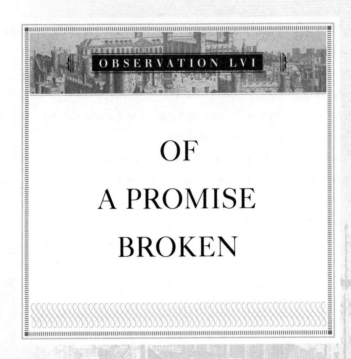

OF

A PROMISE

BROKEN

NOT AN EXACT COPY, THIS BOY before her.

This face was dull. Fine lines etched its surface, prematurely ageing him. The lack of blood had hollowed his cheeks.

She stroked his forehead, feeling the papery texture of his skin. Even though it was not him—for his soul had long left his body—it was such an evocative reminder, like a brother, or a cousin, of her son.

This boy's face was serious and solemn, in possession of a secret weighing him down. His mouth, slightly drawn down at its corners, showed her his disapproval of the attempts to revivify him.

A mild reproach: he understood their choice, but he regretted it.

If he had looked angrily at her, or spoken sharp words, she would have a defence against him, some quick reply, but this gentle chastisement was implacable.

He could only have been indifferent to the experimental trials, the processes and procedures, carried out on him, but it seemed to her as if he must
have felt every cut, every piercing of his skin, every sensation of blood being
moved in and out of his arteries and veins.

His eyes were open and clear, unclouded by decay.

The unblinking gaze was damning.

What had they put him through?

It was his eyes—blue, moving to indigo, identical to her own—which
showed, unarguably, crushingly, it was him. She had hoped they would be
closed. She could then have pretended his death was merely a form of sleep.

Her son would not look away.

✺

THE KING'S DAUGHTER, Anne Lennard, Countess of Sussex, had unwrapped him from her coat, in which she had carried him from Gresham's
College.

Hortense Mancini, Duchesse de Mazarin, had delicately brought him
to the table, laying him onto his back.

Together, they had uncurled him from his foetal position, straightening
his legs, and placing his arms to each side of his body.

His mother reached for a cloth and dipped it in some water from a
porringer. Painstakingly, she washed his face, and then his hair, which
slicked to his head. Not liking the way it clung to the structure of his
skull, she dried it. Then, she cleaned the rest of his body, every crease and
fold, across every plane, over the sharpness of the hips and ribs, along the
length of each limb.

When she reached the wounds going into his legs, she wiped away the
last of the blood coagulated around them, the wet cloth pulled tightly over
her finger, dabbing at them with the tip.

The dates written on him would not disappear. The ink blurred and
smeared at each wound, making it look as if she bruised the flesh.

As if she had hurt him once more.

The constriction she felt, as grief rose from her belly, made her fear she would never breathe or swallow again.

She passed the cloth to Hortense, and placed her hands on the table, thinking she would fall.

Hortense finished cleaning him, while Anne held his mother.

When she had recovered, the three women together took a silk sheet and wrapped him in it. Anne stitched him into the shroud with thread.

Before she finished sewing over his face, his mother bent to kiss his forehead. A last goodbye.

Anne continued with her needle.

Her son left her again, as he disappeared into the silk.

What had led her to give him over to Daniel Whitcombe? His failure coloured her mind, she knew, for if Whitcombe had succeeded, if he had revivified her boy, she would have been forever grateful. She would never have considered the difficulties, or the cost, of success.

She had been desperate—more desperate than at any time of her life—to recover him. Whitcombe had assured her—sworn it to her, as a vow before God—he would bring him back from the dead.

Breathtaking in its arrogance, his promise. His initial self-belief had been absolute, but as the months went by, he became more and more dispirited. More and more distracted. The excuses came. Laid over with medical language and technical terms, but she understood enough to know he was failing.

Towards the end, he had been unable even to look at her.

The three women gently lifted the boy from the table, and placed him into a small, simple coffin. It was wood, only, not lead-lined. There would be no embalming of him. He would be buried, and his human form would dissipate into the earth.

Frances Teresa Stewart—better known throughout the kingdom as Britannia, for so she appeared on medals and coins—stroked her son's hand through the silk.

A last touch, an appeal for his forgiveness.

Her boy had thrived, at first. But then, some fault in his fabric, some weakness—a misdirection in the growth of his heart—had brought him down.

Daniel Whitcombe had convinced her he could return her son to the living.

He could not.

They placed the lid, then fastened it.

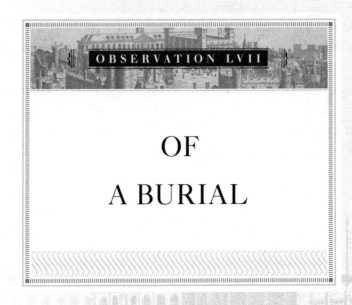

OBSERVATION LVII

OF
A BURIAL

IT WAS SEVEN O'CLOCK IN THE evening. A crowd of mourners gathered in St. Helen's churchyard, just the other side of Bishopsgate Street from Gresham's College. The black trails from every Bishopsgate chimney fell into the sooty cloud hovering and swirling between them, the miasma forcing coughs and sneezes from the congregation.

Many Fellows of the Royal Society, and those who met with Robert Hooke as his New Philosophical Club, attended. By the lanternlight illuminating them all, Sir Christopher Wren, his fingers inky from drawing, inspected the old stone. St. Helen's was one of the few City churches to have survived the Conflagration unscathed. Sir Robert Boyle, Hooke's first patron—at his requirement, Hooke had built the first air-pump—spoke with

Thomas Henshaw, Original Fellow and Envoy Extraordinary to Denmark. Dr. William Holder, inventor of a sign language for the deaf, stood with Sir William Petty, the designer of the *Experiment*, the ship whose drawings the King had explained in his elaboratory at Whitehall. William Croon, Gresham Professor of Rhetoric, Abraham Hill, Council member, and Daniel Colwall, Treasurer of the Society, huddled quietly as a group. John Aubrey and Edmund Wylde shared a flask of genever to keep away the cold. At the back of the congregation waited Sir Joseph Williamson, a keen experimentalist when not busy with his work as Secretary of State. He stood with Mary Robinson, who seemed to have adopted him, yearning to be doing something.

At the front, nearest to the small coffin, were Hannah and Robin Gyles, surrounded by their other children. The husband held the wife, she leaning heavily against him.

Robert Hooke, Grace, and Harry stood just behind. Harry still wore Mr. Hannam's felt cap, pulled down low. He rolled the saliva in his mouth around his tongue, trying to get rid of the sulphurous taste from the burning sea coal.

Sir Jonas Moore, Surveyor-General of the Board of Ordnance, put his hand on Harry's shoulder. 'I must speak with you. A matter of some importance. Not now—you wish to concentrate upon poor Tom's funeral.'

'When, then, shall we talk of this?' Harry asked him, suspecting he had intelligence of Daniel Whitcombe.

'Come to me, at the Tower Armouries. I shall find time for you.'

Sir Jonas stepped back into the crowd.

Harry was sure Sir Jonas's order to preserve the boys, and the King's obvious anger with him when he had discovered it, meant he knew more of the experiments on them.

Happy everyone was now ready to mourn, clearing his throat of the fumes, the minister began his sermon.

'There is a universal standard of truth that God hath set up over all the sons and daughters of men. He hath given the knowledge of it in and through Jesus Christ. This standard and measuring-rule is revealed and manifested in every man and woman, by the light that shines in their hearts, by which they are able to discern, and give a sound judgment, if they are but willing . . . '

Tom had light in his heart. A light now extinguished. Hooke's lodgings would seem horribly silent now. Tom was never able to walk through a door quietly, but instead had to rattle the catch, or shake the handle, and crash it into its frame when closing it.

At Hooke's prompting, Tom had set up a measure in Hooke's turret observatory to mark the transition of stars relative to one another, over nights of stargazing. He had thrilled to the notion a line could be drawn from him—a young apprentice boy in the City of London—to a point above him on the highest celestial sphere. Of course, there may well be no such thing as a celestial sphere, as Hooke believed there was not. The Universe might never stop, and so the light reaching him from the most distant star was an infinitesimally small fraction of the light it sent out from itself. An expanding globe of light swelling out into infinity, overlapping with all the other spheres of light from all the other stars. Every visible star did this, sending at least a portion of its light, tiny though it may be, to him.

Hooke and Harry had taken him to Fish Street Hill and the Monument to the Great Conflagration, to show him it was an immense vertical telescope. One lens was down in its dome-roofed basement and another at its top, mounted inside the blazing copper urn.

Patiently, Harry had explained to Tom the notion of stellar parallax, the changing position of a star at different times of the year, which, with such a telescope, could be used to gauge the distances to other stars.

Hooke's Monument was a 200-feet-tall instrument. Tom and Harry had spent whole days running up and down its stairs, with Hooke shouting instructions up to them. Tom had never been happier. Each of its steps exactly six inches high, the effects of altitude could be measured. Many of these trips had been at night, too, their observations performed by lanternlight, as the vibration of traffic in the daytime hampered precision. They suspended pendula, and they released balls to fall through the airy column inside, to show the rotation of the Earth.

Harry experienced again the impact through the stone column as the man hit the ground.

He could have held him, but instead he let him go.

' . . . This is the standard God hath pitched in every one of our hearts, for the trial of ourselves, either for our justification, or condemnation, of every word and action. Now, to make everyone sensible of the greatness of this blessing, consider: it is not only given to augment and increase knowledge, it is given on purpose to allure and persuade men into a liking of truth, into a love of truth . . . '

Harry stared miserably at the coffin.

Despite Robert Hooke's wishes, he had carried on with the business of the bloodless boys, and with the cipher, and had chosen to keep the progress of his investigation to himself. A childish, egotistical decision. One which had led them tumbling into the depths Hooke had warned against.

After taking Sir Edmund from the waterwheel, Hooke had asked him from where Harry found such disregard for self-preservation. Do you wish not to see old age? An old man's question, Harry thought at the time. But now, he saw the wise judgment behind it. If he had followed Hooke's instruction, Tom would still be crashing about Gresham's, or climbing the spiral inside the Monument, enjoying his childhood, learning his trade.

Tom had wanted to go to sea, dreaming of navigating the world's oceans. Who knows what voyages he may have had, what lands he may have discovered?

Tom now had no existence allowed to him, as these other boys had none.

' . . . The veil of ignorance, that is come over the sons and daughters of men, through sin, transgression, and rebellion, is very great. The Lord our God, that made us, hath not left us in that state of darkness, blindness, and ignorance, but through the riches of his mercy and goodness, hath found out a way, to command that light should shine out of darkness, into our hearts, for all that the Devil did to darken man, to alienate and estrange him from his Maker . . . '

Harry should have left off the investigation before, but he could not do so now.

The voice came to him again.

Which Devil estranged you from your Maker? You cannot take joy from these words, or sustenance. You must find the man who killed Tom. You must find the man who wished you dead, but who instead killed an innocent child.

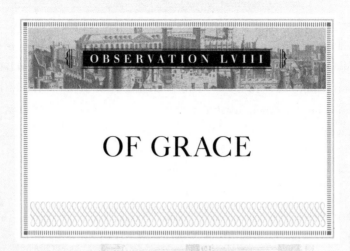

OBSERVATION LVIII

OF GRACE

GRACE LAY IN HER BED, IN her chamber in the upstairs turret room of her uncle's lodgings, trying to fend off waking. She pressed her face into the pillow, luxuriating in its thick, crisp linen. She could feel the hem of her nightgown scratch on her calves, the stitching coming loose. She pulled up her knee and poked the separating hem with her toe, lazily thinking of repairing it at some later time.

After Tom's death her sleep was constantly broken, disturbed by strange dreams of falling from London Bridge, but never hitting the water. Except it was not her: it was a figure dressed in black, like a wicked angel.

She could hear footsteps outside, their sound changing as they left the loose stones of one of the quadrangle's paths and went onto the paved walkway surrounding it. She hoped they would pass on by. She was woken by Uncle leaving earlier, by Mary after that, then she had gone back to sleep.

She picked at a crust of sleep in the corner of her eye and rolled over. Just some more time in my bed, she thought. After Tom's burial last night, it seemed not too much to ask.

There was the knock.

⋙

IN THE BRIGHT sunshine of a crisp London winter morning, the rain stopped and the miasma lifted, Harry had with him more of his notes of Daniel Whitcombe's *Observations Philosophical*. Lacking his keys, he waited for a while with his ear pressed to the door, but there was no sound of anyone inside.

Had Mr. Hooke left already?

He recalled the times when Tom's face had appeared at the window above, when he would shout down if Hooke was in or out, or relay his master's messages to him.

More assertively, Harry knocked again, knowing Hooke became ever deafer. Doubly so, after the explosion in the cellars.

This time—just as he turned to go—the window opened, and it was Grace's face he saw above him. He blinked up at her stupidly, sunlight in his eyes, unable to form any words of greeting for her. Evidently, she had just woken, for her long hair was loose, unbrushed, and she had a map of the creases of her sheets imprinted on one side of her face. He could see the top of her nightgown.

'Why do you all rise so early?' she complained.

'Will you let me in?' Her appearance made him breathless, as it always did, as if he had run the way to Gresham's.

'But no one is here,' she replied.

'In truth, you are here, Grace.'

She regarded him for a moment, then her head disappeared from the window.

Then, footsteps on the stairs, and the key turning on the inside of the door. Grace beckoned him in, stepping back onto the staircase, retreating from the sting of cold from the lobby's flagstone floor, and the harsh air invading from the quadrangle.

'It was always Tom who greeted me, when coming through this door,' Harry managed, sounding hoarse. 'I shall forever think of him when using it.'

To his consternation, Grace's eyes suddenly filled. Although she tried to wipe her sorrow away, the tears refused to stop. She cried silently, her mouth behind her hand, her shoulders shaking.

Harry did not know if he should draw nearer, or stay where he was. He knew he should comfort her, but how?

He put his hands on hers, to calm the shaking of her arms, then took a handkerchief from inside his coat. He softly dabbed her eyes, being careful not to catch inside her eyelids with the cotton, until she took the handkerchief from him.

She looked at him, holding his gaze with hers.

'I wonder—'

His question was never finished.

Grace kissed him, her mouth wet from her tears, holding his head in her hands as if worried he might break free.

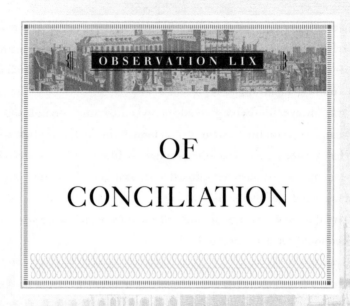

OBSERVATION LIX

OF
CONCILIATION

ROBERT HOOKE SENT A CAUTIOUS LOOK over the quadrangle before locking his door and bolting it, his face still tinged with pink from the fire in the cellars.

'I slept not well,' Hooke told Harry, seeing him in the drawing room as he walked up the stairs. 'I had an obstruction in my stomach, which kept me restless for much of the night. This morning I voided myself of a shit, which lessened my discomfort.'

'Good morrow, Mr. Hooke,' Harry greeted him, smiling to himself. 'I am sorry to hear of your suffering.'

'I have a toothache, too, which troubles me.'

'My mother burned henbane and then breathed in the fumes, for a toothache.'

'Did she? Interesting . . . I shall definitely try it.'

Harry smiled again. 'I stayed up reading more of Daniel Whitcombe. He separated blood using centrifugal force, bringing forth its red, white and yellow parts. He experimented on drying them, then reliquifying them with distilled water.'

Hooke sucked in his cheeks. Harry seemed more cheerful than he should be. This morning he felt a little easier, but could not help thinking of who had killed Tom, and if Daniel Whitcombe would be found to pay for his crimes.

He would go back to his College work as Professor of Geometry, and his Royal Society work as Curator and new Secretary, and his City work as surveyor and architect of the rebuilding of London. Montague House was near finishing. The Bethlehem Hospital already wanted repairs, faulty work having brought down a ceiling. He was worried, too, about its foundations, built into rubble filling the Roman ditch on the other side of their Wall.

Their unfortunate meeting with the Justice at the Fleet had brought only unwelcome danger, and the death of Tom, for which he had blamed Harry.

Now, Hooke saw he himself as responsible. It was he who had brought Harry into the business, by passing him the cipher. He had done this selfishly, in order to follow his desire to replace Grubendol as Secretary.

He should have known Harry, stubborn since a child, would follow the matter as far as he could, finding out those who might help him uncover the meaning of the cipher, and those who might know more of the bloodless boys.

'Have you seen the news, Harry?' he enquired, once they were both sitting at his table in the drawing room. He wondered where Mary was to have let Harry in, knowing he no longer had his keys. He held out a broadside, headlined *The Saviour of the Nation*, its top half devoted to a large woodcut illustration.

'I've been so immersed in deciphering, I've heard hardly a thing of the world.'

'You have heard the bells? And there will be cannons fired. A great pageant—a Procession, they call it—is planned after the death of Sir Edmund Bury Godfrey.'

Harry took the paper, and read of the Procession, to start at Moorgate, going through Aldgate, and finishing at Temple Bar where a Mock Pope was to be burned. All paid for by the Earl of Shaftesbury, busy since his release from the Tower.

The broadsheet also proclaimed Edward Coleman's arrest. The secretary to the Duke of York's wife, Mary of Modena, he had been found with incriminating letters. As Titus Oates said he would be.

'Coleman admits to writing letters to the French,' Harry said.

'There is a chalk as long as your arm between wishing the King's death and seeking monies from France.'

'He'll be drawn to Tyburn, hanged from the gallows there, mutilated, disembowelled, and quartered.'

'He will be already half dead by the time he gets to Tyburn,' Hooke said bleakly. 'He will be stoned and bottled on his journey. With this Procession today, and Coleman's execution tomorrow, London has gone mad. Quite mad.'

Harry scanned through the lengthy report, written in outraged language. There was little mistaking its sentiment, although its logic was sometimes obscure. He folded it in half and placed it on the table between them.

'No mention here of those who seek to use the blood of boys. Only of pernicious papists and assassins looking to overthrow the King and Church. Sir Jonas Moore has asked me to the Tower. He may know who the recipient boy was, to be revivified. Otherwise, why did he press for the boys to be preserved?'

Hooke had his bony elbows on his table, his long chin resting on his hands. 'If you go to him, Harry, you risk being drawn into this too. Retribution against Coleman has been swift.'

Harry stared at the woodcut printed on the broadside sheet. 'This clergyman, Titus Oates, here in the picture. I saw him the night I was followed up the Fish Street pillar. I recognise his big chin. He was with some soldiers, searching into houses.'

'He will be unstoppable now. He is quartered at Whitehall and given a pension to keep him. He will have half of London arrested before we may say Jack Robinson.'

'The Justice suspected Catholic involvement in the deaths of the boys. Yet in Whitcombe's notes I haven't found a mention of those he worked for. If it's all a Catholic plan, then who benefits from his experimental trials?'

'I know not, Harry, I know not. It is all confusion to me. Please have a mind for your own safety—you have shown a scant regard for it since Sir Edmund engaged our help.' Hooke gripped Harry's hand, seeking reassurance Harry would follow his advice.

'If I've learned nothing else in this New Year, I've learned circumspection,' Harry replied.

The clocks in Hooke's drawing room began to chime, a process taking a full minute as each clock reached the hour of ten. As one finished its sounding, another was ready to take its place.

'I must adjust some of those,' Hooke said. His face became uncertain, and Harry knew he had more news troubling him.

'The King bade me go to Whitehall this morning, and he spoke of you. He wanted to know of your capabilities. Indeed, he spoke of little else.'

'What was your answer to him, Mr. Hooke?' Harry asked, feeling flattered, but also puzzled by the King's interest.

'I answered truthfully, and fully. You are a most able Observator, and you will, I doubt not, make for a proficient Curator. You are a natural philosopher, worthy of the name.'

'I should leave for the Tower,' Harry said, with a catch in his voice. He glowed from this tribute from Hooke, who so rarely gave praise it was doubly affecting. 'Sir Jonas has the answers, I'm sure. The way will be blocked by soldiers, and the crowds will be gathering to watch this Procession.'

'You will have a care, won't you, Harry? The Royal Society would not want to lose you, and neither would I.'

'Mr. Hooke, I'm so very sorry about Tom. You were—'

'—You are not to blame, Harry, and you must not blame yourself.'

Robert Hooke stood at the same time as Harry. With an unusual formality, he shook Harry's hand.

'Mr. Hunt.' It was the first time Hooke ever addressed him so.

'Mr. Hooke.'

'I have these for you.' Hooke held out a bunch of newly cut keys.

Harry, his eyes hot, descended the stairs to the lobby, and went out into the quadrangle of Gresham's College.

Inside, Robert Hooke looked for Mary, but she was nowhere to be found. There was no sound from Grace, who presumably was still asleep.

He put some more coal on the fire, sat back down, and continued to read the broadside news-sheet. Then, he wondered how Harry had got in.

OBSERVATION LX

OF
OBEISANCE

HIS EYES ITCHED, THEN STARTED TO sting. He must ignore the feeling.

He thought of other things. Other victories. Other killings he had done.

He started to shake.

He had to look away.

His opponent had won again.

Squeezing his eyes shut, he rolled out the tension from his shoulders, flexed his fingers, and opened his eyes.

He would play the game once more.

They stared at one another, each equally as still and blank-eyed.

But again, he started to tremble, the effort of his concentration showing.

A smile appeared—he could not help it—showing his little narrow teeth. Then he let out his loud, deep laugh.

He looked away from the unrelenting stare of Shaftesbury's automaton and took a pace back.

Pierre Lefèvre was dressed in assassin black. He was ready. His weapon was ready.

He put his heels together, brought himself to his full height, and gave the mechanical scribe his best military salute.

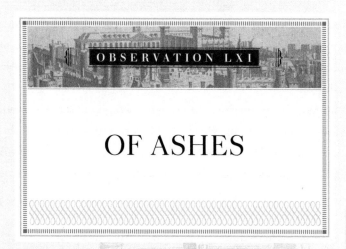

OBSERVATION LXI

OF ASHES

AT ALDGATE, A DOZEN SOLDIERS BLOCKED the way. Harry waited, wanting Whitechapel, edging gradually closer towards the smaller arch for those going through on foot. The main arch had a barrier across it, and carts and coaches queued back along Leadenhall Street, into Poor Jewry Lane and Shoemaker Row, their drivers swearing to themselves under their breath.

On the other side, the queues were even longer. All the people who made their way west, coming in early to get to the Procession, were being stopped. The soldiers were being more thorough, and slower, with those seeking to enter the City.

The figures of Peace, Charity, and Fortune looked down on him from the arch. They were illuminated by the noon sunshine, and Harry could tell from their benign expressions that they saw into his mind, and knew of its wonder at Grace's kiss, and what had happened after. He could not help grinning back at them, but he quickly turned serious when next to be stopped.

'Your name?' The question came from a belligerent sergeant who looked too old to still be soldiering. He blocked Harry with a palm, his other hand resting on the handle of his sword in its scabbard, his fingers opening and closing continuously as he asked the same questions of everyone going through.

'Henry Hunt.'

The sergeant looked him up and down. 'Your business?'

He wished to meet Colonel Fields. He had omitted to tell Hooke of his plan to go back to the old soldier's chapel. Hooke's worries about Harry searching into the matter of the dead boys had kept him from it.

Of all the men he had encountered during his search for the killer of the boys, Fields was dependable, and might say more of how Daniel Whitcombe had changed from being a chirurgeon for Parliament's army, going into slavery on the Earl of Shaftesbury's sugar plantation, to become a *virtuoso* natural philosopher.

Was the Earl of Shaftesbury Daniel Whitcombe's patron? Were Whitcombe's 'employments' carried out for him?

'I'm Henry Hunt, of the Royal Society,' Harry told the soldier. 'I'm the Observator there. I visit Whitechapel on private business.'

'So, not a philosophical business . . . Do you carry anything with you? There's a design on the King's life. We must search everyone.'

'Just some papers.'

'Let's have them!'

Harry produced them from the deep pocket inside his coat and gave them over. The sergeant looked with incomprehension at the first, topmost sheet, with the title *Observations Philosophical*. Without untying them, he rummaged through the remaining sheets, peering under the corners of the paper.

'What's the nature of this private business?'

Harry lied to him. 'Do you know of Mr. Robert Hooke? He's the Curator of Experiments—now Secretary, too—at the Royal Society, at Gresham's College. I deliver these from him, to a man named Colonel Michael Fields.'

'I do know of Robert Hooke,' the sergeant replied. 'We employ his reticle in the aiming of guns. I know Colonel Fields better. A great man, in his time. So, is it private business, as you say, or Royal Society business?'

'I'm sorry, it's Royal Society business.'

The sergeant, regarding the crush of people behind and the mild look-ing, bespectacled youth before him, turned aside, giving back the deci-phered notes. 'Tell the Colonel it was his name took you through.'

HIS THOUGHTS STILL almost entirely of Grace, Harry went against the tide of people going into the City, having to keep to the side of the way, and found the Saracen's Head. He turned from Whitechapel High Street and through the dark archway. He crossed the small meadow in front of the chapel.

As he approached where he had first met Colonel Fields, he slowed, then stopped.

The landscape before him had changed.

The Anabaptist chapel, down in the dip on the other side of the fence, no longer stood. Harry saw charred foundations and a few beams. Only its two columns, which had supported Fields's hammock between them, were still upright, looking like broken ship's masts. Fire had flaked the timber, its texture a black mould covering it.

Harry went through the gate and stepped onto the ashy site of the chap-el's destruction. The roof had fallen in, its emaciated beams folded between the walls. Climbing over them, he knocked against one of the Colonel's burnt chairs, disintegrating it.

The noise was loud. He looked around, suddenly aware eyes might watch him. The repeated sensation of being observed unsettled him, and he searched into the lines of bushes and along the wall of the stables to verify he was alone. There were no sounds other than those he made. Not even a bird stirred. No cows loomed in the fields.

Reassured, he went back to inspect the two scorched columns. The wood crumbled to his touch. There was no trace of the ropes or canvas in which the Colonel had lain. He remembered their first meeting, when Fields was shaving in his hammock.

Harry kicked at the thick grey ash on the floor, which soggily bound together, the rain of the past few days soaking and flattening it. There was nothing of Fields's Bible, or his candle. And there was no trace, either, of a body. No smell of one, and no signs of removal. At least, Harry thought, Fields had escaped.

Harry sniffed at the air again. He could hardly smell the burning of the chapel—the smell of horse manure was far stronger. No smoke rose from the fire. No cinders glowed. Kneeling down to touch a charred beam, he found it had completely cooled. It could not be a recent fire.

Yet just four days ago Fields had come to him to tell him the story of Reuben Creed and Daniel Whitcombe, and Sir Edmund killing Reuben after Worcester.

Surely Fields would have mentioned the burning down of his chapel?

A bright edge of something in the ash attracted his notice. He reached for it, then pulled back his hand immediately. He sucked at his finger, cut by the Colonel's razor. The stool it had rested on must have burnt away. Harry remembered when Fields had come to his lodgings. His head and chin had been covered with stubble.

He wrapped it in his handkerchief. As Fields had returned his boots, he would return the razor . . .

Colonel Fields had returned his boots, after watching him under London Bridge, on the Morice waterwheel.

He had come to Half Moon Alley, and told more of the Wars, and of his two blood-brothers, Daniel Whitcombe and Reuben Creed.

He had presented his Caesar disc.

Fields had been too helpful.

He had known it was Sir Edmund on the wheel. He even said he had reason enough to kill him, for Sir Edmund killed his friend.

Put aside his story of only following orders in wartime.

Sir Edmund's dead body was red, his blood discoloured by the proximity to a fire in an enclosed space. Was this chapel, as it burned, left locked to prevent his escape? The Justice's corpse carried the marks of stinging nettles. Harry saw a patch of nettles nearby, outside the scorched ruins of the chapel, next to a low section of fence leading to the fields beyond.

There could be a dozen such places in London, recently burnt down.

Harry continued to search the site of the fire, seeking evidence in the ash, under the fallen beams, shifting aside sections of the remaining roof. There was little left of the door, and the fire had destroyed any evidence of it being locked or barred to imprison the Justice.

By the collapsed wall of the chapel, near where the door used to be, he discovered a wet, dirty, singed strip of cloth. Studying it more closely, he realised it was a piece of fine lawn cloth. Sir Edmund's wrists had been tied. Harry picked up the cloth from the wet ash and wound it around his own wrists, not pulling the material too hard in case it shredded after its roasting.

Still, he would not allow himself to be certain. Carrying the lawn cloth with him, he further examined the ruins. After a search—which he would have abandoned if not for his resolve to inspect every inch of the place—he found a shiny, yellow strip of cloth, under the scorched remains of one of the chairs arranged for the Colonel's congregation.

The gold band from Sir Edmund's hat.

Now, he was certain. Here was where Sir Edmund had died, after swallowing the paper with *corpus* written on it. After the fumes and the heat of the fire overcame him, the Colonel had dragged him from the burning chapel, redressed him, delivered him to the Thames, and engaged him in the wheel of the Morice water pump.

Then, he had delivered Harry his boots, and talked to him and Mrs. Hannam, eating her tart, giving off no air of guilt.

Sir Edmund must have come here to meet the Colonel, to discuss either the Red Cipher, or their time in the Wars, when Cromwell covertly employed Daniel Whitcombe and Reuben Creed to help escort the King to France.

Had Sir Edmund really hanged Reuben Creed from a tree, frightened he would reveal the details of the scheme?

If so, why had the Colonel waited until now, over twenty-five years later, to take his retribution? It must be to do with the return of the Red Cipher: a letter left on the body of the Fleet boy, another delivered to Robert Hooke, and used to encipher Whitcombe's *Observations*.

Harry pulled his coat tighter to him, more to comfort himself than for warmth, sensing again the unsettling conviction he was being watched.

What best to do?

Who should he go to, to tell of the death of Sir Edmund at this chapel? The soldiers back at Aldgate, Sir Jonas Moore at the Board of Ordnance, or straight to the King himself?

Harry left the site of the Colonel's devastated chapel, crossed the stretch of meadow and walked back to Whitechapel High Street.

He would return to Gresham's College.

Mr. Hooke was the only man to ask, even if Harry had lied to him again.

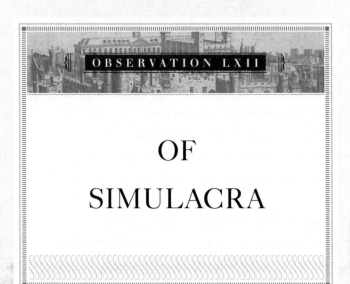

OBSERVATION LXII

OF

SIMULACRA

THE DECISION HAD BEEN MADE, AND the barrier removed. Impossible to search everyone in the crowd.

The people pressed through to the City, aiming for vantage points along Aldgate High Street, or Bishopsgate Street, or Leadenhall Street. Word was, there was no use diverting to the Thames for a wherry to take you to Temple Bar, where the Mock Pope's burning was to be, as the quayside was even worse. Fights had broken out, and wherries tipped. Passengers had been cast into the river.

Their lacerations stinging when exposed to the air, Harry kept his hands deep in his pockets. In the late afternoon, turning into evening, the temperature had dropped abruptly, and the wait to get through the arch chilled him. His bruised legs shivered as well as ached.

'Imagine the City aflame!' a big man bellowed, his voice half carried away by the breeze. 'Imagine all of the great buildings of London blazing by the same popish cruelty that before set it afire! Imagine your father and your mother tied to a stake, as they are cooked by Jesuits. Imagine their heart-wrenching screams in their torments . . . '

Harry tried to block the noise from his mind. Everyone he saw talked excitedly of the Procession. They held bags of vegetables, or baskets of eggs, or pockets bulging with pebbles, ammunition to hurl at the Mock Pope.

He thought of the contents of his own pocket: how much pain it had brought, and how much trouble it could still bring him. He reached for Whitcombe's *Observations*, in case the guard wanted to search him.

'Protestant flails!' a trader yelled, too close to his ear. 'Have a care against the damnable papists!'

Harry shoved him away.

The man waved his flail. 'Are you a one to be wary of?'

Harry turned and grabbed him by his elbow. The trader howled, surprised by the force of the young man's grip.

'Have a care yourself,' Harry snapped. 'Your question is malicious.'

Made nervous by the zeal on Harry's face, the flail seller dropped his eyes. 'I meant nothing by it,' he mumbled contritely.

'Then you merely prattle. Talk such as yours is dangerous, and shouldn't be let loose.'

A trooper looked hard at them, but relaxed as Harry released the man, and the confrontation seemed to be ended.

The people near Harry retreated to give him a little more room, wary of the spots of anger on his cheeks. Harry waited, calming slowly, every so often moving forwards with all the others, hoping nothing more would draw attention to himself. The smells from the crowd shouldering against him were almost overpowering: sweat, something like old bread, wine, smoke, and fat.

Word started up Houndsditch was the way. Those who believed it took the gamble, turning to go north by St. Butolph's.

Harry's shoulders slumped. The flail seller was speaking with one of the soldiers and pointing straight at him.

He just wanted to be back at Gresham's, sitting by the fire, talking to Mr. Hooke and Grace, away from this frantic multitude.

At last, as night fell and the full moon began its arc over London, Harry reached Aldgate. The moon shone brightly, the day's dullness cleared to let it throw silver on those below, as they jostled to watch the Procession.

The trooper stopped him, his voice gruff. 'What was that? With the man and his flails?'

The flail seller still stood there, looking aggrieved.

'I didn't want one, so he took against me.'

The trooper, tall, broad, and doughty-looking, inspected him, holding his lantern too close. The crowd pushed past their conversation, oozing slowly around them like tar. 'Not what he says. Empty your pockets. Take off your hat. There's fear of regicide.'

'I've only got papers.' Harry bridled at the man's close scrutiny, extending to a prodding of the bump on his head that made him flinch. He produced Daniel Whitcombe's *Observations*. 'I'm no assassin. I'm a friend to the King.'

The trooper considered. He was surrounded by enthusiasts, and this one looked no less earnest. Wide-eyed, sweaty, taken up by the same fervour gripping all at Aldgate. He only had papers, which could not be dangerous.

'Please let me through,' Harry said. 'I've news of the killing of Sir Edmund Bury Godfrey.'

The trooper narrowed his eyes doubtingly, then looked to the other soldiers with him. 'Where's the sergeant?'

HARRY COULD HEAR the sound, like a slow heartbeat, of drums approaching. Low and booming, a solemn rhythm. The Procession approached. Everyone pushed forwards or backwards, trying to work out which side of the Gate they should be. The guards went up and down, breaking up the worst of the crush with the lengths of their pikes.

Along Houndsditch, over the heads of the crowd, the Pope's crown was spotted, to shouts of 'The Whore of Babylon!' The crowd seemed to swell, as if a great lung taking a breath.

The way along Shoemaker Row had been too constricted. The Procession instead had gone outside the Roman Wall, along the broader road. As realisation spread, some turned to come back through Aldgate, as others resisted. Those still on the Whitechapel side saw their chance, rushing up Houndsditch to see.

'Push them back! Keep them back!' The sergeant, his voice ruined from shouting, waved angrily, before forcing his way on through the crowd. The trooper saluted to his disappearing back, muttered to himself his decision on this man claiming he knew of the Justice's murder. He took a strip of leather from his pouch.

'Put out your hands, like this,' he said, the insides of his wrists together in front of him. Harry looked beyond him, wondering if he could run, but the size of the man and the push of the crowd gave him nowhere to go. Slowly, he extended his hands, as Sir Edmund must have done for Colonel Fields. The trooper tied him to a bar set in the wall.

A man dressed as the Devil whirled by, knocking those near him, blowing unmusically into a flute. The trooper shoved him away, leaving Harry against the wall, receiving suspicious looks from those passing.

Winding its sluggish progress from Moorgate came the Mock Papal Procession, with drums beating steadily, pipes being played, and a slow, doleful ringing of a bell. At its head were six whifflers, bulky men wearing bright red waistcoats, clearing a path before them.

Harry, pulling against his strap, having to twist to look over his shoulder, could see the red seeping through the crowd, inexorably towards him, the whifflers moving from side to side, swinging sticks to discourage those who stayed too close.

To the sides of the Procession walked men wearing green ribbons pinned on their sleeves and hats, some dressed in green, some with their faces painted green, too. They carried flambeaux and lamps, flickering orange over the scene.

They were the Earl of Shaftesbury's supporters. Members of his Green Ribbon Club. The more boisterous of them styled themselves his 'Brisk Boys.'

Behind the whifflers walked the bell ringer, whose shouts could now be heard: 'Remember Justice Godfrey!'

Sir Edmund Bury Godfrey, dressed entirely in black, rode on a white horse. An excellent likeness of him, even down to the thinness of the lips and the saturnine expression. Only the way he rode, stiff in the saddle, showed he was wood, straw, and wax. Theatrically holding up an oversized bloody dagger, a black-robed Jesuit behind him kept him on his mount.

When they saw them, the people gasped at the murder of the Justice represented. They gasped again at his bloodstained clothes and the deep red weal across his neck. They all knew of the last journey Sir Edmund had taken to the wheel under London Bridge, strangled and nailed through by Jesuits.

'Remember the Justice! Remember Sir Edmund!' They started to chant along with the bell ringer.

As the procession reached him, one of the whifflers tried to push Harry out of the way, but realised he was tied. He looked at the young man, confused, and guided the Procession around him.

Impeded by the constriction of Aldgate, the Procession slowed to a crawl, and Harry could observe clearly, by all the flambeaux and lamps, every detail of those who went by.

Behind Sir Edmund and his assassin walked a tall fat man, dressed in the gown of a Protestant curate, a large black wig on his head. A strange cricket of a man, tiny by comparison, danced with him. His hips swayed and jerked, and his silver hair stood on end, as if tipped with St. Elmo's fire.

'To fall for the demonic tricks of papistry is to become a half-man!' the cricket screamed as he came through the Gate. 'A stunted homunculus, duped by the cruel lies of the anti-Christ! They would yoke us under the tyrannical absolutism of Rome, in diabolical partnership with the French King! Jesuitical spies infiltrate healthy Protestantism, infecting its body with doubts and misgivings, turning its head with diseased evasions and maintenances of grim fictions that fly in the face of reason! Their blasphemous rites, profane, sacrilegious, irreverent, immoral, corrupt, depraved, disrespectful . . . '

It was Titus Oates, Harry realised, the *Saviour of the Nation*, and that must be Israel Tonge with him. With them, they had their own bodyguard, a small group of militia watching constantly for imminent attack.

They went through the Aldgate arch, Tonge still ranting, hands held aloft, fingers splayed out as if to grasp the sky itself, eyes wide and hair shaking, Oates's great bulk beside him.

Behind them came more of the targets of Tonge's vitriol, to jeers and hisses from the crowd.

They pointed at the Catholic priests, robes decorated with skulls and bones, holding huge silver crosses, giving out pardons to those who would murder Protestants. They punched the air at the Carmelites and Grey Friars. The bishops, clad in purple, the breeze flapping their lawn sleeves, ducked as the crowd forgot this was spectacle and hurled eggs and vegetables at them. They sang songs for Queen Bess, and songs calling for the King's wife to bear children, as scarlet cardinals, and the Pope's physician holding Jesuit's powder, and two boys, red crosses on their white silks, swinging incense pots, walked past.

The boys were just in front of the Pope himself, Innocent XI, whose robes, and the chair he sat on, were a glory of red and gold and ermine.

If he were to stand miraculously from his chair, he would have been at least twelve feet tall. He lurched on his platform, which was skirted by a curtain decorated with St. Peter's keys. Lit torches ringed him with fire. Men carried him, handles projecting from each side of the platform.

Despite the hatred against him, his giant hand was raised to bless them all.

Although his face, garishly painted plaster and wood, looked angry: made furious by such Protestant enthusiasm surrounding him, such abhorrence for him and his way of worship.

At each stop and start, the Pope lurched forwards or back, the ropes holding his chair tautening or slackening as he moved.

A clamour of shouts and roars filled the street, as people were thrust one way and another, against one another, all eddying and swirling against the buildings around them. For Harry, strapped to his bar, the noise became deafening.

The Pope stopped before Aldgate. The crowd pressed up to him, and his bearers nearly collapsed under the weight. The men with green ribbons came to his rescue, as the shoving threatened to topple him.

The Pope towered above them all, his golden crown shining against the night sky, lit up by the moon. His wild swinging settled, as more people came to assist, taking the platform he was on.

Crushed against the bar he was tied to, Harry spun around wildly, desperate for breath. Kicks gained some space.

Among all the faces in the crowd pressed against him, one of them stood out, catching his attention.

A man moving smoothly out to the Pope's platform, to take one of its handles at the back.

Something about the shape of the forehead had caught his eye. But when Harry looked again, he had gone.

He pulled hard at the leather holding him, trying to spot the face again.

Dressed in the black of a Jesuit, with a black, wide-brimmed hat.

Harry was sure he had seen the murderer of Enoch Wolfe.

HE PULLED AT the leather digging into his wrists and searched for anything sharp to cut it through. The stone was too smooth. No edge presented itself.

Again, under the Pope. Now, towards the front of the platform.

Unmistakable, even under his hat. The shape of the forehead, the same one long eyebrow across it. The quietness and stillness of him—when all around him shouted, writhed in their displeasure at wicked papistry and the iniquities the Procession showed them—marked him out.

Before, he had worn a soldier's coat and bucket boots. Now, he assumed the clothes of a Jesuit.

That he was a killer, Harry knew, but who in this crowd was in danger?

The man looked in one direction, down Aldgate High Street. He did not seem to be scanning around him for a particular face.

Harry screamed out, but his noise joined the noise of everyone there, barely adding to the whole. All focus was on the Pope and his entourage.

He quietened, and bowed his head in defeat. All he could do was wait for release by the soldiers.

⌇

FURTHER ADVANCE, TO bring the Pope under Aldgate's archway, was impossible. The crowd was so dense it was impenetrable. The music and shouting continued, but the Procession had stopped still. To get ahead of it, people still tried to gain access from Whitechapel.

Harry's ribs could surely no longer hold. Tied to the bar, he had nowhere to go, and his wrists bled from the bite of the strap.

'Is this the one?'

The sergeant, arrived back at Aldgate, forced his way through. The big trooper, carrying a lantern, nodded. Both men looked frayed, breathing heavily. Harry presented their opportunity to leave the crush.

'Says he has news of the Justice.'

'I've seen another in the crowd, a killer!' Harry gasped.

'Get him inside. We may talk in peace,' the sergeant said to his man, producing a large key. 'His Holiness goes nowhere for a while.'

The trooper cut the leather strap with his knife.

The soldiers opened the door to the interior of Aldgate and pushed Harry up the dark staircase. At the top, he was pushed again, into a murky room, the light from the street hardly able to enter through its narrow, barred windows. The Pope's face, glowing orange from all the fire surrounding him, peered in at them from the Whitechapel side of the arch.

Stains and patches mottled the walls and spread across the ceiling from a corner. The plaster smelled like rotten seaweed. The trooper's lantern showed it had once been lived in, but only a few pieces of furniture remained. Just a dull table with a couple of broken chairs stacked on it, pushed up against the wall. A long-disused fireplace had a broken fireguard against it.

The room was small, yet the sudden space around him made Harry dizzy, as when at the top of the Monument after the man's fall. Although the soldiers had not yet started their questioning, his hands were sweaty. All he wanted was for them to believe him, but he expected the sergeant's response to echo the trooper's.

Easily, the sergeant flipped one of the upside-down chairs, to place it on the floor. Wiry, steady-eyed, younger than Harry remembered, he sat and leaned interrogatively at him.

'I remember you from this afternoon. I don't recall your name.'

'I am Henry Hunt, of the—'

'—Royal Society. So said you, when I let you out of the City.'

'I wish only to return to Gresham's College, to meet with Mr. Hooke there.'

The sergeant cocked his head. 'I shall tell you what I know. You went to Colonel Fields in Whitechapel. Some philosophical business. Coming back, you made trouble. Then, you claimed to know of Justice Godfrey's murder.'

'It was the Colonel who killed the Justice.'

The sergeant stood, and the chair scraped loudly on the wooden floor.

Harry took a pace back. 'Going to his burnt chapel proved it to me, for Sir Edmund was killed by fire.'

'The Justice was on the waterwheel, under London Bridge.' The sergeant's voice was getting louder.

'But he died by fire,' Harry insisted. 'I helped Mr. Hooke with the autopsy. His other wounds did not kill him.'

'This news has not come out.'

'The King swore us to secrecy.'

The sergeant took off his cap, looked at his trooper with him, and wiped the sweat from his hair. What the boy claimed could not be true. And opinion was against him—for everyone spoke only of the papist murder of Sir Edmund.

'And now you've seen another killer, in the mob.' The sergeant flicked the sweat off his fingers. 'I think you a rabble-rouser. Or else, your reason slips, like a poor creature of Bedlam, in these fearful times. The King swore you to secrecy, did he?'

'I report what I observed, nothing more. I saw a murder! The killer stands under the Pope, holding him up. He's dressed as a Jesuit.'

'Dressed as what he is? A Jesuit assassin?' The sergeant rolled his eyes. 'Enough of this, boy. I shall tell you what will happen. You will stay here. After the Procession is done, Mr. Hooke shall be fetched. If he vouches for you, he may take you away. Of your story of Colonel Fields, I believe you to be wrong, but it will be looked into. Of your story of the Jesuit, I fear you're overcome by the passions of the day. For an assassin would not work so openly. He would make himself invisible, in amongst the mob.'

'He's made himself invisible, in amongst the Procession!' Harry shouted.

The sergeant picked up his lantern. 'We must go. His Majesty's due.'

He motioned to the trooper, who started to retie Harry with the strap.

'No need for that. This boy's no danger, unless to himself. Henry Hunt, you may watch the Procession from here.'

They did not look back. Harry heard them lock the door, and their heavy descent of the stairs.

❧

LEFT IN THE GLOOM, Harry let out a frustrated howl. He crossed to the window to look on the crowd, and those dressed as Catholics in the Procession.

And the Mock Pope, whose crudely painted eyes observed him interestedly through the glass.

A great noise sounded behind him, from the direction of Aldgate High Street. He went to the opposite window.

Horses and a bodyguard of militia came from Fenchurch Street, avoiding the route of the Procession.

Rather than using a carriage, the King had a chosen to ride: the better for his people to see, the more to show him unafraid of threats made to his person. The greater to convince them he held no sympathies for the Romish way.

The cheering was tumultuous for their monarch.

Waving and smiling, the King joined his subjects by the Aldgate pump. He floated through them, his horse looking half-submerged in them. The people reached out their hands to touch his, his royal hands extended to each side of him, touching them, riding just with his knees.

All wishing the King more careful of his safety, the soldiers protecting him watched nervously about them for the sight of a drawn weapon, or a grenado.

His Majesty insinuated himself into the line of the Procession, just behind Sir Edmund Bury Godfrey, in front of Oates and Tonge.

The drums beat more loudly, with a quickened pace. Since the King's arrival the crowd was more mutable, for the whifflers were able to start forwards, slowly parting the sea of people.

The bell ringer recommenced his doleful chime. Sir Edmund was led forwards on his mount. The King and all the churchmen followed. Israel Tonge resumed his customary torrent, Titus Oates preened beside him.

Under Harry's feet, the giant Innocent was taken through Aldgate, just clearing the height of the arch. Like an immense birth, he reappeared into Aldgate High Street, delivered into the City.

Until he was all the way through, Harry could not see the men who carried him.

There he was. Directly below him, just by the boys swinging incense. The black-robed Jesuit.

In all the frenzy, this man's face was completely still, like an automaton's Harry had once seen.

As again the Pope was settled down, Enoch Wolfe's killer slid his arm along the handle of the platform. Before he had time to readjust it, his sleeve was pulled up.

The glint of a blade.

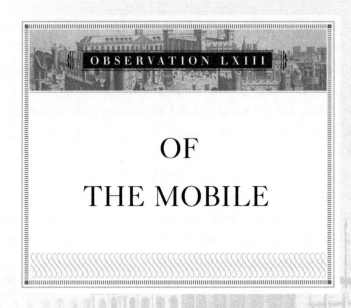

OBSERVATION LXIII

OF
THE MOBILE

HARRY BANGED FRANTICALLY AT THE WINDOW'S glass, his fist between its iron bars. But the crowd's cheering was so loud he knew it was futile. Even when some panes fell from their leading, and crashed on the people below, almost no one turned or looked up, all intent on the King and the papists.

Hitting the door with his fist, and kicking at it, brought no answer either, and had little effect on the door, hardly moving it in its frame.

He tried the window's bars, shaking them with all his strength. Below him to his left there was a canopy stretched over the entrance to a shop. He might be able to climb along the timbers of the old building butting up to Aldgate, if he could traverse the stone of the arch to reach it.

If he could only get through this window.

As the bars were solid, he inspected the sill holding them, seeking for weakness in the stone, or cement gone soft. After, he stared up at the lintel, which held more promise. He scanned the room for something to dig at it with, and saw the old fireguard. Although most of it was charred wooden spindles, it had a rusted metal frame. Carefully prising it apart gave a serviceable edge.

He dug feverishly at the top of one of the bars, his shoulders aching from the reach, but soon realised he could scrape all afternoon—and all night—and not get through. Let alone remove all the bars blocking his way.

Outside, Pope Innocent's height was causing a problem. He was blocked by a balcony projecting over the street. If he were to progress, the requisite reshuffling of people to allow him through needed coordination. This was done by the scarlet cardinals, who bellowed instructions to the whifflers and Shaftesbury's Brisk Boys, who tried their best to shove the spectators aside, out of the way of the Pope.

More of Harry's shouting down through the broken window brought no response. There were so many calls of 'Your Majesty! Your Majesty!' he may as well have been calling to the moon.

Inexplicably, the King turned, and Harry thought he saw him listening, as if he had recognised his voice in the middle of so many. But it was not so, for he started to take his horse towards the Mock Pope, to see if he should take command of its shifting.

As the King approached closer to the Jesuit assassin, Harry screamed to the crowd below, as loud as his lungs would allow.

The killer adjusted the object under his sleeve, and again Harry saw the sheen of metal, lamplight glancing off it. Some kind of contraption strapped to his forearm, with a blade fitted.

Tipped sideways, the people holding him by his ropes, the Pope cleared the underside of the balcony and edged onwards again. The King swung his horse slowly back about, hampered by the crowd, and oblivious to the fact a man with a weapon—a brutal killer—was kept from him only by men pretending to be cardinals, bishops, and monks.

When he saw the King turn, Harry tried to pick up the table to hurl at the bars, hoping if they did not give way, there would be enough sound from the impact to catch the crowd's attention. But it was far too solid and heavy to lift. He struggled even to budge it.

Although the chairs were too flimsy, he hurled them at the window, which only achieved the splintering of two chairs. He pitched their legs down into the crowd, but so many objects were being thrown, most people had been hit by something. So many objects were airborne, it was difficult to tell where they arrived from.

The wooden spindles of the fireguard followed into the Procession below. There were a few disgruntled turns of heads, but no one thought to look above them, to the window over the Aldgate archway.

Harry stood, took a deep breath, and raised his eyes to Heaven. He exhaled, dejected, and took off his spectacles. He extended his arms to shake out his anguish, which had tied knots into all the fibres of his body. Still looking upwards, he replaced his spectacles, and the ceiling, with its patches of damp, came into focus. At one corner, its rough plaster ran with moisture.

Innocent was heading off towards the Aldgate pump. Harry ran back to the table and managed to lift one end of it, straining under its weight. He walked it to the wet corner. When it was far enough along, he climbed up onto it, and took his fireguard knife to the ceiling's plaster, hacking it away.

It fell in wet clumps, revealing wood long rotted. He dug deep into the planking. He twisted, drilled, to make a hole he could push his hand into.

Through the crumbling wood, he could feel smooth, wet metal. As he pushed it, it buckled to his touch, and one edge lifted. Water streamed through the gap he had made between two metal sheets, splashing over his face. Soft lead, badly joined. Over years, the rain had seeped into the wood.

Sawing at it, enlarging the hole he had made, the wood was so soft he was able to pull it away as he cut. When he made a hole large enough, he snapped longer sections of the old planks off, gripping their ends and pulling his feet up, using his weight to break the planks across a joist.

An explosion went off outside. Harry staggered on his table as the Aldgate arch shook violently. The few remaining panes in the windows fell away, onto the Procession below.

Coloured fire streaked the sky. Fireworks lit to celebrate the refusal of right-thinkers to cower before Catholic insurgency, as so bravely exemplified by their King.

A great fan of people teeming along Aldgate High Street, Poor Jewry Lane, and Shoemaker Row, and even those still unable to get through the Gate, chanted their desire for the good health of the King, and their hatred of Catholics.

Once Harry had steadied himself, and broken enough of the planking, he pushed back the lead sheet and rolled it away from the hole he had gouged. He took a great breath of the air coming in, freezing and fresh, then gripped the sides of the hole.

He pulled himself up, and his head went through, emerging out onto the roof of the Aldgate arch.

More fireworks detonated, further noises of bangs and whistles, the sky a spectrum of colours.

Harry scrambled up through the hole.

Looking over the side of Aldgate, between its crenellations surrounding the roof, he tried to map a way down. Although there were holds between the stones, and the alcoves for its statues, it was too difficult. He was sure he would slip, and fall.

Then, there would be no one to warn of the King's assassination.

The roof had an entrance, for the Gate to be defended from up there, but it was an iron-faced door, firmly locked and stoutly hinged. No signs of the rotting of the planks he had cut through.

Since the Procession had moved a distance away, the drumming was quieter. The Pope was now fifty yards or so from him. People filled in behind him as he went, following him and his entourage, joining the flow in spiralling motions, a slowed study in turbulence.

Harry could never get through all of them, or get to the King to alert him. Or confront the Jesuit. The one way off the Aldgate arch was to jump onto the next building, an old inn with a steeply pitched roof. He calculated a way down which involved running to the roof, crawling to a chimney, then sliding to a dormer, seeing a lip across it he could hold.

Convinced this was the only chance he had of reaching the street, but fearing he was about to take off into oblivion, Harry jumped from the roof of Aldgate.

He landed astride the apex of the inn's roof, one side sloping steeply to the street far below and the other to the galleries surrounding the tar-black courtyard of the inn. He straddled his way along, dislodging a tile which slid from its place with a crunch. It fell into the courtyard, taking an alarming duration to land.

He arrived at the chimney, above the almost horizontal of the dormer's roof. He rehearsed his next manoeuvre, staring at the projecting timber across the dormer's edge.

If he missed it, he would be hurled into space, to land on the crowd below.

He took a deep breath and let go of the chimney. Trying to control the speed of his slide, the tiles were too rough and slippery. He bounced across them much faster than he had imagined. Managing to twist onto his belly as he descended to the end of the roof, his toes caught the lip.

Although it gave an alarming crack, the timber held. Able to swing down to the dormer window, he turned and kicked his way through.

He brushed broken glass off himself, standing in a bleak bedroom without comforts or decoration. Servant's quarters. He hurried to the door.

Swinging it open, he was confronted by a woman returning to bed in her nightclothes, grey-skinned, too ill to be outside watching the Pope. She swiped at him angrily with her chamber pot. He had to dodge her to get to the stairway.

She shouted behind him, but no one came to answer her cries of 'Assassin! Assassin!'

At the bottom of the stairs, Harry ran along a passage and pushed open another door, to be enveloped in the smell and warmth of a Turkish coffeehouse. There were rich colours on the walls, and serving men in silks and turbans. It was busy, but all the customers pressed up against the window, watching the Procession, some standing on chairs and tables.

No one noticed him. He ran the length of the room behind them, to the door leading out to the street.

He heard the woman's shout to those in the shop: 'Assassin!'

Coming out onto the street, fireworks still cracking the sky, he saw the Pope's chair, and the top of his crown. The moon shone down from behind him, giving him a satirical halo. As Innocent had met another obstruction, he was swaying impatiently.

Going through the coffeehouse had saved Harry a fight through the Procession in front of the archway, but he was still a distance from the Pope.

Behind him, the door of the coffeehouse opened. A couple of Turks came out, followed by the sound of the woman shouting, 'Brown coat!'

The people pressed against him. When he tried to push through, he found staunch resistance, as they pushed back. He tried to use the movement of the crowd to take him to its heart, as close to the Pope as he could. Those guarding the Pope, Shaftesbury's Brisk Boys with their green ribbons, stood to either side of him.

Harry squeezed his way next to one of these men, who carried a flambeau, and untied the ribbon from his arm, reckoning that with all the pushing the man would not notice some extra tugs on him. Using his teeth to grip the ribbon, Harry tied it around his own.

He pushed his way through the Brisk Boys, nodding at them, pointing at his ribbon, and they let him squeeze through. Once he got behind the Pope, he pulled aside the curtain with St. Peter's keys on it and ducked under the platform. It had legs like a table's, being conveyed by men now exhausted from the weight, and they had stopped to rest him down.

Harry ran in a crouch through to the opposite side of the platform, to find if the man dressed as a Jesuit still lurked at its corner. There was no sign of him.

He reappeared from under the Pope, gave a salute to one of the Green Ribboners, and hoisted himself onto the platform.

When he ran along its length, his action was met by a huge cheer from the crowd. From the height of the platform, he could see what it was they all waited for. Sir Edmund Bury Godfrey, who had fallen from his horse, levitated horizontally over them all, bobbing like a stick in a stream, in a game of passing him from person to person.

Shaftesbury's Brisk Boys were slow to react to the insurgent up by the Pope, as Harry was getting such loud encouragement. The crowd, apart from a few Turks, all saw him as taken up by an excess of Protestant fervour. With the wait for the return of Sir Edmund, it was more entertainment.

He could certainly be no danger to the King, for he was slight, and wore spectacles.

Harry jumped down from the platform, crashing into a priest in a surplice, who turned angrily and swiped at him with his golden cross. The Pope's physician saw him, and went for the interloper, but Harry was too quick. Pushing aside a bishop, avoiding a burly cardinal, Harry carved through the Procession, shouting 'Your Majesty! Your Majesty!'

'Your Majesty! Your Majesty!' the crowd cried, joining him.

From behind Harry, though, more cries, as the woman's identification of him as an assassin was also picked up. It rippled throughout the crowd, proliferated, echoed, multiplied.

'Assassin! Assassin!' became a constant roar, and everybody looked for one, and there was Harry, running towards the King through the line of the Procession.

The King spun his horse, reacting to the chants of the crowd, everyone shouting 'Your Majesty!' or 'Assassin!'. His bodyguards all turned to face the threat from behind them.

Harry pushed aside the Grey Friars, but the Carmelites, tonsures shining from all the flames and fireworks, were ready for him. They grabbed at him, pulling him to a stop. Brown tunics encircled him, and they shouted to Shaftesbury's men to take him.

Harry kicked out at them, shouting, 'I must warn His Majesty!'

He was bundled to the ground, and had his face cruelly pressed into the surface of the road, its stones jagging his forehead. His spectacles fell out of reach, were trodden on, and flattened.

He jerked his head to get his mouth free of the hand covering it, threatening to smother him.

Harry looked up, distinguishing only blackness, as his eyes travelled over the robes of a Jesuit.

The face of Enoch Wolfe's killer looked down on him. The eyes stared into his, and did not blink.

LEFÈVRE PULLED HARRY up from the ground easily, pressing a hard fist into the small of his back. He held his neck in the crook of his arm so tightly Harry could scarcely breathe.

The Carmelites edged back, realising this Jesuit had control of the intruder, and began to reform into their line. Harry tried to twist, to get away, to kick free of the killer, but Lefèvre stood, unmoving and unmoveable, his grip completely secure.

It was like being held by a statue.

Shaftesbury's men, having advanced to take Harry, stayed put, disconcerted by the man's stillness and by the absolute calm on his face.

The King rode towards them, steering his horse through the quietening crowd and the Catholic churchmen, to know what the commotion had been. His militia came with him, a hedgehog of muskets, pikes, and swords.

Lefèvre placed his hand over Harry's mouth. Against his face, Harry could feel a metal object under the killer's sleeve, with protruding bolts and sharp edges.

As the King approached, Harry could only produce muffled cries and sobs.

The Justice's white horse was being brought forwards by two of Shaftesbury's guards. The other Jesuit who had ridden with the effigy of Sir Edmund was nowhere to be seen, and they passed the reins to his substitute. Neither of them looked more closely than the black robes to decide his identity.

They expected the man to swap the horse for his hostage, but he did not let go of Harry. Even being held one-handed, Harry could not release his grip.

Seeing a man dressed as a Jesuit holding his apparent assassin and the

Justice's white horse, the King rode closer. There was something familiar about the assassin's brown coat, which looked to be leather.

'Harry?' he said, dubiously.

Lefèvre's hand still across his mouth, Harry tried to signal with his eyes, widening them, rolling them towards Wolfe's murderer, to make the King realise his danger.

'Unhand him. I wish to speak with him,' the King commanded the Jesuit.

Lefèvre did not.

The King stared at him, perplexed by the man's insubordination. 'Remove your hand!'

Lefèvre stood motionless. Harry squirmed, but the man's grip was firm.

The King turned to a musketeer with him, who levelled his weapon at Harry.

'God's Blood, no, at the Jesuit!' the King cried.

The man's aim shifted, to point his musket unswervingly between Lefèvre's wide-set eyes.

Lefèvre took his hand from Harry's mouth, but still held him securely. 'He meant to kill you,' he said. 'I helped to stop him.'

His voice was strong and steady, but his accent was not of a Londoner, nor of an Englishman.

More muskets rose to him. The crowd began to murmur, as they pondered on this foreigner.

'Your Majesty, he has a weapon!' Harry shouted. 'Under his sleeve!'

The King kicked his horse back a pace, and all his men formed lines of defence, some kneeling, some standing. All well-drilled, pointing their weapons to meet this threat.

A hole in the crowd appeared as the onlookers shrank away, a perfect circle to leave exposed Harry, Lefèvre, and the white horse which had carried the effigy of Sir Edmund.

Lefèvre let go of Harry, and took a pace away. He put his arms outstretched to either side of him, like Christ on the Cross. He gazed unblinkingly at the King, whose horse was snorting and scraping its shoes nervously, trying to back further off.

'Arrest the Jesuit,' the King commanded, struggling with his mount.

Two of his men lowered their weapons and went to Lefèvre, who did not change his position until they produced straps to tie him. Then, he brought his wrists together, as if ready to be taken.

As the first man grasped his wrists, Lefèvre twisted down in a sudden corkscrew motion. He ended in a squat, taking the soldier down with him. The man landed face first with a crunching of teeth.

Lefèvre leapt up, knocking back the second soldier, and squeezed a lever with a quick motion of his fist. A blade fired from the weapon on his fore-arm into the man's chest. The soldier's eyes dulled immediately, his heart skewered through.

Witnessing two of the King's guards go down, people began to scream, and turn, and try to run through the wall of more people behind them. In the panic, Lefèvre ran to the further side of Sir Edmund's horse, placing it between him and the guards. He grabbed its reins and pulled both his feet into a stirrup, bringing up his legs, showing nothing to be shot at.

He spurred the horse, wheeling it in a tight spiral towards the King.

The King's guards had nothing to aim at apart from the Justice's horse, and so were uncertain of their actions. They could not see the Jesuit's plan. They turned as one, keeping between the horse and the King, but unwilling to shoot at the animal.

Harry, comprehending fully the killer's plan, ran to the King in the opposite direction to Lefèvre.

As the horse reached the line of the King's men, Lefèvre brought him-self up in the saddle and pulled back the lever under his sleeve.

His arm pointed at the King.

Harry, taking his sharp piece of the fireguard's frame from his pocket, with just the briefest of thoughts for the animal's pain, stabbed it into the horse's shoulder. It reared, squealing.

A noise like a stage whisper swished from Lefèvre's weapon as its spring released. A blade fired, up and over the King.

Lefèvre somersaulted backwards as the horse went back, landing cleanly on his feet, already looking around him. His tunic's sleeve was pulled back, revealing a complex machinery of struts, levers, and springs strapped to his forearm. In the middle of it all, a magazine of vicious-looking knives, with flights where a handle should be.

He was exposed. Shots fired from the King's bodyguard.

A woman went down, to more screaming from the terrified crowd.

Lefèvre had gone so swiftly it seemed he missed out the space in between, appearing in another part of the Procession. He was back by the cardinals, who fell into the bishops against the Pope's platform, knocking over the man dressed as the Devil.

'Hold your fire!' the King shouted, anxious no one else in the crowd should be hurt.

Lefèvre jumped up to the Pope, still seeming relaxed, as if strolling in St. James's Park. There was no sense of hurry, no sign of fear, yet he moved with bewildering speed.

The crowd shouted 'Assassin! Assassin!' as he climbed.

He was by the Pope's face, on the back of his chair, having seen a way to a balcony, and a window, and a roof.

As he climbed to the highest part of the Pope, over his shoulders and onto his golden crown, shots started again from the soldiers, over the heads of the crowd, but smacking into the walls of the buildings behind them.

Everybody ducked and screamed as volley followed volley.

The King's soldiers all missed, although some shots had gone through the Pope. Holes showed through his fabric, moonlight sending silver threads through them.

As Lefèvre prepared to make his leap onto the balcony, Sir Edmund Bury Godfrey was thrown from the crowd, smacking into the Pope's chair, making it rock.

Demonic cheering rose from the throng, and pebbles and vegetables and coins followed, hurled at the Jesuit. Blood appeared as he was hit.

Lefèvre fired his weapon at the crowd, the blades slicing into them, one after another, until his contraption had emptied.

From every point of the compass, missiles converged on him, making him stagger, but he still kept a hold of the Pope's crown. He reached for the balcony above him, but a bottle smashed against the side of his face, tearing his cheek away.

He shook his head, flinging blood over the crowd. His blood streamed down from the jagged wound, running onto the golden crown.

The people combined to throw the effigy of Sir Edmund again, heaving the artificial Justice at the Jesuit. Sir Edmund hit the Pope's chair, which rocked violently, almost throwing Lefèvre. The chair swayed, and Sir Edmund was thrown again, in the rain of other objects now aimed at the Jesuit assassin.

Lefèvre, still gripping the Mock Pope, took hit after hit.

The crowd's bloodthirst transformed him into a raw homunculus: misshapen, distorted, his robes tattered. Jesuit-black turned red.

Eventually, his hold slipped, and Lefèvre seemed to float down from the Pope, looking like Death's angel, to disappear and be ground down under the feet of the London mob.

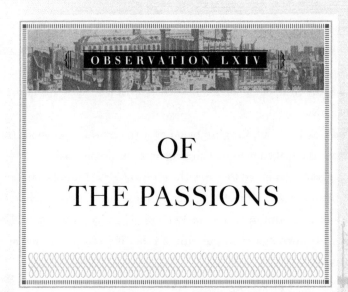

OF
THE PASSIONS

THE EARL OF SHAFTESBURY JERKED THE curtains across the window, blocking the insistent moon.

He could not believe Pierre Lefèvre had failed in his mission of revenge. Nor that Robert Hooke's assistant, Henry Hunt, whom he thought merely an irritant, had obstructed him.

His eyes throbbed. Even the candlelight hurt them, the flames spikes of brilliance piercing them viciously, as spitefully as the pipe pierced his side.

Without the moonlight, the light thrown by the candles was sour. The same shade of greenish-yellow as the juice which had leaked all day. The noxious smell from the wound disgusted him. He was repulsed by his own body, made of sickly flesh and filled with corruption. Rotting before his death. Another shirt ruined, as the fluid from his liver had soaked through the bandages, an acid stain spreading across it.

Every fissure in his skull felt stretched. Every vein in its flesh as if about to split along its length. Every cavity full of gritty slush, as if the liquid inside froze. The rest of him, though, was far too hot. Even without his peruke, sweat dripped from his hair and down his back.

Self-pity, childish and petulant, welled up again, as it had ever since receiving the intelligence of Lefèvre's failure. His own bitterness made him retch.

He did not have John Locke to calm him, to reason him out of his black mood. Locke had left London to escape from its miasmas and fogs, and the particles from the burning of sea coal rasping and clogging his lungs.

Also, Shaftesbury suspected, to be far from the consequences if the attempt at assassination came to light.

The spark. He knew well where it would lead him.

Shaftesbury tried to slow his anger, to regain control of himself. He attempted a prayer, but the words swam meaninglessly, never ordering themselves into significance.

He could not believe the Witch was gone, either.

Daniel Whitcombe, who had promised to revivify the boy. He had promised. He had failed Frances, but assured him, to his face, it was still possible.

Just more time was all he wanted.

No matter. Whitcombe's experimental trials to save their son were at an end.

His mother had seen to that. She had murdered their son, by putting an end to the experiments.

Shaftesbury would never forgive her.

The King had agreed with her, and put a stop to Whitcombe. Perhaps he had ordered Whitcombe to be disposed of, as an embarrassment.

Shaftesbury would never forgive him.

Sir Jonas had been more helpful, but with Whitcombe's disappearance, how could he have done more?

\

Self-pity became resentment—Shaftesbury knew what it would become. He was a victim of his emotions, helplessly in thrall to them. They always defeated him. A form of death, he thought: the civilised part of him murdered by the bestial.

We are centaurs, going only where our horse legs take us.

He could feel violence coming towards him like a driverless carriage. He could hear it.

Droning. Rattling. Hissing. Rushing.

Shaftesbury paced from the library, through the door between the books, and into John Locke's elaboratory.

He crossed the black and white chessboard of the tiled floor.

The air-pump stood before him. All its surfaces gleamed, illuminated by bright lamps placed around the room. The tools, on shelves and in racks on the walls, similarly shone. Oiled, polished, new. Never used.

The room awaited the Witch, as the receiver awaited the boy.

Shaftesbury closed his eyes, wincing at the light. Ever since his year in the Tower, brightness hurt them.

His heart twisted.

His anger burst, *phosphoros elementaris* exposed to the air.

An exploratory cuff. He punched the air-pump's receiver with the side of his hand. His blow bounced off the thick glass. A dull thudding noise was all, the chamber fabricated to withstand forces far greater than a fist.

He punched it again, this time with his knuckles first.

The machine seemed to stare back at him. Indifferent. Dumbly insolent. Shaftesbury's knuckles pulsated with pain. He had split the skin across them.

Daniel Whitcombe was to pursue his work here at Thanet House. John Locke was to help him. As his operator. Assistant. Amanuensis. When they could not find Whitcombe, Shaftesbury had tried to convince Locke to replace him.

But his secretary had refused. Not only did he lack the skill, Locke said, he believed it was against God to try.

The arrogance of the man. Who was Locke to know God's wishes?

Locke had not been squeamish about assassination. Not much Godly about that.

Looking at the air-pump choked him. Shaftesbury took a knife from its place on the wall and stabbed convulsively at the brass cylinder.

His third thrust pierced the brass.

He had managed to injure the machine.

Shaftesbury's elation was demoniacal, his expression one of joy. His face shone, an ecstatic radiance, but it was not enough, this passion—not nearly enough—to satisfy him. To calm him once more.

He stabbed the cylinder again to further mutilate it. Its impassivity made him feel suddenly threatened. The awareness of his impotence against it made his rage burn even brighter. Even if he were to take it apart and disperse its components far and wide, it would have conquered him.

He pushed at the heavy wooden frame, rocking it, then heaved himself against it. The glass receiver swayed, seemed for a moment to be righting itself, swayed once more, then fell from its place. It smashed, scattering splinters and powder over the tiles.

He lifted the frame, pulled it up, over, stamped on it. One of its joints broke with a gratifying crack. He jumped on it, forcing the timbers apart. He picked up the cylinder, panting under its weight, and threw it back down on the floor, denting the brass and cracking the tiles. He wrenched off the stopcock and threw it at Locke's cabinet of curiosities, smashing the glass in its doors.

He pulled out the sucker and stamped on that, too, trying to squash it flat. Until he slowed, from exhaustion.

Shaftesbury bent, leaning on his knees, lungs heaving air in and out of himself. A filament of spittle hung from his mouth, pooling over the floor.

The taste made him retch again.

The broken machine and the room's devastation reappeared, becoming sharp, as the fog of his anger started to clear. He knew the sweet mood of calm approached, as inevitably as anger arrived.

He went to the tools on Locke's workbench, quickly, before the passion died out.

Slowly, methodically, he set about taking the remains of the air-pump apart. At first, his shaking hands meant he kept slipping, once pushing a screwdriver into his finger, but gradually his work became easier, as equilibrium returned.

As he worked, he placed each part neatly beside him. Anger became calm, then misery. His mouth quivered. His chest started to shake.

He worked until the apparatus was dead.

Uriel Aires, his friend since the Wars, was dead. Pierre Lefèvre, the assassin was dead.

His boy was dead. His son. He had a defect in his heart.

God allowed such things, such abnormalities, Locke had told him. So, we must accept them.

But he could not.

Shaftesbury quietly came out of the elaboratory and crossed the library to his mechanical scribe. It was the nearest thing to humanity he could touch.

He clasped the automaton to him.

OF A
PROPOSITION

ALL THESE HOUSES ON THE MINORIES were new. In London's Great Conflagration every house within half a mile of the Tower was brought down
before the flames could reach it. If its munitions stores had blown, then
half of London, north and south of the river, London Bridge, and all of the
ships moored by, would have gone.

Reaching the open ground of Little Tower Hill, Harry looked west,
towards the spot where Archbishop Laud was beheaded. Laud, whose way
of religion had caused the country to go to war with itself.

For what? The King was back on his throne. He had ordered the executions of the men who signed his father's death warrant. He punished
those who opposed him and rewarded those who had paved the way for his
restoration, giving them lands and money taken from the men who had

supported Parliament. He commanded the exhumation of Oliver Cromwell's body. The Lord Protector's head still perched on a pole above Westminster.

He had prorogued Parliament, imposing his authority over it. He ruled as absolutely as his father.

Some fled, preferring the New World. Others hid, fearful of the consequences of being found out, the tolerance Cromwell showed to them overturned.

Men such as Michael Fields could not escape the Wars. Mr. Hooke, too, was wary of the past.

At each side of Harry walked a burly soldier. Two more soldiers, one with his sword drawn and the other with a pistol, walked behind. Ahead was the same ginger-haired captain who had been at London Bridge, after Sir Edmund's retrieval from the Morice waterwheel.

Down to the Iron Gate, at the waterside, and the steps. Harry sensed the chill of the place, rising from the Thames.

They had come for him that morning at Mrs. Hannam's house in Half Moon Alley. He had just returned after buying new spectacles from Yarwell's, at the Archimedes in Ludgate Street. He had paid extra for sides and a sprung steel bridge.

Despite his avowals of innocence, and his assurances he had been a saviour of the King, not one who plotted against him, the captain told him his arrest was by order of Sir Jonas Moore. An order he would carry out. He clouted Harry when he grew tiresome with his protestations.

They marched him over the moat, as far as the Develin Tower. A yeoman gestured them through with his halberd.

Another old, tough man, Harry thought, guessing at what he had done in the Wars. Perhaps he fought against Colonel Fields, at Edgehill, or Naseby, or Worcester. Or with him, if the man had switched allegiance.

The high walls to either side seemed to meet above him, as if they leaned in over his head. This was where the Thames used to be. The mud was soft under his feet, sticking to his boots, every stride an effort.

At the gateway between the Lanthorn Tower and the Salt Tower, the

Board of Ordnance's Surveyor-General waited for him, at once familiar from his portliness.

'Good morrow, Harry.' Sir Jonas Moore had a munificent smile across his face. 'You seemed reluctant to meet with me. I hope my men were not too rough. At least they kept you from being knocked on the head by a Jesuit, eh?'

The relief his arrest had been only to get him to the Board of Ordnance was soon replaced by resentment, confusion, then wariness.

Harry did not return the smile, and only grudgingly shook the hand Sir Jonas extended.

He had steered clear of Sir Jonas, worried he would not welcome being challenged. Instead of waiting, Sir Jonas had him arrested, as a display of his power.

Harry had wanted to be surer of his ground.

Any story men such as the Surveyor-General told him would be the story he was expected to believe. And the one he would be expected to tell. Or, expected to keep secret, their opinion being it was too sensitive to become known.

But what if it were not the truth?

He could not fight such men. He hoped one day to become the Royal Society's Curator of Experiments.

Then he might be worthy of Grace Hooke.

Grinning at Harry's rapid array of expressions, Sir Jonas continued. 'I will explain why I had you brought here.' He dismissed Harry's guards with a flick of his fingers. 'Without ado, it is because the King wishes it. You have impressed upon him your proficiency in natural philosophy, and in your practical action. He spoke to me of the Boscobel tree, in which he hid from the troops of Parliament, until Cromwell's spies could get to him. He said that you looked in the wood, but wanted guidance to the oak itself. He wishes to reward you.'

He made a sweeping gesture across all the buildings surrounding them. 'Since the King's restoration to his throne, we have busied ourselves with building up the strength of the Tower. Its structure and its foundations, and shoring it up against the action of the Thames. We have improved our defences, after our troubles with the Dutch, and the threat from France.'

He led Harry across the Tower grounds and turned towards the Armouries, a large building of red brick housing the Board of Ordnance, responsible for the King's munitions, supplies, equipment, and for the security of the Tower itself.

'We also have a great many people looking at weapons. Currently, we work on a new weapon for the Army, called the fusil, a light musket doing away with a glowing fuse. A glowing fuse is a dangerous thing about barrels of gunpowder. You have recent experience with gunpowder, Harry. You can, I am sure, grasp the advantage.'

By the high wall next to the Lanthorn Tower, a man standing behind a weapon mounted on a tripod waved at Sir Jonas, who waved cheerily back.

The man fired the gun, its ball slapping into a bank of earth pushed up against the wall.

Astonishingly, a few seconds later, he fired again. After a third, soon repeated shot, he poured water over the barrel.

'It has a revolving cylinder,' Sir Jonas said. 'Heat along the barrel is a problem.'

The weapon was fired a fourth time.

'As well as the search for new weapons,' Sir Jonas went on expansively, 'we seek to improve upon the old. Faster rates of shot, better mixtures of powder, directed charges, shapes of bullet, improved grenadoes and grapeshot, breech-loading cannon, greater range, easier manoeuvrability, methods of aiming—Mr. Hooke's reticle is an example—and the rifling of a weapon's barrel to give greater accuracy. And so on. All are trialled within these walls.'

A tremendous detonation filled the inmost ward with smoke. It sent earth shooting up into the air, as high as the top of the stairs leading into the White Tower.

'Ah!' Sir Jonas exclaimed, checking his pocket watch. 'Ten o'clock!'

He helped Harry up from where he had dived for cover. Harry brushed mud from himself, looking shamefaced.

'We look to improve upon ways of killing the enemy. Which means, if you think of it another way, of saving the lives of our own.'

He brushed some more of the mud from Harry's coat, in an oddly motherly manner. 'Always, we look to save the lives of our own.'

Another explosion rocked the ground. 'A noisy place to do one's work!'

Scores of people walked in and out of the Armouries building. Harry observed no one seemed to have their hands free. All carried something, or some part of something, or pushed a cart with something else. The building pumped people and equipment in and out of itself, a great warmongering heart pushing blood around a body.

'Impressed, Harry?' Sir Jonas asked, noting his expression. 'Good, for the King speculates you might work here.'

Harry stopped in mid-stride, astonished by the idea.

Sir Jonas took him by the elbow, leading him up the steps to the Armouries. 'You have a place, if you were to accept it. The philosophical, the mechanical, the analytical, physiological, meteorological, mathematical, and clandestine. All these skills are employed here, as they are in the battlefields of Europe.'

Sir Jonas led Harry up the flight of stairs to the entrance. They went in between white stone columns, and along a wide corridor, Ordnance employees moving aside and flowing around them.

'The Board is not so different from the Royal Society,' Sir Jonas said over his shoulder. 'Both seek an understanding of practical causes, and a desire for practical effects. We have elaboratories, repositories, workshops, libraries, and men of talent to use them. We have experimentalists, and observators, mechanics, and toolmen. Thinkers, and doers. We differ, howsoever, in one important aspect.'

He reached out an enquiring hand, held open before him.

'You have money,' Harry answered for him.

'Yes!' The hand closed, snatching away the money Harry spoke of. 'We have money. Funds, generously given. We pay generously, too, for the right people. Here we are.'

Sir Jonas beckoned him into a large room, its walls covered by shelving and cabinets. Philosophical equipment covered every surface: tools, micro-scopes, flasks, tubes and stoppered jars of glass and brass and silver.

Preserved specimens of organs and their owners, from insects, fish and monkeys, and skeletons stripped of their flesh, including one of a human child, filled the shelves. Arranged in order, they formed a chain of being, displayed to show the similarities and the modifications of form throughout God's Creation.

In the middle of the room stood three air-pumps, their frames larger than Hooke's, now broken in Gresham's cellar, but their glass receivers much the same size.

'This,' Sir Jonas told him, 'was Daniel Whitcombe's room.'

Harry stayed silent.

'I know you know of him,' Sir Jonas said, looking at Harry slyly. 'For the King told me you have his letter to Sir Edmund, and his letter to Mr. Hooke. And I know you have the keyword to his cipher, since I was there when it was found. Inside the stomach of the Justice. And I know he told you the name Whitcombe was known by, ever since Cromwell named him so. The Witch.'

Harry's only reaction was a draining of colour from his face.

'There is more, too,' Sir Jonas said brightly. 'Other rooms go off it, for other trials Daniel made.'

He observed Harry studying everything about the room.

'Imagine such a place for your own. It could be yours, if you so decide. If not, then no matter.' He made a sign of snuffing out a candle flame. 'We shall find someone else to fill Daniel's shoes.'

'Where is Daniel Whitcombe now, Sir Jonas?' Harry asked. 'Is he really dead? Or was his letter a lie?'

'We have lost him,' Sir Jonas replied crisply. 'Or rather, he lost himself. Whether he hides, or put an end to himself, it is no matter.'

'And if I were, as you say, to fill his shoes, would that be my end also? Would I, too, lose myself?'

Sir Jonas contemplated the questions, taking time before his answer. 'Every worthwhile occupation carries an element of risk. If you risk nothing, you change nothing. You need not worry that to refuse us endangers you. As long as you remain silent upon what happens here, you will be free to go about your business, within the law, whatever that may be.'

Sir Jonas strolled across to one of the air-pumps and looked into its empty receiver. He placed a hand on its mechanism and stroked it gently, sensuously, and turned the handle, taking a suck of air from inside the glass.

'Do you desire to dwell in Robert Hooke's shadow all your life? You do not, surely. You have your own way to make in the world. You own too much talent to steer by another's lights.'

He let go of the air-pump and went back to the door they had come through, stopping in the doorway, filling its frame. 'Observe the great purpose of this place. At the striving for improvement. Think of your personal, selfish wants, but think also of the whole. You shall become one amongst many, working for your King and your nation.'

He waited expectantly, then showed no disappointment at Harry's refusal to reply.

'I shall return presently. Let me then have your answer. It is a rare chance we give you, Harry.'

❦

LEFT ALONE IN the elaboratory, Harry took off his new spectacles, as they pinched the bridge of his nose. He massaged his eyes, the struggles of the previous night exhausting him suddenly.

He could not have read Daniel Whitcombe's work without the word *corpus* being left in Sir Edmund's gut. And it was Mr. Hooke who found it there. He could not have known what Whitcombe had done until he found the *Observations*, kept by Henry Oldenburg.

Apart from the grinding task of deciphering, all was given to him.

Whitcombe had wanted Robert Hooke, the Royal Society's Curator of Experiments, and now its Secretary, to have his work. To have his knowledge of how to infuse blood, and his efforts to revivify the dead.

Not the young Observator, Henry Hunt.

Putting the spectacles back on, the leaded frames of the windows looking out at the White Tower sharpened into a grid of lines, black against the bright whiteness outside.

It would be a gilded cage to accept the King's offer.

He ran his hand over the surface of a bench, fondling the grain of the expensive wood. An African hardwood, the bench built to resist cutting, and burning, and corrosive substances poured over it. A natural philosopher's bench.

Of course he must take this position, and this room. He could follow his own philosophical path, and carry out the work directed by Sir Jonas, and the Board of Ordnance.

Sir Jonas Moore had left him there deliberately, knowing the pull of the room itself was more persuasive than any words.

What best to do?

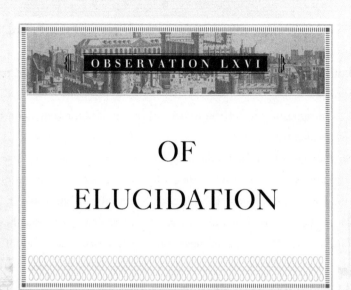

OF

ELUCIDATION

A SMALL DOOR LED OFF FROM the elaboratory, and it opened with an oiled click of its latch. Even the door handles work smoothly, Harry thought.

Inside, the room was dark, having no windows, but by the light from the elaboratory he could make out a marble dissection table, long grooves chased into its surface, a large trough at its foot. Placed neatly along the walls was an assortment of gleaming instruments.

Candles stood along the length of the room, waiting to be lit for the anatomiser to see by. Harry sniffed at them. They were beeswax.

This was the room where Daniel Whitcombe had worked on the boys. This was where they had had their blood infused one into another, and their organs taken.

Where they had screamed in agony and fear.

This memory was in the walls of the room. Harry merely heard its echo. Could he contend with such a trace, endure its presence here?

But why did Daniel Whitcombe prefer to work in a darkened room, lit by candles?

At the opposite end of the dissecting room was another door, and he walked uncertainly to it.

Sir Jonas would return soon and wanted to have his answer. Harry still did not know what it was to be. He could not tolerate the thought of losing all this. He could not bear the idea somebody else might have it, take it from him. Use these rooms and these tools, and have the great luxury of time and materials to make experiments, trials, discoveries, and follow the path of the mind. Have mechanics build apparatus for him at his direction. Have chymists mix preparations by his order.

But it was here where Daniel Whitcombe had killed the boys, in the service of the Board of Ordnance, blundering his way towards a method never found to revivify the recipient boy.

He had expended the lives of twelve others before he suffered the final weight on his soul.

How could Harry step into such shoes?

What would the Board of Ordnance ask of him?

OPENING THE DOOR, Harry stepped through. Sunlight, painfully bright, streamed through a large window. Set out like an office, this room was strewn with documents, laid on every shelf, surface and over the floor.

On the wall, hanging from a hook, was a pair of snowshoes.

Behind the table was the solicitor, Moses Creed, caught midway through the action of writing on paper.

For a long moment the two men stared at one another. Creed gathered the papers on the table together and tidied them into a pile. He placed his pen down on top of it, being mindful, Harry noticed, to line the pen parallel with its edge.

'Mr. Creed?'

'Mr. Hunt.' Creed made his familiar scoffing sound.

'You work with the Board of Ordnance?'

'Only when I am needed.'

'Sir Jonas Moore brought me here. He never said you would be here, also.'

'I catalogue the papers. He wanted a legal man.'

'You know of Daniel Whitcombe's work, then?' Harry asked.

Creed made a moue of distaste. 'Only what I find.'

'You know he carried out experiments on boys, seeking to revivify another?'

'I record what there is. As I have been asked to do.'

Since the Board of Ordnance had ways of going about its business Harry did not know, it should not have surprised him Creed worked for it. He had never questioned what else the solicitor did with his time. He had thought no further than Creed delivering the letter to Mr. Hooke, or being at Lincoln's Inn, or standing in a yard listening to the old Leveller, William Walwyn.

Harry walked closer to the table to pick up the pile of papers in front of Creed. The solicitor shot out a hand to cover it.

Between his splayed fingers Harry recognised the neat lettering and exact regularity of the lines in all the *Observations* he had deciphered, and in the letter sent to Robert Hooke.

'Mr. Hunt,' Creed huffed, 'it is of no help to me you are here. These papers are the King's property, through being the property of the Board of Ordnance. Until Sir Jonas returns, therefore, and tells me otherwise, I shall not let you peruse them.'

'Why do you catalogue these papers, Mr. Creed?'

'At the behest of Sir Jonas.'

'In truth, it looks to me as if you search through them rather than catalogue, looking for particular documents. These papers were pushed all about. A legal man, I think, would more usually work through such a task sequentially, tidying as he goes.'

The solicitor made his supercilious scoffing sound and walked from behind the table to fetch up more scattered documents from the floor. He paused, then indicated the dissecting room beyond. 'Will you wait outside, so I may continue?'

Harry ignored him. Instead, he picked up the document Creed had been busy with when he had come in.

'Your list includes Whitcombe's *Observations of the Light of Grace*, his *Observations of the Light of Nature*, and *of Experience, of Astronomical Magic, of Theology, of Alchemy, of Water, of Fire, of Air, of Life, of Spirit, of Motion, of Minerals, of Vegetables, of the Heart and Blood, of Homunculii, of Automata*, and his *Observations of Lower Species*. Whitcombe called them all together, his *Observations Philosophical.*'

Harry waved the list Creed had made. 'You do not simply catalogue, Mr. Creed. They are not here to be catalogued. You will not find them here, as you will find none of his *Observations Historical, Observations Habitual*, or *Observations Propagational*. Whitcombe wanted them with the Royal Society's Curator of Experiments, Mr. Hooke. He did not want them with the King, nor did he want them with Sir Jonas Moore. And he did not want them with you.'

Although Creed's face was openly derisive, Harry continued. 'For now, I have them, until I decide what to do with them. Whitcombe did not desire you to have them, Mr. Creed, even though it was you who wrote them out. Your list is written in the same neat hand as all of Whitcombe's *Observations*, and the letter you delivered to Mr. Hooke. This then begs a question: are you Daniel Whitcombe, and not Moses Creed at all?'

Creed stood silently, looking down the length of his nose.

'Are you Daniel Whitcombe,' Harry persisted, 'the healer, who treated Colonel Fields after Alton, Major-General Skippon after Naseby, and Oliver Cromwell after Dunbar? Since you are too young, I say not. Colonel Fields spoke of Daniel Whitcombe as a field chirurgeon in the Civil Wars, then taken to the Barbadoes as a slave. You do not bear the marks of such years or harsh experience.'

Harry picked up a small black leather-bound book from the table, with loose papers held between its pages.

'This book I recognise, being that of the Justice of Peace for Westminster, Sir Edmund Bury Godfrey. In it, he wrote of his investigations into the finding of boys left at tributaries into the Thames, and his searching for Catholics plotting against the King. It was with him each time I met him. These sheets, though, within Sir Edmund's book, held between its pages, have writing which is unsteady. Untidily done. A tremulous hand.'

Although arranged in blocks of numbers, twelve along and twelve down, the lines of cipher rose and fell like a wave, and were irregularly spaced. Sir Edmund's copy was far neater than this scrawl, and not disfigured by blots of ink.

'This is Daniel Whitcombe's own letter to Sir Edmund, left on the boy at the Fleet,' Harry continued. 'It has the same seal of black wax, with its symbol of a burning candle, but the cipher is written poorly. I only ever saw Sir Edmund's copy, which I later returned to him.'

Harry placed the book and the papers back down on the table.

Creed made as if to go through the door but checked himself, the sounds of footsteps across the elaboratory reaching them.

It was Sir Jonas Moore's heavy stride, accompanied by another, lighter rhythm, of a more elegant walk.

'I wonder why this enciphered letter should be here, and the Justice's book.' Harry glanced through the dissecting room, looking to see if the two men were there. 'I think it means you were with Colonel Fields at Whitechapel as his chapel burned down, when the smoke from the fire poisoned Sir Edmund.'

'Fields was not there!' Creed mocked him. 'Sir Jonas returns. My business is done. For if you have Whitcombe's papers, then my searching here is futile.'

'It was you who killed Sir Edmund? So not Colonel Fields at all.'

'That old man would not have killed the Justice! He never did so before, in all these years since the Battle of Worcester, though he had reason enough to do so. Fields was not at his chapel. Instead, he trembled at Lincoln's Inn, thinking he was to be taken, or killed. Meeting the Red Cipher again put him in fear, as it did Sir Edmund.'

Harry put his hand into his pocket to hide its shaking. 'Did the Justice kill your father, as the Colonel told me, after Worcester?'

'My father did not even threaten to tell of it.' Creed was almost inaudible, speaking more to himself than to Harry. For the first time, Harry saw no trace of the scornful, ill-mannered solicitor, but only a grieving son. 'He would have kept Parliament's assistance with the King's escape a secret, as it was Cromwell's desire it stayed so. Sir Edmund strung my father from a branch. He admitted it. He seemed pleased to tell me, at the end.'

'The Colonel had forgiven him killing his friend, as Sir Edmund followed orders given by John Thurloe, Cromwell's Secretary of State.'

'His friend! Not his father! Fields argued himself out of taking the action he should have. You have met him. He has lost any courage he once had. He shudders when he speaks of the Wars.'

'He does shudder,' Harry agreed. 'He does. I wonder what else he went through. How did you get Sir Edmund to Whitechapel, though? Did he go to the Colonel as another user of the Red Cipher, having seen it on the boy?'

'I simply sent him a message, telling him I hid there for my own safety. Telling him I witnessed a boy being carried from Somerset House, from the Queen's own rooms, and being left in the Chelsea Physic Garden. Queen Catherine following the Romish way, it made an easy fit for his certainty of Catholic insurrection. He was half out of his mind with the fear of it.'

'But you witnessed no such thing.'

'I took him there myself. He was the last boy Whitcombe worked on. In that room behind you.'

Harry nodded, a slow understanding coming. 'I thought their leaving in tributaries significant, but apart from the boy at the Fleet, and the boy at Chelsea, only chance dictated if they would be found, or not.' He wiped his mouth with his hand, a gesture reminiscent of the Justice. 'Just the boy at Barking Creek re-emerged. The emittent boys—twelve of them—were taken from this room, pushed from the Tower wharf, and disappeared into the Thames. Like rubbish disposed of.'

'I begin to see why Sir Jonas asked you here.'

'But you did not know Sir Edmund had swallowed the keyword to the cipher.'

'I did not. You are clever, but not enough to break such a cipher yourself.'

'I'm not so clever, that's true. You know, I believed you when you told me of the pair in sea-green coats.'

'You made mention of a pair wearing the colour sea green, so I furnished a pair in sea green. It was what you wished to hear. You asked whether the deliverers might be female. I said, *conceivably*. I laughed at you.'

From Whitcombe's elaboratory, Sir Jonas called. 'Mr. Hunt! Are you there?'

'I am here, Sir Jonas. And I have my decision for you.'

HARRY TURNED HIS attention back to Moses Creed. 'Why would you deliver the letter from Daniel Whitcombe to Mr. Hooke?'

'That is simply answered, too. He asked me. I worked as his amanuensis, writing out his *Observations* for him, throughout his last years. His sight, and his steadiness, were failing. He became sensitive to bright light. He could hardly bear any light at all, these last few months. I did not know the meaning of them, only copying out the numbers he gave me. He had found me. He searched out his friend Reuben Creed's son.'

'You yourself wrote out the letter for Mr. Hooke.'

'I did not know Whitcombe planned to disappear, and I did not know where he had lodged the *Observations*. He kept that from me.'

'As he kept from you Sir Edmund's killing of your father.'

'He never told me, for he knew what I would do. He used me as his instrument. His creature. Colonel Fields acquainted me with the story. Your visit to him with the Red Cipher reawakened his conscience.'

Creed studied Harry, seeing a slight, bespectacled young man, bruised, bumped, in a slashed leather coat. 'I wonder what secrets Robert Hooke keeps from his creature.'

Outside the office, in Whitcombe's elaboratory, Sir Jonas conversed with another. The sound of their talking, mostly Sir Jonas with an occasional interjection from the man with him, came through the dissecting room. It had the rises and falls of a heated debate, but too muffled to make out.

'You were not only Daniel Whitcombe's amanuensis, though, were you, Mr. Creed?'

Harry unbuttoned his coat, as if to make himself comfortable. He tried to present a confidence he did not feel, for it leaked away as the boys' blood had leaked away along the grooves of the anatomy table.

'The old man who wrote this letter did not perform these experiments. Whitcombe no longer possessed the strength to handle bodies, or the stillness of hand to infuse blood from one boy to another. He would've missed any artery and missed a vein by more. Your hand, though, Mr. Creed, as your writing shows, is unusually steady. As was your father's. Colonel Fields told me he was a glove maker and stitcher of wounds. It was you who held the knife. It was you who inserted the pipes, to drain blood, and infuse it. It was you who killed the boys. You murdered them. All for an experiment which failed.'

'You are hypocritical! If we had succeeded, the boy brought back to life, you would give not a jot for these deaths.'

Harry gave a brief nod of his head, as if he accepted fully the truth of Creed's words. 'There is one death I care very much about, though.' His face had gone white, except for small red spots of anger in his cheeks. 'Mr. Hooke's apprentice, Tom Gyles, didn't deserve to die, as none of these boys did. Tom was worth no more than each of them. Yet it's his death I mourn, for he was close to me, like a brother. Did you kill him too?'

'It was to save your life, Mr. Hunt.'

Seeing Harry's incredulity, Creed sniffed, unconcerned by his opinion.

'Sir Jonas Moore desired you to be kept alive. The boy's death was a warning to you, to keep you under control.'

'Sir Jonas had a hand in this? He ordered the death of Tom Gyles?'

'Does he not offer these rooms to you? Is that not why you are here? Daniel Whitcombe has disappeared, and the Board needs a replacement. You are the same as him, offered the same choice. The Earl of Shaftesbury, who noticed him on his sugar plantations, brought him back from the Barbadoes. Here he remained, first under Oliver Cromwell, then under the King. His employer changed, but his work just the same.'

'You failed to revivify a boy and murdered a dozen others. And then you killed one more. I'm not the same. I repeat, did Sir Jonas instruct you to kill Tom, by injecting him with smallpox?'

'To be a chirurgeon, to cut into a body, familiarises the heart to a necessary inhumanity. We take nature to task, putting aside our scruples, in order to glorify not the Light of Nature, nor the Light of God, but ourselves.'

'Is that your admission, then? Sir Jonas is not a chirurgeon. He made no such order. You became one, through assisting Daniel Whitcombe. You infected Tom. The disease moved so quickly through him, it must have been the day I met you with Colonel Fields, when we listened to William Walwyn.'

'I needed time to finish here, and thought you too close. It was not Sir Jonas. He is too soft a man. I am to leave for Carolina. The Earl of Shaftesbury is one of its Lords Proprietors. He has a role for me there.' He picked up his list of Whitcombe's *Observations* from the table. 'We are both vain men, Mr. Hunt, but the world needs such vanity. It is the vain, conceited men who have the desire and the appetite to succeed.'

'WHAT TALK IS this of vanity?' Sir Jonas entered the office. 'They sound wise words, though I caught but the end of them.'

Harry looked beyond him, at the other man following him through the dissecting room. He was tall, dark-skinned, with a large black peruke.

'Your Majesty,' Harry said, bowing low. Creed did the same.

'Harry!' The King extended his hand for Harry to kiss. 'You have seen the Witch's elaboratory. And, I see, you have met Mr. Creed.'

'I have. And I have spoken with him of Daniel Whitcombe.'

'You say you have made your decision,' Sir Jonas said. 'Then what is it to be?'

Harry spoke flatly. 'In truth, Sir Jonas, I cannot yet say.'

'Not five minutes ago, you had your answer. You are more dithering than I would have suspected.'

'In the last five minutes, I've found out the man who kidnapped and murdered the boys. It wasn't Daniel Whitcombe, as I thought, though he directed their killing. It was Moses Creed, who I took to be only a solicitor. He was Daniel Whitcombe's assistant, too. Not only his amanuensis, but his operator. It was he who carried out the procedures on the boys.'

'I know this, already, full well,' Sir Jonas answered breezily. 'He is to leave us. You will have the place to yourself soon enough.'

'Twelve boys were killed for these experiments. The boy kept at Gresham's, as I think you know, Your Majesty, was to be revivified. Whitcombe called him the recipient boy.'

The King looked contrite. 'It is a bad business. I guessed at the boy when I saw him in the air-pump. The colour of his eyes, I recognised. I knew the nature of these experiments. I thought I had put a stop to them, then found that they continued. I did not know of all the other boys used. I have chastised Sir Jonas for it.'

He went to Harry, and put his arm around his shoulder, pulling him close. 'But imagine if these experiments had worked, Harry. Hmm? Revivification! It would have been a marvel of the New Philosophy.'

'Who was the recipient boy, Your Majesty? Who was he, seen to be worth the lives of so many?'

The King sighed. 'It was never only about one boy. It would have been a way of keeping alive our soldiers, and our sailors. In war, we would have been invincible. In peace, it would have brought hope to all of my realm.

You cannot ignore the greater good.'

Harry could feel the heat in his cheeks, and realised his eyes were fill-ing with angry tears. 'Who was the boy?' he repeated.

'You are direct,' the King observed. 'A tendency you must guard against.'

That Harry had got so far surprised him. This bespectacled boy, Robert Hooke's assistant, in his leather coat swamping him, making him appear even slighter than he was.

'He was Britannia's son.' The King smiled ruefully at Harry's bewilder-ment. 'The son of Frances Teresa Stewart, the Duchess of Richmond and Lennox. Once, she was the woman I loved above all others. The boy was the son, too, of the Earl of Shaftesbury, who sought to continue the experiments after she insisted Whitcombe end them.'

'Whitcombe had tried for a year,' Sir Jonas added. 'She gave him until New Year's Day, deciding her son had been through enough. His father disagreed.'

The muscle in Harry's thigh had started its tremor. He spoke slowly, trying to keep his voice level, and free from the bitterness he felt. 'Moses Creed, as Whitcombe's *creature*, delivered the boy to Enoch Wolfe at the Fleet. Wearing snowshoes.' He indicated the pair hanging from the wall. 'I saw the trail. He was supposed to take him to the Earl of Shaftesbury. But instead, the boy went to Gresham's College, into Mr. Hooke's air-pump. Whitcombe told Sir Edmund to be there. And Mr. Hooke, too. Whitcombe wanted all his work to go to him.'

'You demonstrate your understanding,' Sir Jonas said.

'Robert is too timorous a man to work here, we think,' the King said. 'He is better situated as Secretary of my Society. We must be quick here, Harry, and have your answer. My Council meets to question Titus Oates and Israel Tonge further on the plot against me. After the go at my life yesterday, I must take them seriously.'

Sir Jonas looked at Creed and shook his hand, in acknowledgement of his work. 'Is your pinnace ready, Mr. Creed?'

'It is moored at St. Katherine's stairs.'

'You have completed your cataloguing for us?'

'I have done all I can do. There is nothing here of Whitcombe's work on the boys, for Mr. Hunt has it—'

'—Sir Jonas. Your Majesty,' Harry interrupted. 'Moses Creed is also the man who killed Sir Edmund Bury Godfrey. He tied him, tortured him, and locked him inside a burning chapel, until the smoke overwhelmed him. Then, he put his dead body on the Morice waterwheel.'

'Catholics did not kill him?' The King's face took on a calculating look. He splayed his fingers as if counting through newly presented alternatives.

Sir Jonas's expression closed. 'Did Sir Edmund die by your hand, Mr. Creed?'

Creed backed away, edging through the door, his supercilious confidence becoming a vulnerable worry.

'For if you killed the Justice, then I fear we are unable to protect you.' Sir Jonas flashed a look at the King, who held up his hand, wanting more time to reflect.

Creed continued, retreating into the dissecting room.

The King waved at Sir Jonas, a sweeping away gesture. 'For all he has done for us, Jonas. No one now would believe anyone but Catholics killed Sir Edmund, anyways.'

Letting Creed disappear into the darkness of the dissecting room, they both stood and watched.

'No!' Harry shouted, and jumped forwards and past them, out from the office and into the dissecting room. 'You cannot let him go!'

Creed broke into a stumbling run, going around the dissecting table. Harry jumped onto it, and almost caught him, extending out a hand to reach for him, but slid on the polished marble. He fell to the floor instead.

Straightening, he felt a point in the back of his neck.

Creed had grabbed a dissecting knife from its place on the wall. He pressed it into the hollow at the top of Harry's spine, cutting into the flesh between the tendons.

'You will let me go, Mr. Hunt, as the King and Sir Jonas let me go.'

Harry raised his hands as if in supplication. The pressure of the knife's point lessened, and Creed reversed into the elaboratory.

'Now all of this shall be yours. I wish you happiness in your employments.'

Creed gave Harry a last sour look, then turned to go, to start his way out of the elaboratory, from the Armouries building, away from the Tower, to his pinnace moored at the Thames, to Plymouth, and then to Carolina.

Harry rose from the dissection room's floor and reached inside his coat. He pulled out Henry Oldenburg's pistol, checked the charge, and pulled the trigger.

The explosion of gunpowder was not loud by the standards of the Armouries, but it was enough to fill the dissecting room. Smoke from the pistol drifted through to the elaboratory, following the path of the ball.

Harry pulled the trigger again, and the pistol—worked on in his rooms at Mrs. Hannam's house, at his little table there—fired again.

And once more, swiftly after.

Moses Creed lay sprawled on his back against one of Whitcombe's air-pumps, his pierced head resting on its frame, a streak of blood showing his journey down the wood.

The second shot had entered his throat. Bright arterial blood sprayed into the air, covering Creed in it, soaking his clothes red.

The third shot had gone into his chest. The blood pulsing from his neck slowed, as the pumping action of his heart came to a stop.

Harry shakily lowered the improved pistol.

'We thought we had the measure of you, Harry,' the King told him. 'I perceive, however, we did not.'

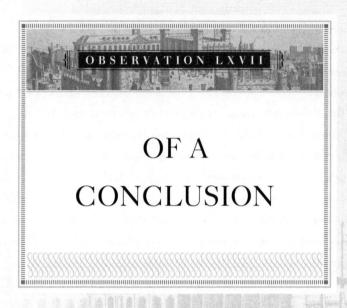

OBSERVATION LXVII

OF A CONCLUSION

SNOW FELL, COVERING GRESHAM'S QUADRANGLE.

Grace's fingers squeezed Harry's hand rhythmically, as if sending him a message. To the other side of him stood Robert Hooke, a drop of liquid at the tip of his long nose, and Mary Robinson.

They huddled around a brazier set up in the centre of the quadrangle, where the paths across it met.

The papers curled, and scorched, and burned.

Harry's work, all the experiments revealed by his patient deciphering. Daniel Whitcombe's numbers, in grids twelve numbers by twelve, using the Red Cipher. Sir Edmund's copy, too. And all the sheets written out in an extraordinarily neat hand, Moses Creed's work as Whitcombe's amanuensis.

All would be consigned to the brazier.

Harry picked up more of them, including the letter from Henry Oldenburg to Hooke, which had been on the package stored in his oak chest, and threw them into the flames.

By order of the King, following the wishes of the recipient boy's mother.

The *Observations* burned well. Their ashes rose up and over the College rooftops, specks haphazardly meandering through the air.

They reminded Harry of Tom Gyles, who never took a straight line if a detour could be found.

Harry committed to his memory the smell of burning paper and ink.

Hooke watched in anguish, regretting the loss.

Colonel Michael Fields, in his tattered campaign coat, stood with them, thinking of his friend Daniel Whitcombe, whom he could never remember without bringing his hand to his scar, where Whitcombe had sewn his flesh together over his skull. And of Reuben Creed, of whom he could never think without the image of him swinging slowly from a rope.

Further back from the heat, by the College repository, stood a glossy black coach-and-four, its windows made of pierced tin. Its driver, a man in a woollen coat, held the reins of its horses, their flanks shiny from the moisture in the air.

Lord Shaftesbury stood next to it, his face pale and pained. With him, but a couple of steps apart, was Frances Teresa Stewart, wearing mourning black. Her image was known throughout the nation as Britannia.

They had asked to watch the burning. The King had permitted it.

Two women with sea-green coats, a colour striking against the whiteness of the new snow, watched too, standing together hand in hand. Hortense Mancini, Duchesse de Mazarin, who many believed to be the most beautiful woman in the land, and the King's daughter, Anne Lennard, Countess of Sussex.

They had sought the boy for Frances. They had reclaimed it from the men of the New Philosophy.

Long after Harry had put the last of the *Observations* into the brazier, and was safely in the warmth of Hooke's lodgings with Hooke, Grace, Mary, and his new friend the Colonel, this quartet remained. Although they all wore expensive, finely stitched gloves, they rubbed their hands together, fingers stiffened by the chill.

As the flames at last died down, they each stepped up into the carriage. Their driver started off. A gentle flick of the whip.

Sheltered in the darkness of Gresham's stables, an old man watched them go. He was wrapped warmly against the bitter weather, his hat pulled low, his scarf covering over his nose.

He wore spectacles with lenses of red-coloured glass, to protect his eyes from the light. Trembling hands betrayed his age.

The carriage moved slowly off towards Bishopsgate Street, the sound of the horses' hooves muffled by the snow, and out into London.

I HAVE ATTEMPTED TO 'REVIVIFY' REAL people. I have also created characters. Events of 1677 to 1679 have been compressed into a busy January. I have used events recorded in Robert Hooke's diary, such as the death of Tom Gyles from smallpox (at first thought to be measles), the fall of a pickpocket from the 'Fish Street pillar', Grace Hooke's engagements, Hooke's campaign to replace Henry Oldenburg as the Secretary of the Royal Society, and Harry Hunt's cataloguing of Oldenburg's correspondences after the Secretary's death.

Oldenburg's suicide, and the disguising of it, are my invention.

The Earl of Shaftesbury's influence over the 'Popish Plot', and of his Secretary, John Locke, I have placed more centrally than historians usually allow.

Sir Edmund Bury Godfrey's murder is one of history's great unsolved crimes. The various accounts and possible explanations I have read have his body found on Primrose Hill rather than under London Bridge. Little is known of his whereabouts during the Civil Wars. His helping King Charles II escape after the Battle of Worcester is my invention.

There were rumours of a child of Frances Teresa Stewart's, born outside her marriage. This is thought to be a girl rather than a boy. I have not found mention of a close relationship, or child, between her and Shaftesbury.

William Walwyn's words are his, but edited.

Daniel Whitcombe's *Observations* are organised in a surprisingly similar way to John Locke's *Animadversions*.

The ♓ symbol, the sign of Pisces, appears throughout Hooke's diaries. Hooke used it to record his orgasms.

ACKNOWLEDGEMENTS

ACKNOWLEDGEMENTS AND THANKS ARE VERY DUE to those who read versions of the manuscript, reacted, advised, and encouraged: Caroline Davidson, Sharon Gregory, Grace Hancock, Victoria Kwee, Rob Little, Sonia Little, Geoff Lloyd, John Lloyd (my father—I miss him), Mark Skinner, Richard Torr, and Jenny Verney.

They are also due to Sonia Land and Gaia Banks at Sheil Land Associates. Gaia spotted the original submission, requested the rest, suggested many changes, and championed the book with astonishing energy and attention.

Also, to all at Melville House Publishing. Especially Dennis Johnson, who found the self-published version and decided he should publish it. And to Carl Bromley, their editor, whose incisive reassessment of the self-published version was expressed so charmingly I hardly felt the sting. Also thanks to Marina Drukman, Beste Miray Doğan, Tim McCall, Michael Barson, and Amelia Stymacks.

Christopher Fowler, author of the excellent Bryant & May novels, found my book in its self-published form and took it upon himself to praise and promote it. (We had no connection previously.) I am truly grateful for his generosity, and for the support he's since given me.

Thanks to the bookbinder in Sheffield who loaned me her customer's *Pharmacopœia Londinensis* by William Salmon. She was happy for me to take this three-hundred-and-fifty-year-old book and photograph many of its pages. (I think she gave me two days to do so.) An act of generosity with somebody else's property I have never forgotten.

Finally, thank you Kate, my wife. She has tolerated much, encouraged always, researched unpaid, and always with more sense than I have. I am a lucky, lucky man.

Follow me on Twitter at @robjlloyd. On Facebook, I'm Robert J Lloyd.

Historical Fiction authors feed parasitically on the hard work of historians, a grubby fact often unacknowledged. So, with heartfelt thanks to them, I include a bibliography. I'm sure I should have read other books, too. These are the ones I did.

ROYAL SOCIETY

Birch, Thomas, *The History of the Royal Society of London for the Improving of Natural Knowledge: From its First Rise*, A. Millar, 1757

Bryson, Bill, *Seeing Further: The Story of Science and the Royal Society*, Harper Press, 2010

Chartres, Richard and Vermont, David, *A Brief History of Gresham College 1597–1997*, Gresham College, 1997

Dolnick, Edward, *The Clockwork Universe: Isaac Newton, the Royal Society, and the Birth of the Modern World*, Harper Perennial, 2011

Gilbert, Adrian, *The New Jerusalem*, Bantam, 2002

Gribbin, John, *The Fellowship: The Story of the Royal Society and a Scientific Revolution*, Penguin, 2006

Hartley, Sir Harold (ed.), *Royal Society: Its Origins and Founders*, Royal Society, 1960

Hunter, Matthew, C., *Wicked Intelligence: Visual Art and the Science of Experiment in Restoration London*, University of Chicago Press, 2013

Jardine, Lisa, *Ingenious Pursuits: Building the Scientific Revolution*, Little, Brown, 1999

Sprat, Thomas, *The History of the Royal Society of London for the Improving of Natural Knowledge*, Knapton, 1734

Ward, John, *The Lives of the Professors of Gresham College*, 1740

ROBERT HOOKE

Bennett, Jim, Cooper, Michael, Hunter, Michael and Jardine, Lisa, *London's Leonardo: The Life and Work of Robert Hooke*, Oxford University Press, 2003

Chapman, Allan, *England's Leonardo: Robert Hooke and the Seventeenth-Century Scientific Revolution*, Taylor and Francis Group, 2005

Chapman, Allan and Kent, Paul, *Robert Hooke and the English Renaissance*, Gracewing Publishing, 2005

Cooper, Michael, *'A More Beautiful City': Robert Hooke and the Rebuilding of London after the Great Fire*, Sutton, 2003

Cooper, Michael and Hunter, Michael (eds.), *Robert Hooke: Tercentennial studies*, Ashgate, 2006

Espinasse, Margaret, *Robert Hooke*, Heinemann, 1956

Hooke, Robert, *Lampas: Or, descriptions of some mechanical improvements of lamps and waterpoises together with some other physical and mechanical discoveries*, 1677

Micrographia: Or some Physiological Descriptions of Minute Bodies Made by Magnifying Glasses with Observations and Inquiries thereupon, John Martyn and James Allestry, 1665

Hooke, Robert, *Philosophical Experiments and Observations*, 1726

Hooke, Robert, *The Posthumous Works of Robert Hooke, containing his Cutlerian lectures, and other discourses, read at the meetings of the illustrious Royal Society . . . To these discourses is prefixt the author's life*, 1705

Hunter, Michael and Schaffer, Simon (eds.), *Robert Hooke: New Studies*, Boydell Press, 1989

Inwood, Stephen, *The Man Who Knew Too Much: The Strange and Inventive Life of Robert Hooke, 1635–1703*, Macmillan, 2003

Jardine, Lisa, *The Curious Life of Robert Hooke: The Man who Measured London*, HarperCollins, 2003

Purrington, Robert D., *The First Professional Scientist: Robert Hooke and the Royal Society of London*, Birkhauser, 2009

Robinson, Henry W. (ed.), *The Diary of Robert Hooke*, Taylor and Francis, 1935

LONDON

Ackroyd, Peter, *London: The Biography*, Chatto and Windus, 2000

Ackroyd, Peter, *London Under*, Chatto and Windus, 2011

Ackroyd, Peter, *Thames: Sacred River*, Chatto and Windus, 2007

Arnold, Catharine, *City of Sin: London and its Vices*, Simon and Schuster, 2010

Ash, Bernard, *The Golden City: London between the Fires 1666–1941*, Phoenix House, 1964

Baker, T. M. M., *London: Rebuilding the City after the Great Fire*, Phillimore, 2000

Bastable, Jonathan, *Inside Pepys' London*, David and Charles, 2011

De Krey, Gary S., *London and the Restoration, 1659–1683*, Cambridge University Press, 2005

Harris, Tim, *London Crowds in the Reign of Charles II: Propaganda and politics from the Restoration until the exclusion crisis*, Cambridge University Press, 1987

Hollis, Leo, *London Rising: The Men Who Made Modern London, Macmillan, 2008*

Jordan, Don, *The King's City: London under Charles II*, Little, Brown, 2017

Morgan, William, *The A to Z of Charles II's London 1682*, London Topographical Society, 2013

Picard, Liza, *Restoration London: Everyday Life in the 1660s*, Weidenfeld and Nicolson, 1997

Pierce, Patricia, *Old London Bridge: The Story of the Longest Inhabited Bridge in Europe*, Headline, 2001

Porter, Roy, *London: A Social History*, Penguin, 2000

Porter, Stephen, *Pepys's London: Everyday Life in London 1650–1703*, Amberley, 2011

Quennell, Peter (ed.), *London's Underworld*, William Kimber, 1950

Weinreb, Ben and Hibbert, Christopher (eds.), *The London Encyclopaedia*, Macmillan, 2010

CHARLES II AND HIS COURT

Bevan, Bryan, *The Duchess Hortense: Cardinal Mazarin's Wanton Niece*, Rubicon, 1987

Blount, Thomas, *Boscobel: Or the History of the Most Miraculous Preservation of*

King Charles II, Tylston and Edwards, 1894

Brown, Colin, *Whitehall: The Street that Shaped a Nation*, Simon and Schuster, 2009

Bryant, Arthur (ed.), *The Letters, Speeches and Declarations of King Charles II*, Cassell, 1935

D'Aulnoy, Marie-Catherine, *Memoirs of the Court of England in 1675*, Routledge, 1927

Fraser, Antonia, *King Charles II*, Weidenfeld and Nicolson, 2011

Goldsmith, Elizabeth C., *The Kings' Mistresses: The Liberated Lives of Marie Mancini, Princess Colonna, and her Sister Hortense, Duchess Mazarin*, Public Affairs, 2012

Harris, Tim, *Restoration: Charles II and his Kingdoms, 1660–1685*, Penguin, 2006

Hartmann, Cyril Hughes, *The Vagabond Duchess: The Life of Hortense Mancini Duchesse Mazarin*, Routledge, 1926

Keay, Anna, *The Magnificent Monarch: Charles II and the Ceremonies of Power*, Continuum, 2008

Masters, Brian, *The Mistresses of Charles II*, Constable, 1997

Nelson, Sarah (ed.), *Memoirs: Marie Mancini and Hortense Mancini*, University of Chicago Press, 2008

Ollard, Richard, *The Escape of Charles II: After the Battle of Worcester*, Hodder and Stoughton, 1966

Spencer, Charles, *To Catch A King: Charles II's Great Escape*, HarperCollins, 2017

Uglow, Jenny, *A Gambling Man: Charles II and the Restoration*, Faber, 2009

Walsh, Michael and Jordan, Don, *The King's Revenge: Charles II and the Greatest Manhunt in British History*, Little, Brown, 2012

Wheatley, Dennis, *A Private Life of Charles II (Old Rowley)*, Hutchinson, 1967

Whitehead, Julian, *Rebellion in the Reign of Charles II: Plots, Rebellions and Intrigue in the Reign of Charles II*, Pen and Sword History, 2017

BRITISH CIVIL WARS

Ackroyd, Peter, *Civil War: The History of England Volume III*, Macmillan, 2014

Atkin, Malcolm, *Cromwell's Crowning Mercy: The Battle of Worcester 1651*, Sutton, 1998

Bennett, Martyn, *The English Civil War: A Historical Companion*, The History Press Limited, 2004

Braddick, Michael, *God's Fury, England's Fire: A New History of the English Civil Wars*, Penguin, 2009

Carlton, Charles, *Going to the Wars: The Experience of the British Civil Wars 1638–1651*, Routledge, 1994

Ellis, John, *'To Walk in the Dark': Military Intelligence in the English Civil War*

1642–1646, Spellmount, 2011

Flintham, David, *Civil War London: A Military History of London under Charles I and Oliver Cromwell*, Helion and Company Limited, 2017

Gentles, I. J., *The English Revolution and the Wars in the Three Kingdoms*, 1638–1652, Pearson, 2007

Hill, P. R. and Watkinson, J. M., *Major Sanderson's War: The Diary of a Parliamentary Cavalry Officer in the English Civil War*, Spellmount, 2008

Kenyon, John, *The Civil Wars of England*, Weidenfeld and Nicolson, 1988

Porter, Stephen and Marsh, Simon, *The Battle for London*, Amberley, 2011

Purkiss, Diane, *The English Civil War: A People's History*, Harper Perennial, 2007

Roberts, Keith, *Cromwell's War Machine: The New Model Army 1645–1660*, Pen and Sword Military, 2005

Roots, Ivan, *The Great Rebellion: A Short History of the English Civil War and Interregnum 1642–60*, Sutton, 1995

Royle, Trevor, *Civil War: The Wars of the Three Kingdoms 1638–1660*, Little, Brown, 2004

Wanklyn, Malcolm, *Decisive Battles of the English Civil War*, Pen and Sword Military, 2006

Whitehead, Julian, *Cavalier and Roundhead Spies: Intelligence in the Civil War and Commonwealth*, Pen and Sword Military, 2009

Worden, Blair, *The English Civil Wars: 1640–1660*, Weidenfeld and Nicolson, 2010

Young, Peter and Holmes, Richard, *The English Civil War: A Military History of Three Civil Wars, 1642–51*, Methuen, 1974

GENERAL

Adamson, John, *The Noble Revolt: The Overthrow of Charles I*, Weidenfeld and Nicolson, 2007

Andrews, William Eusebius, *An Historical Narrative of the Horrid Plot and Conspiracy of Titus Oates, Called the Popish Plot*, W. E. Andrews, 1816

Beloff, Max, *Public Order and Popular Disturbances 1160–1714*, Cass, 1963

Berens, Lewis Henry, *The Digger Movement: Radical Communalism in the English Civil War*, Red and Black Publishers, 2008

Bernstein, Eduard, *Cromwell and Communism: Socialism and Democracy in the Great English Revolution*, Cass, 1966

Carr, John Dickson, *The Murder of Sir Edmund Godfrey*, Hamish Hamilton, 1936

Carty, Jarret A. (ed.), *On the Motion of the Heart and Blood in Animals: A new edition of William Harvey's Exercitatio anatomica de motu cordis et sanguinis in animalibus*, Resource Publications, 2016

Cockayne, Emily, *Hubbub: Filth, Noise and Stench in England 1600–1770*, Yale University Press, 2007

Cooper, Chris, *Blood: A Very Short Introduction*, Oxford University Press, 2016[1*]

Dougan, Andy, *Raising the Dead: The Men Who Created Frankenstein*, Birlinn, 2017

Evelyn, John, *The Diary of John Evelyn*, Everyman, 2006

Firth, C. H., *Oliver Cromwell and the Rule of the Puritans in England*, Putnam, 1924

Fitzgibbons, Jonathan, *Cromwell's Head*, Bloomsbury, 2008

Frank, Joseph, *The Levellers: A History of the Writings of Three Seventeenth-Century Social Democrats: John Lilburne, Richard Overton, William Walwyn* Harvard University Press, 2014

Fraser, Antonia, *Cromwell: Our Chief Of Men*, Weidenfeld and Nicolson, 1997

Garrett, Geoffrey and Nott, Andrew, *Cause of Death: Memoirs of a Home Office Pathologist*, Robinson, 2001

Gregg, Pauline, *Free-Born John: The Biography of John Lilburne*, Phoenix, 2000

Hampton, Christopher (ed.), *A Radical Reader: The Struggle for Change in England 1381–1914*, Penguin, 1984

Harris, Ian, *The Mind of John Locke: A Study of Political Theory in Its Intellectual Setting*, Cambridge University Press, 1998

Hartzman, Marc, *The Embalmed Head of Oliver Cromwell: A Memoir*, Curious Publications, 2016

Hill, Charles Peter, *Who's Who in Stuart Britain*, Shepheard-Walwyn, 1988

Hill, Christopher, *God's Englishman: Oliver Cromwell and the English Revolution*, Weidenfeld and Nicolson, 2019

Hill, Christopher, *The World Turned Upside Down: Radical Ideas During the English Revolution*, Penguin, 1984

Jones, Steve, *In The Blood: God, Genes and Destiny*, Flamingo, 1997

Kenyon, John, *The Popish Plot*, Phoenix, 2000

King, Peter, *The Life of John Locke: With Extracts from his Correspondence, Journals and Common-place Books*, Andesite Press, 2015

Knight, Stephen, *The Killing of Justice Godfrey: An Investigation into England's Most Remarkable Unsolved Murder*, Grafton, 1984

Lane, Jane, *Titus Oates*, Dakers, 1949

Lawson-Dick, Oliver (ed.), *Aubrey's Brief Lives*, Vintage, 2016

Little, Patrick, *Oliver Cromwell: New Perspectives*, Palgrave Macmillan, 2009

Locke, John, *An Essay Concerning Human Understanding*, Penguin, 1997

Locke, John, *Letters Concerning Toleration*, Hackett, 1983

Locke, John, *Of the Abuse of Words*, Penguin, 2009

Locke, John, *The First and Second Treatises of Government*, Cambridge University Press, 1988

[1*] It's not that short.

Long, James and Long, Ben, *The Plot Against Pepys*, Faber, 2012

Marshall, Alan, *The Strange Death of Edmund Godfrey: Plots and Politics in Restoration London*, Sutton, 1999

McDermid, Val, *Forensics: The Anatomy of Crime*, Profile Books, 2015

Moore, Jonas, *The History or Narrative of the Great Level of the Fenns, called Bedford Level with a Large Map of the Said Level, as Drained, Surveyed, and described by Sir Jonas Moore*, 1685

Moore, Wendy, *The Knife Man: Blood, Body-snatching and the Birth of Modern Surgery*, Bantam, 2005

Mortimer, Ian, *The Time Traveller's Guide to Restoration Britain: Life in the Age of Samuel Pepys, Isaac Newton and the Great Fire of London*, Bodley Head, 2017

Norman, Ben, *A History of Death in Seventeenth-Century England*, Pen and Sword History, 2020

Plowden, Alison, *In a Free Republic: Life in Cromwell's England*, Sutton, 2006

Pollock, John, *The Popish Plot: A Study in the History of the Reign of Charles II*, Cambridge University Press, 1944

Porter, Roy, *Flesh in the Age of Reason*, Penguin, 2004

Porter, Roy, *The Greatest Benefit to Mankind: A Medical History of Humanity*, HarperCollins, 1997

Prance, Miles, *A True Narrative and Discovery of Several Very Remarkable Passages Relating to the Horrid Popish Plot: As They Fell Within the Knowledge of Mr. Miles Prance*, 1679

Principe, Lawrence, *The Secrets of Alchemy*, University of Chicago Press, 2013

Rees, John, *The Leveller Revolution: Radical Political Organisation in England, 1640–1650*, Verso, 2016

Robertson, Geoffrey (ed.), *The Putney Debates: The Levellers*, Verso, 2007

Roob, Alexander, *Alchemy and Mysticism*, Taschen, 2005

Roots, Ivan (ed.), *Speeches of Oliver Cromwell*, Dent, 1989

Salmon, William, *Pharmacopoeia Londinensis; Or, the New London Dispensatory*, Thomas Dawks, 1678

Schama, Simon, *Belonging, The Story of the Jews Volume Two 1492–1900*, Bodley Head, 2017

Shadwell, Thomas, *The Virtuoso*, Chadwyck-Healey, 1997

Singh, Simon, *The Code Book: The Secret History of Codes and Code-breaking*, Fourth Estate, 2000

Smith, David L., *Oliver Cromwell: Politics and Religion in the English Revolution 1640–1658*, Cambridge University Press, 1991

Spurr, John (ed.), *Anthony Ashley Cooper, First Earl of Shaftesbury 1621–1683*, Routledge, 2016

Thomas, Keith, *Man and the Natural World: Changing Attitudes in England 1500–1800*, Penguin, 1984

Thomas, Keith, *Religion and the Decline of Magic: Studies in Popular Beliefs in Sixteenth- and Seventeenth-Century England*, Penguin, 2003

Wickwar, J. W., *Handbook of the Black Arts*, Senate, 1996

Willmoth, Frances, *Sir Jonas Moore: Practical Mathematics and Restoration Science*, Boydell Press, 1993

Woolhouse, Roger, *Locke: A Biography*, Cambridge University Press, 2009

Worden, Blair, *God's Instruments: Political Conduct in the England of Oliver Cromwell*, Oxford University Press, 2012

Wright, Thomas, *Circulation: William Harvey's Revolutionary Idea*, Chatto and Windus, 2012

Wrixon, Fred B., *Codes, Ciphers and Other Cryptic and Clandestine Communication*, Black Dog and Leventhal Publishers, 2003

Zagorin, Perez, *Francis Bacon*, Princeton University Press, 1998

WEBSITES

Many, but particularly useful were royalsociety.org and jstor.org

SOFTWARE

Scrivener

ABOUT THE AUTHOR

Robert J. Lloyd grew up in South London, Innsbruck, and Kinshasa (his parents were in the Foreign and Commonwealth Office), and then in Sheffield. He did a Fine Art degree, starting as a landscape painter but moving to film, performance, and installation. His MA degree was in The History of Ideas, where he 'discovered' the seventeeth century, and first read Robert Hooke's Diary, detailing the life and experiments of this extraordinary man. His MA thesis was about Hooke being the first 'professional scientist.'

After a career in sales (grandly, IT solutions) he retrained, to spend the next twenty years as a secondary school teacher. He has now retired from teaching, wanting to return to painting and writing.

Since 2010 he has lived in the Brecon Beacons in Wales. He has three lovely children and an equally lovely wife.